THE DARK HORIZON

The Dark Horizon

THAMES RIVER PRESS
An imprint of Wimbledon Publishing Company Limited (WPC)
Another imprint of WPC is Anthem Press (www.anthempress.com)
First published in the United Kingdom in 2014 by
THAMES RIVER PRESS
75–76 Blackfriars Road
London SE1 8HA

www.thamesriverpress.com

All the characters and events described in this novel are imaginary
and any similarity with real people or events is purely coincidental.

A CIP record for this book is available from the British Library.

ISBN 978-1-78308-2-070

This title is also available as an eBook

THE DARK HORIZON

Simon Hall

THAMES RIVER PRESS

For Mum and Dad, Joyce and Jackie, Arthur and Gill;
Lost on the way, but with us still.

CHAPTER 1

Of all the ordeals of working life, the torments inflicted in this plasterboard box of a tacked-on room had to be a contender for the worst. Hollow, echoey, white and wan, the modern adjunct to the Victorian edifice could only have been placed on the fringes of the building to keep secret what happened here.

Dan had expected the ten gathered around the table to be floundering in the same churning waters of dread. But, scanning the faces, he wasn't so sure. Fearful as the prospect may be, his peers looked as though they were finding the farce entertaining, and perhaps even enjoyable.

It was a rare meeting he hadn't found a way to miss, despite all best intentions. Dan had planned to disappear from the radar a convenient half hour beforehand to a mysterious briefing on a burgeoning story. The long length of the shadows and light newsroom rumbled with journalists, producers and picture editors quietly, efficiently gathered around screens preparing the programme.

It was an ideal cover. He'd been packing up his satchel when a thin and dark presence materialised at his side like an incarnation of the reaper.

'Just on your way, are you?' Lizzie asked.

'Well, err…'

'Because you know how important this meeting is.'

'Yes, but…'

'It's one of the biggest stories we've ever covered.'

'Ok, but…'

'All that bloodshed. The deaths. The controversy, the pitched battles.'

'I know, but…'

'Now coming to a conclusion at last,' she interrupted once more. 'After a year of it. There's no way it'll go off quietly.'

'Yeah, it's just...'

'With this massive Finale Friday jamboree. The eyes of the world will be on us. It's huge.'

'I was just thinking of doing a bit of research on the Cashman,' Dan ventured, hopefully. 'It's such a great story. We've got to find him.'

A stiletto heel ground at the carpet tiles. Of all the desks in the newsroom the area beside Dan's was by far the most worn from such idiosyncratic assaults, a source of pride to the errant reporter.

'What have I told you about your priority?' Lizzie snapped. 'It's Resurgam, Resurgam and more Resurgam. And then some extra Resurgam. Got that?'

'But...'

'I'm going up to the conference room myself,' she added, mercilessly. 'We can walk together.'

There were no squares left for his battleship to hide. Dan suppressed a sigh and resorted to some rapid improvisation. 'Of course I'm coming to the meeting. I wanted to be there early so I can be completely prepared and absolutely on top of every little detail.'

'Good.' As near to a smile as there ever was flitted across the sharpness of Lizzie's face. 'I'm looking forward to how you get on with the team-building exercise.'

★★★

The management consultants had left their unenviable mark. A survey of the workings of *Wessex Tonight* concluded there were *weaknesses in multi-faceted human-orientated cohesion.* Thus it had been decreed that each meeting would now begin with a bonding session, and today it was the wondrous prospect of the *two truths and a lie* game.

With a smile so fixed it could have been the product of a denture grip factory, Dan tried to look entranced while wishing away the precious seconds of his life. Reporters and producers surrounded the plastic, schoolroom-style table, Lizzie at its head.

'I played rugby for England at college level,' Phil, the newsroom trainee began. 'I secretly ask my dear departed gran for help on every story I cover, and my hero is sitting in this room,' the hunk of a young man told the gathering in his boom-bassy voice.

The windows were filled with the winter's night, a clear and icy void. Dan stared out at the frozen trees and distant streetlamps and wondered what excuse he could find to avoid going home.

It was a familiar thought and he was struggling. Too many convenient paths had already been trodden; friends' emergencies, breaking-news stories, forgotten birthdays, even flat batteries. Perhaps tonight he would just head home and finally they would talk.

'I said – Dan!' a voice cut in. 'Are you listening?'

'Err, of course. Intently.'

'Then you can answer,' Lizzie instructed. 'Which of Phil's three was the lie?'

'Um... give me them again.'

'You weren't listening,' the annoyingly observant editor carped.

'I was. I was just deeply contemplating.'

Lizzie gave him a glare, but nodded to Phil and the list was repeated.

The others were grinning. Mouths were forming the word gran, heads nodding in time.

'The rugby,' Dan said.

Now heads were shaking, faces adopting superior expressions.

'Correct,' Phil said. 'But I did play college rugby for...'

'Wales, judging by the occasional hint of a long-suppressed accent,' Dan picked up. 'Not to mention your build. You were a wing forward, I'd say, all speed and strength. But you weren't quite good enough to make the highest level, and that's not enough for you. So you found another career instead. At which, incidentally, I think you'll excel.'

A silence settled on the meeting room. Phil looked a mixture of stunned and flattered. The clock ticked on to a quarter past six.

'Right, my turn,' Lizzie announced, with relish. 'You'll never get this.'

★★★

Even with the heating rumbling away the room felt cold. It was the lurking influence of this mid-December Tuesday, looming in every one of the run of windows, the frost gathering outside.

Dan tried to look interested as Lizzie scribbled her words, black bob twitching in time. On his own notepad, he jotted an outline of something far more interesting.

The Cashman had been captivating the local media and public alike. Over these last four days, the mystery stranger had materialised in four different locations to hand out bags of money containing tens of thousands of pounds to random passers-by.

The motive was unknown and Dan's nomadic curiosity had been tickled to try to find out. But there was little hope of any such opportunity when Lizzie was keeping him shackled to the preparations for Finale Friday.

'Ok,' she announced, looking up. 'I applied to become Director General of the BBC when I was a kid, I modelled in a photo shoot for *Vogue* when I was at university, and I'm a secret knitter when I'm at home.'

Laughter rumbled around the room. 'That's the last one definitely out,' Phil ventured, to general agreement.

'I can certainly believe the photo shoot,' commented one of the reporters, happily confirming his reputation as chief lickspittle.

'Dan?' Lizzie prompted.

'Director General of the BBC,' he said.

'Really? she queried, incredulously.

'Yes.'

'Why?'

Dan glanced at the sycophant sitting opposite and dug in a dig. 'Some might say because if you had, you would surely have got the job. But, in fact, it's because you hesitated slightly, which means you were framing the answer. You also blinked. Plus...'

'Plus what?'

'I can just tell.'

'How?'

He shrugged. 'You know me. I just can.'

'All right, then, Mr Smarty,' she answered, petulantly. 'It's your turn. Let's have some fun guessing your secrets. '

★★★

A strange temptation came upon Dan. It might have been the urge to release the frustrations of the last two months of home life. It could have been the build-up of the years of the way of a loner and all the pressures of the more distant past. Or it may just have been a need to get out of this room and its damn-blast-bloody ridiculous games. But whatever it was, he found himself talking.

'My personal life is a mess. The woman I'm with moved into my flat without asking and I just don't know what to do about it. I think I want to be back on my own, but I imagine life without her and that scares me too. I don't know what to do.'

He clenched a fist, felt knuckles rap on the table, but the mouth kept moving, free from the reins of inhibition.

'I want to be the main presenter of *Wessex Tonight*. I want to be there in the studio, night after night, under the lights, anchoring the programme. I want to be the cool, calm, controlled one, the face of the news. But no one's ever even thought to ask me.'

The room had set very still. People were staring, frowning; uncertain and unsettled.

'And if you think that's bad, I used to be a spy,' he continued, defiantly. 'I was recruited at university because of my brains and perception and I did some pretty bloody horrible things. I even saw friends die in front of me. And you never leave that behind, I can tell you.'

★★★

A silence held the room, long and dense, the kind that binds with an invisible gag. Even Lizzie was quietened.

'Well, um…' she managed. 'Ok… who wants to try guessing which of Dan's list isn't true?'

But no one ventured a thought. No one could. And as for Dan himself, all he could do was stare out of the window to the nothingness of the winter night, eyes feeling strangely sore.

Onwards the clock ticked. The time was half past six, the moment set to put aside the games and discuss the coverage of the opening of Resurgam.

But before anyone could speak, the door flung open. It was Nigel and he was panting.

'We've got to go,' he told Dan. 'The Cashman's done another appearance.'

CHAPTER 2

The trees and bushes of the garden, the birds, even the road was quiet on this iron winter's night. The impenetrable cold had forced a stillness upon the land, a hibernation for all in this little nook of the planet.

Dan hesitated at the doors to the *Wessex Tonight* building. The quickest way to the street was to the right, across the car park. But it was pitted with ice. That way monsters lay, happy to dart out and effortlessly snap a limb.

Instead, he picked a watchful route to the green acre that surrounded the studios and charged, fast crumping footprints in the whitened grass. Pulling on jacket, panting into phone, dodging around shrubs, squinting through the blackness.

The road was ahead, filled with the growing rush of the car's engine. Nigel had led the way, ready for the off. Dan tumbled onto the pavement, battling for balance, a jumble of arms and legs. He grabbed a lamppost, swung in a manner of which a pole dancer would have been proud and piled untidily inside.

'Go!'

As unruffled as ever from all his long years of experience, the kindly cameraman went.

★★★

They were heading for the train station, in the city centre. The traffic was light, most cars now leaving town. They were laden with boxes and packages, the spoils of a hard day's shopping.

'Lizzie wants a phone report into the programme,' Dan said. 'We've got about ten minutes to get it on.'

'The Cashman again, eh? Of all the stories we've covered, he's got to be one of the strangest. And that's saying something.'

Dan didn't reply. He was concentrating on the phone, a recent gift from the Information Technology Department. In the way of IT, the course on how to use it had lasted a whole morning, but the actual amount of understanding being a hard won quarter of an hour's worth.

'Smart phone, non-smart operator,' was Dan's standard explanation for his failure to master the phone's astounding range of abilities. 'I'm a ZX Spectrum kid in an internet world.'

The one feature which had made it through the barricades of his scepticism was Twitter. And tonight, the virtual world was abuzz with excited tweets.

He's handed out thousands, I've got a bag of money!

We love you, Cashman!

Someone recommend him for a knighthood.

I'm off shopping tomorrow, bless that Cashman!

The car sped through some traffic lights, found a straight. Nigel hit the accelerator and they lurched in the seats. Shop windows, buses, the silhouettes of people flashed past.

The station was ahead. A queue of cars lined the road. Nigel slewed around them and pulled up in a space marked "police only".

Time was sharp against them. There were just minutes left of *Wessex Tonight.*

Despite the darkness, Dan donned his sunglasses. 'CID Special Division,' he barked at a man in a uniform who looked to be readying a challenge.

Dan rummaged in his bag and waved the *Detectives on Inquiries* sign, one of the most useful he had borrowed during his various attachments to police investigations.

'We're filming for evidence,' he said, and the petty officialdom evaporated in the barrage of nonsense, as is often the happy way.

★★★

A crowd of a couple of hundred people was massed outside the automatic doors of the station entrance. They were burbling, chattering, charged with the lustre of unexpected luck.

One rotund man was performing a poor attempt at a celebratory jig. The less blessed were ignoring the cold to search gutters and drains, probing the underside of parked cars, scrabbling beneath benches and bins for any booty which may have been overlooked.

Dan grabbed a well-dressed young woman, perhaps an office worker, who was giggling hysterically.

'What happened?'

'I got some!'

She opened a handbag, proffered a fistful of plastic money bags stuffed with the unmistakable colours of ten pound notes. 'A car drew up and he got out and started throwing the bags. There were loads of people round him in seconds. I was right at the front.'

Dan's mobile was ringing, but he ignored it. He glanced at his watch. *Wessex Tonight* was fast running out of airtime.

'What was he wearing?'

'That mask. The one he always wears.'

'Was there anything else in the bags, apart from the cash?'

'Those little notes they talked about on the news.'

She unfolded a square of paper. Typewritten upon it were the letters A B C D E F G H. In black ink, around the E, was a bold circle.

The paparazzi were already here, the white strobes of their flashlights firing through the darkness. People were posing for snaps, holding up their gains.

The dark prince of the pack, Dirty El, appeared around the corner and lumbered over. He stopped stricken upon seeing the other photographers, distress in his sweaty, chubby face. If ever one so devious had a heart, being beaten to the scene of a lucrative snap was a knife through it.

A police car drew in, then another. At the sight of the law and the threat to their gains, the crowd began to thin.

Dan's mobile rang again. 'There's only two mins left on the programme,' Lizzie yelped. 'We need you now.'

He found a corner away from the hubbub, jotted a couple of notes, held the phone hard to his ear. His tight fingers were pallid with the cold, despite his heart hammering hot and hard.

'Finally, tonight's breaking news. The Cashman has just staged another appearance in Plymouth,' came the gruff voice of Craig, the presenter.

Cue Dan.

'This time, each of his moneybags contained 50 pounds,' Dan picked up. 'It seems clear the Cashman's following a pattern. This is his fifth appearance and each time the sum in the bags has increased by ten pounds. From what I've seen here, he must have parted with tens of thousand pounds this evening alone. Again, he said nothing, just threw the bags of money and disappeared. And once more he was wearing that Robin Hood mask. The big question of course, the one so many are asking, and which is still unanswered – who is the Cashman and why is he doing this?'

CHAPTER 3

It was strange, Dan reflected, how the door to the flat had changed these past months. Slowly, yet unmistakeably.

Just a wooden block, utterly ordinary and entirely average, replicated millions of times in the streets and lanes throughout the land. A plain oblong with inlaid panels, albeit newly painted in a smart navy blue.

Even the hinges had been oiled when it was refurbished, back in the happier days of the summer. It was designed to be homely, offer an easy welcome.

And it did. Until two months, one week, and three days ago.

In the yellow lights of the street, at this vacuum time of day, it was a plain and dense black. In the passing beams of endless traffic his shadow ran across it, up and over the walls and away.

She would have heard the car. Would be waiting, know he too was waiting. Yet another unspoken stand-off, this time in the tar-dark freezer of a dense December night.

The cold was omnipresent, all around and everywhere. Ice in the air and sleet in the sky. The crystal teeth of icicles on the windowsills, the glitter dust of frost on the tarmac.

Inside the flat, through the warmed mist of the steamed windows, was another land. Soft lights, rumbling radiators, the hot cocoon of a shower to end this peculiar day.

But still, he hesitated. Stared at the silver edges of the key. Shivered and pulled his jacket tight.

Thought of old friends lost and family long gone. Betrayed promises and dying dreams. Christmases past and all the ghosts of the mind of this most reflective of seasons.

★★★

From inside the door came a slow footfall. Dan straightened, took a breath and turned his key in the latch. Claire was waiting in the half-light of the hallway.

'Hi!' she chirped.

'Hello.'

She waited. He waited. They both waited. Claire leaned forwards and, after a pause, Dan accepted the hug of her outstretched arms.

'Good day?'

'A bit weird.'

'Do you need a shower?'

'After I've walked Rutherford.'

'I've done it.'

'Oh.'

A scrabbling shook the lounge door. 'You shouldn't shut him in like that. He doesn't like it.'

'I just wanted a cuddle without him interrupting.'

'He doesn't interrupt.'

Dan pushed open the door and the dog careered out, a jumble of legs and fur, even now little different from those puppy days. Claire stood watching as Dan knelt and made a long fuss of the Alsatian. His ears were rubbed, his sleek nose stroked, his paws held, his fine mane lovingly ruffled.

'I sometimes wonder if you think more of that dog than me,' she whispered.

There was no answer. Dan had rolled Rutherford onto his side and was tickling the dog's stomach.

'I'll put supper on,' Claire said. 'I've done some pasta.'

'I had a decent lunch. I don't need anything much.'

'A small bowl? It's your favourite. I've made it specially.'

'Ok, then.'

★★★

In the shower, Dan noticed a new line of cosmetics had staked yet another claim to the windowsill. A mat of Claire's dark hair was blocking the plughole. He sighed and picked it out.

From the kitchen a pan clanged. The radio burbled, overly-loud, as ever.

Dan tried to shut it out, think instead about Resurgam towering into the sky, at last almost complete. It was one of the longest running stories he'd ever covered and by far the most bitter. With all that had unfolded over this last year, it would be a strange relief to see it open.

His mobile warbled with a text and he reached through the shower curtain to read it. The message was from El, and unusual. The photographer normally sent only very brief messages, but this was an electronic lament.

You've got to help me! I'm being murdered on me own patch. Them paparazzi from London are everywhere. They're stitching up all me sources with their flash and cash. They're gonna find the Cashman. Me reputation'll be shot. I'll be history, a laughing stock. Help your poor old buddy, please!

A gentle knock sounded on the door. 'The pasta's looking good.'

'Great.'

'Would you like a beer?' Claire asked.

'No thanks.'

'A glass of wine?'

'No.'

'Some company?'

In a strained voice, Dan said, 'I'm almost done. I'll be out in a minute.'

The door slid closed again.

★★★

When Dan bought the flat, it was entrancement at first sight. He delighted in all the rooms, but it was the lounge he loved the most. The great space, the lofty Victorian ceiling, the plasterwork, the expanse of bay window overlooking the city and the white marble fireplace. It needed no television, just a sofa to sit and enjoy.

He had taken care to choose the decor to compliment the bequest of heritage, and the furniture to match. It was a haven of calm, warmth and beauty, an atmosphere it had never lost.

But this evening, the lounge was suffering a look it had never known before, and it was doing so with all the grace of a Hell's Angel forced to wear a tutu.

Tinsel bedecked the dado rail, a caterpillar of red and green. Baubles of shamelessly unconvincing gold and silver hung from the fine stone of the fireplace, turning a little in the caress of the rising heat. In the corner, by the window, stood a small Christmas tree.

'I decorated,' Claire smiled.

'I noticed.'

'I spent hours. Do you like it?'

'It's certainly Christmassy.'

She clicked on the stereo and found some music, a dignified, classical sound. Dan reached for the remote control and turned it down. They sat at the table by the window and ate the pasta, Rutherford stretched between them.

'I saw your report on the Cashman. It's bizarre. Does anyone have an idea what that's all about?'

'Not that I know of.'

'It's quite a mystery.'

Rutherford yawned. Claire picked up her wine glass and took a sip of the claret liquid. Dan traced the line of a wood grain with a finger.

'I bought you a Christmas present today,' she said.

'Oh, right. Thank you.'

'Do you need any ideas for mine?'

'Not really. I'll find something.'

They ate on. One of the strands of tinsel slipped and hung down the wall. Dan's phone rang. Claire glanced at it, a tired, forlorn look.

'You've got to help me find him!' a pained voice wailed. 'I'm being humiliated on me home turf!'

'El, I can't talk now. I'll have a think and get back to you.'

'Promise? Cross your heart, Scout's honour and on Rutherford's life?'

Dan pushed the remaining pieces of pasta around the plate. A gust of wind whistled at the window.

Claire lay down her fork. 'We're going to have to talk.'

'What about?'

'You know what about.' She flicked at her hair. 'Me. You. Us.'

Another piece of tinsel drooped down and swayed with a sad rhythm. Claire got up from her seat. 'I took this sabbatical to try to work it out with you.'

'I know.'

'And you said it was a good idea.'

'I know that. I just…'

'Just what?'

'Just didn't realise it meant you'd be moving in.'

She folded her arms. 'Don't you want me here?'

'I'm not saying that.'

'What are you saying?'

'Just…'

'Should I move out again?'

'I didn't say that.'

'What are you saying then?'

'Just that I'm not used to living with someone. It's the first time I've ever done it.'

'Yeah,' she replied, with acrid bitterness. 'I could tell.'

'I just need some space.'

'Space?'

'It's come as a bit of a shock, that's all.'

'I've been here two months now!'

Dan joined the folded arms club. 'Two months, one week and three days, in fact.'

Claire let out a low gasp. She turned away, the boyishness of her hair highlighted by the glow of a standard lamp.

'All I mean is – it's just… taking some adjusting,' he wheedled.

'Do you want me here or not?'

Dan's mobile began trilling once more. He answered, listened briefly and hung up.

'I've got to go.'

'What now?'

'It's Resurgam again. Another attack.'

'Don't go. Not now.'

'I have to.'

'But I need to talk to you - please.'

'I've got no choice. We can talk… some other time…'

Claire held out her arms for a cuddle, but Dan was already past her and striding for the door.

CHAPTER 4

The wire-and-metal panels of one of the gates lay scattered, a couple of ruby eyes of warning lights still blinking. The hinges had been wrenched from the wall, as if swatted by a mighty force. Lumps of rubble were strewn across the road.

Inside the compound lay a lorry, the axles and exhaust of its underbelly exposed. The tarmac was gouged where it had toppled and scoured at the ground. One door was angled ajar, a fluorescent jacket dangling limp. Oil dripped, glutinous from the engine, forming a dense puddle shining in the darkness.

The guardhouse next to the gates had been demolished, caved in and crushed, as if it had imploded under its own weight. A spray of glass shards covered the road, glittering in the arrhythmic pulsing of the lights of the mass of police cars, fire engines and ambulances.

The bitter tang of scorched rubber lingered in the air, dominating the leaking diesel and background wash of sea salt. The jets of hoses from a team of firefighters damped the underside of the lorry. A sinuous trail of wispy steam rose into the raw air.

A small knot of people was huddled by The Wall, watched over by a couple of police officers. Around them, discarded and forgotten, were the makeshift banners which had been their weapons.

No to Resurgam! Give our city back! Jobs, not follies! Remember Alice!

A couple of the group sat hunched, heads in hands. More hugged each other, a fog of breath surrounding the clutched embrace. Diminished by the cold, shamed by the scene, none could look to the nexus of this night.

A team of paramedics was bent over a corner of the debris, firefighters with them, picking away brick and pulling at metal stanchions. The work was urgent, focused. They formed an uneven line, fighting the weight of a twisted beam.

One, two, three – heave! One, two, three – heave!
In the twilight of the moment, death lingered. Held back for now by the determination of the effort, the shared purpose, but still waiting, hovering on the edge of every set of senses.

A pile of rubble clattered. Brick dust filled the air, a swirling mist in the whiteness of the arc lights.

One more time – heave!

Now the stanchion shifted and clanged to the ground, a mind-splitting attack of sound, decibels ringing to the core of the brain. A stretcher was pulled forwards, the unmistakeable outline of a person lifted onto it.

But wrong, so very wrong. An insult to nature and decency. No living creature should ever be twisted carelessly into such a form.

Unseen as he approached, half-hidden in the shadows, the detective allowed himself one contemptuous glare at the shining glass, steel and concrete edifice known as Resurgam.

★★★

As ever at the start of a major investigation, he had only a drunkard's view. There were blurs and scents, claims and allegations, but no focus or definition.

Adam quickly scanned the miserable group. 'Is this all of them?'

'As far as we know,' the uniformed sergeant replied. 'It wasn't a difficult job. They just stood around waiting to be arrested.'

'Hmm. You think?'

The group was a mix of young and old, all locals as far as Adam could remember. Resurgam hadn't been his case, not even when the protests had turned violent. Only after the first death was his dark expertise required.

These remaining demonstrators weren't the *Professionals,* as they styled themselves. This little group was the set from the community. Committed, passionate or embittered, they had sworn to protest until the day Resurgam opened.

Shock was in each pair of eyes. One woman looked dazed, kept repeating, 'I can't believe it, not again.' The men tried to be stronger, but it was a frail façade. Most were no more than teenagers. One, perhaps only 18 or 19, was clutching a banner. In an untidy legend was painted *For Alice and our Future.*

At the end of the group stood a woman, wrapped in thick layers of clothing but still shivering in the unforgiving cold. A memory surfaced of an elder's role here; comforter of the young, moderator of the radical, a soul of reason and sensibility.

'It's June, isn't it?'

She nodded, but couldn't look at him.

'Chief Inspector Breen. I was part of the investigation into Alice's death.'

Another miserable nod.

'What happened?'

No reply.

'Where is she?'

June turned away, another woman lacing an arm around her shoulders. 'She's too upset to talk to you.'

'I'm sorry, but murder investigations don't allow much leeway for sympathy.'

And now June looked up, her once kindly face pinched and drawn. 'He's not... the man in the guardhouse isn't...'

'That depends how things go at the hospital. But what we do need to know is - what happened?'

'Just a protest,' June whispered. 'That was all. Just another demonstration before Friday.'

'And where is she?'

'Esther?'

Adam's lip curled with the name. 'Esther.'

'It was her idea — for the lorry.'

'I somehow thought it might be. And let me guess - was she driving it?'

'Yes.'

'So where is she now?'

'Off... she ran off ...'

The words faded into a lost silence. Dismal experience said a curtain had fallen on this interrogation. Adam turned to some of the young men, clustered together, sharing a cigarette in shaking hands.

'Where is she?'

No one replied. A fire engine rumbled past, followed by an ambulance, the rising draft pulling at the men's hair.

'Lost your voices?' Adam barked. He leaned forwards, right into their faces, amidst the lingering smoke, waved it away. 'You - where is she?'

'No idea. Just leave us alone.'

There was a fuzz of hair around the young man's mouth, an adolescent attempt at a goatee, but it couldn't hide the trembling lips.

'I can't leave you alone just yet, I'm afraid. Because I'll need to start charging you with being accessories to murder first.'

A foot swung from one of the group, but it was a half-hearted effort, easy to evade.

'To which I'll add assaulting a police officer. That's unless I find out where Esther is – right now.'

'She ran off, ok?'

'Where?'

'I dunno! None of us know, for fuck's sake! Do you think we wanted to be part of this?! She just jumped out the lorry and ran.'

★★★

As if aloof from the human follies playing out at its feet, a great beast amongst mere bacteria, Resurgam continued to make ready for its grand opening.

Flashlights swayed in the dark heavens of the night. From the heights of the Sky Garden, 57 floors above, came the sound of hammering and drilling, the odd spray of sparks arcing in the blackness.

It could have been shrewd marketing. It might even have been a rare sight of elusive truth, but word had been put around it was a traditional *race against time* to get Resurgam ready for its inaugural

20

day. Work would have to go on around the clock in this last week of preparations.

A small team was setting the angles of the sculptures of modern art which would welcome the first visitors; details and adjustments so slight as to be barely worthwhile, except perhaps in the most affected of eyes.

Around the cavernous mouth of the building's doors, engineers fiddled and refined. They stood back in their gangs, hands on hips, pointing and nodding.

The line of low steps leading up to the edifice was smoothed and sanded. The buzz and hum was the backdrop to all that went on that night. Around the ring of flagpoles, final brushstrokes of paint were applied and guide ropes pulled.

While fifty metres from them all, as far detached as could be another time, police officers guarded the remains of the gatehouse as the fingertips of their fellows searched for evidence. And detectives questioned the protesters in a slow path of pained progress, the dispirited responses sullen and monosyllabic.

Workers with pencils and notepads were already assessing the damage to the mass of brick and concrete which had, with an ironic nod to history, become known as *The Wall*.

And across the city an ambulance sped, a blue shrouded spectre amongst the streets, its burden a gravely injured young man. While at the hospital, outside Accident and Emergency, doctors and nurses stood waiting, swinging arms and stamping feet to keep warm and ready.

★★★

A stare as sharp as a broadsword's blade was one of this detective's favoured expressions. With such a lean face, and eyes some said could turn grey amidst the intensity of a major investigation, it was a look he did well.

Tonight, it was set not upon some wriggling miscreant or dissembling recidivist, but a CD. In its mirror shine was a clue, but like the most reluctant of witnesses it wasn't giving up the information easily.

'Security reckons it shows the whole attack,' the sergeant said.

Adam was on his feet before the end of the sentence. 'Then let's see it.'

'That's the problem. The player was in the gatehouse.'

The silent response must have been answer enough, and the man offered quickly, 'There's a machine back at the station.'

'By which time she'll be long gone.'

With impressive speed Adam was out of the van. Striding in a precise, near-military manner, his polished shoes shinier even than the ice, he cut an unerring path, no concession to a slip or slide. Ahead were the gathering lines of the media; satellite vans, radio cars and reporters.

'Where are you going, sir?' the sergeant called, but the crow-black night gave up no reply.

CHAPTER 5

Dan and Nigel had been standing beside the camera, doing their best to keep warm, for a quarter of an hour before other journalists and photographers began to arrive. The duo was eyed with irritation and envy, as befitted those in contented possession of a scoop. Dan took it as a compliment and tried not to look smug.

Across the road, a line of men from the Homeless Mission had emerged to share a cigarette and sightsee. Along the estuary, a sole fishing boat huffed its way into harbour.

Dan's mobile rang. It was the call he had been expecting, but would require artful handling. He listened for a few seconds, said 'Right,' a couple of times, then, 'Can do,' and hung up. He tapped at his teeth and in response to Nigel's questioning look beckoned and whispered in his friend's ear.

The cameraman sighed and pursed his lips, but played along. With a fine flounce, he exclaimed, 'But it's freezing!'

'But if it's there, we have to get it.'

'Why can't you come and help?'

'Because I've got to write the story.'

Other reporters had begun eavesdropping, exactly as the actors in this mini-drama expected. 'What is it?' one asked.

'Nothing,' Dan replied.

'Come on,' another hack joined in, grumpily. 'You've got your exclusive. We're all in this together now.'

Dan managed to swallow a contemptuous snort. 'It's only a rumour. That there was another attack on *The Wall*, right round the other side.'

'And he wants me to film it,' Nigel added, sulkily. 'In the dark and cold.'

'If you'd be so kind,' Dan replied, sweetly. He was about to turn away when the disgruntled journalist added, 'This isn't another of those little tricks of yours, by any chance?'

'Meaning?'

'Trying to get rid of us, so you can have something all to yourself here.'

'Hey, I…'

'It's not like you haven't got form for that.'

The attempted look of innocence made surprisingly little impact on the depressingly cynical pack. 'Yeah,' Dan tried, instead, 'Because I'd really send my cameraman away if there was something important happening here.'

He shook his head with what he hoped was a due weight of sadness and climbed into the satellite van. Nigel tutted to himself, but began walking round the corner. The rest of the pack exchanged glances and trailed behind.

It was only when they were safely out of sight that Dan hopped back down, wandered over to *The Wall* and waited, as he had been instructed.

★★★

From the early hostilities in the Battle of Resurgam, the building had grown to be a fortress. Its seaward side was straightforward to defend; a line of jetties and some unwelcoming wire fencing was sufficient to ward off any attack.

The landward way was harder. There, the faceless figures of power forever known as *the authorities* had opted for the tradition of erecting a wall.

It was a masterpiece of brick and concrete ugliness, topped with spotlights and razor wire. A toothache of a barrier, as incongruous as could be with the Tudor surroundings of the Barbican and the estuary of the River Plym. But, the diktat held, it was necessary and so it would stand, at least until Resurgam was complete.

The wall was salt in the ulcer of the controversy and inflamed the protests further. It became an impromptu art gallery of angry protest; slogans, graffiti and abuse, colourful in image and vehemence, but it did its job. It kept the hordes at bay.

Until tonight Dan reflected, as he paced back and forth along it, arms wrapped around his body for warmth.

★★★

This part of the wall, by the gatehouse, had become the Graffiti Zone. In a munificence of largesse, the authorities decreed that artworks painted here – except the profane, offensive or intolerant– would be allowed to stand. They could be a demonstration of a place for peaceful protest in a thriving democracy.

The problem, of course, was the moment it became licit the appeal vanished faster even than a clergyman making his escape from a brothel. So it was that the graffiti artists turned elsewhere to ply their trade, and out of sight of the security cameras flourished the real feelings about Resurgam. A little along the wall, towards the city centre, Dan found a new mural had been added.

Not in my name, the legend ran.

Beneath it was painted the outline of a silent mass of people, standing together as if gazing at Resurgam. Some held candles, others placards. Beside it, someone had added in a far less cultured scrawl, *Fuck the thing and all the fuckers who built it.*

★★★

Dan wandered on, to the edge of the *Graffiti Zone* and Alice's shrine. He paused as a helicopter chugged its way through the night, slipping behind the indomitable bulk of the skyscraper as it headed along the coast. Stretched reflections of the lights of the waterfront ran in the glass and metal of the building's sheer sides.

From the pinnacle of the pyramid tower, a trellis of aerials jabbed at the stars. Surrounding it, like a crenellation, was the Sky Garden. And beneath that lay the *Night Life Zone,* a variety of bars, restaurants and a club, all sold with the slogan, *Eat, drink and party the spectacle.*

From the ranks of photographs Alice's face smiled out. Her eyes were still bright, even in the embrace of death. Fresh flowers surrounded the pictures, added by the friends and family who mourned her, and the many others she had never known. New messages were left daily, too.

You were worth more than a million follies.

You died for principles – they live without principles.

Sleep easy Alice.

A sharp whistle sounded in the darkness, an unmistakable peremptory summons. Dan rolled his eyes, but turned back towards the remains of the gates.

★★★

The lorry rumbled slowly along the access road, just as many thousands had before. It was dusty and dirty, so everyday as to be unnoticeable. Security was ever alert for gangs of protesters attempting to storm the fortress, but not another delivery. The unseen watching eyes would have glanced over the lumbering beast and given it not a second thought.

Until the truck began to speed up. And by then it was too late.

Along the tarmac it ran, faster and faster. The whiteness of its headlights started to blur, comets racing through the encompassing darkness.

Now the truck broke onto a stretch of road which was better lit. Fencing appeared from the background, daubed amber by the sodium glow of the streetlights. Lampposts too, thin and fleeting markers of the racing progress of the squat and bulky missile.

The image was a little unsteady, the camera moving with the motion, but the action was perfectly clear. And the shock of the ending was one which they already knew far too well.

Ahead lay the gates and guardhouse, a glass box filled with light. The lorry was bearing down fast. Its wheels were spinning, a smudge of driving force.

There was sound on the film, too. A growing, growling roar of the screaming, straining engine.

Only a hundred metres now separated the truck from the gates. They were shut, their thin metal struts a hopeless barrier against the power of the mechanical battering ram which closed relentlessly upon them.

Seventy five metres. The engine was roaring louder still, the image growing ever shakier. In the guardhouse there was movement, the panicked outline of a person, darting back and forth.

Fifty metres. And the lorry was changing direction, gradually shifting its path. Heading not for the gates, but the block of glass and light.

Thirty metres. The door of the cab was moving, swinging, opening. A shape tumbled onto the tarmac.

The lorry careered onwards. Ten metres. The blazing whiteness of the guardhouse dominated the image. Inside, the small, lonely figure of a person stood watching, static and struck.

Impact. A thunderous, booming crash. The smash of shattering glass, split apart and scattered afar. A cloud of smoke and dust, the vague ghosts of faltering lights within the grey, hazy aura. A sudden spray of flame.

Somewhere, a little distant, a man's voice muttered, 'Oh my God.'

The lorry cleared the angry fog of the destruction it had wreaked, pitched onto its side, lay in the compound as if an offering before the might of Resurgam. Crumbling brick fell to the tarmac and settled in pathetic piles of debris.

In the foreground the dark shape of a person rose from the road. It bent down again, searched, scrabbled and picked up an object, something bulky, indiscernible, then started to walk away fast.

Inside the compound a siren wailed, the clamorous ringing of an alarm bell following. And the picture on the monitor screen froze.

Adam reached out and stopped the CD. 'Murder, all played out on CCTV,' he said quietly.

THE BATTLE OF RESURGAM – JANUARY, THE BEGINNINGS

The Deputy Chief Constable of Greater Wessex Police, Brian Flood has a saying of which he is more than fond. His senior officers know it so well it could be ingrained upon their minds in letters of fire.

Flood, or *The Tank*, as he's known, is plenty smart enough to recognise a cliché, but also to acknowledge the truths they contain. So he has adapted one for his own ends.

Come the morning of Thursday, January 4th, when work on Resurgam is due to begin, at six o'clock sharp Flood sits in the Operations Room at Charles Cross Police station. His eyes skip across the wall of CCTV monitors, ears keyed to the police radios. He is the Gold Commander, top of the tree, peak of the pyramid, in control of all he surveys.

He is tensed, prepared and ready for anything, as reminds the man of his days in the Royal Marines. In truth, the weight has inflated since those halcyon times of physical pomp. The jowls, too, have suffered, but the brain is just as sharp.

He's like a toad in his lair. Still now, but don't be deceived. He's ever watchful. And he's always ready.

The plan is in place. Legions of cops await his orders. The eyes of the nation are on his corner of the country, his police force. But it feels as if they're focused only upon him.

Protests are planned. That Flood knows. But the Intelligence Section can't say how many people will turn up, or their intentions.

So, will there be any trouble this morning, a couple of mid-ranking officers speculate? Might there be disorder? Even violence?

'Never on my watch,' Flood barks, as he waits for the first of the workers to arrive at Resurgam, and the first of the demonstrators, too.

★★★

28

Flood had stayed in Plymouth the previous night, just in case the protesters might try for the advantage of surprise and begin their antics early. The hotel was modest, as likely to boast a star as an amateur dramatics' pantomime. But it was cheap and next to Charles Cross, a wise contingency should he be roused unexpectedly.

At half past four, in the dark and constricting cold he stood, in the great car park on Plymouth Hoe and watched over his assembling forces. Had Flood allowed himself the indulgence of romance, he might have thought of generals of yore, amongst the troops as they prepared for battle.

Eight hundred officers surrounded him, silhouettes in a backdrop of snow. All were encased in the armour of their riot gear. Helmets, breast plates - albeit plastic, these days - gloves, boots and knee pads. A fleet of police vans lined the car park, their windows covered in wire mesh, all pointing down the road towards Resurgam. To the north of the city, at Plymouth airport, the police helicopter was waiting.

He should have resisted it, but what was the point of such exalted rank if you didn't flaunt it occasionally? With a little difficulty, Brian Flood clambered onto the bonnet of one of the police Range Rovers.

'I can't say for sure what you'll be riding into,' he boomed. 'But I can say this – whatever may await, I know you'll face it and I know you'll deal with it. With calmness, but with resolution and with certainty. I know you'll do me, yourselves, and your force proud. Now – go do it!'

As he stepped carefully back onto the frozen ground, Brian Flood made sure he kept that little piece of paper safe. One day, posterity may come calling for the words written upon it.

★★★

Into the dark void of the early morning the forces of the law ride. But now comes the subtlety.

Flood has been decried by his detractors as a one-gun cowboy, a man who has but a single strategy for dealing with problems.

With the more minor, such as the disciplinary hearings he oversees, shouting is the preferred weapon. For issues of law enforcement, it is a policing version of the doctrine of overwhelming force.

But no one reaches such high rank without at least a little nous. *Softly softly* has always been the way of British policing, and long may it continue. So, sent to greet the first demonstrators is one everyday police van. It's not modern, nor high-spec, and sans defensive grilles. It contains a dozen officers wearing no riot gear, carrying no shields, protected instead by their uniforms, politeness and pleasantries.

The rest of the massed forces will wait. They'll be close at hand but well out of sight. And now the protesters come, picking their way through the snow. The Control Room, previously rumbling with conversation, goes quiet. Flood leans towards the CCTV monitors.

It is a gang of students, five in number. The officers say good morning and receive a similar reply, interlaced with yawns and comments about the earliness of the hour. The protesters are guided to the area set out for them, a sizeable box beside the access road.

They lean upon the railings. A couple light cigarettes, another hands around some placards and they wait.

Flood says nothing. He waits, too.

On the monitors he watches a couple of cops standing by the protest, exchanging banter. The faces are hard to see, wrapped up in scarves and hats against the cold, but for the most part they're smiling.

More protesters are arriving. A group of four. These are older, a couple even looking like pensioners, swaddled in fattening layers of clothing. They too are guided to the Democracy Zone, as it has been shamelessly labelled.

One is fumbling in a bag. At a command from Flood the CCTV zooms in. He's on his feet, waiting for – what? A brick? A firework? A metal bar? A petrol bomb, even?

No such, and nothing like. This is England.

It's a flask of tea. The woman is handing out plastic cups and sharing it around.

Flood sits back down. The time is quarter past six. The first workers are due to arrive. This is the key moment. If there is to be a confrontation, if that is to be the way of the weeks ahead, it will surely happen now.

More protesters are arriving in ones and twos. Some carry banners, others placards, some carry nothing at all.

They're policed by a total of three cops. The CCTV zooms in again. One of the officers, a young constable, is having a kick about with the students. They're using a snowball for a football.

The time turns to twenty past six. A couple more demonstrators arrive. The protest now numbers around thirty people.

A van indicates, slows and turns along the entrance road. It's approaching the group. They're nudging each other. All have seen it, all are watching. It draws closer.

Flood is on his feet again. Once more the CCTV zooms in.

A couple of arms wave in the cold air and the van is past.

More workers are walking up the road, their yellow jackets flaring in the streetlights. The protesters are watching. A banner is waved and a chorus of *No way, never to stay / Not here, not today*, begins, but quickly dies.

So it goes for the next half hour. A Chief Inspector smiles with the blessing of unspoken victory and asks Flood, 'Shall we start standing the troops down?'

He's greeted by a look like lightning, and a sense of the sudden death of any prospects for promotion. 'It could be a feint,' Flood hisses. 'Never let your guard down.'

By half past seven the protest is down to a dozen. The word from the scene is that some have had to leave, to head for work.

By eight o'clock, the masses of the ranks are released to other duties, for there is always work aplenty for a police officer. But those at the demonstration remain, just in case.

By nine, Flood himself is on his way back to Exeter and headquarters. The Home Office requires an urgent update on an inestimably vital study catchily entitled *On Health and Safety Issues Arising from the Unavoidable Forcible Restraint of Potentially Threatening,*

Hazardous or Violent Juvenile Offenders, Plausibly / Suspected to be Under the Influence of Drink or Drugs (Focus Group, Working Party, Sub Committee).

At Resurgam, the command of the operation is back with a local inspector. Just half a dozen police remain.

A few minutes later, two are required at a car crash, then another pair for a domestic violence call. A further ten minutes pass, and one more is wanted to deal with a suspected shoplifter.

Which leaves a tall and bright-faced recruit of three months' experience as the embodiment of order.

★★★

'Would you like to share our tea?' the older lady at the edge of the demonstration asked. Seeing the young officer's longing look, but also wary glance up and down the street she added, 'We won't tell the bosses – promise.'

He took the flask and sipped gratefully, a microclimate of breath rising around the plastic cup.

'I'm June, by the way.'

'PC Rogers.'

'Don't police officers have Christian names these days?'

She had a distinctive voice, in a lulling fashion. The timbre was kind, but demanded attention with its longevity and wisdom.

'Do you really need to know?' the constable found himself asking.

'We're going to be seeing quite a lot of each other, wouldn't you say? And I always like to know the people I'm responsible for.'

PC Rogers didn't object to the surprising claim, but instead looked pleased to have found a friend. 'Were you a teacher, by any chance?'

'For forty years,' came the smiling reply. 'And a good teacher knows when someone's trying to avoid answering a question. But in this case it can't be because you don't know the answer, can it?'

In response to the meaningful look, a classic of the classroom kind, he climbed down from the battlements of authority.

'It's... Stephen.'

'Steve, you mean?'

'Only if you behave.'

The group of radicals and rebels surrounding the gentle interrogator chuckled.

'You're no good with crosswords, are you?' June asked. She had eyes of a blue so pale as to be the most diluted of tinctures. Faded too by the years was the complexion of her knowing face. Her hands, wrapped in rainbow mittens which matched a tea cosy of a hat, held a copy of a bumper book of cryptic puzzles. 'I can't get twelve across for the life of me.'

'Sorry, not my thing. I did Sports Science at college.'

'I'm thinking about that,' a powerfully built young man in the centre of the line responded. He was handsome, strikingly so, and had been fortunate enough to escape the teenage blight of spots. Perhaps as a result he was exactingly clean-shaven, with a face as strong as his impressive physique. 'Is it a good course?'

'It's much better than just sitting in a classroom all day. You look as though you'd like it. What sport do you do?'

'Athletics.'

'You're a sprinter?'

The guess was a compliment enough to further inflate the young man's stature. 'College champion at the hundred and two hundred metres.'

'I'm a football man myself.'

'I like football, but...'

'What?'

'It's not – well...' The aspiring athlete looked embarrassed, but finally ventured. 'It's a bit of a thugs' game, isn't it?'

'Ok, that'll do,' June intervened, with a demonstration of the old adage that once a teacher, always a teacher. 'Shall we start with some introductions, before we move on to character assassination?'

'I'm Sebastian – or Seb,' the young man said with some relief, and gestured to three others of similar vintage. 'Alice, Esme and Mac.'

The women shook hands with confidence and poise, no trace of self-consciousness. But the subterranean creature identified as

Mac plunged his deep into a pair of capacious pockets and turned away. His long, black hair followed the move with a semi-second's delay.

'Is it worth doing, Sports Science?' Seb asked PC Steve.

'I really enjoyed it. The problem is finding a job afterwards. That's partly why I...' he pointed to the uniform. 'Mind, this job might suit you.'

A friendly nod was directed to Seb's feet, so sizeable that he might have worn the boxes rather than the trainers. At the blossoming of an impressive blush, the policeman diplomatically asked, 'You're a student?'

'We all are.'

A large crane rumbled up the road, yellow lights flashing from its cab, waves of slush fleeing its wheels.

'What are you lot doing here, then?' Steve asked. 'Shouldn't you be studying?'

'We're still on Christmas hols and it's better than revision,' Seb replied, and received an admonishing dig in the ribs from Alice.

He smiled in spite of the rebuke, because that was what men did in the presence of Alice. She was the beauty of this fine cast of youthful spirit, with looks made to please. Her body was elfin, even under the layers of clothes, but she had an elegance which made nothing she did an effort. To complete the artwork her hair had to be blonde, and so it was, aside from a thin streak of rebellious purple. Alice pulled a woolly hat further down over her ears, bunches of its soft flow piling around the dark edges of material.

'It's about our futures,' she corrected. 'It just feels like everything's against us. If we go to Uni we're saddled with huge debts. There aren't any jobs, anyway. The planet's being destroyed. And all the government's interested in is more stuff like this monstrosity.'

Mac grunted, which on the balance of teenage probabilities suggested agreement. He slung a resentful shrug at the nascent moments of Resurgam, nothing more yet than a flat expanse of land being progressively occupied by the forces of development. To make entirely sure no one could mistake his opinion, Mac also raised two fingers and waved them at the building site.

'What's he so angry about?' PC Steve enquired.

'Take your pick,' Esme replied, in a fond tone. 'Our Mac could get wound up by the sun going down at night, then really bitter about it coming back up again in the morning.'

The response was no further guttural utterings, but a deep glower. It was the kind of look a hand grenade might adopt as a warning of detonation. This was a young man swimming deep in the restless sea of troubled youth.

'He's an Emo,' Esme explained, conspiratorially. 'It means he's the emotional type and not afraid to show it.'

'I somehow guessed that,' the policeman replied.

'He's studying art and music,' she continued, as if her contemporary was a favoured dog; well-loved, but unable to speak for himself. 'He plays the bass in a band. Pretty good, too. And he paints. The teachers reckon his stuff is great, full of feeling. But it looks more like a toddler's tantrum to me.'

Mac shook his head, but chose to keep any of the feted passions to himself. The sound of metallic hammering and the thud of a digger working at the icy ground started up, forcing conversation to a shout.

Esme picked at the hem of a boot and tightened the battered buckle on a leather strap.

A frond of coppery hair fell across her cheek. She looked older than her years; aged with the kind of insights which are rare at the outset of adulthood.

'I want to change things,' she said, earnestly. 'That's why I'm here. To make a difference.'

It was the mantra of countless who had gone before. But from Esme, it sounded distinct. There was a purpose to her, a resolution.

Even the fair Alice was eclipsed by her presence, that assurance and certainty. Yet Alice looked admiringly at the gentle oratory. There was no jealousy, no rivalry, between the pair; instead a bond of respect and friendship.

'We're being forgotten,' Esme continued. 'That's how people will remember us - or not, more likely. *Generation What?* they'll call us. And I'm not putting up with that.'

June was nodding in sympathy. 'I'm here because I'm sick of the government wasting our money when it could be spent on schools and hospitals.'

'So let's show them!' came a sudden yell from the end of the line. Mac had darted out into the road, directly in front of the lumbering crane. Its horn sounded a sharp warning, but he stood there unmoving, arms outstretched, until the great machine slowed and stopped.

PC Rogers hurried into the roadway. 'Come on now, Mac.'

'Never! I'm staying here 'til I die! I'm gonna lie down and never shift!'

The young man glanced at the road, ridden with filthy, oily sludge. Then he looked at his trench coat, immaculate in its black leather and decided to stay standing. From the older protesters came a couple of smiles.

'Come on Mac,' the policeman persisted, gently. 'You can demonstrate, but not like this.'

Alice and Esme exchanged a look and each took one of Mac's arms. They whispered to him gently, every word a balm for the wounds of youth. He resisted, but only briefly, and re-joined the line with a moody slouch. The crane rumbled on, the driver shaking his head.

'That's the government brought to its knees,' Esme observed, wryly.

'I think I've got twelve across,' June chirped. 'The last word in steam engines – it's Amen.'

PC Rogers sipped some more tea. Another round of chanting rose from the group, but it was brief and muted.

The Battle of Resurgam was one which began very quietly.

CHAPTER 6

Despite all the pressures upon them this winter's night, surrounded by the images of the destruction of the guardhouse, the two men stopped. The instincts of the investigator were at work.

And then came the action, and how absurd. The interior of the satellite van was a tiny space in which to stage a wrestling match, but in the way of their curious relationship this strange pairing almost managed it.

Adam reached over to eject the CD, but Dan sidestepped in front of the machine. The detective tried to shove a way past and for a man with a wiry frame he was impressively strong. Dan felt himself being levered aside, so he improvised, turned and flipped the master power switch.

The satellite tuner, sound desk and video monitors all clicked, hummed and died. Only the emergency lighting was left, a flickering shade of ghostly blue, like an undersea world.

'What the hell do you think you're doing?' Adam yelled.

'I need a moment.'

'I don't have a moment. Give me that CD.'

'Just a few seconds then.'

'Didn't I mention this is a murder inquiry?'

'Attempted murder.'

'Don't come the hack's semantics with me.' Adam took a step forwards, bringing them face to face in the gloomy confines. 'I haven't made any arrests yet, but I'm willing to start now.'

Dan glanced to the clock. The time had evaporated fast, as was always the way on a major story. It was half past nine.

'Adam! You're not the only one under the screw. I'm on air in an hour.'

'You're trying to compare a news story with catching a killer?'

'I'm trying to help and I've got an idea how.'

'You're pushing your luck.'

'It hasn't fallen over yet. Just a quick briefing. I'll need it if I'm joining you on the case.'

'That's if – *if.*' The detective's narrow cheeks pinched further, but he added, 'One minute only.'

'You tipped me off because you need to find the driver of the lorry.'

'Yep.'

'I'm guessing it's Esther?'

'Genius.'

'Sarcasm aside, I'll need to make a big hit with my report to help find her.'

Dan explained and Adam chewed at his lip, but eventually said, 'And this isn't just spin to make an even better story?'

'No,' Dan managed, with as straight a face as he could manage.

'I haven't got time to argue. All right.'

'It'll take a couple of minutes. Can we step outside?'

He opened the door to a mugger of a wind. Loud was lurking, wrapped up and hunkered down in a coat, embracing the engine to keep warm. He had a face as sweet as a pickled onion.

'Any chance I can come back in now?' the engineer asked sullenly. 'It's an outside broadcast truck, not a bleeding meeting room.'

★★★

The rest of the pack were still away on their grand folly of a hunt, so Dan and Adam stood in the lee of the truck to talk. It was parked along the road from the remains of the gatehouse. The icy swirling air was a sandblasting of dust and grit, a testament to the force of the lorry's impact.

'This didn't come from me.'

'That sounds familiar,' Dan replied, fumbling for his notepad.

'The demonstrators decided to stage a final protest in an attempt to stop Resurgam opening. Esther nicked a lorry. The idea was to ram in the gates, so the others could get through. They were going to chain themselves to the building, the doors, anything.'

'And we're sure about that?'

'It feels right.' Adam gestured to the wreckage of the gatehouse. 'They wouldn't have been up for anything like this. Protest yes, murder no.'

'So what went wrong?'

'We're not sure yet.'

'Esther could have panicked, or lost control of the lorry.'

'It's possible.' Adam looked to his watch. 'Thirty seconds.'

'Is he dead, the lad who was on guard?' Dan asked quickly.

'Not quite. We don't usually bother rushing corpses away in an ambulance.'

Behind them, a crumble of masonry fell from a jagged crack in the battered wall. Another rush of cold wind chased in from the river and tugged at their clothes.

'Any chance of an interview?'

Adam shook his head, spikes of dark hair tussling in the wind. 'I do have one or two other things to think about at the moment.' He turned to walk away, but paused. 'You're right, I might well need your help on this one. We're only three days away from the grand opening, all that bloody Finale Friday rigmarole and VIP nonsense, and...'

'What?'

'Strictly just between us, for now at least.'

'Sure.'

'No, I mean strictly-strictly.'

'Cross my heart and hope to die. Go on.'

Adam produced a scathing look, but said, 'Something very strange arrived at the cop shop this morning.'

★★★

Dan got home just after eleven to find Claire sitting on the sofa, wrapped in a blanket and sound asleep. She looked celestially serene, and for the first time in weeks he remembered how beautiful she was. The ruffled autumnal hair with ridiculously small ears peeping through, those burnished eyes, the porcelain skin.

He stared for a moment, reached out and almost touched her, nearly stroked a stray lock back into place. Dan waited, let the legions of his brain do battle. The hand stretched out again, drew back, reached out, almost touched this time but retreated once more.

He swallowed hard, coughed loudly and she started awake. 'Sorry,' Claire smiled dozily. 'You've had a hell of a day so I thought I'd wait up for you. Would you like anything?'

'I'm just going to sit for a while to calm down.'

'You don't want...'

'No. Nothing.'

He saw the impact of the words in her eyes and added, 'Sorry, I just want to sit in peace for a few minutes.'

'Do you mind doing me a favour first? Can I have Nigel's phone number, and El's too?'

'Why?'

'There's something I want to ask them.'

'What?'

'Nothing you need to know about.'

'What?' he insisted. 'Why?'

'Only that it's Christmas and I'm struggling. All right?'

'Oh. Sorry.'

Claire entered the numbers into her phone, then said, 'Shall I sit with you?'

'If you like.'

And now that look was back, and this time the feeling ran unchecked. 'It doesn't seem so much to ask. I've hardly seen you lately, let alone had the chance to talk. Not to mention...'

'Erm, yeah, sorry,' Dan interrupted, before the momentum of emotion could grow. 'It's just that it's been... busy. We will talk, of course. But can we do it another night? I'm so tired I'm just not up to it now.'

She looked away, picked up a book, one of her crime thrillers, and began to read.

Dan fussed Rutherford, stared out of the bay window at the empty winter sky and let his mind run.

★★★

The outside broadcast had been negotiated successfully. Dan's triumph of the exclusive CCTV footage of the lorry crashing into the gatehouse even prompted an almost congratulatory call from Lizzie.

'That was fairly decent.'

'Thanks, you're really very kind.'

Irony was often a subtlety too far for the Editor of *Wessex Tonight*. Many staff had abandoned the art, believing it ill-suited for a woman they likened to a snowplough working its way downhill against a deadline.

'I want you back on the story tomorrow,' she was saying. 'It's three days to Finale Friday and I want comprehensive coverage. I want up and down, back and front, and inside and out.'

Dan produced a theatrical yawn. 'If I might be permitted to get some rest first?'

'What are you waiting for, then? Get to bed and straight to sleep. None of that sitting around thinking, or Sherlock Holmes stuff, like you do. I'll see you tomorrow – first thing. Oh, except…'

The change of tone was a surprise, and Dan said, warily, 'Yes?'

'The truth and lies game we were playing earlier. I've been wondering if what you said about…'

'So have I,' Dan replied, hurriedly. 'But you're right, it's bedtime. Night.'

★★★

Claire's head was starting to nod. 'Care to accompany a girl to bed?' she asked.

'In a mo. I think I'll have a shower to help me unwind,' Dan replied, and got up before she could say anything.

The water was hot and very welcome. He leaned back against the tiles and enjoyed the cascading currents. The time was almost twelve, so Dan gave his teeth a leisurely brush to the accompaniment of the midnight news. The attack on Resurgam was the second story, after some political row about immigration. With the coming of Wednesday it was now just two days until the grand opening, the presenter announced.

Claire was still awake when he slipped into bed and reached out for a cuddle. Dan held her for a diplomatic while, then turned onto his side and pretended to sleep. But the final discussion of the evening with Adam wouldn't leave his thoughts.

The detective had calmed down, albeit from a category three hurricane to two. A cross country alert had been put out for Esther, with every police force and port watching for her. Adam's mood was further mollified by the discovery of some information about where Esther may have run to, but he wouldn't tell Dan until they met tomorrow. Delayed gratification was one of the detective's most irritating vices.

He was also fixated on what Esther had picked up before she escaped. 'Why not just run?' Adam kept saying. 'For all she knew, she'd just committed murder. What was so important she had to waste time making sure she found?'

The film was too indistinct to tell, so he'd called out Greater Wessex Police's Technical division, the Eggheads, to enhance it. The fruits of their labours should be ripe by tomorrow.

Vehicle examiners were also working on the lorry. Adam wanted to know whether a fault could have caused it to crash into the gatehouse.

'Esther might have meant to do it,' Dan observed.

'Why?'

'A last protest, perhaps. Some final statement just as Resurgam was about to open.'

'But it's never been her way before, something so extreme.'

'Maybe she even meant to die too.'

'In which case, she failed,' came the pragmatic reply. 'Pity, it would have saved me a lot of trouble.'

The Chief Inspector had been about to say goodnight, when Dan said, 'Come on then – *and*?'

'And what?'

'*And*, as you mentioned so cryptically earlier, what was it? The strange thing that arrived at the police station this morning?'

The detective hesitated, rubbing a hand over the dark stubble of a cheek. 'This is strictly not for broadcast.'

'Ok.'

'No, I mean really absolutely utterly strictly. This is off the record, off the record.'

'That's really off the record.'

'I'm not joking,' came the steely don't-be smart-with me reply.

'Ok, ok.'

'It was a copy of the plans of the foundations of Resurgam.'

'What, just the plans and nothing else? No note or anything?'

'No note, nothing else apart from a razor blade.'

Dan frowned as he toyed with the thought. 'Granted that's a bit weird. But it's hardly terrifying. It's just symbolism from one of the protesters, surely?'

Adam shook his head. 'I don't think so. Because those plans have never been seen in public. Due to all the threats to Resurgam and the possibility of an attack, they were classified as secret.'

CHAPTER 7

It was a beautiful morning to hunt a hunch. The stars were so close they felt like fireflies hovering in the air.

Ok, so it was cold, but that was a familiar enemy. Layers were the secret solution. A vest, a T-shirt, a shirt, a scarf, his faithful old body warmer, with a coat on top and he was plenty warm enough. Mittens for his fingers, just enough to keep the hands cosy, but never to slow the pulse of a reaction to snap that sacred shot.

There was the hat too, a thick black beanie, pulled low. Dan once said it made him look like a bank robber. But it did its job, kept his head warm and his reflexes ready.

So here he waited, hoped and hoped again for the hunch to pay off.

Last night, after the call to the attack on Resurgam, Dirty El had done something which didn't come easily. He'd forced himself to sit in his flat and think. Not hang around outside a club or bar, waiting for a snap of a half-cut minor celebrity in a state of indecency. Not tap up some contacts for the latest gossip on who was illicitly entwined with who. But instead, to think.

Of one man. The man, that man, the man of the moment. The Cashman.

Around El, on the dusty floor of his cluttered living room lay the cuttings of the Cashman's appearances. And in his mind a pattern had started to emerge.

Firstly, the Cashman always struck exactly on the hour. That was agreed by the eyewitnesses from each story. Secondly, he always chose a landmark. It was never just a random stop in a street or park to hurl out his bags of cash. And thirdly, since the bizarre legend began, he had struck every day without fail. Which meant tomorrow he would appear again – somewhere.

El took out his map of Plymouth and circled the obvious places the Cashman hadn't yet chosen. There were a few, but not that many.

This was no New York. He would need luck and it would require an early start. Even then, the odds had to be against success, but that was fine.

For the bounty on offer, it had to be worth a try. El would vanquish those other paparazzi, show them who was boss on this turf, and triumph by unmasking the Cashman.

With some difficulty, El pulled his bulky frame up from the floor and waddled off to the kitchen. He made himself a cup of tea and settled upon the location he would choose to lie in wait.

★★★

Of all the landmarks of Plymouth, it had to be here the Cashman would come next. It was iconic, known the world over. The fabled beauty of its views, spanning two of England's fairest counties, the sentinel lighthouse, the great grassy vista. It was an irresistible lure for tourists and locals alike.

So it was that on a bench, overlooking the darkly shifting waters of the silent sea, in the middle of the Hoe, El sat and waited.

It was ten to seven on a December Wednesday morning. Dawn was beginning to kindle her fires in the eastern sky. The Hoe was quiet, just the odd dog walker or worker making their way to meet the day's demands. All were coddled down low in their coats, sheltering from the blades of the morning's cold.

El rubbed his hands together and waited.

The earliest the Cashman had struck was five o'clock in the morning. That had been at the fish market on the Barbican, quite a surprise for the dozens of trawlermen gathered there, selling the day's catches.

Otherwise, he tended to appear later in the day. El wasn't sure whether that meant he should bet his time on lurking in the waning hours of the afternoon, or think it was the moment for another early strike.

A jogger skipped by, panting hard, face flushed, her fluorescent vest glowing in the streetlights. The time slipped on to five to seven.

El rose from his bench, stretched, and began to pace back and forth across the expanse of tarmac.

★★★

The world shrinks in the wintertime. Horizons tighten in the lacklustre light. But still the rhythms of life run, however routine.

From Millbay Docks a ferry glided out, heading for the Channel. In the sky a gang of seagulls swooped and soared, riding on the awakening winds. A street sweeper wandered along the pavement, picking at the discarded litter of the night before. Unseen bottles clinked in a glass symphony as a delivery lorry rumbled past. A car slowed and stopped.

El peered through the half-light. Someone was getting out of the back.

He strained his eyes. Whoever it was had begun putting something on their head.

El didn't hesitate. He began to run, heart lurching to a drummer's beat.

The figure's back was turned. But its arms were reaching into the car.

To find the bags full of money?

Surely. Please, surely.

A bank of cloud slowly shifted. The sun edged above the horizon. The red light of dawn washed across the Hoe, chasing shadows before it.

The figure was turning around.

El's practiced fingers framed the shot. His was the moment and now was the time.

But it was an elderly lady, wearing a hat and holding a leash, a reluctant spaniel peering out from the back seats.

'Lovely day,' she chirped, in a finishing school voice. 'Are you photographing the dawn?'

The camera drooped. Across the city a clock rang out seven. There wasn't another car in sight, no Robin Hood mask, not a hint of the Cashman.

El sat back on the bench and stared sightlessly at the view. The glory of the new day daubing its colours across field and cliff hardly registered in his downcast eyes.

★★★

It was quarter past seven when El's mobile stirred him from the miserable reverie. He answered, then plodded for the car and drove to the bus station. He didn't turn on the radio, didn't put on any music, didn't do anything except drive.

A line of buses was waiting, bottled in the depot by the mass of humanity milling outside. People were hugging each other, smiling, laughing. One man was lamenting how the earliness of the hour meant the pubs weren't yet open.

'Cheers to the beautiful Cashman!' he yelled.

'I'm throwing a sicky to do some shopping,' a young woman giggled, holding up a fistful of bags of money. 'Sixty quid in each. Sixty!'

A couple of discarded sheets of paper blew along the pavement. They bore the letters A B C D E F G H. On both sheets, the F was circled.

El didn't even bother to raise the camera. All the action was over. A distant aftermath never sold a snap.

Particularly not when your competitors had far more tempting fare to offer. And there, around the crowd as though forming a protective ring, were the other paparazzi. The London snappers, with their shiny little scooters, designer leather jackets and top of the range cameras.

And amongst them was the tall one, the one with the pop star stubble and film star looks. The one renowned for some of the most famous shots in paparazzi folklore. The smooth talking one, the rich one. The one all the girls adored and who all El's contacts seemed unable to stop themselves swooning before and spewing their secrets upon.

The one who had charmed his way into the affections of everyone here in this city which was El's manor. His! His home, his patch, his workplace. His heart and his soul.

The one who was waving at El, smiling, so self-satisfied, self-assured, the other paparazzi also joining the taunt.

The one they said had come from Milan to try his trade in a new country, and was doing so with stunning success. *The Italian*, they called him.

El looked down at his anorak and battered body warmer, bulging around the girth of his stomach. His tatty jeans and scuffed old boots.

He turned and trudged away, accompanied only by the cold.

CHAPTER 8

Against the backdrop of the red orb of the rising sun, Resurgam could have been an ancient monolith. Few are the man-made intrusions upon the planet which can rival the effortless spectacles of the natural world. But here, with human ingenuity and endless bloody-minded persistence, was one. It was an affront to nature, a wound in the sky with its soaring presence, high enough to puncture the heavens.

The day began bitter once more, the iciness enhanced by a growing wind gathering at sea. Dan pulled his coat tighter and stamped his feet. They would always be the first parts of his body to register freezing conditions. The phenomenon had only grown worse as he'd reluctantly aged into the decade of the forties.

Nigel had positioned them just inside the long plain of the shadow, to film the moment the light broke through from the building's side. It would make a striking shot to start a report.

Other journalists, cameramen and photographers were arriving, most carrying take away teas and coffees. It would be a sizeable pack which gathered here once more. The talk was all speculation of what they were about to witness, what would be the latest storyline in this extraordinary epic.

Nigel checked his watch. 'You're ok,' Dan told him. 'The great leader's statement isn't for another fifteen minutes.'

★★★

The morning in the flat had run as smoothly as a Penny Farthing trying to negotiate a cobbled street.

They'd both woken just before seven and gone through a yawning, stretching, rising from the covers routine.

'I'll take Rutherford for a run,' Claire said. 'I know you'll be busy today.'

'I was going to. It's how I like to start the day – how I always have.'
'We could both do it.'

Dan thought that an opportune moment to make a cup of tea. Couples jogging together sounded far too much like one of the hits of his personal annals of horror. As he carried the mugs back to the bedroom, the phone rang.

'The Cashman again,' he explained to Claire. 'Got to go.'

In the bathroom whirl of a quick wash the mobile rang once more. Ellen Dance would be at Resurgam at eight to make a statement about last night's attack. The word from the excitable marketing department was that she had incisive views to impart.

Lizzie was suggesting Dan should be there, in the considerate way that people are invited to their own execution. Another reporter would cover the Cashman.

'I've still got to go,' he said, in response to Claire's quizzical look, 'Just for a different reason.'

As Dan dressed, one more call came in to buffet his course. It was El. He was, he bemoaned, lower than a soul singer with a sore throat.

'Yes, I appreciate it's very difficult for you. Yes, sorry, I mean soul-destroying,' Dan soothed. 'No, I'm not sure it is the end of the world as we know it. But yes, I know there's a huge bounty for the Cashman. Yes, I will help, of course. It's just – I'm a little busy right now.'

He slung a coat around his shoulders and made for the door, then stuck his head back in, patted Rutherford and finally pecked Claire on the cheek.

★★★

Ten minutes to the promised revelations. To be a good professional, and to try to distract himself from the cold, Dan fished out a disorganised wad of notes from his satchel and re-visited the profile of Ellen Dance.

It was compiled back in the silly season of the high summer, when *Wessex Tonight* was short of news. Lizzie had become obsessed by an inspired idea to 'give the programme a distinctive edge'.

Dan and Nigel would depart on a little tour of the country. They were to visit notorious environmental protests where Esther had featured to compile a film about her life. Upon return to Devon, they would produce a matching version on the character of Ellen Dance.

The films would run on consecutive evenings, under the heading *Two Women – Two Visions – One Battle*.

It was, Lizzie proclaimed without a dust grain of modesty, rather Hollywood.

★★★

A chance tangle with the Prime Minister brought Ellen Dance into politics. Just over a decade ago, the hapless man was on an election campaign visit to Exmoor, to talk about the importance of tourism. A couple of years before, Dance had bought a small, run-down and ramshackle hotel on the moor, and refurbished it as an upmarket retreat for deer hunters. All of which would have been of no consequence to the nation, had not the great statesman's entourage decided the quintessential English beauty of the village of Exford would make a fine backdrop for the photographers. Out he had emerged, shaken a couple of bemused local hands, and was ambushed.

Dance had seen the photo opportunity unfolding from her window, as if a gift from the Angel of the Heavens whose department it was to look after the little people. 'Point one, bureaucracy,' she hectored in the legendary news clip. 'How the hell are we supposed to run a business with your endless health and safety regulations, inspections, and stupid Whitehall diktats from people who've never even been to the countryside? Point two, the rates. They keep going up, when business is going down. And point three, taxes. You want us to create some wealth, then give us a damned chance and stop bleeding us for every penny...'

So it went on, delivered at a rate approximately twenty per cent faster than most people can think, complete with wagging finger.

'You want my vote, you'd better listen and damn well work for it,' was her fond farewell.

'You should go into politics,' the leader of all he surveyed remarked as he finally made his sweet escape, a heartily unconvincing smile fixed upon his face.

They were words Ellen Dance heeded well.

★★★

First it was election to the district council, then the county. Initially, Dance made her name as a passionate supporter of rural communities, but as she grew more experienced it was business which became her defining theme.

The great controversy over wind farms came first. Unusually amongst her peers, Dance supported them as a source of investment and energy. A battle over a tidal barrage followed, then a new power station in the south of Devon.

The pictures of one protest featured placards daubed with *Dance the Destroyer*. But she had fire and wouldn't be silenced. She visited a picket line, talked to the campaigners, and gave an interview with arguments as passionate as those of her opponents.

'Yes, the south west's beauty is its strength,' Dance said. 'But who's going to live here if there's no electricity, no business, no companies, no jobs? We can balance the landscape with innovation and development, surely? We must, or we have no future aside from being the nation's holiday park.'

★★★

The next shift of ambition came with the creation of Regional Development Councils, to be overseen by an elected President. Ellen Dance ran for the post. Many sneered, said surely it could be only for a bet.

She had always been an independent councillor, time and again proclaiming her only affiliation was the electorate. But with such freedom came a price. Without the powerful party machinery to back her, what hope could Dance have of such high office?

She had an answer to that. Or perhaps her omnipresent aide, Jackie Denyer did, because by this time the two had become inseparable. And the question was raised that had persisted since – which was the true brains, motivation, and street fighter of the partnership?

Their solution to the lack of a party machine was the grassroots. Fundraising and campaigning was run via the internet, creating a network of supporters and activists.

And now came a notable shift in Dance's nature. Opinion polls demonstrated she had a clear chance of winning, and suddenly she became a target for the other candidates. Dance was relentlessly briefed against with the shady whispers that politicians so favour.

Little experience... lacking in substance... questionable judgement... no job for an amateur...

The growing pressure of the campaign was blamed for Dance splitting from her partner of a dozen years. And perhaps for a new bitterness of strategy.

In the fortnight before the election, stories began to emerge in the media about her rival candidates. There were sexual peccadilloes for the Liberal Democrats' woman, flirtations with extreme politics in younger years for the Conservatives' man.

Where they came from remained a mystery, for journalists must always protect their sources. But the suspicion was that perhaps it was the network of Dance supporters feeding information to campaign headquarters, which was then leaked.

Be all that as it may, it worked. Ellen Dance won.

★★★

The early sun was starting to flicker around the edge of Resurgam, like the light cast from a ruby. It crept across the tarmac of the approach road and the discourteous bulk of the encircling wall. Most of the debris from the gatehouse had already been cleared, but there were still a couple of piles of rubble, tumbled pyramids of brick, metal and shattered glass. A pitiful line of masonry formed the remainder of the structure itself.

More barriers had been brought in to reinforce the gate, patrolled by a line of watchful security men and women. A couple of others stood further up the road, stopping any lorries to check their business. A series of trucks was disappearing from view, slipping down the ramps into the underground car park.

It was one of those mornings where anything that lived or functioned was giving off the fog of existence; steamy breaths from mouths, clouds of engine gases from exhaust pipes, plumes of smoke from chimneys and flues.

The great doors of the skyscraper opened and a short, squat woman with cropped blonde hair marched out. She was carrying a fat file of papers and a mobile phone.

'Oh no, here comes Denyer,' one of the photographers whispered. 'Get ready to be organised.'

The woman's eyes were everywhere, like a shrew always alert for any danger. She ran a fast look over the pack, ticking off each from a list. The background for the oration was analysed, then scrutinised. The phone was lifted and within seconds a man jogged out to shift a tub of flowers. Finally, a piece of chalk was produced and a circle and a cross marked on the tarmac.

'I thought it was just Dance giving a statement?' Dan asked, and received a machine gun glare.

'*Ms* Dance will be *one* of those speaking, yes. You will please assemble yourselves here. This interface will last a scheduled ten minutes.'

And with that masterpiece of management-speak, Denyer was back on her phone and gone.

A phalanx of security men began to file out from the Resurgam compound. Each wore a black suit, which they filled with an impressive mix of muscularity and smartness. And all walked upright with the kind of gait that told of years spent in military service. None sported coats, and none offered so much as the slightest of acknowledgements to the morning's cold.

They formed a line in front of the media pack, stared straight ahead, and waited.

★★★

The briefing notes held interesting contrasts in the views expressed of Ellen Dance.

She had become a divisive figure, perhaps a classical politician; both loved and loathed.

One former acquaintance said, 'I'm amazed she's done so well. She was pretty ordinary when we were kids. I thought she'd become one of the local four by fours.'

The translation of the puzzling phrase was helpfully provided. It meant four children by four different fathers.

In Exford however, Dance was well on the way to becoming beatified. 'She's done everything for the village,' one neighbour said. 'She found us sponsorship for the new kids' adventure playground. She got the school refurbished. She even got more bus services running.'

But an anonymous interview came from a different script. It was a former member of staff at the Development Council who had been made redundant.

'Never trust Dance,' the woman said. 'There were ten of us, working on a tidal electricity project. She said we were the future, promised us everything. When this Resurgam idea came along she dropped the project and wanted to transfer us all there, to greenwash it. Some of us refused and were sacked, just like that.'

★★★

Eight o'clock arrived, lingered briefly, and departed. The time had moved on to almost ten past. 'What's she up to?' Nigel whispered.

'Standard politician's trick,' Dan replied. 'They learn it in despot's training school. Always be late. It builds up anticipation and a sense of self-importance.'

'All it's building up in me is a cold,' came the disgruntled reply.

Along *The Wall* another protest was sharing its views, but it was forlorn and felt more like a gesture than a stand. About twenty people stood watching, some holding placards. They were quiet, perhaps out of respect for what had happened last night, or because of the sizeable group of police officers standing around them.

★★★

At the outset, Ellen Dance's time as President of the Council was marked by achievements and compliments. Even her opponents had to admit she was proving effective in the job.

Dance Wins Upgrade at Last one headline announced about the ramshackle rail line from Devon and Cornwall to London. *More Cash for Fast Internet Links* was another.

But, as is the wearing way of life, what starts with a shine will surely tarnish. Other big bids for funding failed. Grumbles surfaced that Dance's head had been turned, she was spending too much time in the power-play land of London, perhaps seeking the next opportunity of ambition there.

A charm offensive was launched with a series of media appearances and Dance recovered some ground. But even that faltered, as what should have been an inconsequential interview for *Wessex People* magazine became both celebrated and notorious.

Interviewer – Tell me about your taste in music?

Ellen Dance – It's a bit embarrassing, but I've always loved The Wurzels.

Interviewer – Interesting. Any particular reason?

ED – They're such great fun. I remember my parents playing them when I was little.

Interviewer – So what would your favourite Wurzels song be?

ED – Err, what's that one about drinking cider?

Interviewer – Most of them, as I recall. Do you mean Farmer Bill's Cowman?

ED – Yes, I think that's the one.

Interviewer – And – dare I ask – I suppose you like cider too?

At that point, the interview was curtailed by the ever-present Denyer. But it left three noteworthy legacies.

The first was a creeping public perception, so dangerous for a politician, that Dance may have lost her touch. The second, and most entertaining, was that amongst her political foes Dance was christened *Farmer Bill's Cowgirl*.

The third probably concerned the elections for the position of President of the Regional Development Council which would be held next year. Dance had already declared her candidacy, and, the commentators concurred, faced a tough fight to hold onto the job.

Perhaps as a result of the pressing requirement for an existence free of gaffes, from here onwards attempts to elicit any kind of comment from Ellen Dance suffered a simple, but unsatisfying fate.

★★★

This refrigerated morning, now approaching half past eight, had abandoned the brief promise of early sun and clouded over.

A rectangular box cranked up the face of Resurgam on ropes and pulleys, so tiny against the mass. A couple of people were going about the Herculean task of applying some clean and polish.

The modern art of the silvery sculptures were also being buffed and shone. Many a story the designs had attracted, and mostly unflattering. More Barbara Cartland than Barbara Hepworth, ran one renowned review. A commonly held opinion was they looked like effigies creased up with the agony of chronic wind.

The superfast lifts that would take sightseers to the top floors began a zipping passage, bullets of glass and steel, effortless in their defiance of gravity. A stream of work traffic edged by, a slowly shifting line of headlamps and tail lights. It was only a couple of weeks to Christmas, the shopping season fast approaching its frenetic climax. Faces inevitably turned to stare at Resurgam, as they had these past eleven months, a daily monitor of progress as it rose inexorably from the earth.

★★★

And so the profile of Ellen Dance turned finally to Resurgam itself. The election was looming and her poll ratings were worryingly bad. It was widely suspected Resurgam was envisaged as the answer; a masterstroke of innovation to woo and awe the public.

The great edifice was the President's project to such an extent that detractors often called it Dance's Folly. No sentence, spoken or written, could mention one without the other. They had become another strawberries and cream, Laurel and Hardy, gin and tonic, England and the rain.

From the Regional Development Council came the concept, much of the backing and most of the lobbying. Compulsory purchase was used against people owning the land which the great building required, as ruthlessly a predator snacking on lesser forms of life. Even when Resurgam claimed the first of its victims, work carried on unperturbed.

We will never give in to violence or intimidation, never bow to the forces of darkness, never waver in our purpose, Dance repeated time and again. *Resurgam is too important to be delayed; a great legacy for the south west, a commitment to its future and a statement of bold intent for the years to come.*

★★★

So Dan's report moved to its summary, the story behind the story.

The first point was of Dance's journey. From her early days as an altruistic councillor, rejecting the spin and manipulations of politics, she was seen as having become that which she promised she never would.

The second was about Resurgam. And on that matter the analysts were agreed. For Dance to have a chance of re-election as President, the great beast would have to open without a hitch and be hailed an unqualified success.

As one of the wittier contributors put it, Ellen Dance was fighting for her political life. And to those in such positions of power, that differed from her actual existence in only one way.

The latter was of significantly less importance.

★★★

From behind the makeshift barriers Ellen Dance approached with the walk of one born to bear unquestionable authority. Nothing could challenge it, nothing mar that measured stride of destiny.

She wore black boots, a long black coat and an aura of grief, regret and respect. Her dark hair was pinned up in a sombre manner and she was holding a resplendent bouquet of flowers. Her look was into the distance, as if not for her surroundings but matters far more weighty.

Walking less certainly alongside was a young woman, probably in her mid-twenties, and a little chubby. She had a face which may once have been called kind, but no longer. Now it was diffuse with the look of the lost.

She appeared jaded and dazed, as if life had suddenly turned on her and refused to relent in its torments. She was sporting too much make up, but even that could not hide the suffering. The suit she wore was grey and dated, and draped her with self-consciousness. She was also carrying a bunch of flowers, but of a more modest ilk.

'So that's our mystery guest,' Dan whispered to Nigel. 'I don't recognise her at all. What's Dance up to now?'

CHAPTER 9

A stasis seeped across the site. It was an invisible, infectious force, moving from person to person with remarkable speed. At Resurgam itself, all activity stopped. The engineers, the construction workers, the cleaners, all were looking over, all with hands clasped before them. It was a masterpiece of choreography.

The pair slowed as they approached the pack. Dance reached out a hand, laid it on the younger woman's arm and carefully guided her towards the remains of the gatehouse. There they waited, waited, waited, let the seconds hang with measured reflection, before softly lying down the flowers.

The morning's breeze ruffled a little at their hair and clothes. On Dance's rich black coat a heavy lapel twitched but refused to shift, the material too fine to be flustered by the elements.

A cloud shifted, allowing a rare few rays of sunlight to grace the grey cityscape. Still the women stood, lost and intent as they stared at the cairn of rubble. Time and reality were inconsequential in this baring of the heart.

Finally, Dance drew herself up, laced an arm around the shoulders of her fellow and turned towards the pack. Her voice was low with empathy, but still strong.

'I'd like to introduce Alannah Lewis. She is the partner of Tommy, the security man who was injured last night. I know you'll appreciate her courage in talking to you.'

The young woman's eyes ran along the massed ranks of the looming, staring media. The photographers and their lenses, the cameramen and their shots. And the reporters noting down every word.

'Tommy and I had only been together a few months,' Alannah began. 'But I knew he was the one. And he felt the same about me.'

She was reading from a piece of paper, the words faltering and hesitant, as though each was a struggle to free from the depths of herself. Alannah toyed with her hair as she spoke, the scuffed toe of one cheap and battered shoe turning continually on the ground.

'We were going to get engaged on Christmas Day. It was a surprise for our family and friends. And now…'

Her voice broke and Dance pulled her closer, whispered sustenance and support.

Alannah's hands were shaking hard. On her ring finger, a jewelled band caught the fleeting sunlight. Dan whispered to Nigel and the camera shifted and zoomed.

'Now…' Alannah continued, her words softer even than before. 'Now, Tommy's lying on a hospital bed. I could hardly recognise him. His body's full of tubes and pipes and surrounded by machines. They're – they're keeping him alive. So, I'm going to spend Christmas in hospital. Holding my Tommy's hand. Hoping he might come round. Hoping that if he does – he'll remember who I am…'

Her head collapsed into Dance's side and she clung on, body shaking with the tears. As one, the line of security men let their faces fall to study the ground.

And now Dance stood taller, as though inflated with the emotion of the moment. She was looking into the cameras but also beyond, a gaze of gravitas, compassion, strength and leadership. With pain and suffering, but also with a certainty of incontestable resolve.

With the draw of a long breath, the clasping together of considered hands, Dance spoke. Her voice was clear and determined, a contrast from what went before as extreme as fire and water.

'You can see what these so called *protesters* have done. Because of their obsession, they have inflicted misery on people who are entirely innocent. I am appalled at what happened here, the dreadful injuries suffered by a young man who should have everything to live for.'

She paused, let her stare rove across the pack, using the ranks of the watching cameras to look the world in the eye.

'This attack will neither stop, nor even delay by a second the opening of Resurgam. To allow that would be to give in to the forces of lawlessness, and that is something I would never countenance.'

And now one more wait, a dramatist's device from a politician in full rhetorical pomp, a stateswoman who sensed her moment.

'I appeal for no more of these protests. Those who wished to demonstrate have had their say, as our fine and free society expects. But we have seen all too clearly where it's taken us. Let us respect our differences. Let us find peace. Let us have no more repeats of the unspeakable events of last night and the heartbreak they have brought.'

★★★

They tried. They knew what was coming, but they tried.

It was their job, their duty, but more, too. Their professionalism, even their pride. Because they suspected what had happened here and they sought to expose it.

So it was that just a second after Dance's final words, from the pack the questions flew.

'Are you trying to use the attack for publicity?'

'Is this a cynical attempt to stop the demonstrations?'

'Are you using Alannah?'

Three questions were all they managed. It was more than had followed any previous Ellen Dance statement of late, but still to the same effect. Not a single answer did they elicit, not even a look which might have betrayed some kind of response.

Except perhaps one.

Dance had already tightened her grip around Alannah's waist and turned her away. Together, stately and measured, they began walking back towards Resurgam.

But just before, in the most fleeting of instants, there was something in Alannah's face. A look at her protector which was hard to read, but might have been realisation.

There was no time, no opportunity to explore it. Faster than a theatre curtain falling, the line of security men coalesced. Body after body came together to form a wall of black suits.

From the largest of the sizeable set bellowed the cry they were expecting. It was cavern-mouthed, parade ground loud and wholly unchallengeable. And it was so familiar, so very predictable.

'No questions!'

★★★

How little they grumbled was a mark of how little they expected. Dance's policy for handling the press had become legend.

There was also more work to be done before the story was complete. Even before Dance and Alannah made their way back to Resurgam, the pack was heading towards the protesters.

It was a simple rule of the news trade. A challenge had been issued, a response was required. The thin line of resistance watched them coming and prepared as best they could. Banners and placards were raised, coats and jackets straightened. And there was whispering in the group too, looks exchanged, nudges and nods. As in days of old, a champion was being selected.

The students were shrinking away. Mac alone held his position, that thickset expression even more overgrown than usual. He resembled an Emo gunslinger, armed with attitude.

'Screw the way she used that poor girl,' he muttered. Esme pulled him aside, a fond finger quietening the rebel lips.

Other men and women were wilting before the pack's imposing presence. Only June stood unmoved, another woman of similarly distinguished years close beside.

With lungs the product of many a hilly run alongside Rutherford, Dan reached the demonstrators first. He thought he overheard the woman next to June remonstrating, 'You shouldn't be here at all, given... and let alone doing this.'

June was wearing a thick padded jacket today, but the woollen rainbow hat and gloves remained. A scarf had been added to the attire, a tartan pattern. It clashed like a discordant cymbal, but she sported the ensemble with such an easy nonchalance that it almost worked.

June regarded the hacks calmly, waited for the pack to assemble in the classic firing squad pattern. Here was matter and antimatter, a leader so different from the one who had spoken only minutes before. Not elected, not expensively clad nor impeccably embalmed in the finest make-up. Not fashionably attired, nor refined in enunciation by the best of elocution experts.

Here instead were crow's feet, clear eyes and the passion of principles. And when June spoke, it was with a calm assurance and mesmeric tone. She could have been years back, dominating a classroom once more, the media mere children before her.

'There are two things we want to make clear. Firstly, we are also shocked by the attack here last night. We condemn it entirely and send our thoughts to the man who was injured and his family.'

And now her words slowed, halted by the formidable impediment of her anger. It was hotly akin to the embers of a volcano.

'But we also condemn a politician trying to turn such a shocking situation to her advantage. The vast majority of people who oppose Resurgam have done so peacefully and in a principled way.'

'Damn right,' a couple of others mouthed.

Esme pushed her way forwards, slipping through the crowd like a coppery river in spate. 'We've lost people, too. Remember Alice. She was my best friend. It's a disgrace what Dance is trying to do.'

'Yeah,' Seb added, in a voice which sounded strangled. 'I miss Alice so much. I… I loved…'

But the words wouldn't come. Arms reached out to support a young man who had learnt far too early the bitter lesson of a broken heart.

And what a toll it had taken. No longer so strong, so sure, Seb had been diminished. He was thinner, that vitality of youth stolen away. He looked around the touched faces and said quietly, 'Alice… we all miss her.'

'In Alice's name, that wall has got to come down.' Esme proclaimed.

The group was reforming, emboldened, clustering closer around June, their unexpected new leader. Unity and belief-infused, the unvanquishable flow of human spirit.

'We will continue to protest,' June went on, her voice building. 'Such a blight, such a monstrosity as Resurgam will not open without it being very clear that many oppose it. People like Alice who died for their beliefs. We will be here each day, and let there be no doubt. However inconvenient it may be for the politicians, however it might be a nuisance for their grand dream, we will be here for the opening day itself.'

★★★

Dan made for the Satellite Van, to sit with Loud, try to keep warm and edit the report for the lunchtime news. It was a simple task; pictures of last night's attack, excerpts of what Alannah and Dance had said and some of June's words for balance.

The microphone was on hand and Dan was about to record a section of commentary when a banging at the door interrupted.

'Come in, Adam.'

'How'd you know it was me?' the detective asked.

'No one else knocks the way you do. It's more like a raid.'

Adam's face was pale, and not just because of the bitter cold. He was carrying a concern, as sure as if it were piled in sacks upon those slender shoulders. 'Come out here. I've got something to show you.'

He led the way along *The Wall*, a couple of hundred metres from the gates. Here the colourful graffiti started to fade, replaced by the odd nonsensical daubing or scrawled abuse.

'Are we going for a long walk?' Dan asked mildly. 'It's just that I did promise my editor I'd knock together some kind of report today.'

Adam was striding hard and not in the mood for forays into the land of humour. They walked up a short but steep hill, rounded a bend and stopped abruptly.

In black paint, in thick letters on the off-white surface, carefully written, was the reason for the Chief Inspector's concern: '**THOSE PLANS ARE THE FOUNDATIONS OF RESURGAM'S FALL**'

THE BATTLE OF RESURGAM
TWO – THE DEFILING

As if to mark the turning of that fateful year, January brought a new character to the city's historic skyline. First it was one, then another, and finally a family of cranes.

The greatest of the group reached high into the sky; a thin trellis of a letter T that could often disappear into the low cloud and sea mists of the intemperate, winter weather. Around it clustered more, each progressively shorter, but all equally industrious.

Every day, from the first light of the colourless dawns to the equally bleak dusks, the cranes stooped and swung, hauled and lowered. Beneath, servants scurried to their bidding; lorries feeding the endless hunger of the site, or removing the debris which was once a part of the land. And around and between all this, the supporting cast worked and worked and Resurgam grew.

The first steel was quickly sunk into the ground, mighty beams, man-made trunks of metal, pounded into the bedrock. Across the entirety of the city the noise beat and banged, to become a background wearily familiar in the months ahead.

Beyond the gates of Resurgam the protest gathered strength, but only a little. More environmentalists arrived, concerned for local wildlife and the effect of the relentless cacophony of noise.

The knot of a dozen regular demonstrators grew to twenty. But the snow continued to fall, the temperatures hovered around zero, and the mainstay of the populace shrugged their collective shoulders and got on with the business of surviving January.

For PC Steve Rogers, Resurgam became his beat. A wise old sergeant at Charles Cross, Richard Wagstaff, commended him on handling the brief outbreak of disorder and put the young officer in charge of community relations. He shared more tea and conversation with Seb, June, Alice, Mac, Esme and the others who came and went from the line, and the charm offensive was effective. There were no repeats of the time when civilisation almost fell, the legendary day a single crane was held up for almost one whole minute.

The tide lapped at the harbour, just as it always had, but this time found the blockade of a line of supply barges. And occasionally, when the site was quieter, a posse of swans, ducks and cormorants would venture over, curious to see what had become of a land which once was theirs. But they never stayed, for it had become a hostile, alien world.

The soft sand of the golden foreshore was now bare rock and hard metal. The waters which used to flow across the small stretch of city beach had dried. And the air no longer smelt of salt, nature, and friendly freedom, but oil, man and machine.

From the landward side, some of the human population felt the violation too, and continued their protests against it.

★★★

With the coming of the thrust of the building work, the might of the forces protecting Resurgam tripled. PC Rogers was joined on his beat by a young man, a little on the chubby side, dressed in an oversized uniform and fluorescent jacket. His coat was open, despite the incessant cold, probably to show off the impressive weaves of shiny braid and ranks of buttons.

'This is Mr Ross,' the policeman told the group of demonstrators. 'He's a security officer for the site.'

June produced a matronly expression of indulgence. 'Don't security men have Christian names either?'

'It's Tommy,' the young man said, pushing an oversized cap up his forehead and shaking hands.

'Welcome to the front line,' she replied, to general laughter.

'Don't be fooled, this lot can be quite a handful,' PC Rogers teased. 'We've already had one nasty outbreak of disorder.'

Eyes shifted to Mac, who emitted a guttural teenage grunt and turned away.

'And this is Phil Rees,' the policeman continued, gesturing to another young man. He sported a shaved scalp and was squat and powerful, looked like an ardent worshipper at the temple of the gym. His eyes were a little closer together than was advisable for true binocular vision, and he was also one of those curious people who find a neck surplus to requirements.

'Alright,' he muttered.

Alice favoured the newcomers with a smile of classic English beauty. 'Don't I know you, Tommy? You were the security man for the shore park here before…' she nodded towards Resurgam.

'Yeah.' Tommy had a quiet voice, difficult to hear above the drills and hammers of the building site. He looked nervous, ill at ease, couldn't quite stand still. 'They offered me a job.' He picked at some of the braid on his cuffs. 'There's not exactly a lot about at the mo, so I took it.'

'Don't you miss the old beach here?'

'A job's a job. You've got to count yourself lucky to have one, these days.'

'But you can't be happy with what's happened?'

'Ok, this isn't an inquisition,' PC Steve intervened. 'Now, who's got the tea today?'

'It's your turn,' Seb replied.

'Are you sure?'

As one, the line of protesters nodded. 'And for biscuits, too,' Alice contributed, in a manner which, if not absolutely irresistible, came very close.

'Chocolate please!' Esme added, with her own brand of more forceful cheeky-charm.

'All right, I'll go get some when I've finished the hard graft of policing you lot.'

'We've got something to show you, too,' Alice added.

'Oh, really? What?'

'Wait 'til you get back,' Esme told him. 'It's a surprise.'

★★★

The promised revelation was a masterpiece of student creativity, a play entitled *Resurgam Defiled*. PC Rogers had the good grace to listen with a fixed expression that he hoped resembled keen interest. But, in truth, his mind did occasionally slip to the weeks of training, and a growing understanding of what the affable old instructor, Sergeant "Happy" Hancock had said so many times.

'No matter what I tell you about, you'll find a thousand times more bizarre on the beat.'

And here he was, not solving crimes, nor even helping old ladies across the road, but listening to a rambling teenage artwork of the soul. Still, it was only a few more hours until he was off shift and tonight, he might just find the courage to ask Kathy whether she fancied sharing a bottle of wine in the Queen's Arms. They would seek out a quiet corner, he would tell her of the fascination of these first few weeks of duty, listen to her stories of life as a nurse, and see where the evening took them.

'Are you listening, Steve?' he was being asked.

'I'm savouring every word.'

PC Rogers, by nature a modest man – he would have asked Kathy out ages ago, otherwise – felt proud he'd managed to keep his voice free of sarcasm.

★★★

Resurgam Defiled began with the life of a headmistress in wartime Plymouth. The year was 1940.

So far, the conflict had little touched the city. Many of the menfolk were away in the forces, the women working the land, or in factories, on the drive for victory. The fighting was abroad, overseas, too far afield to truly feel.

Margaret, as she would be called, went about running her school, keeping the children educated and entertained, trying to make their lives as normal as possible. And in truth that wasn't so difficult, because the bubble of their world floated along much as it always had. Until the night the first bombs whistled their sinister tune through the air.

Three people were killed and Margaret had to lead an assembly to explain what happened. Wide-eyed youngsters, uncomprehending, knowing only that amongst their number one was missing. Would not run with them in the playground, sit with them in class, grow with them into adulthood.

That night, alone in her bedroom, the twins safely asleep, Margaret thought back on the assembly and quietly cried.

But if the tears were a secret plea for clemency, they fell unanswered. The bombing went on and more such assemblies followed the first, many more, for Plymouth was marked in the enemy's mind.

Devonport Dockyard was the principle target. Hundreds of miles away, unseen at sea, the Battle of the Atlantic was being fought. Day and night, a struggle for supremacy which would be so very important in dictating the outcome of the war.

Both sides knew it. And so the enemy pounded Plymouth with a desperate fury, attempting to obliterate the city which dared to nurture the doughty fleet.

In the wartime way, Margaret kept calm and carried on, her upper lip as stiff as a window sill. Despite the fears for her husband, Tony, serving overseas, her family, her neighbours and friends.

'Are you taking all this in, Steve?'

It was Alice, her gentle voice breaking through more daydreams of Kathy. Only five or six times they'd met now, in the local shop and in the Queen's Arms.

At first they'd exchanged brief smiles, then a few words of conversation, as befitted neighbours. But the chats had grown longer and it always felt more than a passing politeness.

She was petite and had such lovely hair, a page boy style in a chestnut hue. It was an alluring combination for a young police officer with few friends in this new city.

'Oh yeah, a hundred and twenty per cent,' PC Steve improvised.

'We'll be asking questions later, to check,' Esme warned.

'I'll get ten out of ten, minimum.'

A knowing look twinkled in Alice's blue eyes, but the plan for the play rolled on.

★★★

The months ran and the year turned to 1941.

Still Plymouth stood defiant. The bombs continued to fall, but the damage was isolated. The personality of the city remained, its core of wood beam Tudor, the smatterings of the arches and parapets of the Jacobeans and the fine stone of the Victorian city centre. It was as it had grown to be, how Margaret had come to know it.

Until the Blitz of Plymouth.

A series of air raids reduced much of the city to rubble, Hundreds of years of history destroyed in a few short hours. But it didn't stop there. Month after month more bombs fell, an agony of endured suffering. The final attack came three years later, an enemy's bitter retribution at a nearing defeat.

Margaret's school was obliterated by a direct hit. But she visited the children at home and set up classes where she could. It was almost a relief, a veil of distraction from the loss of Tony.

She took comfort in the teaching, and in particular the Latin which she had loved from her own schooldays. Perhaps it was that which kindled the idea.

For amidst the ruins, the drifting smoke and the hopeless screams, came one small gesture of defiance. A moment of history defined.

Adrift in the destruction, in the heart of the dying city, Margaret reached her resolution. She found the materials and made her preparations. She walked through a landscape which was no longer familiar to find the mother church of Plymouth. And there, above the door of St Andrew's, she nailed the simple wooden sign.

Resurgam.

And the people watched, and nodded, and quietly dared to believe. It was a comfort, a light in the long darkness.

To this day the entrance is still referred to as the Resurgam Door, a carved granite plaque now replacing the wood. Groups of schoolchildren are taken to stare at it. People of all ages pause as they pass.

It watches over the reborn city. It humbles; history in a single word. *Resurgam* − *I shall rise again.*

A name now to be used for a skyscraper filled with shops, bars, restaurants and a disco.

★★★

'Do you get it?' Alice prompted.

'Stealing a name as important as Resurgam for a bloody shopping centre in the sky,' Seb concurred.

'It certainly makes your point,' PC Steve said diplomatically, handing around some tea and trying to shift the fantasy of a semi-clothed Kathy from his mind. 'What do you reckon, Tommy?'

The young man ruffled his hair. 'I can't say too much. I work for them.'

Phil Rees nodded agreement and flexed his bulky shoulders. This was a man for whom muscles spoke louder than words.

'But you must think something?' Seb persisted.

'It's the little beach I really miss,' Tommy replied. 'I used to love seeing all the kids out with their canoes and windsurfers.'

Alice's face crinkled into another of those special smiles, the single flaw of her beauty spot for once eclipsed by its shine. 'That can be the second part of the play. A security guard who loved the old beach, but needs a job. So he's got no choice but to work for Resurgam.'

Seb nodded hard, but the way he looked at Alice suggested he would have agreed with any words those fine lips formed.

'It can be one man's inner struggle, classic dramatic stuff,' Esme added knowledgably.

'We don't need to stop at turmoil,' Alice added. 'What about if he's driven mad and attacks Resurgam?'

The young police officer decided it was time to quell the rising flames of youthful enthusiasm. 'There'll be none of that while

I'm here, drama or not.' PC Steve nodded hard to emphasise the words, then added, 'Uh oh, here comes that reporter again. I'm off.'

★★★

Steve Rogers may have been an inexperienced officer of the law, but he'd already learnt to recognise the furtive, lurking, unkempt nosiness which betrays many a hack.

The journalist in question was Barnaby Hill, which colleagues joked made him sound like a middle ranking area of London. In fact, the name stemmed from his parents meeting at college, where both studied English and were keen readers of Dickens.

Barnaby was a junior reporter and keen as the north wind to make a name. A sedentary fellow, fond of food and wine in equal excess, he'd always fancied a specialism as the paper's Environment Correspondent. The post offered tempting trips to tropical climes, all courtesy of the newspaper.

Barnaby boasted old school friends who had emigrated from London for the better life of the Westcountry. From them he heard of Resurgam, and convinced his editor there was a scandal brewing in quaint old Devon that was worthy of national attention.

'Make sure you bring me a good splash,' the man begrudged. 'I'm not coughing up for a couple of nights in a hotel otherwise.'

Such it was that Barnaby concentrated his questions on Seb, Alice, Esme and Mac. There he sensed the vulnerability of earnest inexperience, and the prospect of reaping the most fruitful harvest.

'You must fear Resurgam might become a terrorist target?' he inquired, in a manner as leading as a guide dog. 'And it's possible it's being built where the Pilgrim Fathers set out for the New World, isn't it? And something as tall as this, there must be some risk it'll be unsafe? Not to mention the impact on the lovely foreshore and its wildlife...'

Thus gradually, and some way short of scrupulously, it formed; the story which local historians would come to identify as the true beginning of The Battle of Resurgam.

CHAPTER 10

A white van pulled up on the pavement, followed by another. From the first climbed the police photographer, a stick of a man with a top of ginger hair. He took a series of snaps, focusing on the detail of the individual letters.

When the photographer had finished, a couple of men in white overalls and baseball caps emerged from the second van and collected pots of paint and brushes from its innards. They moved in the unhurried manner of the publicly funded workman.

Dan's mobile vibrated its text alert. It was Claire.

Going shopping, anything you fancy for dinner? Be nice if you could get home early so we could spend some time together. X

'We might be able to make some kind of connection between the message and a suspect's handwriting,' Adam was saying, before adding, a little sulkily, 'That's if I can find a suspect, of course.'

The workmen looked over and Adam gave them a shake of the head. The larger of the pair shrugged and picked at a tuft of dark hair protruding impressively from his nose. The other, who was shorter and far balder, started swirling a brush in one of the tins.

'For now, I'm having our little message painted over. We don't want to cause a panic.'

He looked expectantly to Dan, but the intrepid newshound was tapping a finger on the keypad of his phone and staring out at the view. His eyes were way over the horizon.

'Don't you think?' the detective prompted. 'Or maybe I should call the media to come have a look?'

'Yeah, you're probably right.'

'All except that *Wessex Tonight* lot, obviously. They're not be trusted, some of the reporters they employ.'

'Sorry, what?'

'Are you ok?' Adam asked, sharply. 'The least I'd expect is for you to try to film the graffiti, even if I said you couldn't broadcast it yet.'

'Oh, yeah. Good idea.'

Adam waited impatiently, kicking petulantly at a stone, while Dan called Nigel. The workmen had started a kick about of their own, but with an empty paint tin. A hollow clattering mixed with the more distant sound of the building site. Adam tolerated it for perhaps half a minute, then shouted at them to stop. A raggedy, unkempt man limped up the hill from the Homeless Mission and lingered to watch the filming.

'What is it?' the detective asked Dan. 'What's bothering you?'

'I've just… got a lot on my mind, that's all.'

'Well get it off your mind,' came the petulant response. 'It's only a couple of days until this Finale Friday rigmarole. The arrival of the plans and razor blade at the station, plus the graffiti – it's a clear threat. Have you got half an hour?'

Dan checked his watch. The idiosyncratic old Rolex tended to be even more unreliable in the colder months, for a reason which defied explanation. It said half past nine, so the time was probably around a quarter to ten.

'There's ages until the lunchtime broadcast.'

'Then let's talk.'

At his standard strenuous pace, off Adam set. Dan followed, deleting Claire's text message as he walked.

★★★

As was often Adam's way when possessed by thoughts, the offer of a conversation turned out to be the delivery of a monologue.

They settled in a small café just around the corner from Resurgam, close to the Fish Market, in the heart of the Barbican. The street was cobbled, only the odd van juddering carefully past. Some of the fishermen were still in their overalls, others the thick woollen jumpers and hats of the profession's uniform. The smell of their catch was ever present in the air, mixed with the frying of bacon.

A couple of men were talking about the Cashman, speculating how much money he must have parted with during his appearance at the Fish Market. Tens of thousands of pounds was the consensus. This morning's distribution of a similar sum at the bus station was one of the main stories on the radio burbling away in the background.

Dan sighed and stared into his coffee. El had been on the phone again and set a new record on the forlorn scale. The photographer sounded more wretched than a child who'd awoken on Christmas morning to find a note from Santa saying, *Sorry, run out of presents*.

'I'm being diddled, dicked and done, and on me home turf, too,' El wailed. 'I'm thinking of hanging up me camera.'

A few platitudes had done little to lift the lamenter's mood, and so Dan had offered that which he was hoping to avoid. There didn't feel anything like sufficient space in his life for a crazy quest, let alone the enthusiasm. But El was his closest friend and the promise had at least injected a little cheer.

'If you can help poor El, it's beers on him forever!'

'I'll settle for a cut of the purse.'

'Fifty-fifty to you kind sir, I swear on me best camera's life.'

★★★

Dan yawned and rolled his neck. The café was pleasantly warm, and after the cold of outside it had a soporific effect. He realised Adam was tapping his coffee mug. 'Are you listening to me?'

'Of course.'

'Then what did I just say?'

'You said... it was about – Resurgam.'

'Inspired. Truly insightful. Try harder.'

Dan leaned back on his seat. He tried not to wish it would recline so he could lie back, sleep, and let the world tick along without his input.

'I haven't a clue. And to be quite honest, I'm not sure I care. I can't seem to concentrate. I haven't got any energy. I'm just...'

'Just what?'

'I'm… well, lost. I'm not me at the moment.'

Adam sipped at his drink and loosened his tie. 'You're not wrong there. An extraordinary case like this, normally you wouldn't be able to get enough of it.'

'Thanks for reminding me. It's not like I hadn't noticed.'

Leaning forwards, Adam said quietly, 'Is it Claire?'

'No, it's bloody not!' Dan found himself on his feet, his hand waving in the air, slops of coffee spilling on the plastic table. 'Why does everyone think it's Claire? Why does everyone want to know if I'm ok? Why does everyone want to have a go at running my damned life?!'

People were looking over, stopping their conversations. The café had quietened. A face peered through the mistiness of the window, like a ghost in a dream. Adam just sat there, held his friend's look.

'All right, yes it is,' Dan said, as he sat down again. 'I… I don't know what to do. I don't think I want her around, but when I imagine her leaving it frightens me. I think I want to be on my own, but when I am I feel lonely. I just – oh fuck it, I don't know what to do.'

He let out a hiss and stared defiantly at Adam. 'Go on then, laugh.'

There was no reply, save perhaps the slight raising of a well-shaped eyebrow.

'Go on,' Dan ranted, embracing his theme with a growing enthusiasm. 'Enjoy yourself! Take the piss, you with Tom and Annie, your ideal family and perfect life. Have a good laugh at Mr Fuck-Up.'

But laughter wasn't the reaction Dan received. A hand was resting on his shoulder and Adam's voice was gentle. 'Listen a minute.'

'What?'

'Just listen. No one ever really gets the hang of relationships.'

'Yeah?'

'Damn right, yeah. Look at Annie and me. We nearly screwed it up. We could have divorced, but we got through it. Things can work out.'

'Really,' came the sullen reply.

'It's never as bad as you think. Just take your time and take it easy. You're in a very non-exclusive club with relationship troubles.'

'Everyone else seems to do ok.'

'That's always how it feels when you're suffering. Get this - now Tom's finding out about love. He's seventeen, he's fallen for some girl and she doesn't want to know. It's like having a love-sick zombie mooning about the house.'

Dan managed a weak smile and Adam's face warmed too.

'I'm not going to try and do the Dad thing. No one knows what's going on in your heart but you. The only thing I'd say is this – I thought you made a fine couple. Claire's a great woman, you're a good man, so just talk and make some sort of decision. For both your sakes.'

'Both of us?' queried the classical only child, in self-centred surprise.

'She came in to Charles Cross last week to help on one of her old cases and looked wretched. As do you, by the way. It can't go on like this.'

'I know. I will talk to her.'

'Soon?'

'Soon.'

Adam waited while a man collected some plates from a table. 'Now, do you want to hear about the case? And I mean – hear, pay attention and think? I could do with your help.'

Dan nodded. 'Just let me pop to the loo first.'

He got up and picked a path to the back of the café, trying to ignore the watching eyes which escorted him. In the toilets, Dan pointedly avoided looking in the mirror, but spent several minutes splashing handfuls of cooling water to calm the heat in his eyes.

★★★

By the time the emotional incompetent had returned, the café was almost full. The windows had misted across in that way of the winter, when the frozen outside can feel another world apart.

One fisherman, a younger man with a cheery face, drew a couple of pictures on the glass, impressively accurate depictions of a Turbot, Pollack and Bass. But the effect was somewhat spoiled when a compatriot added a beard and glasses to each.

Surrounded as they were, and discussing the sensitive matters of what may come to be a murder inquiry, Dan and Adam leant forwards to talk in subtle tones. They were interrupted only by a waitress who blessed them with an indulgent smile.

'No,' Dan said. 'We're just good friends.'

Adam looked puzzled, rapidly followed by surprised and then aghast. 'She didn't think…' he responded, with an amusing mixture of pique and horror.

'She did.'

'How do you know?'

'I just know. Isn't that what I'm supposed to bring to this relationship – albeit platonic, naturally? The perception thing.'

'Well, yes, but…'

'It's not the first time it's happened, either. We must make a lovely couple.'

Adam emitted an ungracious snort, found his notes and went through a briefing. First, he took out a couple of images from the footage of the lorry hitting the gatehouse.

'The Eggheads have enhanced it, but it's no real help. We still can't tell what Esther made very sure she took before running away. But… we do have another clue.'

He sat back and produced a smug smile. It was a look Dan had grown to know well over the years they'd worked together, but that didn't make it any less infuriating.

'And this clue is?' Dan replied, patiently.

'What else did I say we were looking at?'

'Lots of things.'

'But specifically?'

'Wouldn't it be easier if you just told me?'

'Maybe. But not as entertaining.'

'For you or me?'

'Just think.'

The waitress returned with their drinks and this time kept her face straight. Dan sipped at his coffee and thought, as per the irritating instruction.

'The interviews with the other protesters,' he said, at last.

'All done and all consistent. None had any idea anything like this could have happened. They were genuinely shocked.'

'Ok, then – the checks on the lorry.'

'Done. No mechanical faults which might have caused it to hit the gatehouse.'

'So, it could have been a deliberate attack?'

'It might just have been a dreadful accident. Maybe the lorry started to run out of control, she panicked and bailed out.'

'But she's not the panicking type,' Dan observed. 'Quite the opposite.'

'Nor is she the murdering type. In all those other protests she's been one of the ringleaders. But it's always been largely peaceful. Her only arrests have been for obstructing the highway and criminal damage.'

'There was that other case,' Dan said, thoughtfully. 'I uncovered it when I was doing the profile. That one in Brighton.'

'Assaulting a police officer? Yeah, but that was in the middle of a near riot. It was hardly a premeditated attack.'

'Which then brings us back to the original point. What other clue have you got?'

Adam's smirk widened. He didn't actually say *"Do you give up?"* but Dan suspected he could sense the words hovering in the air.

'The other CCTV,' the detective said, triumphantly. 'Of Esther running away.'

'And?'

'Two things. First, she's got a rucksack on her back. So whatever it was she didn't want to leave behind it's small enough to fit in there.'

Dan nodded slowly. 'Ok, that helps. But it could still be a huge range of stuff. And the other thing?'

'We know where she ran to. The CCTV follows her the whole way, bar one short alley.'

'And?'

'I reckon she had a clear plan in mind. She doesn't slow at all, doesn't hesitate. She knows exactly where she's heading.'

'And that is?'

Adam swigged at his coffee, swirled the remains from the mug and drained those too. 'The big multi-storey around the corner.'

'You're suggesting she went to find a car to get away?'

'She doesn't have a car. Esther hasn't driven since she was at college. She hates cars. She thinks they're destroying the planet.'

'She went to meet some accomplice, to drive her away?'

'Maybe. Because, do you want to hear the really strange thing?'

Adam stood up from the table and put on his coat. They left some money for the bill, which Dan topped up to include a good tip. The waitress deserved it for the discomfort she'd provoked in Adam.

'The CCTV shows her going into the car park,' he said. 'It covers all the entrances and exits, anywhere you could possibly leave. And that's the strange thing – it doesn't show her coming out again.'

★★★

Outside, in an instant, the cold was in their faces and all around; an invisible legion of pinching crabs and biting insects. The wind had picked up, was speeding in from the sea, and under its merciless prompting the freezing air sought every weakness in the flimsy barriers of clothing. The chill seeped its insidious way past scarves, inside collars, along sleeves and through shoes, bypassing gloves and attacking every part of the body.

'Bloody hell,' Dan gasped. 'The Arctic's moved south.'

'You're going soft,' came the scornful reply. 'I used to spend days on the beat like this.'

'That was a few years ago,' Dan pointed out gently.

They walked back towards the gates to Resurgam, passing a line of shops, their windows full of festive lights. The sky had turned a morose grey, a cantankerous contrast to the colours of the festive season.

'About thirty is the answer,' Adam announced.

'To what?'

'The question you should be asking. If you were being your usual self.'

'What question?'

'The number of cars that left the multi storey through the night, after Esther went in. I'm having the owners questioned.'

'Good idea,' Dan managed, by way of response.

'Obvious idea, you mean,' came the acidic rejoinder.

The time had crabbed on to half past ten, in that lethargic way which is the mark of the winter months. The city was begrudgingly coming to life, the braver of the populace venturing out. Shoppers were browsing, sightseers going about their missions. But all were wrapped in the swaddling clothes of yore.

'What are you going to do now?' Adam asked.

'A broadcast is demanded for the lunchtime news. But that's three hours off. In the meantime, I'll probably just sit in the Satellite Truck. I've got a few calls to make to sort some things out. It's media day at Resurgam tomorrow, a sort of curtain raiser for Finale Friday. We're finally going to be allowed inside to do some filming. You?'

'I'm going to see Ellen Dance. I need to talk to her about the plans for the foundations arriving at the cop shop and that graffiti.'

'Do you think the opening of Resurgam should be delayed?'

Adam waited for an older couple to walk past. Sixty years they'd probably been married for, but still held hands and looked entirely content.

'If you stare any harder, you'll frighten them,' Adam observed.

'Was it that obvious?'

'I don't know if you spotted it, but I'm a detective. I tend to notice things. What were you gawping at?'

'It was just – ah, you'll think this is daft.'

'I wouldn't be surprised, knowing you. And particularly not in your current shop-soiled state. But try me anyway.'

'I wanted to stop them and ask what's the secret to looking so bloody happy.'

Adam shook his head. 'You are a bloody diva, sometimes. This might surprise you, but if everything around looks hopeless the problem might not be with the world, but the way it's being viewed.'

They walked on, passing a woman smoking in a doorway. She appeared to be trying to set a record for finishing a cigarette. Ahead, Resurgam appeared a black block in the monochrome of the day.

'Thanks for the pep talk,' Dan said. 'I'll treasure your wisdom forever, if not longer.'

'That's better.'

'What?'

'Some sign of spirit, at last. I thought I was going to have to goad you forever. It was getting tedious.'

Dan was about to return the volley, but decided against it. Adam could be pompous enough, without gifting him another victory.

'As I was saying – should the opening of Resurgam be delayed?'

'That's one for Ellen Dance,' the detective replied, neutrally. 'But it certainly promises to be an interesting conversation.'

They said goodbye and agreed to talk later in the afternoon. Adam began heading towards Resurgam when his phone rang. He listened, then came jogging back.

'We've got a lead on where Esther might be.'

A patrol car swung around the corner, blue lights flaring in the greyness. In the front were two cops, both of impressive stature. Adam hopped into the back. He was about to close the door when Dan grabbed it.

'What're you doing?' Adam protested.

'Getting back with it, as requested. Where are you going?'

'Outskirts of the city.'

'Fancy some good publicity? For a key arrest?'

Adam looked dubious. He rubbed a hand over the stubble on his chin. The cops in the front of the car were watching the exchange, one frowning darkly.

'It'd play well with the High Honchos,' Dan added. 'Show off how quickly the police are making progress. It's a winner for us both.'

And before Adam had a chance to demur, Dan piled untidily into the car.

CHAPTER 11

Traffic had been sluggish around the city for days, motorists ponderously overcautious about the risk of ice. The police driver, however, had no such qualms. He cut through the lines of cars like a shark through a shoal.

They were heading for the Derriford area of Plymouth, home of the biggest hospital in the south west and once largely countryside. But with the constant need for housing, and the persecution of a previously green and pleasant land, it had been filled with rows of new-build faux mansions.

Many were adorned with the black and white beams of the mock Tudor. The wide and leafy byways here were all Avenues, Hills and Crescents, never the unspeakably common Roads or Streets.

The two cops in the front were even larger than on first appearance. One was muttering about being fed up with dealing with traffic shunts and that it was high time for some action. He kept rubbing his hands together, as though readying for combat.

Dan had long enjoyed his occasional trips in a police car. It felt like becoming a VIP. Other vehicles melted away from your path, their occupants staring as you passed. It was an effort not to offer a magnanimous wave.

'Do we need to tool up?' the driver asked Adam, with a little too much enthusiasm.

'No. He's got no record for firearms. Just a fair bit of violence.'

As one, the enforcers in the front of the car smiled.

Dan swallowed hard. 'Who is it we're going to see?' he asked, trying to keep his voice level.

'Are you feeling as lion-hearted as ever?' the detective sniffed.

'You know this isn't my favourite part of police work.'

'All too well.' Adam checked his notes. 'The guy's name is Cliff Larson. He's a builder with an interesting past. A few convictions for assault, also some theft. What's key is that his company had a big contract in the early stages of Resurgam but got the boot for dodgy work. He was mad about it and made threats.'

'And the possible link with Esther is?'

'His car is the only one that came out of the multi storey last night to give us anything of interest. It looks low on its wheels for just a driver in there.'

★★★

The sirens and blue lights were extinguished a mile away from the movingly christened Tree Green Avenue. The police car pulled up a couple of hundred yards from number 92 and they studied the house.

It was detached and set in an expanse of grounds. At both the front and rear were large fishponds. The hedges and trees were well-trimmed and the lawns looked immaculate. A new silver Mercedes sat on the drive. It shone as though it was polished at least twice daily.

There were doors at the front, back and sides of the house. The central heating was on and working hard, clouds of steam rising from a flue. As they watched, a light went on in one room, then blinked off again.

'Time to say hello,' Adam decreed. 'It's one door each, in case he decides to go for a little impromptu morning jog. If you gentlemen would be so kind?'

The two cops hauled their bulks out of the car. They walked stealthily down the hill towards number 92 and disappeared into a neighbouring house. After a few minutes, they reappeared in its back garden and, with some effort, climbed over the wooden fence. One of the officers headed to the rear of the house, the other the side. Both took shelter in lines of trees.

'That's my cue,' Adam said, and got out of the car. Dan remained firmly seated safely inside.

'Are you coming?' the detective asked, patiently.

'Do I have to?'

'I believe it's considered good practice for reporters to be close to the action?'

'It's cold out there.'

'It's just the weather, is it?'

Dan didn't answer.

'I thought journalists were supposed to be intrepid?' Adam continued.

'They're the ones who like war reporting. I work in Devon and Cornwall for a reason.'

'You can hang back out of the way, don't worry. When have I ever got you into trouble?'

Dan gave his friend a sidelong look. 'Do you really need an answer to that?'

'Come on,' Adam coaxed, then ordered, 'Now!'

As if hoping it might offer extra protection against an attack, Dan pulled his coat tight and slowly climbed out of the car.

★★★

The tarmac was white with the days of cold. Adam covered it quickly, his athletic frame striding for the front door. The leaves of the hedge were also patterned with frost. The branches rustled and a bird flew out. Dan spun around, arms raised to defend himself.

Adam looked to the grey of the skies and groaned. 'If you can't manage courage try silence.'

They slipped through the heavy wooden gates and onto the drive. Music was beating within the house, some indecipherable pop tune. Adam gave the Mercedes a quick glance. Inside were a couple of maps and a bundle of papers, but nothing to suggest Esther could have hidden there.

The fishpond was clear of ice despite the chill. Golden shapes swum serenely back and forth. A stone fountain trickled with a forlorn stream.

Adam was almost at the door. Dan started to fall back, positioning himself towards the side of the house where there were no doors.

86

The music ebbed and changed, another equally strangled alleged tune inflicted upon the world. A black cat watched from the side of some trees.

'Please bring me some luck,' Dan muttered. 'Nothing too extravagant required. I'll take continued existence, preferably undamaged.'

Adam raised a fist to knock at the door. The detective never trusted bells, always preferred a good, hard hammering. He described it as heralding the coming of the law in the old-fashioned way he favoured.

Inside the house the music stopped. Dan sensed a sudden stillness. His imagination flew. He could see the man freezing, knowing he was surrounded. Calculating what to do. Reaching inside a cupboard for a hidden gun.

The cover of a handy tree called and Dan found himself backing into it.

Adam knocked again, harder now. 'Gas company,' he called, with a risible attempt at a workman's accent. 'Reports of a leak.'

More seconds edged by. Still no motion inside the house.

Adam leaned forwards to peer through the opaque, distorting glass. He tried the handle. It didn't turn.

And now there was sound. A window was opening. And it was right by where Dan was hiding.

★★★

The panicked mind of Dan Groves concluded there was good news and bad in what was happening only a handful of metres away.

On the positive side, the man was taking time to squeeze through the window. Adam had heard the noise and was running from the front of the house. He was shouting to the other cops to join him. Help was on the way.

But the bad news was considerably more significant. The rescue party wasn't going to arrive anything like fast enough. On top of which, Mr Cliff Larson boasted the proportions of a professional wrestler. He didn't look happy, either.

Larson's face was contorted with a mix of anger and straining effort. His head was shaved and there was a less than fetching tattoo of a large cross on his neck. And despite the freezing weather, he was planning to make a getaway dressed in a vest and jogging pants.

The man-beast freed himself from the window and dropped to the ground. Adam was sprinting over, moving fast, but still twenty metres away. To Dan the distance looked intergalactic.

He thought about running, but his legs had gone for an early lunch and weren't responding to the frantic urges of his nervous system. And anyway, there was no time. Larson was almost upon him.

The creature had thudded into a flower bed and was turning, looking for an escape. He began running towards the gate, a bearing that took him directly through where Dan was crouching.

At the sweet prospect of freedom, Larson's expression changed. He was smiling, but far from kindly.

'Don't hurt me, I'm just a reporter!' Dan wailed. He held up his hands in a gesture of surrender, then thought better of it. Instead he cringed and folded himself into a ball, arms across head, making himself as slight an inconvenience on existence as possible.

And now Dan waited. For the mighty kick in his ribs, the crack of bones, the knife in his back.

But mercifully Larson was too intent on his getaway. Heavy feet pounded on the frozen ground, beating just past Dan as Larson headed for the beckoning arms of liberty.

Mr Courageous opened one eye and dangled out a sneaky shin. The fugitive went sprawling on the frosty lawn, a tumble of arms and legs. And Adam was upon him, a knee in his back and handcuffs around his wrists.

THE BATTLE OF RESURGAM
THREE — THE NEWCOMERS

Of the nineteen who assembled to make up the protest line that Monday morning almost eleven months ago, all except one carried the newspaper. The sole omission was Mac, and that only because of the bitter, soggy and highly unpleasant retribution exacted upon the copy he'd bought.

It was now late January, almost a month into the construction work. Already the building was beginning to stretch its metal arms into the sky. The foundations were dug, bored into the bedrock, shaking and rattling the world around with the endless attacks upon the earth. The building's feet had been laid in place, great pads to hold its immense weight, then encased in thousands of tons of concrete. And from that steadfast base was rising the steel lattice of the superstructure.

The snow still lay on the ground, but in a chessboard pattern. No reinforcements had floated from the sky for several days. The temperature had warmed, occasionally in the afternoons touching a stratospheric two, perhaps even three degrees. Little progress it may have been, but it felt very welcome after the endless freezing hours.

Monday had traditionally been a quiet day for the protest, with two or three figures maintaining a token vigil. But not this time, not now. The group was swollen by the need to share the news which had been splashed across one of the Sunday papers.

Barnaby Hill had written his article. The story made a portion of the front page, with another three quarters of a page within: "TERROR TARGET, ECO-VANDALISM AND A HISTORY BETRAYED"

And were that headline not enough, Resurgam had proved a temptation too far for other newspapers to resist. Several competitors had seen and presumably liked it, for they were running their own versions this winter Monday morning.

★★★

'We'll get bloody lynched for this,' an older man said. 'You stupid students, talking to that reporter.'

'Don't you have a go at them,' June intervened. 'It's hardly their fault if he invents a story.'

Some sharp looks flickered amongst the crowd, but there were no more exchanges. All were too occupied with the paper.

Environmental vandalism is being wrought in the heart of one of our great cities. History is being betrayed, precious and beautiful seashore destroyed. And for what? opponents ask. To build an eyesore, a carbuncle, and not just that, but a monstrosity they fear will become a target for terrorists.

As earnest as ever, and today to the point of tears, Seb insisted to the line, 'That's not what we said at all, I promise you.'

He sounded miserably contrite; as if he'd taken the simple misjudgement of youth to his soul. Alice took his hand, kindness and comfort in a single touch. 'All we were trying to do was tell the truth about what was going on here.' She wound an arm around Seb, who resisted not at all.

'No one's holding it against you,' June replied. She turned to the crowd and held up a fist, clad again in the spectrum of a mitten. 'Are they?'

There was no response so she repeated the words, this time prompting a few sullen mutterings of acquiescence.

'It could even help,' she continued. 'It might galvanise people to come and join us.'

'Fat chance,' Mac grunted, in an unusually comprehensible communiqué.

'We've got to stand together or we won't stand at all,' June rallied. 'What's done is done. It's only the future we can change. Right, is anyone here cold?'

Again, there was no response from the lifeless crowd. The day was too icy, the skyscraper growing too fast, the floes of fate running too hard against them.

'Did you hear me?' she cried. 'Are you cold?'

'Yes,' was the spiritless reply.

'Then this is the message we send!'

And if the speech wasn't quite the beloved Henry V of June's teaching days, if the passing of the years debarred her from leading an army into battle, she had another way.

June collected the newspapers from each of the protesters and arranged them carefully on the pavement. From one of the group she borrowed a lighter and set the pile ablaze.

A couple of the protesters started to clap. Others joined in and together they huddled around the flames, intermittently warming their hands and applauding. A smile ran, as fast and cheering as a songbird greeting the spring. From young to old, man to woman it spread. Hearts beat anew.

From the gates of Resurgam a fire bell began to ring. Tommy Ross and Phil Rees emerged from the guardhouse and came running over, slipping and balancing on the ice.

'You stupid fucks,' Rees yelled, and tried to barge his way past Mac. He got a shove in return and squared up, his bulk dwarfing the young man's frame. June was at Mac's side in a second.

'Leave him alone,' she commanded. 'You big beast of a bully.'

'The fire!' Tommy panted, pulling Rees towards the flames.

PC Rogers was marching over too, fast but upright, as must have been his indoctrination from training college. Rees pushed Mac backwards, the student stumbling and half falling. Now Seb grabbed one of Rees's arms, Alice the other. He shook them off with muscular ease, Alice catching a glancing blow, blood immediately beginning to run from her nose.

The fire was burning well but Rees didn't hesitate, began stamping on it. Seb let out a yell and turned, fists aloft, a red rage filling his face. Some of Alice's blood had spattered onto his jeans.

'I'll fucking kill you for hurting her,' he screamed.

'Yeah right,' Rees called, like a demon dancing amidst the fire. 'Anytime, you little dickweed.'

'Ok, that's enough,' Steve Rogers shouted. Rees took no notice, so the policeman grabbed his shoulder and pulled him away from the flames. 'You,' he yelled, 'Calm it down - now.'

'But it's fucking arson.'

'I'll decide what it is. And swear at me again and you're in trouble. Now – away!'

Rees snarled, but skulked into the background like a wounded caveman. PC Steve made his way to the centre of the group, but unhurried, calm and polite, and stood beside the flames. They were failing now, only a little paper left to burn, most of the fine example of a free press no more than blackened flakes and ash.

'That's naughty,' he told the protesters, folding his arms and producing a wry look. 'We could have the Great Fire of Plymouth on our hands.'

But it was noticeable the young policeman made no attempt to put out the remaining flickers, instead stood amidst the group, watching as the fire dwindled and died.

★★★

Outbreak number two of mass disorder successfully contained, life on the protest line returned to normal. Banners were waved at supply lorries and dissenting pleasantries exchanged with some of the more affable workers.

Rees had been dispatched to the gatehouse, where he stood glowering at the demonstration. One of the cranes was edging a steel beam into position, a crossbar between two others.

PC Steve brought over a tray filled with mugs of tea and handed them around. 'Don't think I'm some liberal, rewarding bad behaviour,' he told the protesters, in a scolding voice. 'It's just my turn.'

Alice was cuddling into Seb, cheek snug upon his shoulder, a reddened handkerchief pressed against her nose. 'We are sorry about that story, really. It's just – we feel so helpless.'

Esme nodded. 'It's like no one's listening to us. And that reporter did. So we talked to him.'

'Not that he bothered to put in any of the other stuff we said,' Seb added. 'There wasn't a thing about our futures being stolen.'

'Yeah,' Esme agreed. 'No jobs, tens of thousands of pounds of debt for an education, no planet left to live on anyway.'

'I know what you mean about the jobs,' Tommy nodded. 'A mate of mine went for some work as a shelf stacker. There were two hundred people in the queue.' He patted his fluorescent jacket. 'You've got to take what you can get at the mo.'

He blew into his tea, enjoying the momentary warming of the air, and confided, 'Between us, I really miss that little beach. I had my first cuddle with a girl there.'

'And a snog?' Esme prompted.

Laughter ran through the crowd. Alice waited for it to quieten, then said, 'They've stolen another name, you know. It's not just Plymouth's history they've tarnished. My gran told me. A friend of hers... she had...'

June put down one of her puzzle books. 'The support society at the hospital, you mean? Maggie can tell you all about that.'

The tall, distinguished woman at her side nodded and said, 'There's a terminal illness club called Resurgam. I started doing voluntary work there after a friend of mine...' Her voice faded, just as Alice's had before, as many would when faced with such a subject. 'It's a wonderful organisation.'

'With a perfect name,' June added. 'The idea of some hope when...'

A lorry rumbled past, more steel jangling in its hold, the driver slowing to offer a wave. Alice waved back, transfixing the man to such an extent that he came close to forgetting how to drive, then asked June. 'Are you ok? You sounded – strange. Kind of choked.'

She rubbed a hand over her chest, and said quietly. 'My, err... aunt was a member of Resurgam.'

'What happened to her?' Seb asked, and received a sharp look from Esme.

'What do you think happens to people in a terminal illness group?' The young man's face flushed. 'Sorry, I meant – what was wrong with her?'

'She had cancer.'

June was looking unusually ruffled, and the diplomatic Alice decided it was time to change the subject. 'Seb's got something he wants to ask you,' she told PC Steve.

'It's not about where babies come from, is it?' He nodded to the intertwining with Alice. 'Now that you're, well…'

Seb reddened further, his face shifting to a shade just short of incandescent. 'No, it was – you made me think about joining the police.'

'It's a good job. You get to meet some interesting people.' Steve offered a meaningful look at the protesters. 'But the trouble is we're not recruiting and I doubt we will be for ages.'

'Same old shit,' Mac grunted.

'He had his name down for an apprenticeship at the dockyard,' Esme explained. 'Just to tide him over, while Mac waits to be discovered as an artist. But they're not taking anyone on, either. No one is.'

They lapsed into silence, all with thoughts for the future. PC Steve's were of Kathy and their first date. The pub had been quiet, the corner welcoming, the wine a deep and relaxing red. It had gone pretty well he reckoned; lots of laughter and no awkward silences. There'd even been a quick kiss goodnight, cut ruefully short by the incessant cold, but perhaps with the hint of more to come.

As for Alice and Seb, the daydream images were of a burgeoning relationship and whether it could survive the college years that lay ahead.

Esme wandered through a world healed by her actions, catalysed to change by the spirit of these protests. Her generation was feted, not forgotten.

And the laconic Mac, for him the visions were far more expansive than his few words; canvases as rich as the artworks he produced.

Upon a stage Mac stood, fans at his feet in dizzy ecstasy as another riff of the bass guitar was sent skywards.

And in the background, unknowing and uncaring, foot by foot and hammer by drill, Resurgam continued to grow.

★★★

A car drew up in a taxi rank, just along from the protest. It was a large green BMW and one of the more aristocratic members of the range. A man and woman got out. Both were rotund to the point of being inflated, dressed in matching bubble jackets and armed with faces harder than a Siberian frost.

'Oh, shit,' Mac muttered.

The couple made straight for the line. The black-clad Emo tried to hide behind a placard, but it was too late. He had been targeted, as surely as if the human eye possessed a laser sighting dot.

'Matthew! What the hell have you been doing? You're all over the papers!'

The woman set a course straight for the prodigal son, an accusatory finger leading the way. 'You stay out all hours, you never talk to us, and this is what you're getting up to!'

'I'm just trying to...'

The attempted defence was as effective as bales of straw before a battle tank. 'All that money we've invested in you and this is how you repay us. All the neighbours are talking about us. I wouldn't be surprised if your poor father gets suspended from the Community Watch Alliance.'

The silent man standing dutifully beside didn't look unduly concerned, until she turned to him. Upon which, Mr Mac's expression transformed to looking like an undertaker with depression. Mac himself had shrunk several inches in height and was trying to submerge himself under the collars of his trench coat.

'You're coming home with me,' the woman continued. 'And I don't want any arguments or you'll be grounded and you won't even be allowed to play that infernal guitar.'

And with that, she turned and headed back for the car. In the trueness of the teenage tradition, the rebellious son hunched his shoulders, but slouched along in the unforgiving parental slipstream.

★★★

It was mid-afternoon, the thin light already fading when the first bus arrived. There were no reporters, no cameramen, no media whatsoever to witness the coming. Which was a pity, as surely the point of the profession is to capture moments of change.

The first of the coaches was streaked with mud and heard well before it was seen, the exhaust blowing hard. The second was painted in swirling psychedelic colours, a drunken pastiche of reds, blues, yellows and greens. The third was nominally white, but more patterned with rust and dents. The fourth was the most modern, and green with white flashes.

Upon the side of three coaches was painted "**ECO WARRIORS UK TOUR**". The other sported the legend "**THE PROFESSIONALS**".

All four pulled up along the road in a zone marked "Strictly No Waiting". From the buses began to disembark young men and women in thick, rag tag coats, wide-brimmed hats and beanies, old boots and wellies, threadbare jeans and combat trousers, and a variety of unkempt hairstyles. Several carried copies of the paper, folded onto Barnaby Hill's article.

And in silent harmony, they gathered and looked to Resurgam, growing above the fences.

CHAPTER 12

Untroubled by the dramas of the human world, the golden spectres were still making their way around the pond. It was a serene and stately procession which would last a lifetime, and sometimes difficult not to envy. Dan stood and watched and tried to calm down.

For the first time in the recent reign of the cold, his feet didn't feel as though they'd been planted in the tundra. It was probably something to do with his heart rate. It was pounding along at a tempo of double time at least.

Adam was contentedly telling Larson his rights, a ritual of the law the detective always enjoyed. The other two cops had appeared from the sides of the house and looked downcast.

'A bit of bloody fun, at last, and we missed it,' the marginally smaller of the two complained.

Perhaps to help lift their mood, Adam let the pair walk Larson to the patrol car. The attempted fugitive had managed to vent a little abuse, but it wasn't particularly colourful. The handcuffs had ended his bid for freedom and eroded his spirit. A couple of neighbours watched from their gardens. They were smiling in a way that suggested Mr Larson may not have been the most popular member of the community.

Adam paced across, flicking some mythical dirt from his overcoat and straightening his impeccable tie. He eyed Dan disdainfully. 'Blimey, you look rough.'

'It might be something to do with staring mortal fear right in the face.'

'Yeah, we appreciate your extraordinary valour,' Adam added, with a double shot of irony.

'It worked, didn't it?!'

'It wasn't exactly the way of a knight.'

'I wasn't attempting to join the Round Table.'

'I'm not sure you'll ever have that option.'

'Adam! I'm not a cop and I don't want to be one, ok? That's your department. I'll take the thinking over the fighting.'

They began walking back to the patrol car. Dan caught a glimpse of himself in a window. He looked like a tramp who'd suffered a shock. More people had emerged to watch Larson being shoved inside. The misfortune of others was always good sport.

Dan's phone rang. It was Nigel.

'We're just wondering where you are,' he enquired, mildly. 'Given that it's quarter to one and we're on air at half past.'

★★★

They reached Resurgam a few minutes after one. The traffic was sticky with Christmas shoppers. Despite Dan's plea, the police driver wouldn't turn on the siren and rush them back.

'It's bad enough we have to make a detour to drop you off,' Adam observed, loftily. 'We're not your taxi service, whatever you might think.'

At least Dan got to enjoy the comfort of the front seat. Adam and the smaller of the two cops sat in the back, squashed each side of Larson. He wasn't saying much, apart from the cryptic, 'All this for a few fish when there's paedophiles walking the streets.'

For the last five minutes of the journey Resurgam rose on the horizon, as if a reminder of the looming deadline. Dots of figures were working on the Sky Garden, making the last preparations for Finale Friday. Some of the building's lights were on, a scattered pattern of glowing blocks in the day's gloom.

Dan tumbled out of the car and almost slipped on some ice, but managed to right himself. Nigel was waiting, holding out the talkback unit which linked them to the studio.

'Hell, you look awful,' he noted.

'I wish people would stop telling me that.'

'What happened?'

'I'd rather not go into it,' Dan replied, with feeling.

'Not been forgetting the day job again, by any chance? Doing too much of your undercover investigator thing?'

Dan's mobile announced the arrival of a text. It was Claire, asking whether he'd seen the earlier message about dinner. He turned the phone off and threw it into his satchel.

'I've got to work on these words. Give me five mins.'

Dan hopped into the Satellite Van to find Loud pulling out tufts of nasal hair with a small pair of pliers. It took but a second to decide to sit in the front to write his lines.

★★★

A banner had been strung along the wall by the entrance to Resurgam. *Grand Opening Friday – Don't Miss It!* Even with a young man lying critically ill on a hospital bed, a marketing opportunity could not be missed.

But the protesters had begun a counter attack. Each held up a sheet of paper and arranged themselves in a phrase which had become a symphony for the demonstration.

TEAR DOWN THE WALL

Security staff eyed Nigel as he set up the camera. He smiled affably, but received only the flinty expression which is the international mark of those so very tough they should not be troubled with.

By quarter past one, Dan had positioned himself in front of the camera, a view of Resurgam and the remains of the guardhouse behind. The protest was corralled to the side, watched carefully by a line of police officers.

Dan had written some approximate words on a piece of paper and was trying to fix them in his mind, but like leaves in the wind they wouldn't stay. On each attempt at authoritative, commanding journalism, he jumbled them up.

'You join me after a marked morning by controversy... yet more trouble flares in the run longing story of Resurgam...'

Nigel was shaking his head. 'You're still not looking great. Permission to take extreme measures?'

The cameraman bent down, scooped up a little icy snow and cupped it around Dan's cheeks. He yelped and recoiled.

'That's better,' Nigel said.

'For you or me?' Dan complained.

'It's got some colour into you. But I'm still going to shoot you in soft focus, if that's ok?'

'How soft?'

'Given the way you're looking – like a valium dream.'

The protesters were watching the pantomime that was television in preparation. Seb and Esme walked over to Alice's shrine. She made sure the flowers were tidy, a large picture of her friend proud above them. He watched, then knelt down, bowed his head and tenderly ran a finger over the photograph.

How he had changed over the past eleven months. They all had, these young protesters, with what they'd gone through, but none more so than Seb. He was thin now, gaunt, almost haggard. When the others asked why, he told them it was because he ran. Around the city, round and around. First two or three miles a day, then, when that wasn't enough, five or six and now nine or ten. He ran and ran, as hard as he could, as if trying to escape the memory of the fate which had befallen Alice.

Esme tried to reach out, but he eased the touch away. Not with anger, but the intensity of profound sadness. There would only be one woman for this heart the simple gesture said, however many years may lay ahead.

The time ticked on to twenty five past one. Dan still couldn't get his lines straight. 'Even as it's due to open, Resurgam is at the controversy of centre again…' Every new attempt swirled the word soup further.

'Are you going to be ok?' Nigel asked.

'No, I'm bloody not. Never mind, only half a million people will see me make a fool of myself.'

'Three minutes to air,' came the director's voice.

Nigel wheeled away to the Satellite Van, flung open the back doors and rummaged inside. He returned with a large square of white plastic and a marker pen.

Dan smiled. How absurdity could ease tension, like a miracle medicine.

'The Idiot Board. I haven't had to use that since I was a trainee.'

Nigel scribbled the key words on the plastic and held it up beside the camera.

'One minute to air. Standby.'

Another gust of biting wind blew in from the harbour. Grey swirls of cloud chased each other across the winter sky. And the opening titles of the bulletin began to play.

★★★

It was, Dan reflected ruefully as he followed the walk of doom, his own idiotic fault.

He'd ignored a basic rule of television journalism. Never relax. Never step so much as an inch into the perilous land of overconfidence.

A couple of colleagues had already given him sympathetic nods and semi-smiles. The long trudge to Lizzie's office was notorious. She wasn't the kind of boss to send out a summons to congratulate you on some wonderful work. It was an adult version of the trip to the headmaster's study.

And it had all been going so well. The lunchtime broadcast had almost passed off delightfully. Thanks to Nigel's fatherly efforts, Dan looked as human and sounded as intelligent as could be hoped, given the raw material.

He'd spoken of the attack on the gatehouse and the pictures had run, precisely on cue. Then Dan introduced Dance's denunciation and June's dignified counter. And so came the simple part, the last few lines.

'Thoughts now turn to the actual opening of Resurgam, the long-awaited day itself. With the protesters here promising to demonstrate to the last, and security heightened following the lorry attack, it's expected to be a tense time when the building finally opens its doors tomorrow.'

★★★

SIMON HALL

Nicola, the latest in a long line of Personal Assistants, produced an understanding smile. Lizzie got through PAs at the rate of one every six to nine months. Life expectancy in the post was only a little better than that of a Tommy in the First World War. The current incumbent had been in the job for four and a half months and her hair was already greying.

Dan knocked and opened the door. The reaction was so fast that he might have trodden on a trip wire.

'Do you know how many calls we've had?' was the charging rhino of an opening question. 'Almost a hundred!'

'Can I sit down?'

The request went unanswered, so Dan did. It presented less of a target and gave him a chance to think.

'It's a terrible mistake,' the carping commentary continued. 'It's something you might expect from a trainee, but certainly not an alleged correspondent.'

The word *alleged* was emphasised in a pitch that would have made an opera singer proud. Just to make unmistakably clear her mood, Lizzie's attire was a double danger warning. She was clad in the blackest of blacks, from polo neck to boots. And they were sharp and spiky.

'Making a cock-up like that! Everyone wants to know if Resurgam's opening tomorrow instead of Friday. It's humiliating.'

Dan studied the carpet. It was a familiar experience and he recognised each stain and join, old allies over the times he'd sat here.

'What the hell's the matter with you anyway? You look wretched.'

The unexpected easing of the assault prompted Dan to look up. 'What?'

'I want to know what's the matter with you.'

'I wish people would stop asking me that!' he protested.

'They're asking because it's obvious. You've been mooning around with a face like a goat with indigestion for weeks. What is it?'

'Nothing. It's – just nothing.'

'Really?'

'More or less.'

102

She paused, considered, but only briefly. Many said this was a woman with a warm heart, whose job demanded she hide it. Dan tended to agree, but such comforting thoughts weren't a help today.

'Look, this is a huge story,' Lizzie continued. 'We can't afford any more mistakes. Do you want me to take you off of it?'

'No! Of course not,' Dan recoiled. 'That'd be... well, I'd be... I don't know what I'd be.'

By no means for the first time of late, he found his eyes felt sore. Lizzie studied him, a sheet of black hair sliding across her face. 'Personal problems are your business, but *Wessex Tonight* is...'

'Who said it was personal problems?' Dan yelled. 'Why the hell does everybody in the whole damn world think they need to poke around in my life...'

He was stopped by her look. It was a surprise, nothing like Dan had witnessed before. And when Lizzie spoke, it was more gently than he could ever remember.

'You get the biggest stories for a reason, Dan. Remember that. You can do the *Media Day* tomorrow, but I've got no choice – if you make a hash of it I'll have to put someone else on to covering Friday.'

CHAPTER 13

Sometimes, however discreditable it may be, running away feels a temptation too far to resist.

This December Wednesday evening, as Dan parked outside the flat, Nigel's words drifted in his thoughts. They were joined by those of Adam and even Lizzie's too, all individual in their phrasing, but variations on the same theme. And the words were growing ever louder, as they had throughout the day.

The front door, which last night appeared so intimidating, had grown in stature. His hand was even shakier as the key found the lock.

The smell of fresh pasta served only to heighten the guilt. The sight of Claire, smiling through her sadness, wearing a rare dusting of make-up and sporting a new top, was another salvo to add to the bombardment of regret.

They were going to talk as soon as he got in. That was what Dan had resolved. No more waiting, no further procrastination, no more putting it off.

But he was hungry after that day. Claire had been kind enough to cook. Why spoil a fine meal? It could wait until after dinner.

And so they ate, and talked of the weather, and Rutherford, and the vagaries of the Christmas post, and the neighbour's new car, and everything and nothing.

The last few tubes of penne took a strangely long time to swallow. Remnants of sauce were pushed around the plate. For once, Claire finished her food first.

Rutherford lay beside the table, his tail unusually still. The music on the stereo, a tender compilation of classical love songs, faded to an end.

And so came the time for talking.

And so they looked to each other.

And so followed a silence.

And on it stretched. And on and on.

And suddenly Dan found himself blurting and burbling, filling the waiting air with a rambling list of excuses and explanations. He babbled about El's predicament, how an old friend so desperately needed help, how he could never abandon a precious companion in an hour of need and made the call.

And Claire just sat, her head bowed as Dan slipped out of the door.

★★★

El was waiting in a corner of the Old Bank pub. He had a couple of drinks, which wasn't a surprise, and a table filled with papers, which very much was.

Although not quite a Dickensian creature, Dan often thought of his strange friend as similarly so. El was a character of the twilight and got by on his wits and cunning. To see him surrounded by cuttings from newspapers, and pages of his own scribbled notes, was as incongruous as finding an archbishop studying a spread of pornography.

As is the way of the paranoid, El habitually sat with his back to the wall. He spotted the new arrival and was on his feet before Dan could make it to the bar.

'No time to waste. I've already bought you beer.'

'I thought those two were yours.'

'No time to drink. I gotta be sharp.'

Always a blur of excitement at the scent of a snap, tonight El was in effervescent form. He was a living memory of one of those school science experiments, when you dropped a tiny piece of sodium into acid.

Dan followed El to the table and took off his coat and scarf. It was wonderfully warm in the pub after the bitter day on the road. There were plenty of people, nursing their drinks and chattering. Christmas was always a handy justification to indulge.

'Come on, come on,' the photographer urged. 'No time, no time. He could be out there now, gearing up to show.'

A draw of beer was the only respite allowed, so Dan availed himself of a lingering ration before turning his attention to the papers. In precise date order were reports of every one of the Cashman's appearances, taken from a variety of sources. There were newspaper cuttings, print outs from internet pages and gossip forums, and even some of El's own observations.

'There's a pattern in there,' the paparazzo whispered, confidentially. 'The Cashman's working to a plan.'

Dan looked up from the papers. 'Really? What?'

El shrugged. 'I dunno. That's your department. You do the thinking.'

'Oh, right.' Dan picked up the bundle which described the first of the strange distributions of money. 'I suppose I'd better make a start then.'

★★★

Approximately ten seconds had elapsed before El leant over the table and whispered, 'Got anything yet?'

Dan sighed and fished in his pocket. 'You've got it, haven't you?' the paparazzo asked. 'Come on, spill it. Tell your old mate.'

A ten pound note was placed pointedly in El's hand.

'What you saying? Is it to do with the money he gives out?' The excited voice rose. 'There's some message, in't there? Tell old El!'

'Go get yourself a beer and calm down.'

El sat back and folded his arms. 'No beer. Don't need it. Don't want it. No time. Gotta find the Cashman.'

'It's part of the deal. No beer, me no look at all this.'

'But there's a queue at the bar.'

'Exactly. Join the back of it. Get yourself two pints to match mine, then come back slowly and drink them quietly. On no account hurry. I need a few minutes to think.'

El thrust out a chubby, sulky lip, but did as he was bid. Dan sipped some more beer and returned to the cuttings.

★★★

The light played through the amber column of liquid and Dan followed the shifting of the surroundings as he let the thoughts run. The pub was a modern conversion which did its best to be a character, but with the usual lack of success. Strings of timeworn tinsel had been tacked up in the corners of the bar. The sight reminded Dan of Claire, probably sitting at home, perhaps gazing out of the bay window, maybe cuddling Rutherford for comfort. He took another drink and returned to the cuttings.

Many of the bigger cases he had worked on contained some element of a riddle. The wonderful artist McCluskey and his Death Pictures had been the best known. Following that, and the extraordinary international media splash the solution brought, several others had attempted to set puzzles in their crimes. It had become almost a fashion.

But the Cashman felt different. Behind this Dan suspected, was another motive. It didn't feel like conceit or egotism, but something else; perhaps a need to make a statement.

As he had with other riddles, Dan started from the obvious features of the Cashman's appearances. It was time for that standard male recourse of a list.

1. Friday, City Centre, outside a line of bars, 6pm. 10 pounds in each of the bags.
2. Saturday, Fish Market, 5am. 20 pounds per bag.
3. Sunday, St Andrew's Church, Resurgam Door, 7pm. 30 pounds per bag.
4. Monday, Plymouth University, Student Bar, 9pm. 40 pounds per bag.
5. Tuesday, Railway Station, 6pm. 50 pounds per bag.
6. Wednesday (today), Bus Station, 7am. 60 pounds per bag.

Amidst the overall strangeness of what the Cashman was doing, there were other minor curiosities. On each appearance, every money bag had also contained one of those pieces of paper, bearing the letters A B C D E F G H.

On Friday, the A had been circled. On Sunday, the C. Yesterday it was the E, today at the Bus Station, the F. That left just G and H.

Two more appearances. Two more chances to catch him.

A couple of pints thudded down upon the table. 'You got anything yet?' El urged. 'You must have cracked it by now. Who is he? Why's he doing this? Where's he gonna strike next?'

Dan took the change and returned a handful of coins. 'You didn't get any crisps.'

'You don't eat crisps.'

'I do now.'

'You didn't ask for any.'

'It was an oversight. Two bags please.'

El glanced back to the bar. 'But there's even more of queue.'

'Quite.'

'Shan't. Won't.'

'Ok then. I'll finish my beers and be off home.' Dan raised a pint. 'Cheers and Merry Christmas!'

The paparazzo emitted a noise which was part frustrated adult, part petulant child. He pulled his bulky frame up from the chair and headed back to the bar.

★★★

Footsteps settled by the table. Dan looked up irritably, expecting an all too early return of the buffoon, but it was a woman. She was attractive and smiling. He hastily shifted his expression to match.

'I'm sorry to bother you,' she said, in a well-enunciated voice, 'But there's something I think you should know.'

'No problem at all. Please, sit down.'

'I'm not interrupting, am I? I can see you're working.'

Dan pushed the cuttings aside and tried to ignore the horrified look from El. 'No, it's just a – little game.'

She was a few years younger than Dan, perhaps in her mid-thirties, and slim, with long blonde hair. He picked up his drink and surreptitiously checked. No adornments to a particular finger.

'I'm Dan, by the way.'

She giggled and prettily, a neat trick. 'I know that. I see you on the TV all the time. I'm Lara.'

They shook hands. Her skin was soft and her hands well-tended.

'I'm guessing you don't dig roads for a living,' said Mr Incredibly-Witty.

'I'm a solicitor.'

'I didn't do it,' Dan replied quickly. 'I wasn't even there when I did the thing I didn't do.'

The reward was another chuckle, however undeserving. 'I won't stay long, I'm having a drink with my friend.'

She pointed across the bar. Dan turned with due dread, preparing himself to see a large and handsome man, probably sporting a scowl. But it was another woman of similar age and just as attractive.

His smile grew. 'You can stay as long as you like. You can even move in to my table if you want.'

This time came a laugh and it sounded genuine. 'I just wanted to let you know – the government's going to close a load of magistrates courts. I wondered if you'd be interested.'

'Yes, of course. That's a big story.'

Dan kept his eyes set on Lara to avoid the animated gesturing of El. He was pointing towards the pile of cuttings lying forsaken on the side of the table and jigging from foot to foot. The effect was much as if he'd swallowed a handful of chillies.

'Thanks for that,' Dan said, when Lara had related what she knew. 'Without being too forward, can I take your number in case I need to talk to you again?'

Without demur she produced a business card, took Dan's pen and added her mobile number. 'Call me anytime. I'd better get back to Ellie now. We're having a night out.'

'Going anywhere special?'

'Just into town for a few drinks. You?'

El now looked as though he was learning the novel art of synchronised semaphore and step dancing. 'The same.'

'Perhaps I'll see you later, then.'

'I'd like that.'

'So would I.'

She rose with effortless ease and glided back to her friend. Dan returned to the cuttings, but found he was struggling to concentrate. Words and numbers whirled in whorls, numbers and words narrowed to nothingness.

Each time he glanced up, Lara was looking over.

★★★

El returned with the crisps, opened a bag and poured the mainstay into his mouth. 'Got anything yet?'

'Some ideas are starting to form,' Dan lied.

'What?'

The visions in his mind were nothing to do with the Cashman, and none that anyone else should know about. Which wasn't to say they were in any way unpleasant.

'I'll tell you in a while.' Dan nodded to the beers, most of which had evaporated almost unnoticed in that way good ales have. 'After another drink or two.'

El downed a pint, the liquid disappearing almost as quickly as had the crisps. 'I suppose I'm getting them?'

But he might as well have been talking to a tree. Dan was watching Lara and Ellie ease on their coats. As they headed for the door, Lara waved, held up her mobile and smiled.

'What do you want this time?' El was asking.

'What?'

'What do you want?'

'Who said I wanted anything?'

'I thought you wanted another beer.'

'Sorry,' Dan replied as he docked back on land. 'I was thinking about something else entirely.'

'So – what beer do you want?'

'I fancy going somewhere else,' Dan heard himself reply. 'Perhaps a little jaunt into town.'

CHAPTER 14

With one of the knowing winks of fate, a bus pulled up just as Dan and El left the pub. They bundled aboard amidst a throng of others. It was standing room only, filled with Christmas revellers, many wearing Santa hats and reindeer antlers.

Frost was starting to form on the pavements, glossing them with nature's own glitter. Few cars were on the roads but plenty of taxis, ferrying their passengers to pubs, bars and restaurants. The party season was careering ever onwards, speeding towards the relative peace of the day itself.

Those braving the cold did so in a stark split of attires. The younger lads wore only shirts, the girls dresses. Some of the frocks were so small it was possible the manufacturers had run short of raw materials. The older travellers were wrapped so well that it was difficult to discern the presence of a body within the layers.

The bus dropped them off at the central thoroughfare of Royal Parade, opposite St Andrew's Church. The smell of sick lingered by a bar and a group of people helped a drunken woman stagger into a taxi. Two bouncers were struggling to keep opposing groups of young lads apart as they exchanged abuse. It was a very English Christmas.

The night was clear, a sliver of moon low in the southern sky. Dan and El decided to head for the Barbican and a back street pub. There was still work to do and a couple more quiet beers to be had, before they ventured into the hedonist's furnace of the city centre.

★★★

El got the drinks again, but out of fairness Dan funded them. They made for the Minerva, renowned as Plymouth's oldest bar.

It was a long and thin hostelry, the type often found amongst densely packed housing. There was a public bar at one end, but in the back was a snug with a sofa unoccupied. Dan dragged over a small table and once more spread out the pile of papers. El was talking to the man behind the bar, which provided a respite for more thought.

First, there was a list of questions to be answered –

1. Why increase the amount in the bags by ten pounds per time?
2. Why the strange pieces of paper, marked A to H?
3. Why strike only at landmarks, and always on the hour?
4. WHY DO THIS AT ALL?

It was that final question which was by far the most fascinating. Dan read through all the cuttings once again, trying to find something he might have overlooked, but could see no hint of an answer. In every one of his appearances the Cashman had said nothing, just thrown the bags of money. The only clues had to be in how he was going about his mission.

'You making any progress?' El asked, as he delivered the beers.

'Not so's you'd notice.'

'Can I help?'

'Same answer as previous, I suspect.'

El took the unsubtle hint with good grace, squeezed himself onto the edge of the sofa and started surfing the internet on his phone.

Dan fished in his pocket for a handkerchief and found himself looking at Lara's card. It was high quality paper, as smooth as the touch of her hand.

He corralled his wandering mind back to work. Something was bothering him about the reports of the Cashman's appearances. There were three photographs of him accompanying the articles, but they'd been taken from mobile phones and were lacking in detail. The Robin Hood mask was clear in each, but there were also differences.

In one picture he was chubby, but seemed much slimmer in the others. Another of the snaps showed him as bearded, the other two clean-shaven. In all three of the pictures, he wore a checked cap. In two, there was no hair visible. In the third, there looked to be a short fringe of grey. It was difficult to be sure as the photos weren't shot with any real context, but it felt as though the Cashman wasn't tall.

El was busying himself making a stack of beer mats. They kept falling down and it was both annoying and distracting, so Dan dispatched him back to the bar for a chaser. The familiar magic blanket of alcohol was coddling body and mind.

It didn't matter if he had a few beers tonight. It would be a good way to relax before tomorrow and Media Day at Resurgam. Lizzie would never take him off the story, there was no need to worry. He would cover it and triumph.

That was, if Media Day still went ahead. Adam had said he would see Ellen Dance to discuss whether Resurgam should open on Friday, given the threats. For once, that was a conversation to which Dan wasn't going to be privy. The detective would be in touch tomorrow morning he'd said, to offer a confidential update.

'Come on then,' El said, as he returned with the whiskies and another pint each. 'You must have worked something out by now.'

Dan took a sip of his drink and a nip of the whisky. It tasted good. He sat back on the sofa and closed his eyes. They were aching again, something which had been happening far too much of late.

Perhaps it was the whisky which swelled the reservoir of feelings and cracked the dam of restraint. But breach it did, and out, unchecked at last, poured the cascade of emotion.

'This is what I've worked out. I want to get pissed. I want the world to sod off and leave me alone. I've had a guts full of work and relationships and just about bloody everything. I don't know what the hell I'm doing with my job and with Claire and your damned quest for the Cashman.' He kicked the table away and it jarred across the pitted stone floor. 'I couldn't give a shit for any of it.'

Dan opened his eyes. He expected to find El uncomprehending, or just keen to urge him to new efforts to find the Cashman. But the Prince of Daftness was nodding.

'You haven't been right for ages. Do you wanna talk about it?'

And strangely, to this dishevelled, unkempt, overweight, scurrilous and devious photographer, Dan found that he did.

★★★

'I'm going to say something that might surprise you,' Dan heard himself confess. 'But the problem is simple. It's... well, it's me.'

El had the decency not to pass out, but the words still registered. Above the well fed curves of his hamster cheeks his eyes widened, and the mouth that was rarely still rested. Perhaps most revealingly, he stopped drinking.

'Claire and I had a heart to heart so intense it was more like a soul to soul,' Dan went on. 'It left me feeling like I'd been spin-dried. She says she's always known she wanted to be with me. She's always thought it would work out between us, despite some of the... difficult times. Most of which...' He considered for a few seconds, before adding, 'In fact all of which were down to me. And despite...'

'Yeah?'

'Well, if you want the truth – despite me being a complete emotional idiot.'

El chewed at his lip. 'I wouldn't be so hard on yourself. We're all that. It's part of the job description for being a man.'

Dan smiled, couldn't help himself. 'Do you know something I've always thought about you?'

'Do I wanna know?'

'You do and it's time I told you. I've always thought of you like some Shakespearean jester. You look like a fool, you act like a fool, but occasionally there's a glimpse of real wisdom hiding somewhere within.'

'Really?' El regarded his ample body with consternation. 'It's bloody well hidden then. I can't ever seem to find it.'

The two men drew at their drinks, slow and reflective sips. Around them the Christmas celebrations continued. Smiles and laughter, cheers and good wishes.

'I don't want to go on about me and my feelings, like some moody teenager,' Dan said. 'But I feel – if I'm honest I suppose it's that I can't live up to what Claire deserves. She's such a great woman. She's beautiful, clever, loyal, loving, caring, everything I could ever hope for. You know this six month sabbatical she's taken from work? She did it to be with me, to give us time to sort things out. She thought I was worth it.'

'So,' El replied slowly, 'What's the problem?'

'It's the same old problem. The standard one, the usual one, the normal one. The one I've had in every relationship every bloody time I meet some woman daft enough to want to have anything to do with me. When I feel someone getting close, I recoil. No, I run. No, in fact I sprint! It's me, it's forever me. I always reckoned I'd be on my own. It's what I expect, what I'm used to.'

El nodded. 'Yeah, but ain't there a danger of that becoming one of those self-fulfilling prophecy things?'

'Absolutely, damn bloody right it is. And that's partly what I'm afraid of.'

They sat in silence. A man came round to clear glasses, whistling Jingle Bells. They both drained the remnants of the whiskies.

'I ain't gonna give you any advice,' El said, at last. 'Women aren't exactly my specialist subject. But I do wanna say one thing.'

'Which is?'

'If you want me to be honest – I like Claire. She's always been good to me. She treats me like I'm human, not some parasite like plenty of people do. She's – I dunno, she's not like a woman.'

Dan chuckled. 'I'll be sure to tell her that. She'll be flattered.'

'I didn't mean it in any bad way. Just that – she's a good bloke.'

'Yeah, as you so beautifully put it, she is indeed a good bloke. But is that going to be enough?'

'I guess you're the only one who can work that out,' El replied, thoughtfully.

★★★

The time was half past eleven. A decision point of the night beckoned.

'We could just go home,' El said with a mild slur, swilling the remains of yet another pint of dark, wintry beer.

'We could,' Dan replied. His voice sounded perfectly sober to him, but that suggested to a distantly sane corner of his mind that his own words were probably slurring too. 'It'd be sensible.'

'Never got the hang of sensible,' El pointed out.

'Me neither. So...'

'So what?'

'Union Street's just ten minutes away.'

'The Street?'

El's tone said it all. Union Street had found fame across the nation, and not for the noblest of reasons. Dan had once semi-jokingly described it as being like a video game.

The half mile stretch of bars and clubs had to be negotiated by an innocent reveller seeking the sanctuary of home. The challenge was first to dodge the whirling arms and legs of the mass brawls which blew up without notice. The knife-wielding undesirables attempting a quick mugging provided level two. Next were the unseen drunkards hurling vomit from doorways, and finally came the unpredictable obstacles of the newly acquainted couples having writhing sex on the pavement. It was quite an odyssey.

But alcohol is the boss, so the decision was a simple one. On the way, they talked briefly about the Cashman. The key question of whether they were any nearer to finding him, or being able to predict where he might next strike, brought a resolutely depressing answer.

'I reckon he is working to a pattern,' Dan said. 'I've just got no idea what it is. It's pretty clear he plans to strike every day, with Friday being the last. Otherwise, why bother with the A to H thing?'

'Which gives us just two chances left to find him,' El observed.

They stopped at a van to buy a hot dog. Only when drunk did Dan consider the dire depths of such faux nutrition, but it wasn't fair to have to watch El pork his way through the drunkard's feast without joining in.

'There are a couple of other possible clues,' Dan managed, amid a mouthful of surprisingly good sausage. 'The Robin Hood mask for one. The Cashman's got some kind of purpose and it's all about taking from the rich to give to the poor. Plus, he's got an accomplice – all the cuttings talk about a car driving up, the Cashman getting out, then him being driven away again. The key to what they're doing is that it's fast. Otherwise someone would have caught them by now.'

'One thing I thought,' El said, carefully picking the remaining fried onions from the wrappings of his meal. 'If his last strike is Friday, is it something to do with Resurgam? Given that's when the thing opens.'

'Like what?'

'Maybe it's another protest. Some attempt to distract attention from the grand opening.'

Dan scribbled a note on one of the cuttings. 'Good point. I'll think more about that when my brain's less fuddled.'

They walked along the Street, edging past a group of cops who were trying to arrest a young man for the new sport of jumping between the roofs of parked cars. For a sizeable chap he was doing remarkably well, which was more than could be said of the cars.

Half way down they found The Sea Lion, which was the Street's version of as posh as it came. Just a couple of its windows were boarded up, there was no graffiti on the wall, and the cluster of smokers outside wasn't huge.

It was only mildly busy, most of the creatures of the night preferring to head to the clubs. Dan directed El to a seat, headed for the bar and found himself standing next to Lara.

★★★

It would have been rude not to, Dan told himself, so he invited Lara and Ellie to join them at the corner table El had secured.

'You didn't ring,' she said as they walked over.

'I didn't think I'd be at my best tonight and didn't want to embarrass myself – or you,' Dan improvised.

She smiled, a look which appeared to draw the attention of the entire male contingent of the pub. 'Maybe later in the week, then.'

Dan nodded. He wanted to keep attempts at actual speech to a minimum. Firstly, he was concerned there would be more than a little slurring, and that was as attractive as acne. Secondly, there was the issue of the onion he'd just consumed. A revitalising visit to the toilets was called for.

He returned, happily onion free, to find El in mid anecdote. He was telling Ellie and Lara about the time they hunted a police superintendent who had been caught drink-driving, and the way Dan lured the man out of his house so El could get a snap.

Lara tapped the bench beside her, so Dan duly sat down. Her leg was pressed against his and he could smell her perfume. It was a light and gentle scent, as much a contrast as could be from the beery, sweaty background of the pub.

'Your job must be very interesting,' she was saying.

'Maddening might be a better word.'

'How come?'

'You never really know what's going on. I often think of it as like a game of three dimensional chess where someone keeps changing the rules.'

The women laughed. Like a practiced double act, El picked up the theme. He told a story about the time he'd dressed as an undertaker and hired a black estate car to get through a police cordon around the scene of a murder.

The boys were drinking spirits now, the women wine, and the glasses were emptying fast. Ellie headed to the bar for replenishments. She too was very pretty, but in a different way from Lara, darker of skin and hair.

With some hopeless effort at good sense, Dan also asked for a pint of water. A group of people arrived and squeezed themselves into the space around the table next to theirs. Lara's body was pressing against him now, the warmth tingling.

Dan's mobile buzzed with a text message. He ignored it. The thought of Claire, lying in bed, wondering what he was doing wasn't something to entertain.

They talked a little about the women's jobs. Both were solicitors, specialising in family law. Divorce was the growth field, sadly.

Lara leaned across Dan to whisper in his ear.

'What?' he said, above the cacophony of the background.

She turned to face him. 'Kiss me.'

'What – now?'

'Yes.'

'Here?'

'Yes.'

Her lips were forming a rouged pool so beautiful it would have been possible to dive into and swim around. Dan could feel El's eyes upon him, but still he moved towards Lara. The skin of her face was as soft as the touch of her hands. Light flashed from a diamond pendant hanging around her neck.

Across the bar, a glass smashed. But Dan didn't hear it. All he could see were those lips, moving closer and closer, parting a little in preparation for the kiss. Dan could sense the hairs on his arms and neck standing, prickling his skin.

And then there was only coldness and wetness, a freezing, soaking shock in his lap. Dan recoiled and sprung up, Lara too.

'Bugger,' El announced. 'Clumsy me.'

He'd reached across for a sip of water and knocked over the pint. Lara was doing her best to wipe away some of deluge. Cubes of ice slid across the floor. El was bumbling his way through a rambling apology, but suddenly stopped.

'Shit!' he yelped, pointing to the window.

An abrupt silence fell, resonating hard after the hubbub of noise. Everyone in the pub was looking, staring, mesmerised, but only so briefly. Because now they were all piling for the door, trying to squeeze out, pushing, shoving, wriggling and crushing, a tumbling, chaotic stampede.

On the pavement outside, clear even through the steamy glass of the windows, was the Cashman.

CHAPTER 15

El was away first, the acceleration of his bulky frame a rebuttal of the laws of physics. Dan clambered over Lara's legs, unsteady with drink and sending a bottle crashing to the floor.

For once, El's insecurity had brought a problem. He'd sat them at the back of the pub, which meant everyone else was ahead in fighting to escape and all assembled were giving it their very best, scrabbling and shoving. There were more than a hundred people attempting to squeeze through a narrow doorway. It was a bottleneck as effective as a four lane motorway suddenly narrowing to one.

The Cashman never lingered for more than minutes. According to the newspaper reports, he climbed out of a car, waited until a few people had seen him and began throwing the moneybags. Within a couple of minutes there was always a sizeable crowd. In five at most he was gone again.

El was dodging, darting, pleading and cajoling, trying to ease his way through the packed mass of people, but making no progress. It was the sort of pub where the punters tended to be on the large side and ill inclined to politely stand aside.

'Come on, shit, come on, bugger,' El muttered and wailed.

'Try a snap through the glass,' Dan suggested.

El raised his pocket camera, shifted back and forth to change the angle and swore again. 'Too much bloody steam and reflections.'

Outside, Dan could just make out the figure of the mysterious man in the Robin Hood mask. He was standing on the edge of the pavement, next to a post box, hurling plastic bags. Scores of people surrounded him.

They were close to the door now. But just ahead, one man had turned on another and pushed him. The opponent shoved back and the pair began to wrestle, right in the doorway. A woman leapt in, then another man, and within a few seconds a tight knot of people were locked together, shouting and struggling, blocking the door like a bung.

Dan grabbed El and headed for the bar.

★★★

In his pocket, Dan found his press pass and held it high. 'Special Undercover Money Laundering Branch,' he improvised. The young lad looked impressed, or perhaps just baffled, so Dan ran with the momentum of his improvisation.

'Which way out the back?'

He was pointed to a plain white door and ploughed through it, El just behind. They were in a damp and half-lit storeroom, towers of boxes of crisps, some old beer pumps, a couple of battered chairs and a cracked mirror.

'Time's running out,' El moaned.

At the far end of the room was a double door, securely shut, but the key was in the lock. The thin metal resisted at first, but then clunked.

They tumbled outside and found a dark, narrow alley, its edges lined with shining ice. To their left was a vertical wedge of brightness, the pumping music and shouting commotion of Union Street. Dan started running, dodging around some bins and a pile of old boxes.

A security light clicked on, stark and white. The alley was coated with mildew and frost, a lethal combination. El slipped, collided with the wall, grunted with pain, but kept running.

Graffiti flashed past, smears of paint, scrawled words, incomprehensible pictures. The alley stank. There were plastic take away boxes, food wrappings, drainpipes half hanging from the sheer walls.

Through all this Dan and El ran, towards the line of light and sound. They were almost at the street.

People were sprinting, jogging and lumbering past, some waving their arms, shouting, 'Cashman, Cashman!'

A siren squealed and blue lights flashed across the gripping narrowness of the alley. A couple of people were hugging each other, faces shining with delight, others slapping friends on the back.

Dan and El stumbled out into the street. Men and women were still scrabbling, some bent double, others on all fours, searching for bags of money. In the gutter Dan spotted one of the strange notes, crumpled and discarded. The letters A to H were again printed upon it, but this time the G was circled.

The paparazzi were already there. A trio of photographers, dressed in black, the Italian amongst them. He was smiling through the haze of cold and commotion. He raised a palm and waved, the gesture of a champion, victorious and triumphant. The others looked towards Dan and El, panting, sweating, unkempt and breathless. One blew a mocking kiss.

El released a salvo of obscenities that wouldn't have been out of place in the exercise yard of a prison. The dejection was instant, as abrupt as a snowball hitting a wall. The air seemed to leave the photographer's body.

'How come they're here so bloody quick?'

'I hate to say it,' Dan replied, 'but I reckon they might have cracked the Cashman's pattern.'

Further up the street, a car was pulling away, gathering speed. Its number plate was obscured by mud and dirt, just a rectangle of black. No one else had noticed, nor even cared. The paparazzi had their shots, the crowd their money.

To the side was a taxi rank. There were two cabs waiting, both with passengers climbing in, and a long queue.

The car trundled further away. Another cab was drawing up, a couple stepping towards its doors.

Dan grabbed the leaden weight of El and pulled him over to the rank. 'His wife's just gone into labour,' he bellowed, with all the emotion of a ham actor at a Shakespearean denouement. 'She's suffering complications. We've got to get to the hospital.'

Some people were nodding their understanding, but not all. And the couple were almost at the taxi.

'Please!' Dan wailed. 'It's my brother's first child. And they've only been married a few months. She's just... err, 19, in hospital with no family and friends there.'

The crowd parted, faces filling with sympathy, and the couple stood back, holding the car doors open.

★★★

Luck was with the fork tongued outlaws. Far too many drivers treated their taxi as though it were a mistress. Not this cabbie. The car spun on its wheels in a remarkably tight circle and accelerated as fast as the engine would allow. Dan and El sprawled across the back seats, arms flailing for a handhold.

'Are you cops?' the man asked with a disconcerting eagerness, after being given the infamous hot pursuit command. 'What're we after? Is it robbers? Terrorists? That Al Jolson lot?'

'Al- Qaeda?'

'Yeah, them and all.'

The driver was young with spiky hair, a large gold earring, and wearing a T-shirt, despite the night's cold. He was leaning forwards, face close to the windscreen, but risked a glance back. 'You're spies maybe? Yeah, you don't look like spies so you must be.'

Dan blessed the fates the man wasn't a *Wessex Tonight* viewer.

'I can't say what we are. Top secret. We just need to keep tight on that car.'

'Roger that. I'm Fizz, by the way.'

'Fizz?'

'Eddie actually, but Fizz sounds better for the girls.'

'I'm – call me Agent Orange,' Dan improvised. 'And this is – Green.'

The unlikely spy with the camera clamped to his eye tipped a finger to his brow but didn't speak.

'I can tell you it's a recon mission,' Dan continued. 'But if we get the chance, we might have to...' he searched his limited knowledge of Hollywood films for the correct parlance. '...take them down.'

Dan tapped his jacket knowingly, hoping the outline of a mobile phone, notebook and pen looked vaguely gun-like.

'Cool. I'm onto them.'

'Not too close,' Dan cautioned. 'We don't want a firefight in a built up area. Can't risk too much collateral damage if it comes to a shootout.'

By Dan's side, El shook his head.

★★★

The cab was heading past the city centre, travelling north, along a dual carriageway. They'd gained ground on the car, enough to see it was small, squat and dark, perhaps green or blue. But any identifying marks were covered in grime, and doubtless deliberately so.

Two people were inside. One kept looking back.

'They're onto us,' Fizz hissed.

'Just keep following,' Dan replied. 'I can always call in back up.'

'Can't get a snap from here,' El whispered. 'Some random car in the gloom ain't gonna sell. We've gotta find him, talk to him, do a shoot with him.'

'You going to shoot him?' Fizz asked, sounding not at all concerned.

'Just concentrate on the driving,' Dan told him. 'We'll handle the engagement.'

Ahead, the figure in the passenger seat raised something to its head. El squinted down the camera's viewfinder.

'I reckon it's a phone. I think the car's a little Nissan, too. My gran's got one.'

'That's a hell of an odd car for a getaway if this is some criminal thing.'

Without a hint of an indicator, the Nissan suddenly wheeled and turned into a side street. Fizz followed, slewing the cab around the corner.

They were in a residential area, the road narrower and lined with townhouses. The tarmac had been gritted, occasional chips flying up. The Nissan slowed. They were thirty metres behind. The passenger looked back again, just as the car passed under a streetlight.

'It's the bloody Cashman,' El gasped. 'He's still got the mask on. We've nearly got him.'

'Apart from working out how to make him stop,' Dan noted.

'We can just keep tailing 'til they run out of gas. I'll pay. The fare won't be a scratch on the loot I'll make.'

Dan leaned forwards. The taxi's fuel gauge read an eighth of a tank.

'That's not going to work. We'll have to think of something else.'

'Like what?'

'Good question.'

The Nissan slowed and indicated left, but instead turned right and sped away hard. Fizz followed, stamping on the accelerator. The taxi slid and swayed dangerously, but stayed on the road.

'Bloody hell,' Dan complained. 'If you could avoid splattering us into a wall I'd be grateful.'

'Sorry, Agent Orange,' Fizz replied. 'But he's not getting away.'

Dan blinked hard and swallowed. His head was still full of beer and a growing sickness was gaining a giddying hold. It was warm in the cab, which wasn't helping. Dan wound down a window and gulped in the freezing air.

'What we gonna do?' El muttered. 'Can't lose him now.'

A few hundred metres ahead was a cross roads and some traffic lights. They were on green. Dan leaned forwards and whispered to Fizz. He hit the accelerator again and span the car into a side street, turned a corner, then another. They were on a main road now, passing a row of shops, heading towards the lights but from a different angle.

Ahead, the red turned to amber, then green.

'Got him!' Dan yelped.

Fizz urged the car on to the crossroads. They were fifty metres away, could see the nose of the Nissan, stuck at the lights.

'Pull up right across him,' Dan ordered. 'Don't give him an inch to get past. Don't worry about blocking the junction.'

El raised his camera. 'Come great God of the paparazzi, sprinkle your love dust on thy poor son.'

'We'll have to be quick,' Dan urged. 'Pile out as soon as we pull up. Stop them getting away. Open their doors, sprawl on the bonnet, anything.'

Twenty metres to the lights. The road ahead was clear. Fizz punched on the hazards and steered the cab across, straight in front of the Nissan. El was grabbing for the door when there was a grinding of gears and their target lurched into reverse.

'Shit!' Fizz yelled, fumbling for the gear stick.

The Nissan span around and headed fast back up the street. The cab reversed hard, smacked into a railing, the iron clang resounding in the night. Fizz hardly noticed. He yanked at the steering wheel until they were in pursuit again.

★★★

'Bugger,' Dan gasped, when he finally managed to secure a breath.

'We'll get him,' Fizz hissed. 'I ain't giving up. It's the SAS way, ain't it boys?'

They were in another narrow avenue, cars parked along each side. Streetlights flared through the cab's interior.

'Did you get any snaps?' Dan asked El.

'Nothing worthwhile. He had that mask on.'

'What about the driver?'

'Wasn't concentrating on him.'

'Him?'

'What?'

'I only saw whoever it was briefly, but it looked like a woman. And I could swear her face was familiar.'

They grabbed for the handholds again as the taxi turned a sharp right. The Nissan was thirty metres ahead, the Cashman on the phone once more. They were passing a park, the tapered outline of trees reaching for the night sky.

A red light blinked on the taxi's dashboard, accompanied by an irritating electronic ping.

'We're low on fuel,' Fizz shouted.

'How much longer can we keep going?'

'Twenty mins maybe. We ain't exactly driving economically.'

'What we gonna do?' El lamented. 'We're so close.'

Dan stared out of the window, tried to think. They spun across a roundabout, still hard on the Nissan's tail.

'How much is the reward?' he whispered.

'Tens of thousands.'

'How many tens?'

'Quite a few.'

'This is no time to be coy. How many?!'

'Sixty grand. Maybe more.'

Dan swore. 'No wonder there's paparazzi everywhere. Ok, call it five grand for the damage to the cab, maybe a bit more. Five grand for the driver to get him to go along with it and twenty five each for us.'

'What?'

'I'm working out if it's worth getting Fizz to ram the car.'

El looked taken aback, a bright red maroon of a danger warning. 'You could kill him.'

'I could kill us,' Dan pointed out.

El scrabbled for the seatbelt and made sure it was tight around his sizeable frame. 'Death versus sixty grand. It's a no brainer.'

Dan checked his belt, too. 'I'd better have a word with Fizz.'

He was about to lean over when a car pulled out of a side street, just metres in front.

The taxi braked hard, the sudden force catapulting Dan and El forwards, arms flailing, flying in the air until the belts caught and yanked them back to the safety of the seats.

The cab was slowing fast, brakes juddering, slowing, bonnet dipping, still slowing, tyres biting into the road, coming to a stop, just a few feet from the car.

★★★

'What the fuck?' Fizz demanded, as he leapt from the cab. 'We're the law!'

The driver was an older man, wearing a hat and peering up through his glasses. 'I do apologise. But you were moving rather quickly and this is a residential area. In fact, I wonder if I should report you to the police.'

'Just get out the way!'

The man fumbled for the gears. Revving roared from the car. 'I fear I can't seem to locate reverse. It does sometimes elude me.'

Dan and El freed themselves from the strictures of the seatbelts and got out of the cab.

The smell of diesel flavoured the air. Further up the road, the Nissan turned left and disappeared. Its pace was now leisurely, almost a taunt.

'Have you passed a shitting driving test?' Fizz yelled at the man. 'Do you want me to shift the bloody thing for you?'

Dan laid a hand on his shoulder. 'Calm now. Just leave it. I can get, err – Agents Blue and Grey to pick them up later.'

El was leaning against a wall, bent over and gasping. He looked as though he was about to be sick. Dan ushered Fizz back into the cab and swayed unsteadily over to his friend.

'Are you ok?'

'Just – the beer, the action and missing him.'

'Know what you mean.'

'That was his strike for today – at one in the bloody morning. He must be getting leery of being caught. There's only tomorrow left now. We had a break and we blew it. That was our last chance, I know it.'

They started walking back to the taxi. The car which had forced them to stop turned past and drove carefully along the road, the man at the wheel not deigning to give them a glance.

Dan took out his notepad and wrote down the car's registration. 'Maybe it's not our last chance,' he said thoughtfully.

★★★

It was after two when Dan got back to the flat. The blood rush of the chase and the fun of the night had worn off, and he yawned hard as he stepped quietly into the hallway.

Fizz took him home, was sworn to secrecy about the *spy games* which had unfolded in Plymouth that night, and was tipped generously for his troubles.

'Anytime you need a hand, just ring Agent Fizz,' had been his parting comment. 'You can rely on me to do my duty.'

Dan sat in the lounge to give himself more time to unwind. Rutherford dutifully padded out from the bedroom to say hello to his stop-out of a master. The dog's fur was sprayed up on the side where he'd been laying.

The flat wasn't particularly warm, the central heating long dormant, but Dan didn't feel cold. He sat, cuddled Rutherford, then washed and made for the bedroom.

Claire usually woke when he came in late and would insist on sitting up for a goodnight chat and cuddle. It was to keep their bond strong through the drifting, sleeping hours, she said.

But this time Claire remained in bed, back towards him, breathing gently. Throughout the night, and even as another December dawn slipped across the frozen city, not once did she turn around.

CHAPTER 16

The waltzes in the dark around the eternal ballroom of the mind had long been a wonder. Commonly they were the more vivid for the input of alcohol, and so it was this night.

The flat's bathroom had nothing to distinguish it, was a mere small white cube filled with the usual suspects of shower, bath, sink and toilet. But the dream that persisted saw Dan astride a bicycle, attempting to ride it around the cramped space, and - unsurprisingly - making no progress.

Following the theme, in that curious way the imagination has, Dan woke to the impression of a wet flannel being pressed onto his face. Opening his eyes, still mostly asleep, a close up of an elongated dog's snout was the first thing he saw that Thursday morning. Rutherford had decided it was time his master arose.

The time was well after seven, the curtains fringed with the lacklustre light of another winter's dawn. Of Claire there was no sign, but that wasn't unusual. She was a light sleeper and would decamp to the spare room if Dan was launching one of his fanfares of snoring.

He sat up on the bed, trying to ignore the sea-sway giddiness and flying white daggers. It took a fair few moments for the constituents of the world to settle into place. By the bed were several pages of notes on The Cashman, some beer-stained, and even more on Resurgam.

Media Day was the heading atop each.

Lizzie's warning sounded in his mind with all the subtlety of an artillery barrage. Dan ruffled the fur on Rutherford's flank. 'There's a big day ahead, old friend. I think we need to wake up.'

Quietly, he got up and slipped on some shorts, trainers, an old T-shirt and thick sweatshirt. Dan grabbed the lead from the hallway cupboard, clamped a hand over Rutherford's nuzzle, crept past the spare room and ushered the excitable dog out of the door.

★★★

The scale of this morning's self-inflicted suffering suggested the usual run, across the road and laps of Hartley Park, was unlikely to be sufficient. Instead, they headed down the hill and towards the city, turning off to the west and Peverell, the two car, two parents, two and a bit children middle class heartland of Plymouth. Along one tree lined avenue after another they jogged, Rutherford for once obeying the strictures of the leash and keeping surprisingly well to heel.

Around them processed the morning's routines. Children climbed into cars for the arduous journey of several hundred metres to school. Parents talked distractedly on mobile phones as they remembered packed lunches, after school clubs and the office business of the day. Front doors clicked closed, goodbyes were bidden, some fond, others less so. In the spectrum of the week faces were looking reasonably content, the sweet prospect of Friday now within reach.

Ahead was the expanse of Central Park, a haven of green amidst the monochrome of the concrete city. With one final, impatient wait for a slug of traffic, they slipped through a gate and into a passable attempt at urban countryside.

★★★

It was another freezer of a morning, sufficient to prompt a hedgehog to abandon the thought of ever emerging from hibernation, the sky colourless with thin cloud. Dan wheeled from the path and began running across the grass, following a line of trees, the compacted ground crunching underfoot.

Freed from the leash, Rutherford ran patterns, sniffing at bushes, sprinting towards other dogs, but always pulling up well short and returning to the safety of his master.

'It must run in the family,' Dan panted. 'You're as brave as I am, hound.'

The park was busy, mostly with people walking a scenic route to work, others taking the medicine of early morning exercise.

To the lengths of his mental list, Dan added a promise he must remember to keep, no matter how busy life became. Phil had asked for a few minutes of mentoring time to help guide his career, and the young man deserved it. He was still awed with the events of the *two truths and a lie* game.

'How did you know about me, Wales and the rugby?'

'Don't ask,' Dan replied. 'I just did.'

'And what you said about wanting to present the programme, your personal life and being a spy... I'd love to know which of yours was the lie?'

'Definitely don't ask,' came the emphatic reply.

★★★

They passed a gang of young lads enjoying a kick about, Rutherford giving them not a second glance. Ahead was Home Park, Plymouth Argyle's stadium. They would run around it, then turn back for the flat.

Rutherford had found a stick, a monster of a specimen in his usual manner, so long he could barely carry it. With the prize delicately balanced in his jaws, the dog trotted carefully over and Dan dutifully did his best to hurl the caber for a couple of rounds of fetch.

In his pocket the mobile began ringing. The time was right on eight o'clock. It was probably Claire, wondering where he was, or work, asking about the plans for covering *Media Day*. But the display was flashing with Adam's name.

'We need to talk,' the detective said, by way of gentle introduction.

'Fancy making me a cup of coffee?' Dan replied. 'Funnily enough, I'm just up the road. I'd rather talk in the comfort of your place than out here.'

★★★

Adam's house was terraced in a Victorian style, and carried off that coveted trick of containing far more space than should be possible. The detective was waiting in the doorway, already dressed in a smart suit and tie, and favoured the gasping, sweating Dan with a distasteful look.

'I suppose he has to come in,' Adam said, with a glance to Rutherford. 'We'll talk in the kitchen then,' he announced loftily and led the way through.

The house was tidy, clean and precisely decorated, but Adam still adjusted one summery watercolour which had the cheek to hang a couple of degrees askew. Christmas stars, tinsel and lights put in occasional appearances.

Annie quick stepped down the stairs and went to kiss Dan, but hesitated. 'No offence taken,' he smiled. 'Second hand sweat won't suit you.'

'Come round for dinner soon,' she replied. 'Far too long no see.' To Adam, she added, 'Tom's still in the bathroom. He's due at college at nine. If you could do the policing?'

'Ha ha.'

Annie grabbed some keys and headed for the door. Her hair had grown, a long sheet of sleek darkness down her slender back

'And don't forget the milk and that DIY magazine,' she threw over a shoulder. 'And the tomatoes.' Adam shuffled a little, but didn't reply. Dan kept his face straight. From upstairs came a loud thud, then another, followed by the rumbling of pipes.

'Still love sick and sulking, is he?' Dan enquired.

'And a teenager,' came the irascible reply.

In the kitchen Dan stood by a radiator to keep warm, Rutherford lying at his feet. Adam thrust across a cup of fresh coffee and sat himself at the table, then stood, adjusted his trousers, and sat once more.

'Plenty's happened,' he announced, and began reading through some notes. 'In order of importance, that graffiti – *those plans are the foundations of Resurgam's fall* – was very probably written by Esther.'

'How probably?'

'85 per cent, I'm promised.'

The graphologist's analysis was very technical and largely impenetrable, based on examinations of the patterns within the writing. There was a particular problem with matching graffiti, the report said. It didn't contain a range of indicators that might be used to compare samples as would be the case with normal handwriting. But a system called *symbolism of space* had led to the conclusion Esther was almost definitely responsible.

'Which tells us she hasn't run far,' Dan said slowly.

'So, why should that be?' Adam replied, meaningfully. 'Why would a woman who's wanted for attempted murder, and knows there's a huge hunt going on for her, hang around the scene of the crime?'

'Maybe she couldn't get away?'

'That doesn't fit though, does it? When she ran, the CCTV shows she made deliberately for the car park. If Esther was running blind she would have headed as far away as she could, surely? She had a plan.'

'And we're absolutely certain she didn't come out of the car park?'

'Pretty much. The CCTV covers all the exits. There's no hint of her coming out. I had the place searched the next day, just in case she might be hiding. All the team found was a stash of drugs, some porn mags, a stolen bike and a tramp sleeping at the bottom of a stairwell.'

'What about Larson?'

'No go. The reason his car was weighted down was he had a tankful of fish in the boot. He's a fish fancier, bizarrely. He bought a load of stolen carp, some exotic species. We've gone through everything and forensics have checked the car to be certain. He had nothing to do with Esther's disappearance.'

Dan sipped at his coffee. 'That's some puzzle.'

'And let me make it worse. I reckon wherever she's hiding, Esther's holed up somewhere near Resurgam.'

'Why?'

'If the graffiti was written by her, then it must have been Esther, or someone working with her, who sent us the plans of the foundations and razor blade. She obviously intended to leave that message on the wall to make sure we didn't dismiss the plans arriving as some crank. She wouldn't want to move around the city much, not with every cop on the lookout for her. That means she's unlikely to have gone far.'

'You're saying that whatever she's up to, she hasn't finished with Resurgam yet?'

'Exactly. And let me add some more ingredients. There was nothing wrong with the lorry, no mechanical faults, nothing.'

'So she either lost control, panicked, or rammed the gatehouse deliberately.'

'And don't forget the original question too,' Adam added. 'What she was fumbling around for in the dark and made very sure she took before she ran off? What the hell can that have been?'

'She must be up to something.'

'My thoughts exactly.'

There was a silence, interrupted only by the odd low thud upstairs. Adam glared at the ceiling and pursed his lips. Rutherford lay his head on his paws and let out a yawn.

'That lot's going to take some thinking through,' Dan said. 'By the way, are you ok? You look stressed.'

'I damn well am,' Adam replied, with feeling. 'I was up half the night thinking –let me tell you what else has happened.'

★★★

The middle-of-the-night call is a common enough phenomenon for both the emergency services and the associated trade of the media. But, Dan knew well from repeated experience, that makes it no less unsettling.

'Half past one, the duty sergeant rang me,' Adam said, ruefully. 'And then I can't get back to sleep of course, because my head's full of it.'

Alannah Lewis's father had phoned Charles Cross and asked to speak to the investigation team. She was still distraught he said, but had taken some sleeping tablets and was now resting.

According to the message the man was angry, and ranted about whether Alannah should have made her statement to the media. She had been used by Ellen Dance, he said repeatedly. She was assured it would help catch Tommy's attacker, but he believed Alannah had become part of a political stunt.

After a few minutes, the rash of ire abated and the real cause for getting in touch became clear. Mr Miles – or Jack, as he had now become, after the sergeant's diplomatic soothing – was rational, reasonable and persuasive.

Alannah had talked little since the attack. It was as if her mind had been submerged by the flood of grief for Tommy. But just before she fell asleep, her father sitting beside the bed, there was a brief conversation that resonated in the man's mind.

'He said he was going to sort it all out,' Alannah whispered.

'Tommy, you mean?'

'Yes, my Tommy. You know he hadn't been himself the last few days? How I was worried about him?'

'Yeah, I remember.'

'All of a sudden he cheered up. When I asked why, he said he was going to sort it. He said not to worry, he'd worked out what he was going to do and everything was going to be fine. He said we'd be together whatever, and that was all he cared about.'

'When was that?'

'The Tuesday.'

'The morning before the attack?'

'Yes.'

By that point, Jack said the tablets were going about their work and his daughter was almost asleep. He'd sat with Alannah a little longer, holding her hand, then left the bedroom, thought about what she'd said and called the police.

★★★

Dan drained the remains of his coffee and set the mug down on the sink. A reproachful glance from Adam prompted him to wash it up.

'What do we make of all that?' Dan asked.

'What can we make of it?' the detective shrugged. 'The problem is that it's all hearsay.'

Heavy feet plodding on the stairs interrupted them, a walk as burdened with the weight of life as ever could be. The door swung open and Tom trooped in. Thin, wiry and with wild dark hair, standing in the kitchen could have been two versions of Adam, separated only by the passing of a generation.

'I'm off to college,' Breen the younger muttered.

'Dressed like that?' the father enquired, and not politely.

Tom was wearing trainers, baggy black jeans and a black sweatshirt with a sizeable rip across the arm. 'It's called fashion.'

'It may have escaped your notice – and manners - but we have a guest?'

'Yeah, right – sorry and all that. Wotcha Dan.'

'Err – wotcha Tom. How's it – um... hanging, dude?'

Dan's attempt at cool ingratiation produced a look which was difficult to decipher, but probably a mix of incomprehension and contempt.

Tom rummaged into the depths of the fridge and emitted a couple of grunts as he found only fresh and healthy food. Instead he searched a cupboard and produced a large bag of crisps.

Adam closed his eyes.

The son mumbled something which may have been a goodbye and headed for the front door. The father maintained a rigid silence of sufferance. Dan busied himself stroking Rutherford. No good ever came from an outsider's involvement in a family's strife.

The door slammed closed, the house reverberating with the impact. After some seconds, Adam re-opened his eyes. Dan tried a smile, which wasn't reciprocated. 'What are you getting him for Christmas?' he asked.

'Hormone therapy,' came the petulant reply. 'And I've got to see Ellen Dance later. The Deputy Chief is coming along, just to add to my troubles.'

'Sounds like it'll be a cosy get together. Are you going to be in the office today, at all?'

'If I'm lucky to have a spare second to call my own.'

'I was wondering if you might do me a favour.'

'What?'

It's nothing arduous, hardly anything at all. There's just this car I could do with tracing.'

Adam folded his arms, came to the conclusion further disapproval was required and wagged a finger instead. 'Naughty and no. Not unless you've got some good reason.'

'Like what?'

'Like it potentially being involved in a crime.'

The clock on the wall – a precise, digital model - said the time was half past eight. Sweat was drying uncomfortably on Dan's back.

'I'd better get going. I've got to cover Media Day.'

'What time does all that nonsense start?'

'Noon.'

Adam looked thoughtful but didn't say anything, so Dan added, 'What are you thinking?'

'What do you reckon?'

'You're going to see Alannah.'

'Almost. We're going to, if you've got the time? Bitter and disheartening experience has taught me that you do the empathy bit better. You might get more out of her. And it sounds like what she's got to say could be important.'

'And the business about the registration plate?'

'May get sorted later. If I'm in a better mood - which will depend on how we get on with Alannah.'

'I'll have to clear it with Lizzie. She won't take kindly to me going missing on a day like this.'

'Try tempting her with this. If you can come, I might just let slip – on a strictly un-attributable basis, naturally - about the police seeing Ellen Dance because they're worried going ahead with the opening of Resurgam tomorrow may not be a good idea.'

THE BATTLE OF RESURGAM
FOUR — THE VIOLATION

January was finally coming to an end. A month that somehow contrives to feel longer than any other took the hint and prepared to depart.

The snow fell anew, a spin of helixes and flurries filling the air and smothering the ground. With a handful of days left of the month, the weather forecasters were already talking of the most hostile January since the infamous Big Freeze of 1963.

Of all this, Resurgam was oblivious. Like a mighty metal giant rising on a city beach, it was dizzying how fast it grew. From a flat plain of shoreline to begin its dominance of the urban sky.

The foundations were established, deep and firm. The footings were encased in thousands of tonnes of steadfast concrete, the structure so secure it could have been a part of the bedrock. And from them a trellis of steel sprouted. First the vertical beams, then horizontal counterparts, layer upon layer of metal boxes forming in the air, like some vast toy. Lorries rumbled to feed the endless appetite of the growing beast. The family of cranes twisted and swung, and the new background beat of the city sounded incessantly, hammer and drill, hammer and drill.

Beside all this, in their allocated space along the access road, the protesters made their point. The original demonstration of locals and students was closest to Resurgam, the new arrivals of *Eco Warriors* and *Professionals* a little further away.

Initially, between the groups there had been words of friendship, statements of joint endeavour, a mixing of the two camps. But it had never been quite wholehearted and a separation started, as sure as oil and water will dissociate, no matter what forces are applied to encourage their bonding.

A small set of the new protesters had begun standing back, a clique within a clique. They eyed Resurgam with looks that could have been missiles and slings. They pointed with hateful fingers.

They blew the smoke of their roll up cigarettes at it with the force of all their contempt. And they whispered to each other, with words that could only be heard amongst themselves. For the moment any outsider should approach they would always fall silent.

★★★

In one of the question and answer sessions at training college, Sergeant Happy Hancock had been asked about the secret of longevity in the police. His reply was smiling, but purposeful.

Don't be a hero, leave that to a TV show.

If in doubt, make sure you shout.

The little rhymes stayed with PC Steve. As a boy he had always liked verse, perhaps because of the bedtime stories his mother would read. Edward Lear and Dr Seuss were the favourites, filled with the fun of words.

A lad of middle class upbringing, Steve was never the most comfortable with what his parents distastefully called *society's fringe.* In their little Cornish village of Chacewater, not so far from the county capital of Truro, such creatures were rarely sighted.

Those had been idyllic days, a memory to carry through life. He and Lucy, siblings who actually got on, taking the bus together to school. Mum waiting for their homecoming in the evening, dinner prepared, Dad back just an hour later, full of tales of the day's business in the bank. In these modern times when no one seemed to have a spare second, when families were defined more by division than unity, it felt a bygone age.

The instincts learned in the training college days alerted PC Steve to the coming of trouble, and at first sight of the busloads of new protesters he called Control. Within an hour more officers had arrived, meeting Steve around the corner and out of sight of Resurgam.

'I'm going to try to talk to them,' he briefed the group, as they sheltered beside a wall. 'You wait here, just in case.'

'Yes sir,' someone muttered, sarcastically.

'What are you expecting?' one of the older cops asked. 'Mortar fire, petrol bombs or kidnapping?'

'Look, it's my first real job. Bear with me, will you?'

The appeal to a fair play spirit won the day. PC Steve adopted his best upright gait and headed over striding through the fresh snow. Along the way he reminded himself of the importance of being even-handed.

Diversity enriches us all, he repeated, another of the slogans of his training days. From a different corner of his mind, PC Steve tried to banish one of his father's favourite sayings – *My definition of diversity is three real ales on a bar.*

'Morning,' he bid the line of protesters, jovially. 'Welcome along.'

Eyes turned to find him, some peering, some watchful, a couple affable, a few openly hostile. A terrier started barking, an unpleasant high pitched yap, one of the newcomers bending down to soothe her.

'Where are you lot from then?'

No reply. Just more looks. Some pulled their coats closer, others itched at wisps of beard. An older woman let out a long yawn, a man coughed hard and spat on the ground.

PC Steve refurnished the fading smile and tried again. 'Who's your leader?'

'Why's everything gotta be some kind of Scout troop?' a young woman sneered.

'Sorry. I just wanted to know who I should talk to?'

'Talk to us all – if you must.'

From one of the buses came sudden music, a guitar screaming, drums and cymbals crashing with it.

Old MacDonald had a farm, ee-i-ee-i-oh,
And on that farm he had a piglet,
Ee-i-ee-i-oh!
With an oink oink here, and an oink oink there…

'Talk to me,' a young woman said, quietening the song as surely as if with a remote control. She had a deep, husky voice, was in the centre of the group, less dishevelled than the rest. Although short, she seemed somehow taller, with a presence that drew the eye. She wore a battered denim jacket over layers of jumpers, combat trousers and army boots, and sported a couple of piercings in her nose.

'And your name is?'

'Esther.'

'Here she goes again,' someone muttered, and Esther turned, eyes like embers in the gloom, muting any further dissent.

'Pleased to meet you.' Steve held out a hand, but there was no response so he lowered it again. 'Are you planning to stay long?'

Esther folded her arms and angled her head. Snow was settling in her hair but she was impervious, above the mere efforts of the elements.

'If you are planning to stay we need to have a word about those buses. That's a no waiting zone.'

Still Esther didn't reply. Her jacket was decorated with writing on one of the arms.

London – Wanker Bankers, Brighton – Motorway Madness, Swansea – Estuary Ecstasy, Coventry – New Town Naughtiness, Hinkley – The Power Plant Parade, Inverness – Industrial Estate Action.

At the end, in letters far fresher upon the old denim was *Plymouth – Resurgam Wreckers.*

Steve adjusted his cap, tried to keep his hands steady. 'Well, we can talk about the buses later. I just wanted to introduce myself. I'm in charge of community liaison, so if there's anything I can do please say.'

'Get the fucking Resurgam thing torn down,' came a man's voice from the back of the crowd.

'There's no need for the language.'

'Bollocks there is,' a woman replied.

Steve put his hands behind his back and puffed out his chest. He scanned the crowd, giving them no fear, not a hint, exactly as Happy Hancock had said. He was the law here and the law was him. The structure of society with a smile on its face.

'All right, that'll do. I respect why you're here, but keep it decent and peaceful and we'll get along fine.'

As he turned to walk away, upright with moral authority, another couple of shouts of *bollocks* followed from the crowd.

★★★

A little further along the access road, PC Steve found the kind of radicals more to his taste. June and Maggie were talking to the students and without a word of abuse.

'I ain't going to bother,' Mac grunted. 'No way I'm taking out half a bloody mortgage just for some bit of paper.' To emphasise the point, his fingers emerged from the leather caves of his pockets and played a defiant riff on the air bass.

'But university's not just about a degree,' June told him, with her habitual indulgence. 'You have a wonderful few years, the time of your life. I made friends who've stood by me whatever.'

She smiled fondly at Maggie. It was a warming look, heartfelt, one filled with the bond of the formative years. 'You learn all about yourself too,' Maggie added. 'That's just as important – more so.'

'But where are the jobs when you're done?' Esme asked. 'You can't live off friendships.'

'That's what bothers me,' Alice joined in, the blueness of her eyes heightened by the white of the snowy backdrop. 'Take out all this debt and then what? You end up being the best qualified burger chef in town.'

Seb was toying with his phone whilst keeping a tight arm around Alice. First love; as plain as the colours of spring, and just as beautiful.

'The Resurgam site says they're ahead of schedule,' he told the group, then added, 'Did you know a couple of teachers at college still live with their parents because they can't afford a place of their own?'

'I don't want to be like that,' Alice said, wistfully. 'If I'm going to spend years studying, I want my own flat at least.'

'It's not so much to ask,' Esme nodded. 'Some dignity.'

A large lorry rumbled past, moving carefully in the compacted snow.

'Why aren't you lot back at college then?' PC Steve asked.

'What's the point?' Alice replied. 'We might at least be here, trying to achieve something.'

'Even if we're not,' Mac added.

'Not that anyone's even noticed us skiving, either,' Esme added. 'We've got no voices. *Generation What*, that's us.'

'Come on, it's not so bad,' Steve jollied the disaffected band.

The sullen silence suggested the consensus was otherwise. Another flurry of snowfall whirled around. From Resurgam came an attack of angle grinding, followed by drifting acrid smoke, tainted with the smell of flame on metal.

Amongst the other protesters, further up the road, the clique of whisperers had reformed. But this time they were looking over with undisguised hatred; pointing not at Resurgam, but the young police officer trying to cheer the crowd.

★★★

Through the white mist of snow, Tommy and Phil emerged from the compound for a patrol. They were so wrapped up they could have been Tweedledum and Tweedledee setting out on an arctic expedition.

'It's got to be better than staying in there,' Tommy explained over the background of industrial din. 'The noise is doing my head in.'

The pair began walking towards the Eco Warriors, but Alice reached out a hand and stopped them. Little intervention was needed. Few were the men who wouldn't wait for Alice.

'Before you go, and you PC Steve too – it's my birthday next month, my eighteenth.'

'Mine too,' Seb interjected.

The teenage couple cuddled closer together. They made a fetching pairing; his growing strength, her gentle beauty, and both were filled with the subtle anticipation of life, the shared joy of the great journey ahead.

'We thought we'd have a joint party,' Alice continued. 'You're welcome to join us.'

Phil Rees nodded, even if the invitation had never been directed towards him.

'Are you sure it's not an engagement do?' Steve teased.

'He's just jealous,' Tommy chided. 'That's really kind, I'd love to.'

'You can bring your girlfriend, too.'

And now Tommy looked self-conscious, as if a great fault had been exposed. He said quietly, 'I don't have one.'

PC Steve spoke quickly, a kind attempt to cover the awkwardness. 'I'll see what I can do about coming along. I'm not sure it's a good idea as I'm supposed to be policing you lot.'

'We won't tell anyone,' Alice smiled. 'Consider it part of the job. You can keep an eye on us to make sure we don't do anything too naughty.'

★★★

'More pigs,' a voice grunted as the law-enforcing trio trudged through the snow towards the Eco Warriors.

'Hippy wankers,' Rees retorted.

'That'll do, all of you,' Steve intervened. 'I want to introduce two more people you'll be seeing a fair bit.'

Tommy and Phil were duly presented to the crowd. Esther pushed her way to the front, the group parting easily. A large man followed, blonde and wearing a hoodie which was pulled up over his head. He was young and almost a match for Rees in stature. As if two boxers readying for a bout, the men stared at each other.

'That's one big fucker,' Rees mumbled, making himself as large as possible but less cocksure than usual.

'His name's Simian,' Esther replied. 'He likes looking after me.'

'Hello Simeon,' Steve said, politely.

'It's *Simian* – because he climbs and he's good at it. Held the cops off for ages in our little tree houses in Brighton, didn't you?'

'They can't have been trying too hard,' Rees said.

'You reckon?' the big man retorted.

'Yeah.'

Simian pushed out at Rees, but the security guard was surprisingly quick. He dodged aside, let his opponent stumble past and kicked his backside, not hard, but mocking. Rees put up his fists, taking guard, but found PC Steve in the way.

'That'll do!' the young cop shouted. 'You,' he told Simian, 'Back to your friends.' He turned to Rees, genuine anger in his face. 'You should know better. Back to Resurgam – now!'

Both men looked sullen but did as they were told. A few of the crowd jeered at the denial of some sport. Rees kicked out at the snow as he skulked away.

Esther was calming Simian, her hands on his arms, talking fast and low. He nodded a couple of times and she sent him away to one of the coaches.

'I wouldn't let your man provoke him again,' she told Steve and Tommy. 'He can get carried away.'

'I don't want anyone provoking anyone,' Steve replied, sternly. 'This is going to be a nice lawful protest.'

Esther gave him an impenetrable look, the expression of someone who knows a secret. She turned to Tommy. 'I hear you're not so happy about this thing being built.'

'Who told you that?'

'Word gets around.'

'I've got a job to do.'

She looked him up and down, unblinking, straight through the pale defence of skin and bone, exploring memories and opinions, hopes and fears; the map of a man in seconds.

A smile formed. The sudden touch of humanity changed her face to reveal an unexpectedly attractive woman.

'Do you live in Plymouth?' Esther asked.

'Yes.'

'Alone?'

'Err – yeah.'

Tommy had shrunk a little before the intensity of the interrogation. He looked daunted, even intimidated, but flattered too.

'What's the city like?'

'It's great. I love it.'

'Good places to go?'

'Lots.'

Esther took a step closer, to the edge of Tommy's personal space. He shuffled, eyes flickering, but stood his ground.

'I'd like to see them,' she said. 'I'd like to get to know some of the locals too.'

Tommy began fiddling with the lapel of his jacket. Esther reached out and stopped his fumbling hand, held it for a second, then placed it back by his side. Never once did she break the look she had fixed upon him, the gaze which was warming the security guard as surely as a heat lamp.

★★★

Through the white gauze of the snow a slight figure picked a way towards the protests. It was wearing a parka, the furred hood pulled tight, and carrying a take away coffee. It passed the *Eco Warriors* and moved on towards the original demonstrators, scanning left and right, clearly looking for someone.

'Do we have a new recruit?' June asked.

PC Steve turned to find the sacred gift of a hot drink being held before him. 'Kathy!'

'I thought you'd be cold. I was in town doing some shopping so I brought you a present.'

A gentle chorus of *Aaaahhh* rose from the crowd.

'You shouldn't have,' he replied, but took the drink and sipped gratefully. 'Let me introduce you to the rebels.'

Kathy shook hands with all in the line. She was gentle, sounded kind and genuine. Her face had paled with the cold, but she wore dimples of pure cuteness and had sweet lips, as dark as port. June gave her an approving look, a special of the aunty sort, and offered a maternal wink to PC Steve.

'I don't want to interrupt,' Kathy said. 'But – dinner at my place later?'

Such was the effect upon the young man's face that the offer could have been one of eternal life, to be spent at a utopian beachside retreat, forever in the company of a certain woman.

'Are you sure it's not you who'll be having the engagement party?' Esme teased.

'Ok, ok,' Steve replied, reddening by the second. 'Don't go embarrassing me.'

'Bring Kathy to our party too,' Seb said. 'If you'd like to come?'

'I'd love to.'

Steve walked her a little way along the road, taking care to skirt the lines of unkempt demonstrators. They stared as the couple passed, silently contemptuous, glacially hostile.

'Kiss her then,' June called, as the pair stopped to say goodbye.

Kathy pulled back the hood of her parka, like a bride with a veil, and smiled. Steve hesitated, then bent and pecked her on the lips.

Another chorus of *Aaaahhhh* accompanied the brief embrace.

She began walking away. Steve watched every step, his face soft with the trance of the invisible drug. Only when Kathy was starting to fade from sight in the flurrying snow did he turn back.

Right into the snowball.

The crack of bone could be heard across the Resurgam compound. But it was nothing compared to the young man's agonised scream. It stayed forever in the minds of those who heard it, a memory that could never be escaped. It was too horrible, too traumatic to ever forget; the sound of obscene violation.

Steve fell to his knees, hands clutching for the bloodied orb where an eyeball had been.

CHAPTER 17

One of the few challenges to be addressed smoothly when Claire began moving into the flat, was finding space for her clothes. In the main bedroom were two built-in wardrobes, aged but spacious. One was occupied with Dan's wear, the other largely untroubled.

It was used most commonly after Christmas, to secrete the unpleasant objects and misshapen articles that distant family would send under the guise of being presents. Claire cleared a way through the dusty piles of tacky bric-a-brac with ruthless efficiency and quickly established a base for her outfits. The only real conflict had been her usurping of a couple of drawers, and both for knickers. How any woman could require upwards of forty pairs when she did a wash once a week was well beyond Dan.

His own wardrobe was lightly populated, with a handful of pairs of trousers, shoes, shirts and jackets. The only fashion to prove a weakness was ties, and loud ones, particularly as they were useful for disguising the appearance of the same jacket or shirt on a run of occasions.

Rarely did Dan suffer from what he quietly called *Adam Breen syndrome*. It involved long periods of inner turmoil suffered while trying to calculate what to wear. But this morning, the matter of wardrobe was one Dan was trying hard to get right.

For a man who must have carried out thousands of interviews in the years of his career, it was always these which lodged in the memory. The times he'd spent with the bereaved or heartbroken were the narratives of the darkest nights. For this meeting with Alannah, Dan wanted to look his best.

He chose a navy blue jacket, his favourite, and a light blue shirt to go with his eyes. The tie was trickier, nothing too bright required, and eventually Dan settled on a subtle floral print.

The time was quarter past nine. They were due at Alannah's house at half past. Outside, Dan heard Adam's car draw up, the detective precisely on time, as ever.

Claire had been missing on his return to the flat. She left a note, saying she'd gone to meet a friend for a coffee.

As he made for the front door, Dan noticed Claire had laid out some clothes on the spare bed. They were sorted into neat piles and quite a range, even shoes too, a large suitcase standing waiting. She must be having a clear out, planning to take the discards of fashion to the charity shop.

★★★

Alannah lived in Eggbuckland, only five minutes' drive from the flat. She was spending most of her time at the hospital, by Tommy's bedside, and had initially suggested that was her preferred place to talk.

'Are you sure it's better to see her at home?' Adam asked, staying exactly two miles per hour below the speed limit, in his traditional manner.

'She'll be more relaxed on home territory and far more likely to talk easily. Besides…'

'What?'

'It'll give us a chance to have a look around. You never know what we might pick up.'

'You stick to the insight bit,' came the huffy reply. 'I'll do the detective work. On the subject of which…'

He launched into a rapid briefing on Alannah's background. Bright was the consensus of her former school, achieving a range of good GCSEs. But she had little taste for education and left at sixteen to join the navy, a familiar path in Plymouth. She became a wren, served for five years and was identified as having the potential to be an officer. But the allure of the seafaring life had worn off and she left to return home.

Several mundane not-much-and-nothing jobs followed, before Alannah joined a firm of solicitors as a receptionist. Once more, her intelligence had been noted and she was offered training which could lead to a formal legal qualification.

'That's how Dance got her to do the appeal,' Adam said. 'The old mutual back scratching thing. Alannah works at Dance's solicitors.'

'Do I detect displeasure?'

'It was a unilateral operation, that appeal. A word of consultation would have been appreciated.'

'It's certainly even more of an indication she was used by Dance, to put out that spin about stopping the fighting over Resurgam,' Dan noted.

'There's one more thing the briefing mentions,' Adam added. 'Apparently Alannah's got quite a temper.'

'I'll bear that in mind when I frame a question.'

Eggbuckland is a curious locale within a modern city, possessed of at least a couple of personalities. The landscape is hilly and has an incongruous number of parks, bounded with old housing and dense modern estates. In one of these, a small semi with a history dating back no more than a decade, lived Alannah. They were pulling into the street when Dan's phone rang.

'Where are you?' Lizzie barked.

'On the way down to Resurgam,' he replied, ignoring Adam's sidelong look.

'Not in the newsroom, then?'

Sometimes the temptation of sarcasm is just too strong, however inadvisable. 'You're not wrong.'

'Explain yourself.'

'I wanted to get down early. To make sure I'm on top of every last detail. To make our coverage as brilliant as it can possibly be.'

The flannel may have been overly moist and excessively applied. But, as with many tyrants, supplication was a weakness.

'That's acceptable. But remember what we said – cock it up again and...'

'There is one other thing,' Dan interrupted, before Lizzie could add any further turns to the emotional thumbscrews. 'I'm going to see a... police source.'

At mention of the words Adam lifted his chin, as sure as a Guardsman on duty.

'Why?'

'In confidence...'

'Tell.'

'Really top secret.'

'Tell instantly.'

'There's been a threat against Resurgam. The cops think it might not be a good idea to open it tomorrow.'

'And we can report this?'

Dan let his look creep across to the silent detective, who raised an eyebrow.

'It depends on my negotiations.'

'Then negotiate like a battleship. I want that story!'

Adam parked just up from Alannah's house, taking care not to obstruct any drives. He checked his reflection in the mirror and straightened his tie. They climbed out of the car into the white teeth attack of the December morning.

The temperature had only tentatively edged above freezing. A postman strode by, his arms heavy with Christmas cards and presents.

'It wouldn't be anything to do with you expecting Dance to have none of your requests to delay the opening, by any chance?' Dan said, as he opened the gate to the house. 'This leaking of the threats to me. To put some pressure on her?'

'I have no idea what you mean,' the Chief Inspector replied, unusually unconvincingly by his standards.

★★★

Alannah was dressed in the same dark grey suit which she wore to face the cameras yesterday. A closer view revealed it to be threadbare in patches. She greeted them with a quiet voice and a handshake so ephemeral it could have belonged to a ghost. The young woman felt a long way removed from the world.

Her father stood alongside. He was a tall man with receding hair, a strong physique and his handshake was a contrast as could be, a real bone squeezer.

Adam went through the introductions, again using the words that made Dan wince.

'This is nothing to worry about,' the detective habitually said. It tended to put people at ease in the same way they might feel when visiting the dentist for root canal work at a time of a shortage of anaesthetic.

They talked in the lounge, a small box of a room, but homely enough. It was decorated in the creamy white that often seems the default colour for English households. Following the tradition, both carpet and curtains matched. The room was warm, much more so than the hallway. Like many families who weren't well off, perhaps one room was where they spent most of the time in the winter.

Opposite the television was a two-seater sofa, which Alannah and Jack occupied, and a couple of chairs. Pictures lined the mantelpiece, the Lewises and Tommy at a football match in the green of Plymouth Argyle, the Lewises and Tommy all waving on Plymouth Hoe, the Lewises and Tommy surrounded by the rocky tors of Dartmoor.

Jack said, 'He was like a son to me.' Alannah's head drooped and her father realised his mistake, reached out and hugged her hard. 'I meant he *is* like a son to me. Come on now, he's going to be ok. He's a fighter, isn't he, our Tommy?'

She nodded, but it was a tired gesture. Her face was pallid, eyes shrunken and puffy. Adam asked, 'How is Tommy doing?'

'He's stable,' Jack replied, abruptly. 'The doctors say the next day or two'll be critical.'

The resulting silence felt persistent and dense. Adam looked to Dan. As it was no time to thank the detective for his fine work in easing their passage, Dan ventured, 'I would have mentioned it yesterday, but I didn't have the chance – I found that moving.'

'What I said?' Alannah replied, softly.

'And what you were wearing.' He pointed to her finger and the unique rays of the diamond's sparkle. 'That's the ring you were going to show the family on Christmas Day?'

'Yes.'

'You're wearing it so Tommy will know you're thinking of him?'

'We chose it together. When he... the crash – after I got back from the hospital I put it on. You used a picture of it on the news last night.'

'I hope you didn't mind.'

'Not at all.' She managed a weak smile. 'I was glad.'

Alannah was holding a mobile phone and tightly, not once looking ready to put it down. She kept glancing at the screen.

'Photos of Tommy?' Dan guessed.

'And video too. Dad took them.'

'May I?'

'Why?'

She was suspicious and guarded, sore with the rawness of the emotional wounds. It was a delicate part of the interview. They'd reached a gateway, and it was ready to open or close.

Dan got up from the chair, moving slowly, giving the moment some respect and allowing himself a few seconds to think. He headed for an icon, to be found in every home, and a trick he'd used many a time before.

'I met him once or twice when the protests were at their height, although we never really spoke,' Dan said, pointing to Tommy in one of the photographs. 'But I have heard about him. A gentle and kind man, wasn't he?'

Alannah nodded, pride laden with sorrow.

'We'd like to get a better sense of Tommy. It might help the investigation.'

She stared at Dan, then the photograph and Tommy's smiling face. Alannah pressed a pattern of buttons and held out the phone. The image was of the couple dressed in shorts and T-shirts, walking along a beach. They were hand in hand, both with the rare looks of true happiness, a ruddy sun setting away to sea.

'It's from Bigbury Island in September,' she explained. 'We had a lovely day, but it was a bit cloudy. Just before we left the sun came out and we had a last walk.'

'You've been playing it a lot?'

She swallowed hard. 'I've been playing it to Tommy.'

Dan nodded, Adam too. 'I think it's time to find out why the attack happened,' the detective said. 'Can you tell us what Tommy was like in the days before?'

★★★

The view through a lover's eyes may be coloured with the sepia of affection, but the picture of Tommy was a charming one. For the first time Alannah talked fluently, the words free with the flow of feeling.

'I should tell you how we met – if you've got time?'

'Of course,' Dan said, before the painfully pragmatic Adam could find a dissenting word.

'It was on a bus on the way into town. I'd seen him a few times, but we'd never talked. One day the bus was really busy. He got a seat first, but it was the last one so he gave it to me. He insisted. He stood beside me, we got chatting and that was it.' She smiled in a self-conscious, attractive way. 'Well, mostly it.'

'You were waiting, but he didn't ask?'

'How did you know that?'

Dan pointed once more to the photograph. 'It's in his look. Warm, but shy.'

'That's my Tommy,' she smiled. 'When we got off the bus, we just stood there looking at each other. He said it was nice talking to me and I said it'd be good to meet again soon. You men are so rubbish with hints sometimes!'

A thought of Claire and the tortuous procession that had been their relationship jigged through Dan's mind. 'That's very true,' he agreed, sadly.

'We just stood there some more, then he said he'd better be getting to work and went to shake my hand. He was so hopeless and cute! I giggled and tapped my cheek and he just looked at me, then kissed it.'

'And then?'

'He was still standing there. And I don't know what got into me, I'd never normally do this, but I said *I'm free tomorrow night.* We exchanged numbers and that was it.'

Tommy had been living in a bed sit. In the way of many a bachelor he'd found a place so inhospitable that Alannah stayed there only once. The sound of mice scuttling at night, and the screaming from the house across the road kept her awake. He had been introduced to Jack, they'd got on well and Tommy began to spend more and more time at the house.

'He asked my permission to marry Alannah,' Jack added. 'He was so scared he was shaking. But I didn't hesitate.' Recalling his error of earlier, Jack made sure to find the present tense. 'He's a top man. I'll be proud to have him as a son in law.'

As the relationship progressed, Tommy opened up more. He'd only had a couple of girlfriends Alannah said, neither long term. It was at that point he made a confession. It came after several pints of fortifying lager, much preamble and procrastination; asking her to promise not to be angry.

'That's some build up,' Dan noted. 'You must have wondered what you were going to hear.'

'I did. But do you know all it was? When he met me, he'd been kind of seeing some other girl. Not a proper relationship, just an on–off occasional thing. He said it wasn't working anyway and as soon as he met me he ended it.'

Adam leaned forwards at the scent. 'Did he say who the girl was?'

'No. I got the feeling he was – well, ashamed. He never talked about it again.'

Another silence. Dan and Adam exchanged a look, the detective nodding slightly, his eyes full of thought.

★★★

Tommy Ross was a quiet and placid man, so much so that Alannah could make a rare claim about their relationship.

'We never rowed. We had the odd word of course, but it wasn't like shouting and screaming. That just wasn't Tommy.'

He had loved the job as a Security Guard for the little stretch of city beach. When plans for Resurgam were first mooted Tommy had been photographed on patrol, talking to some children on a canoeing expedition.

'He kept his views quiet,' Alannah said. 'He had to. But he hated Resurgam. He thought it had stolen something precious from Plymouth. He was looking for another job, but there was nothing about. He couldn't have handled being unemployed. Plus we needed the money for the wedding.'

At mention of the word, her fingers found the engagement ring and fiddled it back and forth.

'And what do you think about Resurgam?' Dan asked.

The simple sentence could have been charged with electricity. It struck like a shock. The tenderness of the memories of Tommy were gone, replaced with an incandescent anger.

'I hate the thing! I fucking hate it! And that Ellen Dance too! Everything was going fine. We'd got enough money put away for a little wedding do and a deposit on a house. We were talking about starting a family. And now… because of it… that fucking skyscraper…'

Jack pulled his daughter close, whispered soothing reassurances. Dan studied the ground and tried to ignore the thunderstorm of a look Adam was glowering in his direction.

'So your domestic life, normally, was like what?' the detective asked, with an attempt to ease the atmosphere and unusually clumsy syntax.

Alannah shrugged. 'Just like everyone's. We'd get home from work. One of us would cook something. Dad doesn't charge much in the way of rent, so we cook for him as part of the deal. Tommy does a mean Shepherd's pie, doesn't he?'

Jack nodded. 'Just like you do a great curry.' He patted his stomach. 'They keep me going.'

'Then we'd just watch TV,' she continued. 'Maybe go out to the pub sometimes, but that's about it. Both of us liked to get to bed early.'

'So how did Tommy change?' Dan said. 'And when?'

She stared through the air. 'It was about a week ago, maybe last Thursday.'

'Just over a week before Resurgam was due to open,' Adam noted.

'Yeah.'

'How did he change?'

'It was... weird. First off, he was really quiet. He was always a bit quiet, but even more than normal. When I'd try talking to him, he'd like – jump in fright.'

'As if something was bothering him?'

'Yeah, maybe.'

'And it got worse?'

'Yeah. One time – I think it was the weekend – I said to him *Are you ok?* And he snapped at me and said something like *I'm fine, stop bothering me will you!* It really took me back. It wasn't like him at all.'

'He didn't want to go to the footie on Saturday either,' Jack added. 'We usually do, but he said he didn't fancy it. Good match, too.'

'And was there anything else that was odd?' Adam said.

'Sunday,' Alannah replied. 'That stuck in my mind. You'll think this is so silly...'

'Go on.'

'I did him some toast and it was a bit burnt, just blackened on one edge. But he went off on one, even swore at me. And he never swears, Tommy. Never at me, anyway.'

'And the rest of the day?'

'He was really quiet.'

'Did he say what was bothering him?'

'I didn't ask. I was a bit – well, scared. I thought...'

'Yes?'

'I was worried he was having second thoughts about us getting married.'

Alannah's voice was even quieter now. Dan and Adam were both leaning forwards on their chairs, to be sure to catch her words. Jack laced an arm around his daughter's shoulders and hugged her.

'Course he wouldn't, never. He loves you, you know that.'

'And that night?' Adam prompted.

Her fingers were on the engagement ring again. 'Nothing much. Just – he didn't sleep, was tossing and turning, getting up to the loo. It kept me awake.'

'And Monday?'

'He was quiet again in the morning. But that night – he'd changed.'

'How?'

'He was back to being Tommy. He came home and he was smiling again, the first time I'd seen him grin like that for days. He was talking about where we'd have the wedding and what house we were going to buy.'

'And did you get any sense why he'd cheered up?'

'He just said he'd worked out what he was going to do and everything would be all right.'

'And that was it? You didn't ask him what happened?'

'Yeah, course I did. But he just said not to worry. That things might be tricky for a while, but he'd sort it all out and we'd be together. That was the only thing that was important.'

'And he never said what had been bothering him?'

'No. Not a word.'

Adam leaned back on his chair and rubbed a hand over the stubble on his chin. Dan studied Alannah. Her expression was lost, filled with fog and mist.

Some called it the thousand mile stare. But Alannah's eyes were for only a handful of miles away and her fiancé, lying unconscious on a hospital bed.

★★★

Before they left the house, Adam requested a brief look around Alannah and Tommy's bedroom.

'Why?' she asked, more fear and defensiveness in the single syllable.

'There might be something which could help us to understand, well...' The detective paused and Alannah immediately sensed the reason. At the start of this interview, she was focused only on grief. Now some of the haze had cleared and her eyes were bright and shrewd. Watching how fast her mind worked, Dan understood why those who contributed to the briefing judged her to be highly intelligent, and she was perceptive, too.

'You think the attack was deliberate? That someone meant to kill him?'

Adam breathed out heavily. 'Please understand, there's a limit to how much I can say. But yes, I think it's likely Tommy was deliberately targeted.'

And now pain was piled upon hurt, suffering upon suffering. 'But – why? Why? He was only a guard. Just my Tommy.'

'We don't know why. But whatever was bothering him in the days before the attack could explain it.'

'I – I don't know if I want you in the bedroom. It's – ours.'

'I understand. But it could help us find whoever attacked him.'

Alannah slumped into herself again, reached out for the comfort of Jack. 'I don't understand any of this,' she sobbed. 'Why would anyone hurt Tommy? He was nothing to anyone except me. Why is all this happening?'

'I know this is hard,' Adam soothed. 'But we just want to help you.'

The anger was back, as fast as a flashlight, another instant shift of mood in this tormented woman. 'Just like that fucking Ellen Dance? She used me, didn't she? Like a little wind-up toy.'

The detective remained calm, but Dan could see the impact of her words. Few were the insults that could make it through the defences of such an experienced investigator. But this was well-aimed, hitting the plexus of Adam's principles; the unspoken promise that ran throughout his career.

'Not like her, I promise you,' he said, levelly. 'We're trying to help. And seeing your bedroom could be important.'

The decision was made by Jack, who'd used the seconds to study Adam and weigh his integrity. He took his daughter's hand and led the way up the stairs.

The room was even smaller than the lounge and poorly lit, just space for a double bed and some drawers, a pile of washing on a chair in the corner.

Adam asked which drawers were Tommy's and began a rapid search. Initially Alannah turned away, but then looked back and watched carefully, following the detective's every movement. She was trembling, fingers continually toying with the engagement ring.

The confines of the room meant Adam's work was brief. When he'd finished checking under the bed, the detective emerged and asked, 'One final thing – have you got Tommy's mobile phone?'

'Yes.'

'May I borrow it?'

'Why?' Alannah asked, and now her voice was different. There was still fear in the timbre, but it was of a unique kind; the dread of betrayal. And Adam, who had seen it as a motive so many times, recognised the emotion immediately.

'It's not what you think,' he said, with genuine kindness.

'I don't think that. He wouldn't, never. We were happy.'

'I just…'

'We were happy!' she screamed, her voice so loud it made them recoil. 'And now… now… I don't understand any of this.'

'It just might help us to work out why Tommy was different for a few days, then back to normal again. That's all.'

The tears were flowing fast, cascading down Alannah's face. She stared out of the window, at the lines of roofs running down the valley. Some were patched with snow, others bare and black.

'Alannah?' Adam prompted, gently.

She gulped in a tearful breath, but opened a drawer on her side of the bed and took out a phone.

★★★

Back in the car they had a couple of minutes to talk, no more. Deadlines were wrapping their iron chains around both men.

Dan grabbed for the seat belt as Adam accelerated away, much faster than his cautious norm. He turned on his mobile to find a couple of messages.

One was from El. The first few seconds were filled with husky complaints about the thickness of his aching head, rapidly followed by another long lament bemoaning their chances of ever finding the Cashman. Upon both bended knees, the paparazzo implored Dan to undertake one final exertion of supreme effort.

Predictably the other message was Lizzie, demanding a progress report from Resurgam. The time was a quarter to eleven.

Dan quickly rang Nigel and asked the cameraman to pick him up from Charles Cross Police Station.

'Bloody hell! Where are you? Do you realise how big a deal this is?! What on earth are you playing...'

'Don't ask,' Dan interrupted. 'We don't have the time. Just help me out, please.'

'When do I damn well not?'

He put the phone away and was about to ask Adam a question when a memory intruded, an important question which hadn't yet been answered.

'Hey!' Dan exclaimed theatrically, spinning in his seat. 'I reckon the bloke who jumped into that car back there was carrying a knife.'

'What? Are you sure?' Adam asked, suspiciously.

'Well, no, not sure. It's probably not worth going back, given we're both so busy,' came the carefully judged response. 'But you'd better check he's not a nutter, storing up weapons for some dreadful crime.'

Adam didn't reply, so Dan prompted, 'Hadn't you? It'd be negligent not to.'

'And no doubt you got the registration plate, like a good citizen?'

'It's funny you should say that. I did just manage to scribble it down.' Dan passed across a piece of paper, which the detective received with haughty ill grace.

They were heading down the hill towards the city centre, just a minute or so away from Charles Cross. As the car pulled up at the police station, Dan had the opportunity to say only, 'It's Esther, isn't it? That other woman of Tommy's?'

'It sounds like her way of working,' Adam agreed. 'I'll get his phone analysed and talk to you later.'

CHAPTER 18

The time was almost eleven o'clock. They had just an hour to work through a formidable list of tasks; get to Resurgam, come up with a plan for a live report for lunchtime, make sure they filmed every important detail and covered every interview. And there was something else Dan very much wanted to be doing but feared the scarcity of time would never allow.

That familiar nagging thought set sail on the choppy seas of his mind, the one that usually appeared with a figurehead in the guise of Lizzie. There was the line, bright and yellow, unmissable and unmistakable, and there was Dan Groves about to cross it – again.

Adam would be less than impressed too, and probably launch into one of his little tirades. But what the hell, there was plenty enough dung lingering in life at the moment. Some more would hardly hurt.

Nigel was waiting, as requested, engine running, keeping a twitchy watch for his errant reporter. Unusually for such a sociable man, he said nothing as Dan clambered into the car.

It was overwhelmingly warm after the freezing interlude of outside, a sudden cocoon of heat. Dan massaged his temples. The beer of last night had coalesced into jackhammers in his mind.

Cars whipped by, streets and shops too. It was a couple of minutes before Nigel spoke, and when he did it was with a curiously quiet voice.

'Claire?'

'Not this time.'

'Doing your Sherlock Holmes thing?'

'Maybe.'

Nigel rapped a hand on the steering wheel in a rare show of anger. 'I'm not sure if you missed it, but it's quite a big news day.'

Dan managed to keep his voice level and ignore the sarcasm. 'I haven't missed it.'

'And given yesterday's … issue, it's more than a little important you get the story right.'

And that was enough, the final nudge to upset Dan's fragile balance. 'For fuck's sake I know that, all right? But what I've been doing this morning, the *Sherlock Holmes thing* as you so sneerily put it, is pretty damned important too!'

Nigel reached out a hand, but Dan shrugged it off. 'Calm down,' the cameraman soothed. 'I'm on your side, remember?'

'Yeah, and I'm really feeling the friendship.'

'All I'm saying is maybe it's time you concentrated on your proper job.'

Another rocket of a reply was well in preparation and being readied for launch, when Dan yelled, 'Stop the car!'

'What?'

'Just do it!'

Nigel did, slewing into a bus bay. And if there was any doubt about what was to unfold, that swinging manoeuvre settled it. Dan piled out of the car, grabbed at a bin and threw up. He held on hard to the cold certainty of the metal rim as the world dipped and span.

'Are you ok?' Nigel asked, as the wretched creature returned.

'Yeah, I'm tip top and dandy. Well, no actually as you might have noticed. Ah, bollocks. Sorry if I was – well…'

'Forget it. We're under enough pressure without us falling out as well.'

'You got it absolutely right,' Dan confessed. 'I'm trying to do two jobs at once. They can both be buggers and sometimes it's too much. Not to mention – well, the domestic stuff.'

'Maybe you could just stick to one job, then – for the next few hours, anyway?' And in words of pure kindness, sufficient to reach even an entrenched cynic like the one brooding in the passenger seat, Nigel added, 'I was hoping to work with you for a bit longer.'

Dan patted his friend on the shoulder and glugged some water. He checked his reflection in the mirror. It was far from the sort of vision which would appeal to an artist, except perhaps one who specialised in the covers of horror novels.

'There's just one more thing, to help us on our merry way,' Nigel ventured. 'You should know that Lizzie's in a manic mood.'

★★★

They were on the Barbican, rumbling slowly through the narrow streets, almost at Resurgam. The day was still gloomy and the sky a lank, disinterested grey, the great monolith a black block towering above the seaward horizon.

Lights were on in most floors. Tiny silhouettes scuttled across the Sky Garden, disappearing and reappearing between the outlines of foliage. The express lifts were zipping up and down, bullets of light in the semi-darkness of the December day. Cops were on the streets, patrolling or parked up in cars and on motorbikes, polite and smiling, but ever watchful.

They passed the Homeless Mission, a couple of men enjoying the pageant unfolding around them. One was holding a tin of super strength lager, the sort of stuff which can clear drains. He waved it happily at anyone who passed by, but never spilling a drop.

Nigel turned the car along the access road, into a line of security officers. Dan groaned at the inevitability of a hefty delay. They had no time to mess about. He fished out his press pass and wound down a window.

'Hello again, sir,' one of the women was saying to Nigel. 'Please carry on.'

He thanked her, put the car back into gear and they drove into the compound.

'How'd you do that?' Dan asked.

The few remains of the Gatehouse were gone, a couple of benches and plants brought in to mask any memories burnished in the concrete. Workers strode around, some carrying brooms, brushing away miscreant specks of dust.

The silvery statues were tolerating a final polish, but looked no less anguished for the attention. The gloom of the day coloured as spotlights began illuminating Resurgam's facade in slowly changing shades.

Nigel parked by the outside broadcast truck. The satellite dish was already up, the camera set upon its tripod, microphone laid along its top. The door was open, Loud sitting with his feet on the edit desk, reading a paper.

'How'd you do all this, too?' Dan added.

'I got in early. I thought you might be a little distracted. I've also got a plan for how to do the lunchtime live, if you're interested?'

Dan reached out a hand to shake Nigel's. He found his voice curiously hoarse. 'Thank you.'

'It's ok. We are trying to look after you.'

There was something in the sentence which made Dan frown. A peculiar inflexion, the hint of a hidden meaning.

'We? Meaning what?'

'Never mind for now. You'd better ring in.'

Many a song or poem has been written to the wonder of friends. This morning, had he not been so preoccupied, Dan could have added another to their number.

★★★

Lizzie was as agitated as a tap dancer on hot coals. But she was at least passably mollified by the reassurances Dan offered.

'What about the exclusive on the cops and Ellen Dance?'

'The meeting's later. We should have it for tonight.'

'Should?!'

'Almost definitely.'

'Almost?!'

'Got to go, got an interview to do,' Dan lied.

Inside the compound, but contained in a penned off area away from the main building, a group of demonstrators had been allowed to gather. The pitch was as prominent as the cupboard under the stairs.

Jackie Denyer was patrolling the area like a human frigate, gliding back and forth. With a cosmetic smile, she explained the magnanimity of Ellen Dance extended to encouraging the democratic right of protest, even after the dreadful events of Tuesday night.

'I suspect it's more a case of Lyndon Johnson and his tent, isn't it?' Dan asked, mildly.

'The media will assemble at 11.50 at the main doors,' she replied in a haughty voice, with a wave of the clipboard. 'The President will give an address, then at noon precisely you will be allowed inside to film. And before you ask; no. Ms Dance will not be answering any questions.'

The protest group was a dozen strong, the maximum allowed by the grace of the authorities, made up of the students and local people who had been at Resurgam from the start. The faces had grown only a little older in that year, but far wiser. The main placard they carried now said simply *Why?*, although there was also a large one dedicated to the memory of Alice.

With an irony that was probably unintended, the group had been corralled next to The Wall. *No way, never to stay. Not here, not today*, the chant began. Some started banging fists on the bricks to emphasise their point.

All eyed Dan carefully as he walked a tentative approach, June producing a guarded smile, the faces of the students as cold as the day.

Dan checked his watch. It said eleven, so the time was probably around ten past.

There might just be the time to attend to the intriguing shades of that other business after all.

★★★

They watched him approach, every single step, as wary, as ever. They'd been through plenty enough to make them that way, this little group.

'Morning,' Dan offered.

'Morning,' June replied, cordial but cool. The rest of the set were silent. Fists gripped hard at the placards and banners, the loyal standards of their battle.

'I need to have a chat.'

'About that?' she replied, with a disparaging look towards Resurgam.

'In a minute, of course. But... there's something else.'

'Yes?'

'You won't like it.'

'Try us.'

'Really, you won't.'

'I don't think much is going to shock us now. Not after...'

'This might.'

'Go on.'

The pleasantries, as sparse as they were, had already been exhausted. No charm, no humour, no diplomacy was going to crack this ice. Years of experience of softening tearful or angry interviewees were feathers upon granite here. Sometimes the direct way was the only way, no matter how it might be received.

'It's about Esther,' Dan ventured.

The frigid cold of the icicle air chilled further. There were a couple of intakes of breath at the taboo of the name. Words were being mouthed, and far from the kind which would be welcome at the church fete.

'We've got nothing to say,' June stated, in a voice which only the bravest would challenge.

'Not to you,' Mac added forcefully.

'Which means?'

'You're one of them.'

Dan kept his voice as level as possible, given the provocation. 'Them? Them who?'

'Them bastards.'

'Them, all of them,' Seb joined in. 'Just... them. The lot of them.'

The group were clustering around Dan, tightening the space, shading out the grey winter light. The infection of the mob was running free. They had been wounded too many times to be unthreatening any longer. But Dan held his ground, filling with a resentment of his own, the challenge to a standard he had carried proudly all his adult years.

'Them?' he said again, and with meaning.

'Yeah,' Mac grunted. 'The politicians, the cops, the bankers, the business wankers, the fucking lot.'

Dan felt his blood abuzz. Of all the many goads he faced in life, this was an electric wire to the core of his brain.

'Miss something, did you?' he replied, with a hard-won calm.

'Like what?' came the replies from the group. 'Arsehole. What you talking about?'

'I was one of those people who exposed the MPs' expenses scandal. Remember that? And kept banging on at the bankers about their bonuses. And got some action there, too. Miss that too, did you... *arseholes?*'

'So what about...'

But Dan was tolerating no interruptions. However outnumbered, no matter how unwise, his mind kept firing and feeding the passion of his all-too-willing mouth.

'And let me guess – I live in a luxury house, not a flat, right? With top-of-the-range cars and so much money I use it as bog roll? With servants running around at my every whim? Or maybe I do this job because I believe in it?'

There was no reply, but the passion had made them listen. They'd ripped to the heart of a rebel. In days long gone it would have been a young Dan standing here on the protest line, thinking and feeling the way they did. And maybe – just perhaps – little had changed, despite the passing of the decades.

'And I still believe in this job,' he ranted onwards, 'Even if some of my old college mates earn more in a day than I manage in a year. And take the piss out of me for doing what I think is right. And others run the country and ask what the hell I'm doing here? Understand that, can you?'

Still no response from the group. But on some of the faces there was a hint of surprise and recalculation.

'Yeah, but…' Mac ventured, but even he, this densest of a barrier, was overridden by the momentum of Dan's anger.

'And do you know what I'm most proud of? It's the youngsters who've found jobs they love because of the careers work I do. Who would never have managed that, otherwise. And every Christmas, when I get a load of cards from them, thanking me – that's one of the best moments of my year.'

Seb pushed his way to the front. He was so thin now it was pitiful. But today his suffering was invisible, hidden by the force of rage.

'You work with the pigs. Everyone knows it.'

'Yeah,' came a couple of mutters from the group.

'After what they did to Alice you should be ashamed. Go on, fuck off back to your pig mates.'

Dan stepped over, so they were eye to eye. 'Yep, you're right, I do work with *the pigs*. And do you know what? I'm damn proud of that, too. Do you want to know how many murderers and rapists and other criminals I've helped catch?'

And now a silence. Two armies of anger, two sides so certain in their beliefs had fought and been becalmed.

People passed, more arrived. Cars trundled up to Resurgam, dropped off passengers. But here, in the far corner of the compound, in the shadow of the skyscraper, there was quiet. And the group stared at Dan, and he stared right back. Today, for once, courage had found him.

'Let me guess,' he said slowly, to taunt and to hurt, but also with the calculation of a thinking mind. 'You're still feeling sore about what happened to Tommy?'

'Fuck off,' Mac snorted.

'Because you've realised the truth, haven't you?'

'What truth?'

Seb joined in with his friend, shoulder to shoulder. 'Yeah, what truth?'

The words found echoes in the crowd. 'What truth? What fucking truth?'

More feet were edging towards Dan, bodies starting to press harder against the pen. But still he held his ground.

'What – fucking – truth?' Seb spat.

'You were set up. By Esther. Used... to cover the lorry attack. You were little patsies.'

The words struck like a silent missile. There was no reply. No response. Nothing.

Now Seb raised an arm and Dan tensed, ready to parry the blow. It was the one he had been waiting for as he set off on this perilous path. But there was no swinging fist, no impact, no pain.

Esme had taken hold of Seb's wrist. 'Yes,' she said quietly, in a voice husky with remorse. 'You're right.'

'I think we have realised,' June agreed, moving to stand next to Esme. 'We were used.'

Dan nodded. 'And I'm trying to find out why Tommy was attacked. And finally getting the answer to some big questions about Esther could help.'

One by one, the little group looked to June. In her thick coat, rainbow hat and gloves, she was perhaps one of the most incongruous leaders ever ushered forth by history.

She let those wise old eyes run over Dan, up and down and right through, and asked, 'What is it you want to know?'

CHAPTER 19

It had taken a week to put together the profile on Esther's life, to match the one on Ellen Dance, and it was a fascinating assignment. Few people were happy to speak openly. It required all the dark arts in a hack's armoury; a mix of charm, guarantees of anonymity, and more than a little manipulation.

As he sat in the front of the satellite truck, Dan leafed through his file of notes, mind adrift in what June and the others had just told him. There were only minutes left before Dance's speech, but perhaps enough time to finally fill in the missing pages of an unfinished story.

The quest began in Berkshire at Esther's childhood home. Longstaff was a village in the way only those in the London commuter belt can have the front to so describe themselves. Five pubs, several restaurants, a butcher, greengrocer, delicatessen, hardware store, hair salon and plenty more other shops besides. The moment Dan and Nigel parked and set up the camera, the gossip was running faster than a white water river in spate.

Nigel started filming while Dan began asking questions. The answers he found were consistent. Yes, people knew Esther. But they did so in that nodding, knowing manner. No, they would rather not talk about her, thank you. The refusals were as polite as any finishing school could wish for, but steadfast. Something was awry.

Progress came at last in the place it so often does. The Red Roe was the current inn of choice for the village drunkards, scandalmongers and bores, and there Dan and Nigel settled under the cover of lunch. To bait the hook all the better, they took the camera along and laid it obviously upon a bench.

The pub was a little tatty and the multitude of horse brasses certainly made a statement, but it was comfortable enough. Within five minutes they were fielding questions about their work. Within a quarter of an hour, Dan had bought a round for their newfound friends. By the end of lunch they had secured plenty of information, plus a surprisingly passable Chicken and Mushroom Pie.

Esther had been adopted and was the only child of a city banker and a public relations executive. They were wealthy enough to afford a lofty Victorian house on the edge of Longstaff. Both parents were renowned for disappearing for days into the metropolis, the young Esther being looked after by a nanny.

As soon as she was of age, Esther was sent to a boarding school. From then onwards she was rarely seen around the village. At that stage there was nothing to feed the hunger of the gossips, for every time they were spotted the family wore a veil of contentment.

That was, until the fire.

★★★

The archives documented it with the stark facts of a reporter's eye. But as so often it was the unspoken subtext which was far more interesting.

The fire was intense and took several hours to bring under control. The house was badly damaged and required many months of painstaking renovations.

It was April, just before Easter. The fire broke out in the middle of the night. It was Esther who discovered the blaze, roused her parents and made sure they escaped. For weeks, she was feted as a hero.

The paper contained a couple of follow up stories, short paragraphs about progress in restoring the house. Only a month later did it become a lead story once more, a reporter writing of a police visit to the home to investigate the possibility of arson.

The gossips filled in the rest. No one was charged. But the whispers were as sharp as razors in the dark, and all angled towards Esther. As for a motive, even the cluster of drinkers who gleefully passed on their views in the Red Roe admitted they couldn't say for sure.

But one theory had grown to become accepted currency. It was a cry for attention from a young girl who felt she was far from the centrepiece of her parents' lives.

★★★

Despite the traditions of her school, Esther didn't go on to university. In that way the world has, fate, luck and chance intervened.

Her closest school friend was a girl called Mollie. June and the students had the most to say on her, because Esther talked about her friend on several occasions. Blonde haired, gentle, intelligent, principled and charming, Mollie sounded like a perfect companion through the teenage years. And it was Mollie, and what happened to her, which left Dan with a new understanding.

Esther's alma mater was a castle of a place, with a reputation for sending students to a career on the stage. She was remembered as someone who delighted in performance; an impressive actor, perhaps good enough to become a professional. But before that familiar dream could become reality, a different stage beckoned.

The school was set in the idyllic countryside of Herefordshire. But the never dormant beast of development would sometimes visit even that fair county. A new road was planned, a dual carriageway designed to beckon investment to a nascent science and business park.

The route would cut through classical hills and aged woodland only a mile or so from the school. The plod of the planning process was negotiated and building work began just a week after Esther turned eighteen. Protesters converged, peace camps were set up and the newly found adult decided to mark her majority by joining the demonstration. Mollie, a couple of months older, followed.

Protesters laid in the way of bulldozers and chained their bodies to trees. There were scuffles with the police, abuse hurled at contractors, chases though the woods, and all in the sunshine of the English springtime.

On the scale of these things, it was a minor battle with an inevitable outcome. A week of skirmishes passed, the demonstration waned and the road was built. But it was there, another anonymous interviewee told them, that Esther developed her taste for protest; the theme which would come to define her life.

'She was hyper about it, absolutely buzzing,' the woman said. 'She asked everyone what demos they'd been on, for tips about how to stop the bulldozers, where the next protest was. She just couldn't get enough.'

★★★

Brighton was their next destination. It wasn't such a difficult journey, in part due to the failure of Esther's efforts.

Perhaps it was the similarity to her first protest that drew the young woman to the edge of the South Downs, where another new road was planned.

Summertime was all around, the fields a pallet of wild flowers, the distant sea coloured that sparkling blue it boasts only in the happiest of seasons. On a hilltop, beside the remains of a small wood, Dan and Nigel found a ramshackle camp. Where once its views were of unspoiled hills, now it was within a few hundred metres of an incessantly roaring road.

A couple of banners were strung between the trees, sadly forlorn in their messages. "*Done, but not forgotten*" one read, "*Look what you've lost*", the other. But if the drivers who passed took any heed of the plea there was no sign. The traffic rushed ever onwards.

The natives were friendly enough, five of them, staying for the summer. No longer to try to stop the development, but instead to goad a few consciences.

'We reckon you press people did us proud here,' a thirty-something, shaven headed man who called himself Jimbob told them. 'You're welcome to share a cup of tea with us.' And that, despite Dan's askance look at the battered mug, they did.

The group remembered Esther and Mollie. The pair were still close, inseparable the word that was again used. 'Esther was the boss, though,' Jimbob said. 'She was like an older sister to Mollie.'

The demonstrators had heard about the protests in Plymouth and of Esther becoming a fugitive. 'Not much we can tell you,' Jimbob said, apologetically. 'Secrecy of the sect and all that.'

'I understand,' Dan replied. 'But if I don't get to hear a little about her...'

'What?'

'Oh, nothing.'

'Go on – what?'

'Look, I don't want it to feel like I'm putting pressure on you,' said the man who did, 'It's just without a story about Esther, all I'll be broadcasting is an item on the developers at Resurgam. It'll be like an advert for them.'

The group looked to each other. There were a couple of shrugs.

'Well, if you can't help,' Dan said, turning away with no intention of leaving.

'Suppose it can't do any harm if we just tell you a bit,' Jimbob said. 'Tessie knew her best, didn't you?'

'Pretty well,' an older woman with long hair and a leather jacket replied. 'She was a good tunneller, really got stuck in. Nice kid too. Said she felt at home with us, always chatting and smiling. Until the pigs moved in.'

The camp was well-established, a hundred or so protesters. One day, just before dawn contractors came to begin the building work. They were escorted by police in full riot gear, creeping through the fields and woods. The great machines which would strip, chop and cut anything nature had the cheek to place in their way were poised and ready to follow.

'We was infiltrated,' Jimbob said bitterly. 'They picked the morning after a little party we had. They knew. They was on us before we had a chance.'

None of the protesters made it to the subterranean fortress. A handful managed to chain themselves to trees, but that was it.

Esther was young and quick and had almost reached an old oak when a policeman grabbed her.

'She tried to fight him off,' Tessie said, proudly. 'Put up a hell of a show, she did. But some other cops got her too and that was it.'

'She really fought them hard?' Dan asked.

'Like a demon. Gave one of the cops a lovely black eye. Got some fire in her belly when she needs it, that one. I wouldn't wanna cross her.'

★★★

That afternoon, in a very passable hotel near to Brighton's marathon promenade, Dan made a series of phone calls. In the London campaign against bankers' bonuses there was no official record of Esther.

The protesters were well-prepared. They wore hoodies, scarves, shades and baseball caps for disguise and few were arrested. A call to Dan's best source of information, petulantly though he received the request, revealed that Esther was suspected of involvement.

A small gang had split from the main body of demonstrators, dodged through a maze of side streets and made it to the stone-clad headquarters of one of the capitalists-in-chief. They daubed the edifice with a new style of paintwork of which Jackson Pollock would have been proud.

A couple of witnesses spoke of a noticeably young woman leading the gang. Her hoodie had come off in a struggle with a security guard and the description was suggestive of Esther.

CCTV footage agreed, although with a distant, indistinct image. It also showed the gang repeatedly turning to the woman for instructions. The final pictures were of her blowing a whistle and the group dispersing instantly, all heading in different directions. They were followed by a squad of police officers, who the CCTV showed suddenly tripping and sprawling to the ground for no apparent reason.

'Fishing line,' Adam explained. 'The clever little anarchists had strung a load between some pillars.'

There was a quirk to this demonstration, another suspicion without proof. The protesters seemed to know precisely what security would be in place at the bank and how to circumvent it.

'I can't tell you why with any certainty,' Adam said. 'But an internal investigation at the bank resulted in a security guard being quietly dismissed. He was suspected of having a relationship with a protester who used him to get inside information.'

'Esther?'

'As I said, there's no proof. But work it out for yourself.'

A hunt for Esther was launched, but soon abandoned. The problem, Adam said, was the evidence was too uncertain to make for any charges. Besides, there was a practical issue. Esther had no known address and there was no way of tracing her.

'Interesting,' Dan mused. 'She's learning. And she's growing more confident, or cunning – or maybe both.'

★★★

With Lizzie for an editor, the idea of a blank cheque could be discarded to the extremes of fantasy. Dan's suggestion of an extra week on the road, to visit Inverness, Newcastle and Coventry, places which also bore suggestions of Esther's work, was summarily vetoed.

'One week, no longer, bring me a brilliant report,' was the reply.

So next they headed for Swansea. In truth, a week away was sufficient for both, homely sorts that they were.

'I miss James and Andrew,' Nigel said one evening, over a beer.

'I miss Rutherford,' Dan added.

'And Claire?'

'That goes without saying,' agreed the man who hadn't said.

Swansea's attraction to the protesting tendency was a new marina. It would, conservationists claimed, cause all manner of irreparable damage to a precious estuary. And here came an event of great significance; both for Esther's life and perhaps her vendetta against Resurgam.

The maritime development presented a challenge, it being problematic to chain oneself to water. So the demonstrators gathered in hired, coerced and pilfered boats. The fleet was sufficiently unseaworthy to be more of a danger to themselves than anyone else, although they did succeed in briefly delaying work.

Dan and Nigel found a couple of the group still living on a houseboat, she being pregnant and they having developed an attachment to the area. Both were in no doubt that in this protest Esther was taking the lead.

'It was her idea to get the boats in,' Olly, a young man with bleached blonde hair said.

He was sitting next to K, as she introduced herself. She was a little older, both ears and half her nose perforated with piercings.

'Cool kid, Esther,' K agreed, hands protectively across her belly. 'When the media turned up she waited for a wash from a security boat and capsized one of ours. The pictures were great, we really hammed it up, flailing around and screaming. It made them look like bullies.'

'What was she like when she was here?' Dan asked.

'Real intense, even scary like,' Olly replied. 'Totally focused on trying to stop them buggering up the river.'

Dan was about to leave, when a final question occurred to him. 'She was very young. Why did people follow her?'

It was a few seconds before he got an answer. K and Olly both chewed at the air, then she said, 'Dunno. We just did. There was something about her. Some sort of… certainty. She made you believe.'

It was only at the end of the demonstration, when the protesters had been dragged from the water, that the dreadful realisation came. One was missing.

A young woman had fallen from a boat, perhaps hit her head, and been under water for several minutes. A rescue operation was launched and she was found. The efforts to save her were successful, up to a point.

The deprivation of oxygen left her in a coma, which was later diagnosed as a persistent vegetative state. She was in hospital in London receiving the best care available, but the outlook was bleak.

Quickly, Dan sped through his pages of notes, looking for confirmation of that which he already knew. And there, on a faded old cutting, he found it.

The young woman's name was Margaret Hollis, commonly known as Mollie.

★★★

On the way back to Devon, Dan called one of the barroom bores from the Red Roe. According to June, Esther had once mentioned a childhood memory being part of her obsession with Resurgam. The connections were snapping together in Dan's mind. The treasured old friend of intuition was at work.

Yes, he'd be returning to Longstaff soon, he assured the man. And yes, they would share another drink or two. But first, a little information...

Now Dan came to mention it, yes, Esther and her parents did go on an annual summer holiday. And yes, Devon was the destination. When pressed, the barroom crew agreed it was somewhere in the countryside near Plymouth.

A woman was called into the conversation, a lady named Jan. She used to clean for the family when Esther was much younger. Yes, she did remember the summer fortnight to the coast as she kept an eye on the house while they were away. And yes, now it was mentioned, there was something about it which had always stuck in her mind.

Esther had once drawn a series of pictures on her return from one of the breaks. The first showed a young girl at home, on her own, looking out through the window of a large house. Around the walls she'd drawn railings. There were tears on her cheeks.

In the next, a woman and man were on either side of the girl. They were walking across a beach, all smiling broadly. Behind was a blue sea, crested with rolling waves.

Picture three had the trio sitting at a table, eating together, all still smiling. The man was tucking into a piece of toast, the woman drinking from a cup, the girl sipping at something ginger and fizzy.

In the fourth picture the family was making sandcastles. Rock pools covered the beach and a brilliant sun shone in the sky.

The last picture was similar to the first, the girl back at home, alone once more. The sky around the house was filled with clouds.

Did Jan remember the young Esther talking about beaches, all those years ago, Dan asked? Of course beaches featured, she recalled. They would, wouldn't they? Every kid loved a beach.

Was there anything about Plymouth? Perhaps a memory of a beach there?

There was a pause before the reply came. Jan couldn't be entirely sure, but yes, that did seem to ring a vague and dusty bell.

★★★

Esther lived in the shadows, eschewing mainstream society and the media. There were no interviews with her, and only one example of her speaking out that Dan had been able to find. It was a grainy video, taken by an undercover journalist who was reporting on a protest camp at Hinkley Point Nuclear Power Station.

She was surrounded by countless people as she talked about the importance of their movement. It provided a strong insight into the motivation of the woman, and why people followed her.

"For those who say we haven't achieved anything, look at our history", Esther orated, in a voice surprisingly loud and carrying easily above the mass of people. "In the 1980s, we greened even Margaret Thatcher! We saved the ozone layer. We've made people across the world aware of the damage they're doing to the planet and forced countless governments to listen to our demands. We've ended the horrors of nuclear power in Germany, we can do it here in Britain."

There was spontaneous applause, the crowd clearly entranced with the words of this young woman as she rallied them together.

"We've become mainstream politics, forced every party to think about the environment. But the pace of change is still too slow. Together we can continue to advance and save this wonderful earth for future generations, instead of the selfishness of using it and abusing it just for ourselves."

And now her voice fell, grew deeper and more emotional, a change of pace and tone.

"We've made such sacrifices. We've lost people along the way. Someone I loved lies in a hospital bed because of her commitment to our cause. But we will never be bowed, never give up, because our promise to future generations is resolute. We know our mission is the most important there is on this beautiful planet."

★★★

The last page of Dan's notes contained material which didn't make it into the profile, but which he kept for interest. Attached was a tatty cutting from one of the national papers.

The Militant Greens, the story was headlined. It was about the disillusionment of those who had demonstrated on environmental issues. The item listed a top ten of major developments, all of which had proceeded as planned, despite protesters' attempts at disruption.

"This lack of success has led to a hardening of attitude in some quarters," the story continued. "A minority are now considering violent protest as the only way to hamper major building projects. They argue their actions would be justified, as nothing less than the future of the planet is at stake"

There were a couple of quotes from unnamed sources to that effect. But it was the conclusion of the article which Dan highlighted.

"We have learned that two environmental activists – a man and a woman - have been arrested and questioned by anti-terrorist police. It's believed they were researching methods of making explosives using readily available materials. No charges were brought, but police sources have expressed concern, saying the development is a worrying indication of the ever more extreme views of some in the green movement."

The pair were not named. But the paper did detail the well-known environmental protests of which they had been a part.

Dan ticked off each. The list matched those where Esther had played an increasingly prominent role.

He sat back, breathed out hard and scribbled some words to summarise his thoughts.

Tommy lonely - used by Esther for inside info on Resurgam – like security guard in London?

Unhappy childhood - Mollie, the sister she never had, grievously injured in a demo.

Esther's only good childhood memories - beach where Resurgam now stands.

Alice very like Mollie? That why Esther so fond of her? Death of Alice means Esther absolutely set on destruction of Resurgam – revenge for both Mollie and Alice?

★★★

Nigel knocked on the window of the Satellite Truck. The time was twenty to twelve. A line of security men was assembling outside Resurgam.

Dan stepped down onto the tarmac, flinching at the bitter embrace of the pitiless cold.

The press pack was gathering around the doors. Nigel had already reserved his space with the traditional cameraman's marker of an emphatically planted tripod.

Dan had just begun walking over to join him when the compound was rocked by the blast of an explosion.

THE BATTLE OF RESURGAM FIVE – ALICE

The snow changed colour that January day.

Collapsed amongst the pasture of white was the black uniform of a young policeman. PC Rogers was still conscious, despite the dreadful wound. He was hunched in a ball, fearful fingers probing a shattered socket and shredded remains where once an eye had been. He was a child again; helpless, crying, screaming and sobbing, 'Kathy, please. Kathy help me.'

Following the attack came a stillness. The Ecowarriors looked on and to each other, one or two with perhaps an edge of remorse, but most expressionless. The students and rest of the original protest just gaped.

It was June who broke the incantation of horror, her quiet strength taking control. She demanded a mobile phone from Seb and called 999 as she ran over to the stricken man.

Alice and Esme followed, compassion conquering their revulsion. Silently they moved, for there was nothing to say, nothing that could be said.

Mac and Seb remained in the safety of the group. Young men rendered lost by the brutality of life.

Moving fast across the snowy tarmac, June reached PC Steve. He flinched away, tried to hide, protect himself from another attack. But he found instead humanity and empathy, gentle hands reaching for his own.

June took off her scarf and hat and laid them under Steve's head. Drips of blood seeped onto the rainbow colours, spreading like blots of red ink. The man was whimpering, a strange, inhuman sound.

Maggie pulled his coat tighter, a pathetic defence against the unvanquishable cold and pervasive fear. She began whispering to him, soothing words that could never mean a thing; that everything would be all right, the ambulance would soon be here, that he'd be better in a few days. And June, so tender, even with shaking hands cradling Steve's head.

Esme and Alice just stood, cuddled together, unable to move, unable to help, unable to do anything except share the shock of the moment. The pair were as pallid as the surrounding snow.

This protest, this righteous gesture, had turned from frivolity to barbarity; the land of childhood forever lost. No one, no matter what their radicalism, their hatred, nor how embittered, could look at the vile offence of the incision into a young man's face.

Inside the group of protesters, Seb turned away and spat bile. Mac muttered, 'No, no, no,' to himself, fists clenched hard in those deep leather pockets. In the distance, the siren of an ambulance wailed.

And from the Resurgam compound Rees and Tommy came running, picking a way through the thinnest patches of the snow. Rees was in the lead, stronger, fitter and faster. He reached the crumpled police officer and shoved June, sending her sprawling across the pavement into a bank of icy slush.

Maggie tried to remonstrate, to intervene, but was also pushed ruthlessly away, stumbling to her knees beside June.

'You fucker!' came a shout. Mac was sprinting, full tilt, filled with the irresistible momentum of uncontrollable anger, careering towards the security man; a teenage rebel who could no longer hide his heart.

He launched himself into an arc of flight and the pair went spinning, tumbling into the snow, Mac's fists a blur of beating fury. Rees twisted, kicking out, trying to free himself, but not a chance, not from the power of this red spirit released.

A group of the Ecowarriors began running towards the melee. A police car span around the corner, followed by another. Cops jumped out, took in the scene in an instant and pitched into the fight, trying to push through the crowd and pull the pair apart, fending off flailing arms and legs.

The phoney war was over. The Battle of Resurgam had begun.

★★★

All around, the fires of conflict spread. A pack of cops forced their way through the melee to where PC Steve was lying, the paramedics following. They knelt in the slush beside the injured officer and began a quick and expert examination, a couple of officers standing guard. Experienced though they may be in the insanity of the world, neither could look at the treatment being given to their young colleague.

Two more cops forced Rees and Mac apart. Rees was protesting, Mac just looked stunned, perhaps with what he'd witnessed, maybe with himself. His fists were raw, bleeding with the force of his attack.

Seb was alongside Alice, holding her, pulling her into him as if trying to cocoon her, protect her from any more of the torment this savage new world could inflict. Maggie was picking June up from the slush, fussing gently. 'I'd better get you to a doctor, given… '

'I'm fine, I'm all right, I'm staying.' June shook off the attention, but her voice was thin. Her greying hair was damp with dirty melt water and her coat streaked with icy grime.

In the gutter lay a rough snowball, one side smeared with blood, the jagged edge of a piece of flint protruding.

'Who did this?' a sergeant demanded, voice filled with the reckoning of the law but more besides; an unmistakeable blade of emotion.

It was Richard Wagstaff, only the turning of a calendar away from the end of his service, but tall, lean and fit, with a kind face. Good natured enough, even after all these long days of policing to be nicknamed The Wag, today humour was an alien land. For this was the man who gave PC Steve the beat of Resurgam.

And now trying not to let the toxins of the thought spread. That this would never have happened if… that maybe it was too much to ask of a probationer…

The Ecowarriors stood in their pack, a block of sullen defiance. Hands in pockets, faces unyielding.

'Who – did – this?'

The Wag's words were quieter now, but ridden with infinite menace. There was going to be an answer to the question.

Yet nothing came in reply. Traffic was backing up the road, a long tail of a jam. The paramedics were shifting PC Steve onto a stretcher. The young officer was crying.

And now, at last, a voice replied. 'It's always us, eh? Whenever anything happens, it's straight to us. Why not...'

'We're not having a debate,' Wagstaff cut in. 'It's simple. Tell me who did this - right now.'

'Or what?' Simian grunted.

'Or I'll arrest the bloody lot of you.'

Around the sergeant uniforms were gathering. Each cop, bulky with their stab vests and coats, eyes set on the protesters. Staring at the men and women before them, in their threadbare jackets, jeans and hats. It was primeval now, no longer professional and detached, but two opposing gangs.

'Last chance,' the sergeant said. 'I've got a young lad with a gaping hole in his head where his eye was. You talk now or you do it at the station — but you're going to do it.'

'You reckon?' Esther replied, with the hint of a mocking smile. And that was enough.

Wagstaff grabbed for her, but found his arms caught by Simian. The two strained together in an equilibrium of loathing, the rest of the cops pitched in and the battle began anew.

★★★

Unseen by most in the unfolding melee, something curious happened. Tommy was standing beside the police lines, watching as they waded into the pack of protesters. He looked to Esther, a gaze that felt meaningful, even imploring, and mouthed some words. But she gave him nothing, not even an acknowledgement, a snub as hard as a cigarette crushed under the heel of a boot.

The opposing battalions were unfairly matched, more than double the number of demonstrators to the forces of the law. But the siren of the ambulance as it took their fellow to hospital was everywhere and plenty enough to even the odds.

Some of the Ecowarriors had already been arrested. They weren't resisting, but weren't cooperating either. They'd slumped onto the icy ground, a few lying in pools of slush, others tucked up on their sides. Policemen and women were trying to shift them, haul them away, but there were too few for the leaden mass of resistance.

Esther was glowing. It was as if she'd absorbed the heat of the battle, savoured its fiery sustenance. Diminutive by comparison with most, she was still dominant. With fast eyes and quicksilver thoughts, Esther was taking in all around her.

She slipped to the back of the group, whispering to anyone she passed. In turn they spoke to their neighbours who spread on the words.

On the front line Simian was still struggling with the sergeant, locked together in a wrestling dance, other cops trying to grab and hold him. But he was strong, resisting hard, continually shifting and slapping away their hands, kicking out with heavy, swinging boots.

Amongst the demonstrators the whisper was spreading. From the back Esther was watching, always calculating. Only when she was sure everyone had understood did she shout, 'Now!'

Each of the rag tag band began running. In all directions they headed, a human explosion. Some made for the small fleet of ramshackle coaches which had brought them here, some for Resurgam, others along the road.

A group of women linked arms and lay down in the oiled mire of the street. More spread themselves across the access road.

Protesters were emerging from the coaches, armed anew. Glass phials flew through the snowfall and the foul stench of stink bombs curdled the winter air. Smoke canisters were being hurled too, trails of white and grey fattening and lingering. Cops were everywhere, trying to chase down the haze of movement, but they were outnumbered and outmanoeuvred.

Some of the Ecowarriors had made it to Resurgam. A couple of men jumped into the bucket of a digger and were hurling grit and snow at police officers. A group of women were handcuffing themselves to the steel skeleton of the building.

More police cars were converging, the air punctured with the screams of their sirens. But otherwise the sound of the battle was curiously subdued. There was the occasional shout or yell, but most of the noise was the panting of men and women as they ran and dodged, feinted and grappled.

June sat on a bench, a hand on her chest, Maggie holding a coat around her. Mac had been escorted to a police van to calm down. He walked with a curious mix of pride and self-consciousness. Rees was still remonstrating angrily with an officer. 'Let me go, I'm on your fucking side,' he kept saying, gesturing wildly, as if trying to rouse an invisible orchestra.

Esme and Alice had been standing, watching the battle. A woman ran past and went to lay down on the access road, but was grabbed by a policeman and hauled away.

More snow was falling, light and drifting, gentle flakes of white. Esme flicked some from her hair and found a decision. She began walking towards the line of protesters in the road, lay down and linked arms, became absorbed in the mass. Alice watched, blue eyes shining with admiration. She followed, but was intercepted by a policewoman.

A shout rose from across the street. Esther had been standing on a bench, like a general of olden days commanding an army. She jumped down, careered into the officer's back, knocking her over, grabbed Alice's hand and pulled her away towards Resurgam.

★★★

More police poured into the area. In lines they formed and advanced, hunting in packs, surrounding and dealing with each pocket of resistance.

Simian took four cops to subdue him, one for each muscular limb. 'Bastards,' he roared, time and again. 'We'll have the fucking thing down one way or another!'

The police helicopter was hovering above, filling the compound with a buffeting, roaring downdraft. Snow sped around, spinning whirlwinds in the air.

Cops were pulling at the line of women who were blocking the road. Slowly, muscle by sinew, the chain gave. One after another they were hauled up and away. Esme was the first to be arrested. She looked abashed, but managed a wan smile at the cheer from the rest of the protesters.

Esther was still running, towards Resurgam, pulling Alice with her, but found the gates shut and chained. She stopped, hesitated, checked back on the battle. Most of the demonstrators had been arrested, just a few still resisting.

'We should stop,' Alice panted.

'Never!'

Esther darted for a van parked by the gates, clambered up onto its bonnet and then roof, balancing carefully on the slippery, icy surface.

'Come on!'

Alice took the proffered hand and also climbed up. Esther was laughing, her face flushed with a rush of delight, her arms in the air. She was the master of this stage, the creator of a storm, intoxicated by her power.

The police who had ended the protest in the road were brushing themselves down, ready for the next stage of the campaign. At a word from one they began advancing on the van.

Esther grabbed Alice's hand. 'Stay with me.'

'Shouldn't we come down?'

'Never.'

'But...'

'Never!' Esther yelled. 'How far did your little camp here get you? And now... we'll be all over the TV. And more like us will come.'

'But – Steve. Poor Steve...'

Seb had seen what was happening, was running over, shouting, 'Alice, Alice!' Fear filled his every movement. He was stopped, held back, flailed and struggled, reached out desperately for Alice, but could make no progress through the gathering cordon.

A ring of police officers surrounded the van. 'Come down,' one said. But Esther just smiled and clutched tighter at Alice's hand.

From along the road a group of demonstrators began running for Resurgam, sprinting hard. They dodged around a police car, as practiced as rugby players, headed straight for the gates.

The engine of a police van started up and it accelerated towards the compound, white headlights bouncing in the gloom.

Seb had stopped struggling, was still now, just watching. It was as if he'd been petrified by a sense of what would happen next.

Below Esther and Alice, a policeman found a foothold on a tyre. He climbed onto the bonnet, advancing carefully. Esther edged backwards, pulling Alice with her.

'That's enough messing about,' the officer said. 'I want you both down.'

'Where's your manners?' Esther mocked. 'We haven't even been introduced.'

'Look you…'

'No names, no coming down.'

'I'm PC Warr,' he said, heavily.

'Nice name for a keeper of the peace. But you forgot the magic word.'

The policeman breathed out heavily. 'Come down… please.'

'Shan't!' Esther called, and kicked some snow onto the watching ring of cops.

The police van was close, speeding towards Resurgam, engine roaring. PC Warr took advantage of the distraction and reached for Esther's leg. But she dodged, stepped aside and slipped on the frozen roof. She flung out a panicked hand, found Alice's jacket and grabbed at it.

The support steadied Esther, but the sudden movement knocked Alice off balance. She teetered for a second, arms grasping at the icy air, then fell backwards, right into the path of the van.

Brakes screeched and jarred. Alice screamed. The driver pumped at the pedal, trying desperately to stop. But the tarmac was far too slippery, the van moving too fast for there to be any hope. And a little way down the road, a young man's life was forever frozen in that winter moment.

CHAPTER 20

On this December morning, a day dedicated to parading the glory of Resurgam, a hiatus held the compound. It was the canyon between action and understanding, the time taken for synapses to flip and realisation to seep.

An explosion... an explosion...

Then came the shock. Hacks, cameramen and photographers shouting and swearing.

The line of security men holding fast, as the honour of the job demanded. But eyes were darting around, seeking the threat, muscles tensing in readiness.

The protesters, a few open mouthed, others gripping tight to their placards. The multitudes of staff stopping their sweeping, polishing, all awaiting to see what happened next.

Which was nothing. There were no more explosions, no screaming, nothing aside from the usual grumbling traffic backdrop of an urban winter Thursday.

'It came from outside,' one reporter was saying. 'Bloody close.'

'A car backfiring?' another asked, with a marked lack of conviction.

'No chance,' a photographer scoffed. 'It's got to be to do with Resurgam.'

They were all looking over the barrier of The Wall, to the city skyline. And there, perhaps a couple of hundred metres away, a column of dark smoke was rising.

The time was almost ten to noon. Any second now, the doors would slide open and Ellen Dance emerge to make her statement. And then, for the first time, they would be allowed inside to capture the spectacle.

As the marketing people put it; the moment you've been waiting for.

'What do we do?' Nigel whispered to Dan.

'It can't be a coincidence.'

'Well, no. But...'

'What?'

'Can we risk missing the opening?'

Dan swore. From behind the line of security men Jackie Denyer appeared. 'Nothing to worry about,' she soothed, 'Just a gas bottle in one of the local pubs, apparently. Standby please. It's one minute to Ms Dance's statement.'

She beamed out a smile. It was wide and white, as carefree as a mother watching her children playing at the seaside. But this was a master of manipulation, with a thousand expressions ready on demand.

The pack waited, hesitated. The pillar of smoke was growing.

Nigel looked to Dan. 'What're we going to do?'

Dan swore again, but this time with far more élan. Even in the bitter cold, he was sweating.

'Is there time to get the newsroom to send someone else?' Nigel suggested.

'They'll miss all the action if it's something big.'

'And if it's not, we'll miss the shots of Resurgam opening. And it could be your job riding on this.'

'Thirty seconds to Ms Dance,' Denyer called.

Hacks were looking to each other, dilemma in their faces. Police officers were jogging along the street towards the explosion.

Dan studied Denyer. That smile was fixed, immovable. But she was a bluffer. And so was he.

'We're going,' Dan shouted.

'I can assure you it's nothing...'

'We're going anyway. We'll be back later.'

'If you leave, I warn you - we won't be able to let you back in.'

Dan let his eyes hold hers through the icy gloom. Denyer stood stout in a fine black coat, perfectly upright, commanding the situation. The smile never faltered.

But one fingernail, a rosebud of red, was scratching distractedly at the pile of papers in her arm.

Dan grabbed Nigel and they started running.

★★★

No quest of a reporter's research this, it took only an instant to find the source of the explosion. Smoke was still rising, a smear spreading in the misty sky, an accusing finger pointing to the detonation.

Police officers were cordoning off the area, pushing people back. They were working outwards from where an old-fashioned red phone box had stood. One of the few remaining, it had become a fondly admired anachronism in a mobile phone world. But no longer.

The lines of windows had been blown out. Daggers of fragmented glass were strewn on the road. At the rounded top the smart red paint was blackened and charred, the panels which invited people to *phone from here* were warped and melted, like the wax of old candles.

The box was filled with black fumes, some still billowing from the shattered windows. A bitter smell of scorching tainted the winter air.

A family was being ushered away by a policewoman, a young girl crying, holding tight to the hands of her parents. Both looked dazed, disbelieving. By the Homeless Mission, a ragtag line of men had emerged to watch, some holding cups of tea.

'Bloody good call, coming out,' Nigel whispered, without straightening up from the camera.

'Bloody good job,' was Dan's infinitely relieved reply.

The smoke was clearing from the box, pulled free by the freezing, gusting wind. The receiver hung down, its hardy plastic deformed by the force of the blast. The insides of the box were streaked with soot.

A group of onlookers had gathered, all watching in a strange silence. A line of cops began ushering the crowd further back.

'No need to panic,' one was saying, with hollow words. 'It's only a precaution.'

A police car drew up and Adam got out. He studied the remains of the phone box through narrowed eyes and said grimly, 'I think someone's trying to tell us something.'

★★★

People were being moved back and back, further and further. They packed the narrow streets and seeped into the side alleys.

An inspector with a loud hailer was piping the standard messages of such times, and just as unconvincingly as ever. 'There's nothing to see here, nothing to worry about.'

A constable tried to shepherd Dan and Nigel away, but Adam stopped him. 'I need a word,' he said.

The time was five to twelve. Dance had probably just finished her little oration. Resurgam was about to open its doors for the first time.

If they were quick, they could get back and make it inside to film. That was, if they were allowed in.

'I don't have a lot of time,' Dan said, as calmly as the pressure would allow.

'Five minutes,' Adam replied, in that detective's way which made clear dissent was futile.

'I don't have five minutes.'

'This is important.'

'So is keeping my job.'

'And so is attempted murder, and...'

'Dan has got a point,' came an unexpected interruption. The tone was mild, but no less surprising for that. 'He already does far more than he should for you.'

Adam eyed Nigel coolly. It was a curious confrontation; a sharp suit versus a pullover and anorak. 'As we've discussed, I believe,' the cameraman added, with meaning.

'Hey,' Dan interjected. 'What have you two been up to, talking about me?'

'Not now,' Adam said. 'I need five minutes.'

A group of people were trying to get into Resurgam. The security detail turned them back, as effortlessly as a harbour wall repelling waves. The sole photographer who had followed Dan and Nigel to the phone box was also sent away, despite his remonstrations.

Denyer was standing behind the barriers, shaking her head at the man. It didn't take a lip reader to understand the message - *You were warned.*

'Actually, I might just have a minute,' Dan said, brightly.

'For God's sake...' Nigel began.

'That's if you'll help us in return, Adam?'

'Why does there always have to be a price with you?'

'It's the commerce of camaraderie.' Dan nodded towards Resurgam. 'Please?'

'I'll see what I can do.' Adam gestured to the police car. 'Now, let's talk.'

Nigel held out his arm and waved his watch. 'Five minutes only.'

★★★

The car felt stickily warm after the ice bath of outside. The clock on the dashboard said three minutes to noon. Dan sat in the driver's side and pushed the seat back to give himself some room. Nigel was standing by the bonnet, pointedly checking his watch.

Adam passed over a piece of paper. The sheet was A4 sized, a line across the copy showing the original had been folded in half when delivered.

Today, a demonstration.

Tomorrow, people WILL get hurt – unless the opening is cancelled.

'It arrived at Charles Cross this morning,' Adam continued. 'It was too vague for us to do anything, apart from put plenty of cops around. Recognise the writing?'

Dan studied the sheet. 'Esther's?'

'The graphologist's pretty sure.'

'So she is definitely still around here somewhere.'

'I'd say so. Particularly when you consider the peculiarity about the explosion.'

'Which is?'

'Think.'

Dan pointed to the clock. The time was 11.59. 'Thinking takes time.'

'What do explosions normally do?'

'Go bang?'

'Don't be fatuous.'

'It wasn't the smartest question I've ever heard.'

'It had a point.'

Through clenched teeth came Dan's pained reply. 'Then perhaps you should just make it.'

'No one was hurt,' Adam relented. 'No one was even injured. Because no one was anywhere near the phone box at the time.'

'The bomb was deliberately small.'

'Yes. And?'

'Must have been detonated by someone watching the phone box – so they'd know when no one was about.'

'Exactly. A wireless link, we reckon.'

A young boy was studying the police car, running a hand over its bonnet. Adam tried a tolerant smile, but must have been too deeply in detective mode. The lad recoiled, whipped away his hand and ran off.

'Where does all that leave us?' Dan asked.

'Firstly, we need to find out more about Esther and how she was behaving. Particularly in the run-up to the attack on the gatehouse.'

'Ah.'

'*Ah* what?'

The gallop of Dan's mount balked at the size of the next fence. Long experience of Adam management suggested it would be better to take time to prepare the detective for what he was about to hear. But today time was not an ally.

'I… might have a little confession to make.'

'Which is?' Adam asked ominously.

'I could be able to help you with the Esther question.'

'How?'

'Say you won't be cross.'

'Unlikely. What - have - you - done?'

'A little investigating of my own. I kind of – thought I'd check some of the stuff about Esther myself. With the protesters.'

Adam swore, and forcefully. 'How many times have I told you? You're not a cop, however much you might like to think you are. I could arrest you for that.'

'But you won't.'
'You could cause all sorts of problems.'
'Or find some solutions. Look, given what happened with the Battle of Resurgam, who were they more likely to talk to? A cop, or me?'
'This is the last time I'm going to tell you. In future...'
'Guilty and sorry,' Dan interjected, proffering his palms before Adam could waste any more precious time. 'Never again, ever.'
'I've heard that before,' Adam retorted.
'I did find out some very interesting information, if you want to hear it?'
As can often be the way in life, the absence of a reply was answer enough.

★★★

As always it does, no matter how inconvenient, the time moved on. It was 11.59. The inside of the car was starting to steam up, adding to the gloom of the day. Dan wiped a window with a sleeve, found his notes and briefed Adam on what June and the students had said.
'Esther didn't have a lot to do with the other demonstrators. But as to how she was in the days before the lorry attack – they say unusually quiet, even withdrawn. And on one occasion, June says she tried to ask if Esther was ok and got a very nasty reply.'
'Really?' Adam said, slowly.
'June said Esther seemed very tense.'
'Which ties in with the way Tommy was before the attack.'
'Yep,' Dan replied. 'And the protesters say the only other person Esther appeared to bother with was Tommy.'
'So just as we were thinking, there might indeed be some kind of connection between the pair.'
'The same trick as she used in the London protests. But this time, when something goes wrong, it forces Esther to take drastic action.'
'Then if that's the case – what was it that went wrong?'
'Well, it can only be to do with Resurgam.'

Adam slapped his forehead. 'I'm so glad you're here. I'd never have thought of that.'

With supreme self-control, Dan rode the irritating breaker of sarcasm and confined himself to another nod towards the clock. Morning had turned to afternoon.

'Did you get anything from Tommy's phone?' he asked.

'Nothing. The only calls or texts were to Alannah, or a few mates. We've checked them all. No go.'

'So, with Tommy unconscious and Esther AWOL, we can only speculate.'

'Then start speculating,' Adam grunted. 'And make it good.'

Dan's mobile buzzed with a text message. He sneaked a hasty look, expecting the newsroom, but it was El: *I'm taking action. I got me a Cashman plan. It's me reputation, me future, me life. Ring yer old mate later, please, please, please!!!!*

A layer of snow was gathering on the windscreen. The clock clicked on to 12.01. Dan's phone began ringing and wouldn't stop. Lizzie must have heard about the explosion.

'You know what's still bothering me?' Dan said. 'It's what Esther was carrying when she ran from the attack on the gatehouse. The thing she made very sure she didn't leave behind. I reckon if we can work out what that was, it might help sort this case.'

'We've also got to ask the more fundamental question again,' Adam replied. 'Why is Esther still here? Why the hell is she hanging around when she could be long gone?'

'It's part of the plan, isn't it? It has to be. About Resurgam and trying to stop the opening tomorrow. On the subject of which...'

Dan nodded towards the skyscraper, gave Adam a knowing look and received a begrudging nod.

'I'm going to see Dance now. She's been avoiding me all morning, but no longer.'

They got out of the car, just as the clock was showing 12.02. Dan took the tripod from Nigel and the strange trio headed towards Resurgam.

CHAPTER 21

Adam checked his reflection, straightened his tie and carefully assembled his "don't mess with me" face. It was designed for one simple message; whatever the argument, wherever it may be and whoever with, I will prevail. It was hard as the granite of a Dartmoor Tor, the product of a generation of a life of policing.

He set off along the access road and towards the security line with a straight and determined stride, snow billowing in his wake. Dan and Nigel fell into step behind.

Always a thin man, this morning Adam looked gaunt. It might have been the cold light through which he walked, or the momentum of his purpose. But his features were lined with focus and shaded with the stubble that forever accompanied him.

The crowd which had gathered to see the aftermath of the explosion was fraying, patches of people starting to drift away. Adam cut a line through the remains of the throng, men and women instinctively understanding the invisible authority and stepping aside.

Ahead, beyond the security line, the doors of Resurgam were wide open. The elevators began their smooth, insistent journeys up its sides, the outlines of a pack of people within the steel and glass tubes.

With Adam bearing down upon them, the security men packed together, bicep by bicep, ready to meet the challenge. He made for where Denyer was standing, right in the middle of the line.

'I need to see Ms Dance.'

'She's very busy, I'm afraid. If you'd like to leave your name and a contact number...'

Adam's warrant card materialised in front of the woman's eyes. To Denyer's credit, she too had steel. She held her ground, hands grasped around the files she habitually carried.

'Police – investigating terrorism,' Adam spelt out. 'Resurgam - implicated. Get Dance here - now.'

'As I said, if you'd care to…'

'Last chance. Get her now, or you get arrested.'

At the raising of the stakes the security men bunched even closer around Denyer, like forwards readying for a scrum. And it was a formidable pack.

Sensing the support, Denyer smiled. 'Then you'll have to arrest all of us.'

And now Adam matched the smile, and raised it. He beckoned to a police van which was parked just along the road. 'There's plenty of room in the cells. And I'm sure a criminal record will do you all good when this place is closed down and you're looking for work.'

A couple of the men shuffled their feet. Eye by eye, they looked to Denyer. She stared at Adam and he stared right back, entirely impassive, utterly expressionless.

Don't mess with me.

'You'd better come through,' she huffed, finally.

Dan and Nigel made to follow, but Denyer said, 'Not them. They were warned.'

'They're witnesses. They're coming.'

The detective didn't even break stride. Dan kept quietly to the magnificent slipstream and walked on. Loud was sitting in the doorway of the Satellite Truck, a phone wedged under his chin, pointedly holding out a palm. As they passed, Nigel threw over the memory card holding the pictures of the aftermath of the explosion for Loud to send to the newsroom.

They reached the doors, fully open for the first time, the inside of the skyscraper looking like a great modern cathedral of commerce. All three, as preoccupied as they may be, nonetheless couldn't help but stare.

'Wait here,' Denyer said brusquely and bustled into the mall.

Dan went to step inside, but Adam stopped him. 'A mutual friend,' he said, passing over a piece of paper upon which was written a name and address.

Nigel set up the tripod and began to film their first shots of the inside of Resurgam. With a couple of the pans back and forth to try to capture the extent of the cavernous space, all shining, everything new, he let out a whistle of awe.

Dan turned his phone back on and apologised to Lizzie for being unable to speak earlier. Sometimes, sorry was the only word. But sugared with the explanation they had been busy securing the pictures of the chaos outside, it worked. Dan also texted El, typing simply *Tonight we find him.*

One last tilt down of the camera, slowly from the distant reaches of the upper levels to the marbled floor, and they walked into the building.

★★★

For all the trouble Resurgam had caused, the deaths and the injuries, Dan had set himself determined not to be impressed. A building was just a building, however grand. But indifference wasn't an option. He found his eyes floating with the sights that surrounded them.

'Where the hell do we start?' Nigel said. 'I could spend all day filming here.'

Facing them was a vast piazza. Around its sides was the monoculture of the well-known stores common to every high street. Their glass frontages were so new, so polished as to make the sight dazzling.

The doors were open, staff standing smart. All were impeccably dressed, many a uniform sufficiently new as to still bear creases. They were waving, smiling, beckoning, in a way so atypical of the British definition of service that it could surely only last a day or two.

Christmas decorations accompanied each display, but not the familiar cheap and distasteful mass. No plastic reindeers here, instead there was holly and mistletoe. Even the gold and silver baubles were expensive and elegant.

Curving lines of wrought iron street lamps wound their way through the level, guiding shoppers to the different zones. Their contours were dusted with a suggestion of snow. From each hung baskets of flowers, sprays of colour sprouting and tumbling, the freshness of their scents filling the mountain of air.

At the centre of the floor was a series of high marbled steps leading up to a fountain. Its waters giggled and gushed, splitting the light and casting a mirage of rainbows. The first few layers of stone were bare apart from wooden slats, a welcome place for weary shoppers to rest. The higher levels were filled with ferns and other plants, weeping their way downwards.

To either side of the fountain a couple of escalators, humming smoothly with hidden power, led the way to the next floor. Beyond that level rose two more, all dedicated to shopping, above them an artwork of a ceiling. It was patterned with frescoes, ships and sailors, hints of the seafaring history of the city where this monolith had grown. Great lights hung down, wrought with shining brass.

Even the electronic signboards managed not to be bright and brash, but subtle in their changing displays. *Welcome to the High Street*, they were informed. For the Fashion Market, boutiques, fine foods of the world, sports and leisure, electronics and computing, the awed onlooker should travel ever upwards.

The time on the board flicked and changed, crystals shifting to 12.15.

'Just a little more here,' Dan told Nigel. 'Then on we go.'

★★★

Adam had been waiting only a couple of minutes when Flood arrived. As if the might of the forces behind Resurgam had reconsidered their strategy, the Deputy Chief Constable was escorted into the mall by two security men. Both wore smiles that looked as uncomfortable as new shoes.

'You can leave us now,' Flood told them, taking off his coat and shaking free a layer of snow. Some settled onto the marble of the floor. One of the men produced a horrified look, which Flood entirely ignored.

'You *will* leave us now,' he ordered, and the men slipped back out of the doors.

'How's Dance behaving?' Flood asked Adam.

'Evasively.'

'I'm not surprised. If this doesn't go smoothly she can kiss goodbye to any hopes of re-election.'

Footsteps on the hard stone of the floor announced the return of Denyer. 'Ms Dance will see you now.'

★★★

Level Two was entitled the *Backstreet Boutiques*. Here the shops were smaller, independent outlets boasting all the outfits a human could want for every kind of weather and any season. It was less industrial than below, some of the space given over to coffee lounges and café bars.

The snow had stopped, the weather even offering a hint of blue in the southern sky. Dan grabbed a pair of take away coffees, and with a humanitarian afterthought for a barely human creature, one for Loud.

Nigel picked up a quick few shots, colourful details of the rows of spring dresses in one ladies' outlet and the spangles of the Christmas numbers. For their efforts, each was rewarded with a discount voucher. 'For the lady in your life,' the smiling assistant said.

'How is Claire, by the way?' Nigel asked, as they made for the escalator and the next floor.

'Fine.'

'What's she up to today?'

'Having a clear out, I think. There were bits of clothes and suitcases everywhere when I left.'

Nigel nodded thoughtfully, but didn't reply.

The third floor was a mass of televisions, computers, mobile phones and the latest in games. Screens filled the shop windows, moving fast with the action of pop videos and trailers for films.

The ambience had changed again, the lighting harsher, the electronic signs more brash. The time had moved on to 12.25.

'I reckon we've got enough commerce,' Dan said. 'All we need now are the lifts and the Sky Garden.'

★★★

The two police officers were led through a concealed door to a flight of stairs. Here the glitz of the public face of Resurgam had fled. It was cold concrete, hollowness and echoes, smelt a little of damp, could have been part of a multi storey car park. Up to the fourth floor they walked and emerged into a level which was deserted.

'Wait here please,' Denyer said and disappeared through another door.

Adam walked over to a balcony. Below, journalists and paparazzi rushed through the brightness of the lights, interviewing shop managers, photographing the spectacle. But here it was half lit and abandoned, no Christmas decorations, no plants, no flashing signs, the shop fronts dark and empty.

'Maybe Resurgam isn't doing quite as well as they'd like us to believe,' he said.

The far door opened and Dance emerged. Her walk, as ever, was authoritative, but perhaps a little slower, a hint more trepid than usual. Her hair was again pinned up, but this time tighter, with more severity. She shook hands, favoured the men with that politician's smile and asked, 'How can I help you?'

'We want you to consider putting off the official opening,' Flood replied, with his usual directness.

Dance took the blow without flinching, a true game player. But beside her, Denyer uttered a little gasp. Sacrilege had been spoken in the temple.

'On what grounds?' the President of all she surveyed asked.

'The most important grounds – public safety.'

'We have received a series of credible threats against Resurgam that leads us to believe it may be subject to an attack tomorrow,'

Adam explained. 'What happened earlier indicates whoever is behind this is serious and has access to explosives.'

Dance shifted her stance to favour Adam. 'My security people say that explosion was tiny. It might have been some ridiculous prank.'

'That's not my view.'

'And your evidence?' Denyer asked, sharply.

'We believe it was remotely detonated, by someone wanting to send a message. Plus there have been other threats.'

'Like what?' said Dance.

'I can't divulge...' Adam began, in his traditional detective's way, but was interrupted by Flood.

'We've been sent plans of the foundations of this place. Documents that were kept secret for security reasons. Plus, if you hadn't noticed, a man was nearly killed here on Tuesday night.'

'And you think all these events are connected?'

'It'd be a hell of a coincidence if they weren't.'

'But still possible,' Denyer interjected.

'Let me put this as straightforwardly as I possibly can,' Flood intoned. 'Greater Wessex Police are formally advising you to put off the opening of Resurgam. Go ahead and you risk the safety of large numbers of people.'

Dance put a hand on her chin and stared up at the ceiling, to a serpent coiling its way around a sailing ship. 'Give me a moment,' she said and paced away.

***

An attendant welcomed Dan and Nigel to the lift. He wore a uniform so laden with buttons, bullion and braid that it would shame the doorman of one of London's finest hotels. 'Hi guys, I'm Jezzy,' came the portly young man's chirpy greeting, in a horribly faux American accent. 'Prepare for the ride of your life!'

'I do hope that's not the case,' Dan countered, dimming the man's smile not one Watt.

Nigel set up the tripod so the camera was looking out at the harbour. 'I'm rolling.'

'Hold onto your eyeballs!' Jezzy cried, and with the finest of theatrical flourishes pressed an ornate button.

The force of the acceleration was like a mighty invisible hand pushing down on the tops of their heads, trying to squeeze their bodies through the floor. With a low whine the lift set off up the side of Resurgam, moving at a speed that left each passing level a whispering blur. Before them opened up a view of the waterfront and the Barbican.

Two other lifts zipped past on their downward path, so fast it was quicker than a blink. Within seconds, the ride was over.

'Behold, the wonder of the Sky Garden!' Jezzy cried, as the doors slid open.

Slowly, dazedly, still adjusting to the near instantaneous transportation so far into the atmosphere, they stepped out.

★★★

'Look around you,' Dance said in an unusually quiet voice as she returned to the waiting policemen. 'Just look - please.'

There was something in her tone, and they did as bid; at the darkness of the surrounds of vacant shops, then the bright lights below.

'We've achieved so much. All the cynics, all the critics said it couldn't be done. But we raised the investment, we fought to make sure it happened and we did it.'

Dance's hands had bunched into fists. She took a couple of steps towards a shop front. A small poster on the door read "To Let. Don't Miss Out, Be Part of the Dream!"

'Are you locals?' Dance asked.

'Look...' Flood began, but she interrupted.

'Just bear with me. For what you're asking I deserve to be heard.'

'I grew up in Cornwall - Launceston,' Flood conceded.

'I was born and raised in Plymouth,' Adam added.

'So, we're fellows? And you love Devon and Cornwall, like me?'

Both men nodded, although Flood did so begrudgingly.

'Let me be honest with you, then' Dance continued. 'We haven't got quite as many companies here as I'd hoped. Not sold quite enough of the flats, not let all the office space. There are plenty more people interested, but they're waiting. They want to see how Resurgam goes.'

She tapped a finger on the *To Let* sign. 'Resurgam has to be a success. A hundred per cent, unequivocal, undisputed success. If that happens, this wonderful beacon of investment is lit and we thrive. But if not...'

From below came the sound of a string quartet tuning up, the notes slow and melancholy, but rising easily to this level.

Dance turned the sole of her boot on the stone of the floor and adjusted one of the lapels of that fine black coat. Now she spoke again, but this time with the timbre of finality.

'So, you see what would happen if the opening was put off? Because of a terrorist threat? That's what you're asking me.'

Denyer walked over to stand beside her boss. Together, the two women looked to the pair of police officers. Below, the music was slowing, the notes falling, reaching a nadir of sadness.

Flood cleared his throat. 'I understand, Ms Dance. And I'm sorry. But we're talking about a matter of public safety, so my advice to you must remain the same.'

★★★

It was akin to walking in a wooded sky. Around them was a dizzying mix of trees, plants, clouds and air.

To the distant south lay an expanse of mercury sea. Westwards was Cornwall, farewell county of England, a patchwork of fields and nestling villages. To the north the dark lines of the lurking, brooding Dartmoor. And to the east, the run of rugged coast that gave way to the woodlands and easy Devon countryside of the South Hams.

The whole of the city was set out like a map, the angles of the hills, the glass towers of the university, the dockyard, the lattice of roads and the countless houses. Dan raised a finger and picked out

Charles Cross Police Station, his flat and Hartley Park behind it, then the *Wessex Tonight* studios.

The Sky Garden was laced with paths, wandering a route through the foliage. For such a height it was curiously calm. A display board boasted of some clever quirk of the design which baffled the attack of the wind and made it possible for a range of plants to survive.

Even on a grey winter's day the Garden felt vibrant with colour. Amidst the greenery heaters protruded, panels of fire to shift the season to a perpetual spring, coddle the plants and welcome the people who came to visit.

The ferns were damp with the melt of the earlier snow. Nigel lowered the camera and filmed a close up of a droplet hanging on a leaf, a shot full of detail and beauty, the like of which make the medium of television.

No horticulturalist Dan, the extent of his interest in the shared garden at Hartley Avenue was to sit in it with Rutherford. But here, for once, he could understand the draw of the green dream.

There were so many colours, a waterfall of coned red flowers cascading from a small hillock of rocks, sprays of tiny stars of blue. Flecks of yellow, twinings of white, crescents of violet, pokers of orange. And all against a background of every green the eye can comprehend.

The smells of the display drifted around them, some subtle, just a tint to the freshness of the air, others sweet and exotic. They were an instant transportation across the miles to the Mediterranean. The textures also challenged the senses, from the dainty fragility of the tiniest of flowers to the waving plates of waxy leaves.

Atop a mast flew the Devon flag, the white cross on green, waving proud in the breeze, below it a pennant embossed with a golden "Resurgam".

The time was twenty to one. 'Five minutes here,' Dan said.

★★★

Dance and Denyer backed away, cloistered together and held a whispered conversation. They were standing below one of the few fluorescent strips working on this floor. It cast the pair in shadow and light and highlighted their gestures. Denyer was animated, her cropped hair twitching as she spoke. Dance was mainly listening, occasionally nodding, offering the odd monosyllabic comment. There was fascinating material here for those many who had speculated about the dynamic of power in the pairing.

Below, the strings started up again, a chirpier number this time, the notes jaunty and optimistic. A few bars played, then the momentum faltered and the music stopped. Flood just stood, hands behind his back, gazing into space, a memory perhaps of his military days. A man awaiting an enemy's advance.

Adam wandered a little way past the rows of shops. Each was deserted, fish tanks without a single fish. In the door of the largest was a pile of post, several letters marked from a debt collection agency. Adam paced on, the footfall of his leather shoes loud in the quiet of this forlorn floor.

The two women turned and walked back over. They were moving more briskly now, with determination, kept close together. Allies forever in mind, word and deed.

'We've discussed what you have to say,' Dance announced, brusquely. 'Can you definitively tell us there's likely to be an attack tomorrow?'

'No,' Flood replied. 'But we have to take the possibility seriously.'

'So what you have is just a theory.'

'A scenario,' Adam corrected, 'Which if played out could result in the deaths of many people.'

'If.' Denyer pounced, with strong stress on the single word. '*If.*'

'I've given you my advice,' Flood told her. 'If you go ahead with opening Resurgam tomorrow, it will be a matter of record that you did so against the wishes of Greater Wessex Police.'

They stared at each other, the two women side by side, the two men facing them. In the twilight of these strange, forsaken surroundings, silence held the moment. The only movement was the twitching of a shadow under the flicker of a failing light.

Dance took a long breath. When she spoke, she sounded tired but still resolute. 'You want me to put off the opening when tens of thousands of people are planning to be here tomorrow. When it's all timed for the peak of the Christmas shopping period. When we worked day and night to get to this point. When all is in place and everything finally ready.'

'Just give us a few days to catch whoever's behind this threat,' Adam said gently.

'If you'd done your job and caught them already, we wouldn't be having this problem at all,' Denyer snapped.

'Now look…' Flood began, but Dance put a hand across her aide and said, 'Let's not have a scene. Deputy Chief Constable, if we go ahead you'll naturally ensure security is as tight as it can be?'

'That's our duty.'

'And we have every confidence in the police, of course,' Denyer added, snidely.

Flood's complexion was colouring dangerously, the veins on his neck so pronounced they appeared to be struggling to break free. The Tank was readying for battle.

Dance spoke quickly, before he could remonstrate further. Something had changed in her voice. Before, it was uncertain. But now it had the confidence of a familiar script.

'I believe that to put off the opening would be to show cowardice when courage is demanded of us. It would be to give in to terrorism. That is not our way, and never will be.'

The belief was pouring back into every feature of her face, the determination shining through. The rhetoric was gathering force, the words rising to a rousing finale. The politician, the orator, the stateswoman was in command once more.

'I have no intention of becoming the first leader in this country's history to submit to coercion, to bow to the forces of darkness. We stand undaunted, we will move forwards without fear and we shall win through. So, if you'll excuse us, we have work to do to prepare for tomorrow – as no doubt have you.'

CHAPTER 22

This late afternoon, for once, there was no hesitation at the front door. The tiredness wouldn't permit it.

The time was coming up to five, the dense darkness of the midwinter settled upon the land. The perpetual cold accompanied it, a partner in crime, harder, sharper now than during the daytime hours.

To get home at such a time was a rare indulgence. One of Lizzie's encyclopaedia of edicts was that reporters must be in the broadcast gallery when *Wessex Tonight* graced the airwaves. In fairness it was a standard of the industry; there could always be last minute queries about the story, or updates which needed to be added.

On this afternoon though, she had discovered an unusual mercy. The way Lizzie expressed it could have been kinder, but, as the old saying goes, you can't have everything.

'Hell, you look rough,' she commented, as she stood in the edit suite to approve the report. I hope you're not coming down with something.'

Dan was about to voice appreciation for his editor's pastoral concern, when the words were strangled in his throat.

'It'd upset our plans for tomorrow. Plus you'll have breathed your germs all around here.'

'I'm just tired.'

The incredulity in her voice could have blown the light bulbs. 'Tired?!'

'I have been working quite hard on this story.'

'You've been working adequately, yes. Get home early then. I want you fresh for tomorrow. It's a big day. Bed by nine for you, got that?'

The bizarreness of Dan's boss telling him what time to retire meant no retort was necessary, or indeed possible. He packed his satchel and made to slip out to the car park when Nigel intervened.

'Off home?'

'Given half a chance.'

His friend's avuncular face registered the sarcasm and Dan apologised. 'I didn't mean to be sharp, I'm just feeling jaded.'

'That's ok. It's been quite a time.'

Dan was about to get into his car when he noticed Nigel had taken out his phone and was involved in some rapid texting.

'What you up to?' Dan asked. 'Got a date?'

'Just, err - checking on the boys.'

It was mostly dark in the car park, but Nigel was blushing. A kind, honest and open man, he could compete with a nun for the inability to lie convincingly.

'It must be some new woman,' Dan said to himself, and tied a mental knot to find out more tomorrow. So, the evening was his. And for once Dan could honestly say he was looking forward to seeing Claire. The tiredness wasn't unpleasant, like an invisible duvet. It was pushing away any concerns for the future and thoughts of the conversation that must someday come. But not now, not just yet, not for a while.

A night on the sofa, hopefully with the input of some of the pasta that Claire cooked so well, a film, a tin or two of beer, Rutherford at their feet, would be just what Dan needed. And if he didn't make it to bed by nine o'clock, as instructed, then it would probably be soon after.

He pushed open the flat's door to find Claire in the hallway. She was dressed in a coat and surrounded by a couple of suitcases and a pile of boxes. And she was crying.

★★★

A day which had gone so well now fell over the edge of the cliff.

Dan had found a rare quarter of an hour over coffee to give Phil some words of advice. As so often, the young man just needed some reassurance. News is a selfish trade, with few journalists having time for much outside of their story of the day.

'You're well on the way,' Dan soothed. 'Lizzie's already trusted you with some important reports. That's the highest praise she can give.'

'But she never says anything about how I'm doing,' he replied.

'And she never will. That's just her way. But she'll soon pipe up if she sees something she doesn't like. Take silence as appreciation.'

Phil had returned to his research duties a much happier man. At the canteen door he paused and added, 'About the *two truths and a lie* game...'

'Maybe some other time,' the unlikely mentor of men replied. 'Probably when I'm about to retire.'

★★★

Dan was covering the opening of Resugam tomorrow, as if there had never been any doubt. His error of the broadcast of yesterday would not be forgotten by an editor like Lizzie, and forgiven might also be too strong a word, but it could be overlooked. The plans were in place and all was well.

Lizzie was even moved to a modicum of traditionally churlish praise for the reporting of Media Day.

"Pretty acceptable" was her moving commendation. No one else had the pictures of the aftermath of the explosion, nor the revelation about the police warning of the dangers of opening the skyscraper.

That, in itself, had proved an interesting diversion. As Dan and Nigel were emerging from one of the lifts, they saw Adam and Flood pacing out of the building. Flood's face was sufficiently incandescent to suggest a detonation was imminent.

Dan had no intention of talking to his friend with such a senior officer for a chaperone. But Flood was a cop and a good one, and had already spotted the lingering presence. A few words to Adam and the detective approached.

'Mr Flood said he seemed to remember you and I know each other.'

'Did he?'

'He did.'

216

'And did he go on to add anything?'

'He did.'

'Which would be what?'

'That he wouldn't be surprised if news of the police's conversation with Dance leaked out.'

'Really?'

'Provided, of course, that it could never be traced back to the source of the information.'

'From which I take it the little chat didn't go brilliantly.'

'How remarkably perceptive.'

'And judging by the look of him, Mr Flood is not best pleased.'

It's a difficult art to nod ironically, but Adam managed it. 'You certainly haven't got where you are for nothing.'

He turned to go, but Dan said quickly, 'Do you really think there might be an attack on Resurgam tomorrow?'

'Yep.'

'What kind? How?'

'If we knew that it might just occur to us to stop it.'

'Sorry, daft question.'

'I would agree.'

'What I meant was – any ideas? Any theories?'

'It could be anything. So far we've had a lorry and an explosion. Take your pick what's coming next.'

'Bloody hell. That ups the stakes.'

'Quite.'

'So what're you going to do?'

'Whatever we can. All leave's been cancelled. Every cop going is being called in.' Adam eyed Resurgam with an impressive dislike. 'Let's just hope it'll be enough to stop this bloody thing causing any more deaths.'

★★★

It had been a day of significant developments in the long-running story of Resurgam. On the way back to the studio, sad news came through from Tamarside Hospital. Tommy Ross had died from the injuries he suffered when the lorry crashed into the gatehouse. Alannah was at his bedside.

Dan could imagine her sitting in a ward, head lost in hands, the tears dripping onto the sterile floor. Her father would be beside her, Jack trying his best with the impossible task of offering some comfort. Nurses would offer cups of tea which would never be drunk. Perhaps they would have to gently unfold a hand from that of her lost fiancé and lead her away, to a small and quiet room which had seen so many moments of such emotion.

A brief, but caustic statement had been issued in Alannah's name, with a request that the media allow her to grieve in peace. Dan saw the pain turning fast to anger, a need to hit out at the cause of the suffering.

"Tommy was my world. My life, my heart, my soul. And now he's gone, and for what? Just some building. Just concrete, steel and glass. The people involved in all this should reflect on the pain they've inflicted on so many innocent people and hang their heads."

The statement was carried in full in Dan's report, along with a recap on some of the other traumas the construction of Resurgam had seen. The grievous injury to PC Steve Rogers, the death of Alice and now the loss of Tommy too.

A veteran of many an intense story, they nonetheless took a quiet toll. The wonder drug which is adrenaline had seen Dan through his reporting day. But as the time neared five o'clock, he began to long for the comfort of the flat.

That was the great thing about being part of a couple. It might not work all the time, it may even have little hope of a future, but some days the support was a wonder beyond words.

So in the hallway this December evening, as he stood nonplussed, the only question Dan could find was the dazzlingly redundant, 'Claire… what are you doing?'

★★★

From the hallway, each door except that to the lounge, was open. The flat was as tidy as Dan could ever remember it. The kitchen suffered no ramshackle mess of cutlery and crockery on the draining board and all the surfaces were brightly clean. The spare bedroom had been vacuumed, the racks burdened by far fewer clothes than had been the way for...

Two months, one week, and five days.

The main bedroom was impeccable, too. No boots wilting, spread-eagled or intertwined on the floor. No line of women's tops on the front of the wardrobes. No pile of books by the near side of the bed. No collection of half empty glasses to go with them.

Claire followed Dan's look and said, 'I wanted to make sure everything was... the way you want it. The way it was before...'

And now he looked to the suitcases and boxes, a neat array on the hallway floor. On top was a notebook, a pen clipped to it. At the head of the first sheet of paper was written, *Dear Dan*. Below were a couple of damp blotches.

'You... you're leaving?'

She didn't reply.

'You're moving out?'

'I – I didn't think you'd be home yet. I thought you'd be doing a live thing at Resurgam tonight. I was just going to leave a...'

Claire's words faded into a gulp. From behind the door to the lounge came scrabbling, followed by a couple of pitiful whines.

'Why?' Dan asked.

'Why?'

'Yes. Why?'

Again she didn't reply, just stared at him, her eyes indistinct with the tears. Downstairs somewhere, a door slammed shut.

'Why?' came the word once more, this time swollen with disbelief. 'Why?' Claire said again, and now there was an eternity of emotion in her voice. 'Why? Why do you think? Why do you bloody think?'

'Well, I don't – I mean...'

He got no further. Dan's words were swept aside, as easily as confetti in a hurricane of feeling.

'Why?!' Claire shouted. 'How can you ask why?!'

'I don't...'

'I'll tell you why! Because just about all I've felt since I moved in is resentment. That's why! Because every day I think you'd rather I wasn't here.'

'But...'

'I've tried everything to please you. I've loved you, I've looked after Rutherford, I've put up with your bloody moods, your miserable damn ways. I've swallowed all the times I've felt like yelling out, or crying. And you haven't even noticed! Or maybe you just didn't care.'

'But...'

'You never even asked me to move in! I took a sabbatical for you, to try to work it out between us. I put my life on hold for you, my career, everything. You never said thank you. You never even said you appreciated it. I had to sneak in here like some bloody squatter, bring all my stuff in myself. You weren't even here when I did it! You were out covering some shitty story. You didn't even leave me a note!'

'But...'

'I have to sit here with you and try to work out how to behave. I have to cuddle you when you need it and leave you alone when you're having one of your damn depressions. I wait up for you while you go out drinking. I have to listen to your pitiful whining when you've got everything going for you! You've no idea how lucky you are! And do you know how many times you've asked about me? How I'm feeling?'

'I don't...'

'I'll tell you how many. None! That's zero. Absolutely fucking none! I sometimes wonder if you even notice me, let alone care.'

'But...'

'Do you know how much I've gone through for you? I didn't expect it to be easy, but for God's sake, Dan! Why must you wallow in this pit of self-pity? Do you ever think of anyone but yourself?'

'I...'

'There was the time when I was pregnant and you didn't even realise! There was the time afterwards when I really needed you, and all you could do was mope and tell me how hard it was for you. And then you went off with that other… that bloody scrubber! Did you think I didn't know about that?'

'Well, I…'

'But I forgave you, and do you know why? Because I thought, at heart, you wanted me. Because I thought you wanted to be with me. Because I thought I could get through this bloody self-inflicted suit of misery. Because I was stupid enough to think you were worth it!'

'Claire, I…'

'And do you know the worst thing? All I've ever tried to do is love you. That's it, that's all, that's the lot! I've tried to love you and make you happy. And in return, I've got… oh, fuck it all, and fuck you! Go on, go live on your own with your damned dog and your misery, just like you've always wanted.'

Claire stood rigid in the dimness of the hallway and stared at Dan with a starburst of defiance. And all he could do was reel, mouth agape.

Another scrabbling shook the lounge door. And now, through the beating numbness of the barrage started to prickle a feeling. It began to grow, spread fast through his body, outwards from heart and soul to vein, muscle, sinew and limb.

Claire grabbed the handle of one of the suitcases and started for the door. But Dan reached out and held her arm.

'Stop. There's something I want to say.'

★★★

If a picture can be worth a thousand words, then sometimes a look can summarise a chapter in a life. Filling Claire's eyes now was the repressed anger and hurt of the last two months, and all the wounds Dan had inflicted on her over the years.

He took his hand away from her arm. She reached for the door.

And now Claire waited. She was balanced, absurdly like a tightrope walker, arms outstretched, caught between leaving and staying.

'What do you want to say?' she asked. 'What can you say?'

Dan found he couldn't look at her. His eyes fell to the tatty old linoleum. Claire had asked several times whether she should get some catalogues to look for a replacement floor.

The answer was no. He liked it the way it was.

The memory wasn't a wise one for this moment, so Dan shifted his gaze to an abstract painting he'd picked up at an art sale, a charcoal jumble of shapes. Claire had nurtured a potent dislike for it, particularly in the hallway where it would frighten guests, she said. The request was that it be moved to the spare bedroom, if it had to stay at all.

Dan said no. He liked it the way it was.

He looked to the aged barometer discovered in a second hand store. It had never worked, in an act of lunatic optimism for England perpetually prophesised sunshine. Claire had repeatedly offered to get it fixed.

No, Dan replied. He liked it the way it was.

Perhaps it was time to close his eyes and concentrate on what he had to say.

Claire shifted her weight a little towards the door. 'Well?'

'I want to say...'

'Yes?'

'I have to say...'

'What?'

'I need to say – sorry.'

'Sorry?'

'Yes.'

'Just sorry?'

'No.'

'What then?'

'I'm... very sorry. Very, very sorry.'

'Are you?'

'Yes. I'm so sorry. So very sorry.'

Many times in his life Dan had said the word. It must have been tens of thousands. Often without thinking, automatically and inconsequentially. Just a reflex because it was expected, without any real feeling, meaning or understanding.

But now came a surprise. This version of the little word felt like no other. It set his body trembling. Sentences were tumbling from Dan's mouth. He had no idea where they were coming from, but they were certainly coming. With little in the way of breath, hesitation, or reflection, out they poured.

'You're right. I've been an idiot. Worse, in fact. An absolute award winning, Nobel laureate, category one, gold plated, top ranked, presidential, high flying, world beating, flag waving, Olympic champion of an arsehole.'

There was no response. But that didn't matter. Nothing was going to stop these words. They felt strangely good, pure catharsis, the breathless release of a long-stored bile.

'You've been wonderful. You've done everything. You've tried to make me happy. You've done all you can for me. And in return I've been a miserable, sulky, resentful, ungrateful shit.'

Dan hesitated briefly for a gulp of air, then ploughed onwards.

'I know the sacrifices you've made. I know how you've suffered because of the way I am. I know you've been patient and tolerant in a way I had no right to expect. And I've treated you with contempt. I'm such a dickhead.'

The floor creaked. Dan would have opened his eyes to see what Claire was doing, if she was moving towards the door, but he didn't dare.

'The problem's never been you. It's me. It's always me. I'm so selfish, wrapped up in myself, too preoccupied with my own problems to think about anyone else. I've treated you dreadfully. I'm such a prick.'

Another complaint from the floorboards and a couple of sad barks from Rutherford. Dan found he was feeling light headed and fumbled for the support of the wall. But still he couldn't open his eyes.

'All I can say is that I'm sorry. Sorry and please give me a chance... one more chance - please.'

And there the rambling stopped. He had said what he could, all that the strictures of his heart would allow. And the walls whispered the words, time and again. In the darkness of his imagination and the silence of his fear.

She's leaving. She's going. She's leaving. She's going…

In Dan's mind he could see Claire reaching for the door. To walk out and never return.

Tonight he would be alone, just as he had wanted. And tomorrow night, and the night after that, and all the nights to come.

And he was afraid.

The moment roared. Colours and sound, a vortex of vision. One of the fulcrums of a life. Burned into the memory, never to be forgotten, the true meaning of fateful.

Dan felt a soft breath in his face. With a leap of unsuspected, perhaps even unwanted courage, he opened his eyes.

Claire had taken her hands from the suitcase and door. She was close by, looking into him, as though she could see through to his soul.

And she could.

'A chance?'

'Yes.'

'Why?'

'So I can be what you want me to be. What I want me to be.'

'Why should I?'

'Because… I – I think… I might be able to…'

'Can you?'

'Yes.'

'Really?'

'Yes.'

'You sure?'

'Yes.'

'So – how're you going to start?'

'What?'

'Showing me you mean it.'

She took a step closer. Their faces were only air apart, both still blurred, but neither running with tears any longer.

Tentatively, so hesitantly, Dan placed a finger on Claire's shoulder. The touch felt like a passage to another world. It wasn't deflected, not resisted at all, so he let it slide down further, lower, and took her hand.

'I'll help you unpack.'

'Try harder.'

'I'll give you extra drawer space for your knicker collection.'

'Harder.'

'I'll take you out for dinner.'

'Harder.'

'I'll cook dinner.'

'Harder.'

'Blimey, even harder than that?'

'Yes.'

'You can have the best seat on the sofa,' Dan said, before adding hurriedly, 'For tonight, at least.'

'And?'

'You want more?'

'Yes.'

'Is there more?'

'Yes.'

They were so close now, the last of that terrible separation closing fast.

'How about… the greatest gift I can give?'

'Which is?'

'Joint custody of Rutherford?'

At the sound of his name the dog scrabbled again at the door and let out a long, mournful howl. Dan clicked the handle and Rutherford bounded in and nosed his way into the cuddle.

'You can do even better than that,' Claire whispered. 'But I need you to be absolutely sure. So you can do it tomorrow evening, ok? I don't want to overburden the emotions of an idiot like you.'

From the sky, a cricket ball of realisation hit the back of Dan's head. 'You're talking about,' he floundered, 'I mean, you're saying… what I think…'

She pressed a finger to his lips. 'Shhh. That's enough for now. Let's leave it to tomorrow.'

★★★

SIMON HALL

High dramas of the domestic world dispatched, this strange couple managed to sit down for supper in time to watch *Wessex Tonight*. Dan's mobile rang a couple of times, but he ignored it. Diplomacy and a demonstration of commitment of even the most basic kind suggested that to be the correct course of action.

'It's going to be quite a day tomorrow,' was Claire's verdict on the Resurgam story. 'Do you really think there'll be an attack?'

'Adam says there's a good chance. You're not a bad cop yourself. What do you think?'

'I'd say whoever's behind the attacks has certainly shown they're not afraid of violence. Plus there's enough bitterness with all that's happened around Resurgam to prompt something dreadful.' She held out a hand and Dan took it. 'Be careful tomorrow. You never know, I might still need you.'

They finished the remains of the pasta to the weather forecast. Another cold day was in prospect for Finale Friday, but at least the prognosis was no more snow. Dan's phone rang once more.

'You'd better answer it,' Claire said, gathering the plates. 'And a little tip - remember next time that different types of pasta take varying times to cook.'

Dan was already on the mobile. 'Oh shit, I completely forgot with all that's been going on,' he apologised. 'Yes, I do appreciate how important it is. I know I promised but I'm really tired and...'

He was interrupted by an agitated burble on the line. 'Ok, I'll check if I can pop out for a couple of hours.'

Dan looked to Claire, who raised her eyes to the heavens but nodded with the forbearance of angels. 'This is the address,' he told the phone. 'I'll see you there in quarter of an hour.'

A perfunctory attempt to help wash up was dismissed with a good-natured wave. 'But just before you go,' she said. 'I need to know - are you ok?'

The answer came surprisingly easily, almost without thought. And perhaps that was the problem; he had been thinking too much and feeling too little.

'I'm more than ok. I feel like… maybe that a very long hangover has finally lifted. It's like this dense cloud has gone, as if the world's come back to me.'

A beautiful smile was the response, a real lighthouse of its kind, and it was all that he needed. Dan kissed Claire, grabbed his coat and headed for the car.

'And don't you forget what we talked about earlier,' she called after him. 'I'm looking forward to tomorrow.'

CHAPTER 23

The house could have come from a factory line of featureless modernity; a new build semi in a neat suburban street. If it held a clue as to the identity of their quarry, there was no outward sign. Dan and El stood a little way along the road, just out of sight, studied what there was to see and planned their plan.

El had a tendency to regress to toddlerhood at times of excitement and tonight was ruefully no different. He grabbed the sleeve of Dan's jacket and repeatedly shook it. 'What we do, what we do? Come on, come on!'

'Shh! I'm thinking. Or trying to.'

The house had a small drive. Upon it sat the car that had ended their chase through the streets of Plymouth in the early hours of this morning. Squared and immaculately shorn hedges bounded each side of the property. The curtains of the lounge were tightly closed but backlit, and there was a hint of light in an upstairs bedroom.

'Come on!' El babbled again. 'He's home, he's in, he's there.'

'Brilliant observation, thank you. Now shush!'

A sulky lower lip protruded. 'El's only trying to help.'

'Then El should try imitating a gatepost.'

'What?'

'Be perfectly still and utterly silent.'

Dan continued his study of the house. Only a few words they'd exchanged with the man who lived there. But his manner was educated, which suggested the daunting credentials of intelligence and principles. A straightforward knock on the door and question as to the whereabouts, and, more importantly, whoabouts, of the Cashman was unlikely to deliver the bounty.

'Let's have a look around the back,' Dan suggested.

They found a narrow alley, lined with wooden fences and intermittent gates. It smelt of creosote. A tidy pile of recycling boxes stood at one end. The gate of number 44 was just a little too tall to see over.

'Down you go,' Dan told El.

'I'm not a stepladder.'

'How much do you want to find the Cashman?'

Even in the darkness of the alley, there was greed in the photographer's eyes. 'Lots, plenty, buckets and tonnes.' He rubbed a hand over the camera dangling from his neck. 'Snappy snappy makes El happy!'

'Down you go, then.'

Reluctantly and inelegantly, El formed his bulk into a step and Dan levered himself up.

'Ow! How much do you weigh?' asked the makeshift platform.

'Not as much as you. Now shush.'

A double glazed back door gave onto a small patio, occupied by a couple of stone statues of a cherubic nature. There were flowerbeds and a lawn, but nothing else of note. Here too, the curtains were tightly drawn.

'What you got?' El asked, as Dan hopped down.

'Nothing.'

'So what we gonna do?'

'Good question.'

They walked back to the end of the alley. The cold had marshalled its forces and progressed from icy to bitter. Dan swung his arms in an ineffectual attempt to keep warm. El had no such needs; his fat reserves were of the whale genus and sufficient insulation against the spite of an English winter.

'We gotta find him,' El moaned. 'Tomorrow's the last chance. And I reckon that Italian and those others know where he's gonna make a last stand. We gotta get him first.'

He rambled through a requiem that Dan had suffered twice tonight already. Earlier in the day El had been in the city centre, trying in vain to pick up any clues about who the Cashman may be. He'd bumped into the other paparazzi and they'd delighted in distributing more taunts.

'Can't find him, little fat man?' the Italian said, in his fine English. 'Don't worry. It'll all be clear tomorrow.'

'And we'll be splitting the reward,' another added.

'You know what he's gonna do?' El couldn't help asking. But all he'd received in return were broad smiles.

A car swished past and turned onto a drive further up the road, the beams of lights clicking off.

'They know,' El mourned. 'They've broken his code. They're gonna clean up. I'm flat packed and washed out to sea. I'm more history than the dinosaurs. Hey, where you going?'

Dan had set off up the road towards number 44. 'If all else fails, try the obvious.'

★★★

The bell produced the melodic ding dong so beloved of the English middle classes. In the opaque glass of the front door lights shifted and brightened.

'He comes, he comes,' El whispered, breathlessly.

The dark shape of a person approached, moving carefully. Dan put on his best smile and adjusted his satchel so it was close to the letterbox.

The door slipped open, but only a crack. 'Roger,' Dan exclaimed cheerily, as if to an old friend.

'Who is it?' asked a suspicious voice.

The man was peering around the door, blinking hard to see through the darkness. Dan manoeuvred his satchel a little further forwards, but the gap wasn't quite sufficient.

'Don't say you don't recognise me?'

The door edged further ajar. But still not quite enough.

'Who are you?'

'Oh Roger! I just can't believe you don't recognise me. Roger Franklin, really! And after, well…'

Dan let his voice tail off. And as so often, the bait of curiosity was too tempting. Now there was enough of a gap, but also recognition in the man's face.

'How did you find me…' he began, before reconsidering and instead trying to shove the door shut. But the delay was just enough. Dan dropped his satchel into the wedge of space.

'Clumsy me,' he said, placing a foot on top of it.

'I want to shut the door. Kindly move your bag.'

Dan craned his head for a fast reconnaissance. In the hallway he could see a sideboard set with some plates and a vase of flowers. In pride of place, at the very centre, stood a photograph of a woman. She was in her sixties, about the same age as Roger Franklin. Her expression wasn't the forced smile of so many portraits, but filled with unmistakeable sorrow.

'If you don't move I shall call the police.'

'Will you, Mr Franklin? And risk scandalising this lovely little neighbourhood? Becoming the talk of the street for months? Because then I'll have no choice but to broadcast your role in the story of The Cashman.'

Now Franklin's expression changed. And Dan continued working away at the weakness.

'There's no need for any of that, after all.' He pointed towards the photo on the sideboard. 'Not given what happened to Mrs Franklin – which is how you met the Cashman, I think? And why you're helping with his plans.'

Franklin said nothing. But he'd stopped trying to push the door closed.

'If we can just pop inside for a few minutes and have a chat, I think we'll be able to work out something which will suit us all,' Dan added. 'Because if I'm right, it's a story which very much needs telling.'

★★★

It was a plain little lounge, its uniformity interrupted only by a couple of old maps of Devon, which looked like originals. Dan and El sat on the sofa, Franklin in the armchair.

'I fear you're wasting your time,' he told them. 'I've made a promise and I have every intention of honouring it.'

Dan nodded. 'I understand – and why it's so important to you.'

His hair must once have been very fair, but now the lustre had faded and was a lank grey. Franklin sat upright, a tall and lean man who hadn't filled out with the years, as was the curse of so many of his contemporaries.

There were three boxes beside the sofa, two filled with books, one ornaments. The room had that slight echo which said it was a little barer than would be homely.

'I take it you haven't lived here long, Mr Franklin?' Dan ventured.

'Just a few weeks. I moved after ...'

Dan waited for the seconds of sensitivity to pass, before prompting, 'And her name was?'

'Louise.'

'I'm sorry.'

'Thank you.'

A silence took hold. A carriage clock on the television, which might as well have sported a tag saying *retirement present*, told of the time reaching eight. If they were to have any chance of finding the Cashman tonight rapid progress was required.

'Can I ask about the maps?' Dan ventured, just to have something to say. 'They look fascinating.'

'I used to be a geography lecturer. I've collected scores. I just don't seem to have the heart to put the others up.'

'They're beautiful.'

'Thank you.'

'You've lived in Devon all your life?'

'Most of it, apart from when I went to college.'

'And you were married for...'

'Forty years. Well, almost forty.'

Franklin's voice caught and he looked away.

'Almost?'

'Louise died ten days before our anniversary.'

'That's cruel.'

'Yes.'

'And without wanting to upset you ...'

'It was cancer. Not sudden, but slow.'

'She was treated at Tamarside Hospital?'

'Yes.'

'Where you both met the Cashman?'

Franklin studied Dan, fingers on his chin, but didn't find any threat in the question. 'So, you think you know what this is all about?'

Dan managed a half smile. 'Perhaps a reasonable idea. But I'd say there are still more questions than answers.'

They held a look, but Franklin was impassive and gave nothing away. Instead, he said, 'May I ask you a question?'

'Of course.'

'How did you know I was a widower?'

'It was this house,' Dan replied. 'It struck me as classic downsizing – or perhaps escaping a memory – or maybe both.'

Franklin nodded sadly. 'You're quite right. Look, I don't want to be rude, but this is bringing back all sorts of memories and as I said...'

'I appreciate you've made a promise,' Dan interrupted. 'And I can sense a man like you won't break it. We'll leave in a minute.'

'Thank you.'

'It's part of a journalist's job to know when to make a dignified retreat.'

Dan got up from the sofa, ignoring a horrified look from El.

'There's no point asking, because you won't tell me who the Cashman is.'

'That's correct.'

'Or where to find him.'

'Correct.'

'Or where and when his last appearance will be, when it comes tomorrow?'

'Also correct.'

'But...'

'But what?'

'Louise was a member of Resurgam, wasn't she? The terminal illness club at the hospital?'

'She was.'

'And she didn't like the name being used for a skyscraper either, did she?'

The guess hit its target. A strange noise escaped the man. It was part sigh, part snort. 'She hated it, as did I. She was a Plymothian through and through. She thought it a scandal that some ugly, unwanted building should bear that sacred name.'

'So I wouldn't be wrong in thinking Resurgam, and its opening tomorrow, has some significance in the Cashman's plans?'

Franklin looked as if he was about to answer, then stopped. The kindling of emotion had revealed some of the story. But he was too in control to give away any more.

'You must think what you wish. Now, if you wouldn't mind…'

He led Dan and El towards the door. By the sideboard, Dan paused. The face in the photograph could have been staring at them, eyes sharp, even though the melancholy.

'Louise looked a very fine woman.'

'She was.'

'This is all about Resurgam, isn't it?' Dan asked, quickly. 'And maybe as the focus of some even bigger protest?'

'Please, it's time for you to go.'

'But it is?'

Franklin opened the door. 'You're very shrewd. And I admire your tenacity. But…'

'But what?'

A biting draft was blowing into the hallway. Dan and El stepped out into the night. The hedges were rustling, as though irritated at their presence.

In the doorway, Franklin stopped. 'Without betraying any confidences, I can tell you this. However much you might think you know, you've still got one very big surprise to come.'

★★★

This was no time for a late night, but it can be the way of life to leave little choice. Dan sat on the end of the sofa, surrounded by his notes on all the Cashman's appearances, and tried to work a way through the puzzle.

He closed his eyes and let the thoughts free. He and El had left Franklin's house with the photographer so agitated it wouldn't have been a surprise if he'd laid an egg.

'What'd all that mean? What was he saying? What do you know? What's happening?' El repeated time and again.

'We're almost there,' was the best reassurance Dan could offer. 'I'm going home to do some more work on it. Tomorrow we'll find the Cashman.'

'Not tonight?'

'That is part of the generally accepted definition of tomorrow.'

'Tomorrow?'

'Still yes.'

'You promise poor El?'

'I think so. Or maybe hope is a better word. I reckon we're close, but there are still a few missing links in the chain.'

Claire had a little surprise of her own to impart when Dan got back to the flat. She was returning to duty.

'Mr Breen called,' she said, referring to the chief inspector in her traditionally respectful way. 'He needs every cop he can muster tomorrow. Given our conversation of earlier, I think we've sorted out what we needed to and I can go back to work?'

'Uh huh,' Dan replied, from amidst the jungle of his thought-trek.

'So my sabbatical's over and I'm on the Resurgam case – no doubt working with you.'

'Uh huh.'

'You're not really listening, are you?'

'What?'

And so they sat, and she read, and he contemplated, ruminated and deliberated, pen working back and forth across the notepad. Rutherford lay at their feet, gentle music played on the stereo, and all was a picture of domestic contentment until just after half past eleven.

'Shit!' Dan yelled, making Claire drop her book and Rutherford sit up dozily and offer a half-hearted bark.

'Oh no! No, no, no,' he wailed, with a mixture of excitement and disbelief. 'It can't possibly be that simple, can it?'

THE BATTLE OF RESURGAM
SIX – THE INVASION

Now they came in numbers. Undeterred by the late January snow and the relentless cold, they travelled from across the nation to these few acres of land.

There were more of *the professionals,* some hitch hiking, others arriving in their battered minibuses and coaches. They, however, were relatively few compared to the swathes of those referred to as *the general public.*

They were summoned by the horror of what happened to a young woman. They had purpose in a collective mind and a statement to make.

It was less than an hour after Alice's death that her photograph began to appear on tribute sites on the internet. Another hour and it was accompanied by scrolling pages of eulogies. The next hour saw her picture on the 24 hour TV channels and news websites, and the following day upon the front pages of the papers.

It mattered not the rights and wrongs of Alice's story. That she was part of a protest, trespassing, and would not otherwise have suffered such an ending was forgotten. That there were evils and abuses on both sides was largely overlooked. Even the grievous wound inflicted upon PC Steve went mostly unreported.

The photograph was sufficient. The bright eyes and the blonde hair. The indescribable beauty of the sunshine of youth. The innocence lost to unfeeling concrete and steel. Alice was the fallen standard around which they gathered.

The police had suspicion of what was to come, and then warning. Brian Flood was called away from another fascinating Home Office conference, this time on *Policing the Divide, an examination of the rationale and reasons for the criminalisation of the emerging underclass and a prognosis for the future of the concern.*

Reports were coming in of a flux of people making their way towards Resurgam. Increasingly strident intelligence briefings indicated the next demonstration would be when the majority of the workforce clocked on, at half past seven tomorrow morning. And so, that freezing Tuesday night, the opposing sides arrayed their forces and laid their plans.

***

The familiar maxim of *softly softly* had served the law well before. It would, Flood decreed, be employed again.

On Wednesday morning, just after six o'clock, a mass of police once again assembled on Plymouth Hoe. Lines of vans, officers pulling on riot gear, just as it had been at the start of work on Resurgam.

This time, Flood deigned a rousing oration unnecessary. Cakes, as Mrs Flood sometimes said, could be over-iced. He checked all was well and then departed to Charles Cross to take up his position in the warmth of the Control Room.

Most of the legions of the law again waited well out of sight from Resurgam. A small detachment of smiling, polite and pleasant officers took up station along the access road.

By seven, the protesters started to arrive, wrapped up in coats, scarves and hats, a baffle to the icy breath of this winter's morning. They formed in their allocated positions, behind the barriers along the access road, and positioned their placards and banners.

Seb was there, Esme to one side, Mac the other, both with arms of support around the young man. Even in the darkness and occasional swirl of snow, it was obvious his face was filled with loss.

A young man had aged overnight. Once charming, warm and engaging, his conversation had become a monologue.

'I can't believe she's gone,' he repeated. 'And for that bastard Resurgam monstrosity.'

June was there too, Maggie alongside as ever. Both hugged Seb and tried to find soothing words that could never hope to ease his suffering.

Esther was further along the road, surrounded by a group of the professional protesters. Only Simian was missing. The *I fought the law* stance singled him out as the sole member of this familiar cast to remain in custody.

From the entrance to the Resurgam site Phil Rees and Tommy Ross watched, both dressed in the fluorescent jackets and ill-fitting caps of low authority. Rees would sometimes shake his head at the demonstration gathering before them, contempt further hardening his face.

But despite the numbers of people and the passion of their motives, all began calmly. Police officers walked up and down, exchanging brief greetings with anyone who would respond. Some of the demonstrators just stood, others waved their banners, some hugged themselves or stamped their feet to keep warm. Seb held his placard the highest, arm as outstretched as it could possibly be, as if waving aloft a beacon. On the thin wooden board was painted *For Alice*.

At quarter past seven, the first carful of workers arrived. Now the police officers stopped their patrols, watched the saloon's slow progress. A blinking indicator, wheels churning slush, a careful turn onto the access road.

From the crowd on either side rose a chorus of booing. A couple of half-hearted shouts of abuse followed. But the car continued its passage undaunted, trundled onwards and reached half way along the road.

Placards lifted and waved in the darkness. All eyes followed the car, streetlights shining from its windscreen, the hint of pale faces within.

The police were poised, ready, waiting. In his Control Room, with a steaming cup of coffee untouched, Flood watched. The officers parked up around the corner clustered by their radios, set to climb into their vans and speed off.

And the car reached Resurgam and disappeared inside.

In the eastern sky appeared a hint of the dawn's light. Protesters looked to each other, chatted a little, pulled coats tighter, hats lower. Police officers resumed their winding patrols through the crowd.

And now another car turns along the access road. And there's a shout, and movement.

It's Seb. He's young and quick and he's fuelled by the feelings filling his heart. He's past the police before they can react. He's into the road. Without a hint of hesitation he's thrown himself down, is lying in the dirt and grime, slush and snow. He's in front of the car, forcing it to stop.

And now he shouts, with a voice so loud it could have carried across the city. 'For Alice!'

Mac's with him. Sullen Mac, taciturn Mac, the originator of the very idea for this blockade, and now he finds the courage to carry it through. He's on his back, that long leather coat planted firmly in the filth of the road. And for once, the rebel looks strangely contented.

Esme's with him, also serene in the incontestable morality of what these three young friends are doing. Together they lay in a line in front of the car.

They don't say it. But they don't need to. Everyone knows who is laying, invisible, beside them.

A semi-second's stillness hovers, encompasses, lingers. Just time for the briefest of considerations, a thought and a decision. And it's made as one, in every mind that lines this road.

People are pouring over the barriers, flooding into the street. The first ones lie alongside Seb and join arms. And more follow, many more, in a tumbling rush.

Before the police can act there's a mass, a solid block of humanity. And some of the professionals are fumbling in the thickness of their coats and handing out objects.

Watching his monitors, Flood cranes forwards. Whatever they are, these things, there are lots, being passed quickly through the crowd.

And being used. Snapped around wrists. Linking people, limb to limb. They're handcuffs. Plastic, lightweight, but robust.

Now there are scores of people in the road, some reaching so far across the tarmac as to lock themselves to the barriers and lampposts.

From Resurgam emerges a Landrover. Rees is at the wheel, his face like a hammer. He drives up to the dam of bodies, moving slowly, until the wheels are almost upon a woman. He revs the engine and inches forward a little further, so part of her body is under the bonnet.

She begins screaming, twisting, trying to get away. But she can't, she's locked to those all around. They're shouting, yelling, begging for the Landrover to stop.

But it edges forwards again. The man at the wheel is smiling; one single expression of genuine pleasure amidst the melee. And a sergeant runs over, hammers on the glass and shouts at Rees to back off in the kind of language the young man understands.

The protesters are starting to sing. An old song, but here and today undeniably appropriate.

We shall not be moved,
We shall not be moved...

And indeed, for many hours, they were not.

★★★

Flood's mantra changed that day. *Softly softly* was out, *Tomorrow will be different* was in.

Work on Resurgam eventually resumed just in time for it to end for the day. It was almost four o'clock when the final demonstrators were cleared from the road. Freezing they may have been, covered in filth too, but they were buoyed by their success.

Seb was one of the last to be hauled up. Surrounded by journalists and cameras, the centre of all attention, he shouted repeatedly, 'For Alice, it was all for Alice.'

Despite the near-darkness, the cold and grime, Seb burned with righteousness. 'Never forget her... we'll never forget,' he called to the news crews who followed his path to the police van.

In the chaotic aftermath of the protest, with the police busy processing all the dozens to be arrested, no one noticed that Esther and a group of the professionals were not amongst them.

★★★

Thursday, as Flood had promised, would indeed be different. But not quite in the way he had envisaged.

As the protesters began to arrive at Resurgam, in the darkness just after seven, they found themselves outnumbered. All along the access road were police officers.

The barriers which once were a polite waist height had grown to well above the level of the average pair of eyes. The wire was thicker too, and the line of fencing was held together with strong metal clamps.

A group of police vans had parked a little further along the road, their back doors deliberately open. On display was a range of tools which would have made a start on breaching the Berlin Wall. No matter how a mass of demonstrators might attempt to link themselves together, today the bonds would be no match for the waiting blades.

It was a little warmer this morning, perhaps minus two rather than four. It must be that, the cops said to each other, which is prompting the grins amongst the demonstrators.

It was five minutes later that the first workers' car turned along the access road and the ritual booing began. Placards waved, but the slow passage passed peacefully. So it was with the second car.

The response to the third was very different. A voice shouted 'Now!' and a group of perhaps fifteen men and women began running towards the entrance to Resurgam. Within an instant, a mass of police were in pursuit, more coagulating ahead.

The officers formed a line to face the charge. More cops were converging from other directions, holding onto helmets as they ran, panting in the cold. The rebels were outflanked and greatly outnumbered.

As they reached the police line the runners slowed. From behind, and to each side, other cops were approaching, encircling the little group.

Their leader, a young man with a beard befitting a disciple of Marx, said cheerily, 'Morning.'

'Morning,' grunted a sergeant, with all due suspicion.

'We fancied a little jog. To ward off the cold, like.'

'Did you now?'

'Yeah.'

'Well, how about making our day and jogging back again?'

The opposing sides eyed each other. Cops scrutinising the little knot of men and women, searching the outlines of their clothes for handcuffs, missiles, anything that might mean more disorder. But the expressions they received in reply weren't angry. They were amused, perhaps even mocking.

'Sure,' the young man said. 'I reckon that's long enough.'

In the pack of officers there were a couple of puzzled looks. It was only when a radio squawked that an answer to the unspoken question came.

'Resurgam compound, now – bloody quick!'

★★★

With a bow to literary history, the three men agreed that when arrested they would give their names as Jay, Harris and George.

Last night, after some quiet hunting of the foreshore, they had found that which they sought. It was rickety, precariously so, but this would be only a short voyage.

Come the morning, at six o'clock precisely they met, retrieved the vessel from where it had been hidden and climbed carefully aboard. In the small and silent rowing boat they paddled gently through the darkness until they made landfall on the one remaining corner of the city beach. And there they waited.

Harris alone had a mobile phone. When its screen lit with a text message – *Now!* - they slipped through the site and headed for their target.

This small detachment of the professionals had been chosen for their stealth and stamina, but also one other talent. In neat formation they hopped down into a ditch, bent double, creeping through the crumping, frosty snow. And at last, they rounded a digger and came upon a patch of open ground.

It was perhaps fifty metres across and well lit. On the far side stood their destination. And in their path, a couple of security guards sharing a sneaky cigarette.

'We can't wait,' Jay, the youngest of the three, whispered. 'The second message'll come through any minute.'

'We've only got once chance at this,' George replied, picking at his teeth. 'They won't be able to keep the cops occupied for long.'

'Esther said it'd be ok if two of us made it,' Harris added. 'That'd be enough.'

'I'll give them some entertainment then,' Jay decided. He took off a rucksack and handed it over. 'You'd better take this.'

Harris strapped the carrier over his own and he and George put on gloves. The three joined hands in a brief farewell and Jay was away, sprinting across the open space, heading for the rising steel beams of the infant skyscraper.

'Hey!' one of the guards shouted, and they both set off in pursuit. 'Stop!'

Not a chance, not a hope. He led them a fine dance, zig-zagging into the hollowness of the growing structure, weaving through stanchion and pole.

George and Harris began their own running, towards the focus of their plan, standing tall in the dark sky. As they reached the metal trellis, both looked up to the red, winking jewel so high above, and began climbing.

★★★

Resurgam grew not at all that Thursday. The modern day three men in a boat achieved their mischievous aims. And as happens comically often, the law came to the aid of the lawless.

Harris and George made it to the highest reaches of the crane. And there they posed a beautiful dilemma for the police and Ellen Dance.

'We don't have time to mess about. We're up against a deadline,' Dance reminded Flood, again and again, before the fragile temper of the Deputy Chief Constable yielded. 'And your bloody skyscraper will never get built if we've got dead protesters decorating its foundations.'

The Health and Safety automatons were called. They sucked in air through teeth and pored over checklists, before issuing the inevitable list of decrees for the eradication of risk.

In fairness, on this occasion they had a point. The agitators had thought hard and planned well.

In their rucksacks George and Harris carried a range of sizeable stones. At the sight of any approach, missiles would be hurled. Work could not begin again until the pair were removed. And that may only happen when suitable contingencies had been put in place in case they should fall.

Most of the day passed in setting up safety netting around the crane. The operation was painfully slow, as the workers had to be protected from the occasional flying stone. The light was starting to ebb when a cherry picker was brought in and both George and Harris dislodged.

At the access road, the demonstrators delighted in a day of baiting the police and goading the workers. It was only as afternoon became evening that the authorities secured a form of revenge.

To keep them entertained, the demonstrators built a large snowman at the end of the access road. Stones made up a mouth and eyes and an old hat was angled upon his head. Phil Rees stewed his loathing until the artwork of ice was finished, before climbing into his jeep and gleefully ploughing through it.

★★★

On Friday the battleground changed, and how.

Overnight, under cover of darkness, reinforcements were brought in. Facing her self-imposed deadline of opening Resurgam by Christmas, Ellen Dance hired just about every contractor, worker and piece of machinery she could find. Together they set about making the site impregnable.

Maritime specialists worked the seaward side, installing jetties, fencing and wire to resist any further incursions. Teams of builders deployed along the landward front, set up rows of dazzling lights and began their work. At seven o'clock, when the first protesters arrived, *The Wall* was already beginning to grow.

Flood too had been far from idle. A blow to The Tank's pride was more painful than if it had been delivered to his substantial body. Lining the approach road to Resurgam were not just ranks of cops, but horses too, and police dogs. The fencing had been reinforced again, the gates to the site fortified, and even more officers deployed.

The protesters assembled and found nowhere to go. They were channelled, corralled and kettled. They would be allowed to make their point from two pens, one on each side of the road. The demonstrations could be vocal and visual, legal and legitimate, but nothing more.

Seb, Mac and Esme were there, despite a conditional discharge all round and a ticking off from a Magistrate. 'I admire your ideals and respect your views,' the woman lectured. 'Even I was young once. But you went too far. It must not happen again.'

'It'll never stop me coming back,' Seb told his friends, this dark Friday morning. 'Just 'coz she's gone, doesn't stop me loving her. I'm gonna be here every day.'

'I'm with you,' Esme replied, a hand on his shoulder. 'For Alice.'

'For Alice,' Mac grunted.

'And for PC Steve too,' Esme added. 'Another of the victims of Resurgam.'

June gave them one of her motherly smiles, as proud as could be. 'And they say today's young people don't care about the world.' She hugged the three in turn and ruffled Seb's mop of hair.

Workers arriving suffered the ritual booing, but it was less spirited today. It was hard to show real feeling from within the confines of a cage, the demonstrators agreed.

★★★

Across the road, in the opposite pen, Esther was surrounded by a group of the professionals. Despite the limited space the respect was such that no one got too close, like a delegation of subjects before a monarch.

'We reckon it's time to get going,' a chirpy young man said. 'We've done our bit. They're fortifying the place. We'll get nowhere now.'

'And work's gonna begin soon on that big rail thing in the midlands,' a woman added. 'We should get up there, start digging in.'

'No.' Esther's answer was unquestionable. 'We stay.'

'But...'

'We stay.'

A sullen muttering broke out in the fringes of the group. *She's feeling guilty about that Alice... she ain't thinking straight.*

'But being here is pointless...' one began.

'No!' Esther snapped, her diminutive frame filled with passion. 'No more do we give up and walk away. No more compromise, no more desecration, no more damned monstrosities like Resurgam. There's always a way to fight. And we will fight. We'll fight, and fight, and fight some more. We'll never stop fighting. We've given up too many times. But not here, not now, not this time. This time we stand and we force them to take notice.'

Her voice fell, but it no longer needed to be so overawing. Because all around her were listening, as they always did.

'We've lost too many people to give up,' Esther continued. 'We've all lost friends, those who were precious to us, in the name of their gods - *progress* and *growth* and *development*. As if bricks and glass and steel and money were more important than our people and our planet. Yeah, ok, if you want the truth, I do feel guilty about Alice. I never stop thinking about how she died alongside me. But she was here willingly. She was one of us. And if we walk away now, we betray the memories of those who've fallen and we abandon the future – and that was the very thing they stood with us to protect.'

The power of the speech left the professionals becalmed, doubts banished by the belief of this young woman. In the silence that followed, Esther looked to Resurgam. A crane was swinging a steel girder through the lightening sky. The framework of metal was growing inexorably, day by day, never resting, always rising.

Her expression said she wanted to smite it down with one mighty, triumphant blow. Trample upon the foundations until they were dust, erase Resurgam from the history of the planet as if it had never existed. Restore this little stretch of city beach where once a young girl had played so happily.

'Something's got to be done about this thing,' she said, more calmly now and with all the certainty of her soul. 'And it will be, believe me.'

'You got some plan?' a man asked quietly. 'You're up to something, ain't you?'

But to that, the only reply was, 'I've always got a plan,' along with an emotionless, enigmatic smile.

★★★

Over the weekend there was a little push and shove, some shouting of insults, but that was the sum of it. A woman was arrested for trying to damage one of the fences that penned in the protesters. But real disorder there was none.

Far above the juvenilia of the human world, Resurgam continued to grow. The Wall was completed and suffered its first graffiti attack. Concise, if far from eloquent, the untidy message was "Fuck This".

And that came to be how many of the demonstrators felt. When Monday dawned with more snow, the numbers fell a little further. By Tuesday, the protest was half the strength of last week.

The police maintained their watchfulness. The dogs, the horses, the hordes of officers remained on duty. They had been caught before. They would not, Flood decreed, be caught again.

By Thursday many of the professionals, those not so deep in Esther's thrall, had slipped away. A new greenfield battle was in prospect further up country. But they left behind one final sting, a twist in their departing tails, a trap that was thundered into with lethal effect.

As a farewell gesture the demonstrators built another effigy, taller even than the first. In the spirit of equality, this time it was a snowwoman.

She was further away from Resurgam, on the road towards the Barbican, and a fine specimen of her kind. An ice cream cone was begged from a local café to form a nose and a scarf purchased from a charity shop to keep her warm. With a frisson of mocking flair, the ice woman was christened Ellen.

On a patrol along the fortified gates of Resurgam, Phil Rees saw the new artwork and once again filled with enmity, as surely as a cyst will swell with toxins. When the protesters returned to their pens, he clambered into his jeep, crunched it into gear and headed towards Ellen.

It was unfortunate he was such a couldn't-care-less type, and thus unconcerned with strapping on a seatbelt. Who gave a shit for the law and the bleating of safety campaigners? This would only be a short trip. Not to mention another hugely enjoyable one.

Faster and faster he drove, past the lines of wanky, stinking, hairy-arsed protesters. His boxer's face was alight with the malevolent anticipation of scattering Ellen into her component snowflakes.

It was only the shocking, shrieking warping of metal and the shattering of glass as the jeep imploded that a final thought filled the dying mind of Phil Rees. And it was a mark of the man that it ran "those fucking hippy twats only went and built the shitty thing over a fucking post box."

CHAPTER 24

That night's sleep felt like a perfect suspension of life; a cradle of warm darkness with an escort of benevolent dreams.

There were plenty of cares which could have come visiting. The opening of Resurgam, the pressure of the day covering all that would unfold and the possibility of an attack on the skyscraper. There was also the fascination of the quest for the Cashman, and how that would end. But they were kept easily afar by a modest, yet extraordinarily powerful weapon. It was one which had been missing for too long in life.

Dan awoke to a strange conviction he had been sleeping with a smile, and Claire's look was likewise. As befits their bizarre family, even Rutherford joined in. The dog was sporting his tongue out, happily lopsided face as he scampered around the flat.

'Come on, sleepy,' a vision of Claire chuckled. 'We've both got big days ahead. I've put the oven on low so it's a quick run, then back here for a pain au chocolat.'

Finale Friday was set to be another freezing day, but at least dry and clear. The inseparable companions of ice and frost had skipped through the night and left their footprints everywhere.

Hartley Park was deserted save for a prowling cat, which needed but one look at Rutherford to depart. On the stern instructions of his doctor, a man used to dealing with a tiresome diet of sprains and strains, Dan went through a warm up. He began a quick walk, then a jog and finally a full run, but still taking a while to catch up with Claire and Rutherford.

Together they lapped the park, wearing a footpath in the brittle grass. Dan took Claire through a quick and often breathless briefing on the case. Just as he expected, she analysed the information in seconds and listed the key questions that remained to be answered.

'Just what did Esther take with her from the lorry crash and where did she go? What's the connection with Tommy and what's she planning? And how can Esther hope to do anything with all the security there's going to be around Resurgam?'

A fast final lap of the park interrupted the list. The sun was rising, bringing no warmth but at least some light for the long suffering inmates of the jailer of the winter.

'Don't forget the other question,' Dan puffed. 'What's the Cashman to do with all this?'

'Which all makes for one hell of a day in prospect,' Claire noted.

They began walking back to the flat, to prepare as best they could for the hours ahead. She reached out a hand and Dan took it without hesitation. It was remarkable, he reflected, how yesterday this would have been unthinkable, but now...

They were about to cross the busy Eggbuckland Road, Rutherford carefully on the lead, when Dan's phone rang. He expected the newsroom, full of questions about the coverage of Resurgam, but it was Adam.

'Can you two get down to Charles Cross ASAP?' he asked, in a voice that was tight with pressure. 'Another bloody warning's arrived.'

★★★

A high esteem for your partner should be part of coupledom, even if it's often unfortunately otherwise. But it's always a pleasure to see that others harbour a similar respect.

The curse of working in television meant Dan was used to being recognised. The long association with Adam also made him a familiar figure in the corridors of Charles Cross Police Station. But today, Dan was very much the warm up act compared to the delight prompted by the return of Claire.

'Great to see you!' a woman detective exclaimed, giving her a hug. 'So glad you're with us again!' a man added. 'We've missed you.'

And that was just on the ground floor. By the time they'd traversed the claustrophobic stairs to reach the third level, Dan had counted nine hearty welcomes. But the effusion prize went to a uniformed probationer, so young he could have been recruited from primary school, who came close to genuflecting. 'Sergeant Reynolds!' the infant squealed. 'You've made my day!'

Dan tried, but mostly failed, to overlook how the young man's eyes escorted Claire's figure up the stairs. But he had a point. Claire had resurrected one of her collection of black trouser suits for this day, and was filling it with style.

When at last they arrived at the top floor, Adam was waiting with that irascible impatience he did so well. There was no time for greetings, just a hasty ushering into the Major Incident Room, or MIR, and a thrusting of two photocopies of the note and its abrupt message: '**LAST CHANCE**'.

It was Esther's writing again, but this time it wasn't the words which held their attention. A photograph had been attached, a colour reproduction of unusual quality and sharpness.

It showed a thick steel girder, intersecting at a right angle with another. In that corner were strapped some large plastic packets. Laced around was black tape, holding them tight to the frame. And protruding from one end were several electrical wires in a variety of colours. They ran to a small, black box, with a row of tiny lights on the front. Only the top light was illuminated, with a steady green glow. A couple of thin antennae sprouted alongside.

The background was poorly lit, out of focus and indistinct. But it looked like earth and concrete, smattered with mud and perhaps a little snow.

Dan and Claire looked up from the picture at the same time. Adam was standing, arms folded, against the window. In the distance, the backdrop now to all city life, was Resurgam, only hours away from its grand opening.

'Shit,' Dan whispered.

'Quite,' Adam replied.

★★★

The span of windows along the MIR was akin to a ship's bridge. The view was the one commendation in a police station which was otherwise a graceless block of brutal functionality.

It was said in the early days that every department coveted the top floor, but CID pulled rank and squatted. For that, Dan was always grateful. The panorama of city and distant sea helped him reflect and let his mind explore the alleyways of a case.

The time was a few minutes after nine, the roads still clogged with the daily gloop of commuters. The MIR started to reverberate with the sound of rotors and the police helicopter laboured past, heading towards Resurgam.

'Every cop we've got is either here or on the way,' Adam explained. 'And you two are here because thinking's your thing. So get thinking.'

'That picture,' Claire said. 'Is it what it seems?'

'The experts have had a look. The way it's set up is credible. But it's impossible to tell if it's a real bomb or a hoax.'

'And it's inside Resurgam?' Dan asked.

'The boffins say *the layout of the steel is consistent with Resurgam's foundations.*'

'But not definitely inside?'

'Nothing's bloody definite!' Adam snapped. 'That's the problem.'

'Anyway,' Claire intervened, adopting her traditional role as arbiter, 'if we assume it is a bomb, could Esther have got the materials?'

'You know how easy it is to make explosives,' Adam replied. 'Plus we have evidence Esther was looking at that kind of thing before.'

'So how could she have planted a bomb in the foundations without it being found?'

'An inside job,' Dan and Adam said together.

'Tommy?'

'It has to be,' Adam continued. 'He plants it when he's alone at night, probably with her help. They hide it somehow, in plastic bags, under some other materials and the building grows around it.'

'But,' Dan said, 'From what we know of Tommy he's not up for something like that.'

Adam shrugged. 'Esther can be persuasive. Or she could have told him it's not really a bomb. Just designed to look like one to stop us opening Resurgam.'

'But wasn't Esther supposed to be dedicated to peaceful protest?' Claire observed. 'Which is presumably why she's giving us these warnings. She wants to stop Resurgam opening, but not hurt anyone.'

'That changed though, didn't it?' Dan noted. 'I got a sense of her becoming more and more embittered. And when Alice died...'

They were interrupted by a man offering cups of tea from a tray. The pungent smell told of the traditional police stew of a brew. Adam and Claire helped themselves, Dan decided to pass. It wasn't a day to risk a bumptious stomach.

'There's something else,' Adam said. 'How the hell is Esther posting these threats to us? We're pretty sure she's still hiding somewhere around Resurgam. I had surveillance teams out all yesterday watching the area. But no one saw anyone who looked anything like her.'

And to that question the only answer was a thoughtful silence. In the distance the helicopter was flying slow circuits of Resurgam.

'I take it the theory is this bomb – if it is one - is radio controlled?' Claire asked.

'Yep.' Adam replied.

'But would it still work? It'd have been planted almost a year ago.'

'The boffins say it could. The technology, the batteries, they're all pretty robust now.'

'And could it still be detonated through all the metal and glass and everything else?'

'They think so.'

'You've carried out a search?' Dan asked.

'Oh!' Adam exclaimed with all the mockery of a virtuoso satirist. 'I hadn't thought of that.'

'Dan means - did you find anything?' Claire soothed.

'No. But then most of the foundations are encased in tonnes of concrete anyway. We've tried the dogs and explosives detectors. Nothing.'

'So it might just be a hoax, or no bomb at all,' Dan pointed out.

'Or it might just be well-hidden and too deeply buried to find.'

'But even if there is a bomb, surely it wouldn't do serious damage to Resurgam?' Dan asked. 'It's such a huge building, so strongly designed.'

'No one's prepared to guarantee me that,' Adam replied, quietly. 'And how do you feel about taking the chance when there are going to be thousands of people in there?'

★★★

With all the security in place, the fabled *ring of steel* which must feature in every modern policing operation, they decided to walk to Resurgam.

It was one of those classical winter days that feel good from the right side of a window. Up in the MIR, with the low yellow sun stretching across the city, a stroll was the obvious idea. But emerging from the police station, the temperature change was as sharp as plunging into a fjord.

They walked fast to help keep out the chill, traversing the stark shadows and bursts of dazzling light. Adam went through the remainder of the briefing as they strode. There had been another exchange between the Deputy Chief Constable and Ellen Dance regarding the latest threat.

'Exchange?' Dan queried, knowingly.

'Ok, fight then.'

Dance had seen a copy of the letter and photograph and dismissed them as the work of a crank. Once more she had taken refuge in the stateswoman's stance; that terror, bullying and coercion must never prevail.

'In fairness, she has got a point,' Dan ventured. 'That picture – it could have been taken anywhere.'

'I'll mention that to the relatives of the scores of corpses we end up dealing with,' Adam retorted. 'I'm sure it'll be a huge comfort.'

The police had scored one victory. If they couldn't prevent Resurgam from opening they could at least tell the Duke of

Lyonesse that his presence would be inadvisable. The regal dignitary, the day's VIP, had duly pulled out, diplomatically citing family issues. Undaunted, Ellen Dance herself would now carry out the opening.

'I can hardly wait,' Adam added, sullenly.

The timings of the big day that was Finale Friday were unorthodox. Resurgam would open at 3pm. The explanation ran that it was designed to allow people who had been at work to enjoy the fiesta. The stores would stay open until 11, the restaurants, bars, Sky Garden and nightclub even later.

The main anchor of *Wessex Tonight,* Craig, was being sent to front the coverage. Dan would cut the report on the grand opening, the culmination of all these months of waiting.

'Not feeling a bit put out, are we?' Claire teased. 'Having your glory stolen?'

'I would have been, but – not given what I reckon I'll need to be doing at one o'clock. That's going to be really something.'

'I still can't see how this Cashman nonsense is connected,' Adam complained. 'If it even is.'

'It is,' Dan replied. 'You wait.'

They walked along a cobbled street and turned the corner. Ahead, one side lit bright by the sun, the other black in shade, Resurgam towered into the perfect sky.

★★★

It was almost six hours until Resurgam opened and the temperature was bitter enough to make a husky think twice about venturing out. But already the crowds were gathering. Even Adam, that most practical of pragmatists, stopped to take in the sight.

'Hell,' he said. 'Make that hundreds of corpses if there's an attack.'

The area around the skyscraper had been closed to traffic and taken over by a wedge of humanity. The access road, the streets, the pavements, all were filled with the slow trudge of visitors and sightseers, chattering and gawping.

A queue had formed to be the first in, stretching back along The Wall, around the corner and out of sight. The people at the front were being photographed, filmed and interviewed. Security staff paced the line, offering tea and coffee to those towards the front.

'We've been queuing since midnight,' a pair of young women shouted excitedly as they enjoyed the attention. They were wearing duvets and sleeping bags around their coats.

The police helicopter was hovering out to sea. Cops on motorbikes, in cars and on foot were everywhere. Some were armed, cradling sub machine guns. As if to counterpoint their menace jugglers and magicians roved, working their tricks. By the gates a fire eater sent plumes of flame into the sky.

Adam, Dan and Claire began picking a slow way through the mass of people. As they rounded a family, young children on the shoulders of two men, Claire's hand found Dan's and squeezed it. The children were beaming with smiles, waving little flags with Finale Friday blazed upon them.

By the gates to Resurgam an area had been penned off for the protesters. The barriers were laced with banners. Several read "For Alice, never forgotten".

June stood at the front of the group, those rainbow gloves warming her hands, as they had from the start of the campaign. She was the leader still, had only grown through all the battles of Resurgam. But the long days here had taken a toll. She had aged beyond the year since this started, looked paler, but also more serene.

Alongside was Maggie, holding one of June's crossword books. She was even more concerned for her old friend now, stood watchful and caring.

The students were there too, Mac scowling out that teenager's look from amidst his long leather coat. It bore the wear of the protests, scuffed and scraped, but did so with pride. And hidden upon his shoulder was a tattoo, a cause of such parental horror; the dark outlines of a flock of flying birds. Mac had never said why he had it inscribed, but all around him knew.

Seb wore a body warmer and was still horribly thin, his face even more haunted than in the days following Alice's death. Time had been no healer here; he carried the pain through each passing minute.

He would rub at the soreness of his thighs when he thought no one was looking. Only Esme knew the truth; about the hidden wounds where the young man cut himself, time and again.

She had tried to help, but Seb would allow no one close. Not any more, not after what had happened to Alice. The death of a first love in the most brutal of ways, and played out before him. Seb had become a block of ice, always refortifying himself, never permitting a single breach in his frozen defences.

Esme huddled down in a parker, the fur of its hood framing her face. Much of the mischief of her soul had left over this past year, the fire of her spirit quenched too. She had become quieter, that coppery hair less vivid, the cheekiness gone from her smile.

She shared Seb's suffering, and all the worse for being able to do nothing about it. At night, sleepless and with no one to talk to, she browsed websites that she found frightening, but nonetheless alluring.

At the other end of the pen was a set of the professionals, returned for one last demonstration on this seminal day. Simian's bulk rose above the rest of the group, as he eyed the patrolling police officers with undisguised, unblinking contempt.

Along the access road a couple of large police vans had parked. Sitting in the front of the first was a young man, an eye patch bisecting his face, a pretty woman with short, dark hair beside him.

'Isn't that Steve Rogers?' Dan asked.

'We found him a desk job,' Adam replied. 'It was the least the lad deserved. For some reason he wanted to be here today.'

'And that's his girlfriend, Kathy?' asked Claire.

'His fiancée now. She's looked after him throughout.'

Love surrounded the pair, if not unbridled happiness. They were holding hands, but Steve's one surviving eye was only for Resurgam. It was a stare of repugnance and revulsion.

'An eye patch?' Claire asked, quietly. 'They can do much more, these days.'

'He didn't want anything else. He's wearing that patch for a reason,' Adam replied, with a disdainful nod to the skyscraper.

★★★

The foreign paparazzi were standing on a bench, taking shots of the crowd. The Italian was in the middle, wearing a black woollen jacket of impeccable cut and impenetrable, fly's eyes sunglasses. He kept looking at his watch and chattering to his friends. They were all smiling.

'Bugger,' Dan muttered.

'What?' Claire asked.

'They know. I'm sure they do.'

'About the Cashman?'

'Yep.'

'What're you going to do?'

'Err – I'll come back to you on that.'

Jackie Denyer was watching from behind the gates, a clipboard in one hand, a mobile phone clamped to her ear. She paced up and down as she spoke, as if urged on by the importance of her work. It was all over her and within her; upon these moments so much depended. She kept staring up at the great monolith as if it was a god. Of Ellen Dance there was no sign.

The crowd thickened, a slow wave of motion shifting along the access road. They struggled through, Adam to the fore, carefully forceful as he edged along. It was dark and close in the tightness of the pack, strangely warm in the cold of the day.

The viscous river of people broke to reveal a surprise. Standing beside a bench was Alannah, all dressed in black, her father too. Her eyes were boring into Resurgam and she was mouthing some words. It was impossible to make out what she was whispering, but it could have been *fuck you*, time and again.

Alannah looked brittle, her complexion like aged china, delicate and fragile, so frail it could shatter with the slightest of knocks. One hand was deep in a pocket, but in the other she held a photo of Tommy.

She spotted them at once and visibly started, looked panicked, cast her eyes around as if seeking an escape. But the mass of onlookers was too dense.

She stared for a second, that look filled with fear and loss, but anger too. Dan was taken aback by the rage contained within the young woman. There was resentment, loathing, detestation; all in a brief glance before she turned away and hid her face.

Jack leaned over and said bluntly, 'Leave her be, will you? She's suffered enough. She insisted on coming here. God knows why, all the trouble the bloody thing's caused.'

Dan followed Adam and Claire as they made their way towards a block of police vans. They were parked in a bay just along from the Homeless Mission. Again today, a handful of rough sleepers had emerged to watch. Resurgam had provided them with many a month's free entertainment.

Adam plunged into a rapid conversation with a sergeant. 'No sir, nothing,' the man kept saying. 'Nothing unusual, nothing suspicious at all – so far.' Another cop leaned out of the van and handed down plastic cups of coffee.

The time was almost ten o'clock. More people were arriving, walking down the road in bunches and swathes, some stopping to take photographs. A public address system boomed through the background of chatter.

Welcome to Finale Friday. Only five hours to go!

Claire was sipping demurely at her drink, eyes upon the skyscraper, when she flinched as though hit by an electric shock.

'What?' Dan asked.

'What?' Adam joined in.

'Don't turn around,' Claire said quietly, 'But I think I might know where Esther's hiding.'

CHAPTER 25

For all the quirks of his character, Dan had come to the view that Chief Inspector Adam Breen had three fundamental drivers. Firstly, he was a family man and utterly committed to Annie and Tom, however much he might complain about the latter. He was also a policeman, with a powerful sense of justice. And lastly, but only just, he was a man of action.

This moment, this morning, with Claire's insight of inspiration, that trait surged to the fore. It took a second, perhaps two at most of thought, before the strategy was set and the orders issued. Claire hopped up into one of the police vans to do her bidding. Dan received a peremptory beckon and they set off towards the Homeless Mission.

'Any chance we could have some back up?' he asked, nervously. 'I'd prefer not to go through another Cliff Larson experience.'

Adam groaned. 'We're after one young woman. Not a posse of desperadoes.'

'Yeah, but…'

'And you heard what I told Claire.'

The tone indicated further argument was redundant. Dan duly quietened and followed, weaving through the relentless flow of people heading towards Resurgam. Even in his urgency, intent upon what might easily be the last moments in the case, Adam was unfailingly polite, issuing an "excuse me" to everyone he had to navigate.

The Mission was an austere stone building, probably Victorian, perhaps even older. Two rough sleepers were standing outside, both smoking. They watched warily as Adam approached. The ability to spot a police officer was learnt early amongst those who live on the wrong side of the law.

If the men were expecting arrest, or an order to move on, then Adam had a surprise. He moved close, to within inches of their faces. They muttered and shuffled with discomfort.

The first was tall, an inch above six feet and quickly discounted. But the second was much shorter and suffered the full scrutiny of a detective's eye. Adam reached out and gave the man's beard a sharp tug.

'What the fuck!' he bellowed, in a voice worn by cigarettes and drink. More remonstrations followed, but they were vented at the air. Adam was satisfied with his unorthodox investigations and already inside the Mission.

★★★

The place might once have been a hotel, for there was just the hint of long-forgotten style. Fading and crumbled plasterwork lined the heights of the yellowed walls. The stone floor was tiled with the memory of mosaics, more missing than present, now just the odd curl of colour. A smell of bleach and pine dominated the atmosphere, but everywhere behind it was decay; stale urine, body odour and sickness.

In what was probably once a reception area stood a large wooden hatch, and inside a tired looking middle-aged man. He was wearing a scruffy shirt and jacket, which hung open around an impressive gut. The effect was similar to the curtains on a stage being almost drawn, but instead halting as they gathered round a remaining prop.

The man bent down to fumble with some unseen issue beneath the hatch. Adam coughed and was ignored, so he rapped hard on the wood with his wedding ring.

'What?' asked a disembodied voice.

'Police is *what*.'

The head reappeared. 'Oh.'

The man attempted to introduce himself and got as far as David Haddock when Adam interrupted. 'I need to see the list of people you've had in over the past week.'

'That's confidential.'

'Not when I'm investigating murder and terrorism.'

'You got a warrant?'

'No. But I have got thirty cops standing outside looking for a place to get warm. And I wonder what they'd start finding if they joined us in here and had a poke around.'

Without further ado a threadbare A4 book was produced. Adam began scanning the list, tracing the lines with a finger, quickly going back over the days.

Dan favoured the unfortunately named Mr Haddock with a smile and asked, 'Is it only men you have in here?'

'Yeah. There are a few women rough sleepers. But this place is men only.'

'Here,' Adam said, pointing to an entry. In neat writing, on the page marked Sunday, was the name Winston Smith. He flicked through the sheets. Smith had been in residence every night since.

'That's the one,' Dan said. 'And she couldn't resist a little barb, even now. Winston Smith, the quiet hero who stood up for what was right.'

'She?' queried Haddock, rubbing a hand over his girth. 'What you mean, she?'

'Is Smith in his room?' Adam asked.

'Think so.'

'Which one?'

'Number seven. Just around the corner.'

'Tell me about him.'

Haddock shrugged, the drumlin of his stomach moving in time. 'Not much to tell. New arrival. Said he'd probably be here until Friday – sorry, today I mean.'

Dan and Adam exchanged a look.

'Kept himself to himself,' Haddock went on.

'Anything unusual about him?'

'Not really.'

'Describe him to me.'

'Not tall, bit short in fact. Not fat or thin. Didn't speak much.'

'I bet he didn't,' Adam noted. 'But when he did, what was his voice like?'

'Hoarse. He sort of whispered, like a lot we get in. The drink does that.'

'And it's a hell of a good way of disguising a voice,' Dan observed.

'Was he carrying anything?'

'Like what?'

'Like a rucksack.'

'No, nothing.'

Adam hesitated and Dan could see the thoughts running. 'She could have dumped it after she changed clothes,' he whispered.

'Thank you, I had thought of that,' Adam replied in a piqued voice, before turning back to Haddock. 'Was there anything else unusual about him?'

'Nothing really. He was just – average.'

'A grimy face? Dirty?'

'Yeah, but that's pretty standard.'

'And what about smell?'

Haddock pulled a face, like his namesake might use to communicate puzzlement at suddenly being netted and hauled out of the sea. 'His smell?'

'Smells can be harder to disguise,' Dan tried to help, albeit unsuccessfully judging from Haddock's expression.

'Disguise? Look, what's going on…'

'Just answer the question,' Adam commanded.

The man considered, then raised a thoughtful finger. 'You know, there was something. He didn't smell like the others. He was sort of – cleaner.'

Heavy boots on the stone floor interrupted the observation. Claire was striding towards them, followed by two large police officers. Both were carrying guns.

★★★

They huddled in a small alcove just along the corridor. Adam sent Haddock back to close the main doors, reassuring him that the Mission should be shut for no more than an hour. The two marksmen began checking their pistols.

Dan found himself watching the skilled manipulation of the squat, black guns, the magazines of small brass cylinders. Both men were remarkably young for what they may be asked to do.

'We've only got minutes before word gets around we're here,' Adam said. 'And there's a risk Esther could detonate the bomb from her room.'

'So we enter unannounced,' Claire continued.

'And if she goes for anything, shows even a hint of trying to reach something...' Adam added, and the two marksmen nodded in time.

'Get it right and we finish this here. End any threat of an explosion and the loss of countless lives. We're all heroes and everyone has a happy afternoon.'

Dan felt himself gulp. He edged a little further into the background.

'You ready?' Adam asked.

'Yes sir,' the pair replied together.

★★★

Quietly they paced along the corridor. Both the marksmen wore police issue boots, tough and protective but soft of foot, and stepped without a sound. Adam's predilection for fashion meant anything less than leather soled shoes would have been heresy, so he adopted a curious exaggerated gait. As for Claire, she just glided with a nonchalant defiance of gravity, as only Claire could.

At the rear of the little party Dan hung back. Several times before he'd been amongst armed police and he had grown not in the slightest any more comfortable with it.

The occupants' rooms were numbered from the reception area outwards. They passed a door with a one on it, no sound from within. Number two whispered with the suggestion of a little shuffling. Number three was silent.

From outside the Mission came the muffled bark of a sudden loudspeaker. *Welcome one and all to the wonder of Resurgam. Only four and a half hours to go!*

The doors were all plain wood, differing only in their degree of wear. They passed number four, its handle drooping a little, a large crack bisecting its face.

Ahead was a blind turn. At the front of the group Adam stopped and held up a hand. He crouched, almost onto his knees, and carefully peered around the corner.

One of the marksmen raised his pistol.

Behind them, away in the distance, a door thudded closed. Dan wheeled around. There was no one there, nothing.

Adam stood up again and beckoned. They paced around the wall to find an identical corridor, leading deeper into the building. It was darker here, all shadows and half-light.

Door number five was a dense black. A crack of daylight edged from its base. But there was no noise, no sign anyone was inside.

They paced on, even more slowly now. A patch of the stone floor was stained with a coagulated darkness. Adam stopped, studied it, picked with a fingernail.

'Blood,' he whispered to Claire.

'Could be anyone's, sir.'

'You think?'

The sound of the police helicopter crept through the thickness of the building's walls. They reached door six. Its number hung askew. From inside came coughing and a loud sneeze followed by swearing. The voice was unquestionably male.

Room seven was just feet ahead. Adam inched onwards, holding to the edge of the corridor, furthest from the door. He stopped directly opposite. The marksmen took up positions on each side.

Claire slipped back a little, Dan even further behind. All was silent.

Adam stepped forwards and gently pressed his ear to the wood. For several seconds he listened, eyes closed in concentration.

After perhaps half a minute, the detective straightened and nodded his head. He held up a hand, the four fingers and thumb outstretched, then pointed to his chest. Both marksmen nodded.

Adam steadied himself by the door. He dropped his thumb, then a finger. Three to go.

Dan edged a little further back along the corridor.

Another finger folded. Two left.

One of the marksmen let out a long breath.

A final finger remaining.

Both the cops trained their pistols on the door. The barrels gleamed in the dimness, unwavering and unerring. Calm fingers hovered above the metal curls of the triggers.

The last digit dropped. Adam raised a foot and smashed it into the door.

With a roar in the silence the wood cracked, splintered, and the door flew open. Adam lurched inside, scanning around fast, the marksmen following, their weapons roving for a threat, a target.

And all stopped, as sudden and shocked as a bird flying into a window. Adam, the marksmen, the three just froze and stared.

The room was basic; a bed, wardrobe and a chair. Peeling, damp-stained walls and a grimy window. On the floor was a small pile of clothes, some food wrappings and a couple of plastic drink bottles.

And on the bed, surrounded by a dark slick of blood, lay a body, a knife protruding from its neck.

CHAPTER 26

They were some of the stranger surroundings in which to try to solve a murder, but there was little choice. With Resurgam less than four hours away from opening, and crowds and hubbub everywhere, any hope of peace was a precious rarity.

Dan watched as Adam and Claire slipped calmly into full investigative mode. The room and corridor were sealed off, forensics and scenes of crime officers summoned. Mr Haddock was informed the hour's delay was to become far greater, with any attempts at protest ruthlessly overridden.

It took the two detectives but a few seconds with the corpse, and another handful to scrutinise the room, before they knew all they needed for now. With a bulky policeman of a guard in place, they headed upstairs to the Mission's Association Room.

Sizeable and surprisingly light, it must have been decorated courtesy of one of those art in the community projects which transform dully distasteful places into brightly distasteful versions. Murals covered two walls, grotesque, spray painted representations of human forms.

There was an aged pool table, large television and an old radiator which gave out as much heat as an electric torch. The room was only a begrudging tad warmer than the temperature outside.

The far wall was dominated by a large window, which looked out onto the Barbican. Once it would have boasted an uninterrupted view of the harbour. Now it had an outlook in which Resurgam owned a controlling interest.

Set around the window were some old and battered armchairs. Dan sank gladly into one and found it remarkably comfortable. Claire poised elegantly on the edge of another and Adam folded his arms and paced back and forth, as was his wont.

Neither of the two detectives spoke, so Dan asked, 'Well then?'

'No forced entry,' Claire said. 'No struggle.'

'Then whoever killed Esther, she must have let them into the room?'

'Spot on,' Adam replied. 'And more to the point, how did our killer know she was there anyway?'

The room filled with the spectres of thought. Outside the crowds milled, swirling in a slow vortex around Resurgam. A clock on the wall said the time was well after eleven.

Dan's mobile rang. It was El. He switched the call to the answer machine.

'She's been dead for no more than a few hours,' Claire said.

'Suspects?' Dan asked.

'Take your pick,' Adam grunted. 'Just about everyone in this case might have a reason for wanting her dead.'

'And we've seen all of them around Resurgam this morning,' Claire noted.

'But how could any have known where Esther was?' Dan persisted. 'She was hiding for a reason.'

'Maybe she had an accomplice,' Claire suggested. 'Perhaps they turned on her.'

'Maybe someone was smarter than us and just worked it out,' Adam added, rather sulkily. 'We haven't exactly been distinguishing ourselves.'

His mobile rang and he listened for a few seconds, then outlined the contents of the call. Esther's room had been searched. Little of interest was found, apart from a box of batteries, along with some electrical wiring.

'But nothing that could be a detonator,' Adam concluded. 'Just what we might suspect could be spare parts for one.'

'So,' Claire said, 'Whoever killed Esther, it looks like they took the detonator.'

'Which means this isn't over,' Dan observed.

'More genius!' Adam exclaimed. 'I think we could just about safely assume that.'

'Look smart arse, I know you're under pressure, but...'

'That's enough,' the traditional referee cut in, before the squabbling schoolboys could revert to type. 'We don't have time to waste arguing. Let's think about what we do.'

'Arrest anyone with a motive for killing Esther?' Dan suggested.

'A bit of evidence wouldn't hurt first,' Adam replied, more calmly. 'We can't just go and round up everyone. Plus, we've got to be cleverer than that. If they do have the detonator we need some kind of plan to stop them using it.'

Adam glared at the window and its view of Resurgam. But Dan and Claire were looking in the opposite direction, over the detective's shoulder. Standing in the doorway was Ellen Dance.

★★★

Dance stepped into the room. She was as impeccably attired as ever. That fine black coat flowed around like an old fashioned cape, and her dark hair was pinned up in a style which radiated authority.

The message was as clear as a cannonade. For this day, above all others, everything must be perfect. Dance carried her usual self-confidence, but couldn't hide an edge of trepidation in her movements. Each was a little hesitant, as if fearful of what she was about to hear.

Denyer followed just behind, as ever. Her eyes skitted across the room, taking in everyone, continually calculating the situation.

'I hear something's happened,' Dance said. 'You've got Esther?'

'Kind of.'

'Meaning?'

Adam didn't reply, just stood, arms still folded across his chest.

'You can't keep any information back,' Denyer piped up, gnawing impatiently at the silence. 'We've got a right to know.'

Dan could see that Adam was deliberating what to tell them. Another blast of the public address system boomed into the room.

Just three and a half hours to go! Keep moving along, please, make space for others to come enjoy the wonderful spectacle of Finale Friday.

The queue for the skyscraper was stretching along the road and out of sight. More people were joining it, more and more. Police officers were trying to keep the line in some kind of order but it was an impossible task, like to trying to herd cats.

'Well, Chief Inspector?' Dance prompted, the tension clear in her voice.

'Yes, we do know where Esther is.'

'Which is?'

'Downstairs. And dead.'

'Dead?'

'She's been strangled.'

He briefly explained how Esther's body had been found, watching carefully the whole time for any sign of a reaction. Dance and Denyer listened intently and then turned to each other and embraced.

'I'm glad you're finding murder so enjoyable,' Claire said, in a voice like an arrow sculpted from ice.

'She murdered Tommy Ross, remember?' Denyer shot back. 'Not to mention...'

'We have a quaint tradition in this country called justice,' Claire interjected. 'Not vigilantes.'

'But the point is,' Dance replied, loftily, 'Everything's all right now?'

'*All right?*'

'You mean apart from the deaths of Esther and Tommy?' Adam asked, matching Claire's disgust and raising it. 'And all the others who've suffered...'

'You know what I mean,' Dance interrupted.

'Opening your building.'

'Opening Resurgam, yes.'

Claire rose from the arm of the chair. 'I'm so terribly sorry to mention it, but there is just one little problem.'

'Which is?' Denyer asked.

'Whoever killed Esther took the detonator. And I can only think of one reason they'd want to do that.'

'It's a bluff,' Dance said quickly, as if fearful an inconvenient truth might escape and begin breeding. 'There never was any threat.'

'Which no doubt means you intend to go ahead with the opening?' Adam asked, heavily. 'Despite the growing pile of corpses you're kindly helping to create, and the danger to thousands of people. Well, you surprise me.'

Dance ignored the jibe. She drew herself up and swathed herself in the comfort of the new mantra. It had become unchallengeable, a boast of the strongest of leadership, the loudest of clarion calls.

'Resurgam will open, proud and unfettered, just as I promised.' She gestured towards the window, her voice rising. 'It will welcome with open arms all these fine people who have come to delight in its wonder. Now, please excuse me. I have a speech to finish.'

★★★

The crowd had grown so dense it was difficult to find a path through. The walk from the Homeless Mission to Resurgam, no more than a few hundred metres, took the best part of ten minutes. People jostled, pushed and weaved in the slow moving mass as it oozed around the skyscraper.

Four times on the short journey Dan's phone rang. On each occasion it was El. When at last he answered, Dan was greeted by a near hysterical burbling.

'They know, I know they know. They're everywhere, the Italian and his mates. How're we gonna get the Cashman to ourselves? And how're we gonna get him anyway in this crowd? I'm screwed, washed up, hung out, dicked, danged and done.'

Never a great respecter of the English language, at times of stress El could thrash it more efficiently than a combine harvester. Dan managed some soothing reassurances and told the photographer to meet him at the gates in a few minutes.

Here, by the entrance to Resurgam, the crowd was at its thickest, a solid block of people. He edged and wheeled his way through the final lines, showed his press pass to the security men and stumbled gratefully into the compound.

The satellite vans were parked against The Wall, a line of them, technical staff and journalists from a range of broadcasters milling around. Dan found Craig and Nigel and checked all was well for the lunchtime broadcast.

'Everything's sorted,' the perpetually tanned face of *Wessex Tonight* told him. 'But that's the easy bit. It's when the thing opens it's going to go crazy.'

The time was coming up to twelve o'clock. Dan wasn't due to meet El for a few minutes, so he slipped into the front of the van to take one final look at his notes on the Cashman's appearances. There were still questions to be answered and they were nagging quietly away.

The timings made sense. They had to indicate his final stand would come at one o'clock. And the countdown of days tied the Cashman's plan to the opening of Resurgam.

The only remaining mystery was the letters, the enigmatic A, B, C, D, E, F, G and H, one circled for each appearance. Today it would be the turn of the H.

Dan doodled on his notepad, scribbled a couple of thoughts, but no inspiration came. He braced himself to face the crowd once more, and walked over to find El.

★★★

By the gates, there were almost as many police officers as visitors. Their fluorescent bibs flashed through the throng.

And that was just those in uniform. Adam said there were many more in plain clothes, looking for any of their suspects, the people who may have the detonator. On surrounding buildings, watching from windows and rooftops were yet more officers, continually scanning for any hint of a threat.

Dan had left the Homeless Mission as Adam and Claire went through a fast list of thoughts about what to do next. They had just over three hours until Resurgam opened.

'We can be pretty sure Dance or Denyer didn't kill Esther,' Adam said. 'They didn't react when I said she'd been strangled.'

'But they're also the least likely to want to blow up Resurgam,' Claire pointed out. 'And that still leaves us with the rest of the suspects. There's the Professionals, Simian and co., say because of some conspiracy, then a falling out with Esther.'

'And any of the locals,' Adam replied. 'Seb, the other students, June and her friend, because of what happened to Alice.'

'Then there's Alannah and Jack.'

'Yep. After the attack on Tommy, they could hate Esther enough to want to kill her and maybe even bring Resurgam down too.'

'Then there's the more difficult possibility,' Claire added. 'Steve Rogers.'

Adam nodded. 'We have to consider it.'

'Should we arrest them all?'

'That'd be a hell of a drastic step. We wouldn't be able to do it quietly. With that crowd outside it could cause panic.'

'We may be left with no choice,' Claire replied. 'Not when hundreds of lives could be at stake.'

The forensic examination of Esther's room was almost complete. Adam decided to wait to see if any more evidence was found, before going ahead with the arrests.

'This day is just getting more and more damned tense,' Dan said, as he was about to leave the Association Room. And with that observation, no one disagreed.

★★★

In the years of their collaborations, El had always brought Dan more than a few concerns. But today he was forcing his gift of peculiarity upon a group of innocents.

The photographer was balancing on the edge of a bench on the access road next to a family. It was an outing of the generations, a trio of children stood between a mum and dad, with three grandparents at the far end.

Dad, a youngish man with short hair and a very pale face, had positioned himself next to El and was eyeing him warily. At Dan's approach, El yelled, 'At last, at last, come on, we gotta sort it out, gotta!'

The man leaned forwards and discreetly asked, 'Is he with you?'

'Kind of,' Dan replied. 'I suppose I'm the nearest to a keeper he has.'

'Is he alright?'

Dan was pondering how to answer that broad and perceptive inquiry when the man went on. 'I was about to call the cops. He's been fidgeting like he's got some disease and muttering away to himself. He's frightening the children.'

'Right, calm now,' Dan told El. 'What's the matter?'

'Look!' came the disconsolate reply.

A series of other benches lined the access road and frontage of Resurgam. Upon each stood a member of the foreign paparazzi gang. They were scanning the crowds with the lenses of their cameras. Each also had a walkie talkie strung around his neck.

The Italian had taken a bench in the middle of the line. He was wearing that beautiful black leather jacket and had slicked back his dark hair. He looked over to Dan and El, smiled condescendingly and waved.

'We're sunk, stuffed and screwed,' El wailed. 'We're outgunned, outnumbered and outthought.'

'Shh,' Dan replied. 'I need to think.'

The time was a quarter past twelve. The crush of people was getting worse. Further up the hill a line of police officers had formed a cordon to stop anyone else walking down to Resurgam. Finale Friday had become like one of those dreadful nightclubs of younger years, with a one in, one out policy.

An ambulance was trying to make its way into the mass of people. Progress was slow, barely perceptible. Another two followed. Dan squinted through the winter brightness of the day. Someone had fainted in the press of bodies.

A figure was being lifted onto a stretcher and into the back of one of the ambulances. It set off towards hospital, the other two remaining, parked up and ready for the next casualty. In this crush a customer would surely come, and soon.

El's head was whipping back and forth like a spectator at a tennis match. 'What've you come up with?' he urged.

'Shh,' Dan repeated. 'I'm still thinking.'

'Come on, come on, come on!'

Dan wedged himself by the side of the bench to avoid the glutinous flow of the crowd and once again took out his notes on the Cashman's appearances. One o'clock, it had to be 1300 hours for his final stand. That made perfect sense. And it was all to do with Resurgam, so it had to be here. But where exactly? And how could they possibly grab the Cashman for themselves amidst this crowd, and with the other paparazzi watching for him?

The PA system barked into life once more. *Welcome all, to the wonder of Resurgam! It's half past twelve. Just two and a half hours to go!*

From the bench, El let out an anguished moan.

★★★

Over by the police vans Adam was surveying the crowd. He looked grim, his face heavily lined. Cops were still patrolling, winding their way through the masses, smiling and chatting, but always watching for anything suspicious.

Dan's mobile buzzed with a text message. It was Claire.

Look after yourself out there. I don't want anything denying me tonight, not after all this time! x

Amid the squeeze of people, the pressure of the day and the relentless whimpering and moaning of the village idiot, Dan nonetheless smiled.

'What you laughing about?' El groaned. 'There's no sign of him. What we gonna do?'

'I was smiling about Claire.'

'Yeah, great, glad we've sorted that. Now, minds back on the job.'

Dan gave the oaf a look. 'What do you mean – *we've sorted that*? And how did you know it was sorted anyway?'

El shook his head so vigorously his chipmunk cheeks rolled. 'Never mind, never mind, we gotta get the Cashman!'

The police helicopter made a slow pass overhead. The time was moving ever onwards. It was twenty-five to one.

'I'm not so sure about this anymore,' Dan muttered.

'What?' El yelped.

'It's just – everything the Cashman's done so far has been meticulously planned. If he was making a last stand here, surely it'd be at the gates. But with such a crush of people there's no chance of that working.'

'So?'

'So… I'm wondering if we're in the right place.'

El's face crumpled. 'What? No! No, no, no! But the Italian and all that are here.'

'But they're not necessarily right. All the clues point to the Cashman's last appearance being here and now. But…'

'But what?'

'Shh!' Dan urged, for the third time. 'Just give me a moment.'

He grabbed at the bench and pulled himself up, looked around. There was no sign of anyone who might be the Cashman, no hint of anything unusual.

Dan let his eyes roam, tried to concentrate. Resurgam was towering into the blue sky, awaiting its moment, so soon to come. The crowd was quiet and good-natured as they too waited.

Only the little pen of demonstrators was more active, occasionally waving a placard and airing one of the familiar chants.

No way, never to stay, not here, not today.

But something had changed. Someone was missing.

Dan scrabbled through his notes and found the pages dedicated to his attempts to crack the Cashman's code. At the top was written A B C D E F G H – *why?*

And now he knew.

'Shit!' he hissed.

'What?' El babbled. 'What, what, what?!'

But Dan didn't answer, instead grabbed for El's watch. The time was twenty to one.

They'd never make it. Not through this crowd, not that journey.

'What?' El yelped. 'What?'

Dan paused but only briefly, then whispered into El's ear.

'No!'

'Yes.'

'Really?'

'Yep.'

'You sure?'

'It all adds up.'

'Oh my God!'

The photographer gasped in a couple of shallow breaths and clamped his hands over his heart. His knees sagged and he folded to the bench, then rolled down and came to rest on the freezing tarmac. The crowd edged back, forming a space around him.

'Help me!' Dan yelled. 'My friend's having a heart attack!'

He grabbed for El's jacket, tugged at it, tried to give the stricken man some air. El looked up, then past him, away to the distance, vision unfocused, lips trembling, hands still clutching at his chest. Slowly, his eyes slipped closed.

CHAPTER 27

For all with their duties, missions and quests this afternoon, time was seeping away. Like the blood from a wounded body, or the waters from a breached lake, it was unplugged, unstopped and unstoppable.

Time was what they needed, and time they didn't have. The old foe was once again going about his business with emotionless, silent efficiency, and deserting them.

For Dan and El, Adam and Claire, time was eroding away the hopes of finding their resolutions. And for the Cashman, and the faceless killer whose hand was upon the detonator, it was another edge closer to their culmination.

Over the year of the biography of Resurgam, many stories, many individual paths had been set in train. And on this cold winter's day, not yet half done, the destinies of all the players were converging, as surely as beads of water will swirl together into a plughole.

★★★

'Flood's on the way,' Adam said. 'He wants this sorted, he says.'

'So do we,' Claire pointed out, with her usual calm logic.

'I did mention that – or tried to. He wasn't in the mood for a discussion. It was the *never on my watch* thing.'

They were standing beside one of the police vans, looking down the hill towards Resurgam. The city was at a standstill. Hordes were here already, many more trying to get to the opening.

'There must be tens of thousands,' Claire observed.

'Storm through it with me,' Adam urged. 'We've got a few mins before Flood arrives. Who killed Esther? Who's got the detonator?'

Claire let her look run over the layers of humanity milling around Resurgam. A man was lifting a young child from a pushchair, balancing the boy on his shoulders. The woman next to him stood on tiptoe to try to take in the sight.

In the distance the sea blazed in the winter sunshine. It was only a little warmer than earlier, the air above the great crowd a haze of bodyheat.

The forensics teams had carried out an examination of Esther's room, albeit with reluctant haste. The results were quick, but unhelpful. There were plenty of hairs and fibres in the room, but many people might have been there, aside from Esther and the murderer, and they would take days to analyse. No fingerprints had been found on the knife. The killer had worn gloves.

'Which wouldn't have looked out of place in the winter,' Adam noted. 'So Esther wouldn't necessarily have been on her guard.'

'Which in turn helps to explain the lack of a struggle,' Claire added. 'So we're left as we were. Esther must have known the killer.'

'Then who was it?'

'Steve Rogers?' Claire ventured. 'He's got a strong motive.'

'With his fiancée helping? Or at least suspecting? It doesn't sound likely. And why does Esther let him in and not be wary?'

'Maybe he spins her some story about how he hates Resurgam for what it's done to him. He's come round to her cause.'

'And how does he find her?'

'He's a cop. He'd have seen what was happening in the investigation. He might have been looking for her, got a break, spotted something.'

'That's worth thinking about, 'Adam nodded thoughtfully. 'Alannah? She's got a hell of a good motive too.'

'A possibility, but − has she got the guts?'

'Maybe, maybe not. One of the other protesters then? Or perhaps more than one?'

'And a motive? They'd be turning on their own.'

'With the local lot it could be because Esther hijacked their demonstration and look what that led to. With one of the so called professionals, maybe a feud or falling out.'

'That's certainly possible,' Claire mused. 'And you reckon Dance and Denyer are out, after your little test?'

'Not definitively. They could be good actors. They're certainly smart enough and they've got the best motive for wanting to get rid of Esther.' Adam let out a frustrated hiss. 'We're just guessing. Flailing in the bloody dark.'

Along the road, a siren wailed. A police car had become mired in the crowd. The passenger door opened, Brian Flood climbed out and began pushing his way towards the vans.

★★★

The ambulance picked up speed as it broke free from the stickiness of the mass of people. El was lying prostrate on a stretcher, his eyes closed, one hand across his chest. An oxygen mask was strapped over his mouth and his breathing was sharp and thin.

The young paramedic, who had introduced himself as Chas, began attaching a series of sensors to the ample body of his latest unfortunate.

'Try not to worry,' he told Dan, over his shoulder. 'He's in good hands.'

'Ok, but – it's so hard seeing him like this.'

Chas turned around. He was a young man, perhaps on the home stretch towards 30, with short, dark hair, designer stubble, and a narrow but smiley face. The expression looked natural, but might perhaps have been learned in medical training school. He had oddly large feet, encased in shiny black air-soled shoes. Combined with his tall and thin stature the effect was to create a comparison with a golf club.

'Are you his brother?' Chas asked, in a friendly way.

The well-intended words unleashed an unusual affliction upon Dan. He was rendered speechless. And before he could rebut the blasphemy, the silver tongued medical saviour blithely iced the cake of insult with, 'You do look quite similar.'

Dan eyed the rotund, freckle faced, shock haired specimen of primitive humanity lying upon the stretcher and probed pointedly at his own face. 'We're not related,' he managed eventually, and added very deliberately, 'No one's ever said we look alike before. That's no one. And never.'

The ambulance jarred and rattled as it negotiated some turbulence on the road. Dan forcefully reminded himself to keep quiet. This was no time to be difficult.

'It's good news so far,' Chas chirped. 'His heart's looking ok. The rhythm is strong and sound.'

'Thank the gods for that,' Dan gushed, in a manner he hoped was suitably convincing.

'Don't you fear, we'll soon have him right as rain.'

'Yes, please. I'm so worried.' Dan glanced at Chas's watch. The time was a quarter to one. 'Will it take long to get to the hospital?'

'Try to relax. It'll be five minutes, no more.'

'That's perfect.'

★★★

Brian Flood was filled with sufficient purpose not to bother with even a perfunctory greeting. He stepped into the police van, instructed the sergeant and another cop who was sheltering from the cold to leave, and beckoned Adam and Claire inside. The door was propelled shut with a force that rocked the suspension.

The space was cramped and smelt of diesel. Monitors flickered with varying CCTV pictures of the crowd. A radio crackled with intermittent chatter.

'I've got thousands of people out there, quite likely a bomber running loose, and the bloody Home Office on the phone every few minutes,' Flood barked. 'We've got two hours before Resurgam opens and possibly the worst case of mass murder the country's ever seen. What do we do?'

Adam quickly outlined the list of suspects and their possible motives.

'But no indication who has the detonator?'

'No sir.' Claire answered. 'If there even is one. If there's even a bomb, and if it's even viable.'

'We have to assume there is. We can't take any risks with that mob out there.'

Flood nodded towards the screens. The area around Resurgam was entirely filled with people, from seafront to inland. All the surrounding streets, going back for perhaps half a mile, were also packed.

'We're going to seal the area off,' Flood said. 'There are too many people here already. If there's an attack it'll be carnage.'

The radio barked with an order to get to the Harbour View pub. One of the monitors showed a group of men pushing each other. The smallest of the set swung a fist, another a boot, and the others rapidly joined in, producing a stumbling, scrapping melee. Police officers were attempting to get to the fight, but it was taking time to find a way through.

'Bloody hell,' Flood grunted. 'It's tense enough out there as it is.'

'Realistically there's little chance of identifying who might have the detonator before Resurgam opens,' Adam said.

'So if we want to be sure, the only option is to take out every single suspect,' Claire added. 'We've got them all under surveillance.'

She tapped one of the screens. The picture kept changing, from the group of protesters by the gate, still waving their placards, to Steve Rogers and Kathy, standing outside a coffee shop.

There was Alannah and Jack by a bench on the access road. She was shaking, kept opening her mouth to draw in trembling breaths. Jackie Denyer was standing behind the gates watching the crowd.

'You're suggesting we lift them in that mob?' Flood asked. 'There'd be panic.'

Adam leaned back against a wall. 'It's even worse than that. Whoever has the detonator has already killed to get it. Which means we have to assume they'd use it. Tasers are no good – the electric shock could trigger the detonator. So it's got to be an armed operation – with the order to shoot if someone looks like they're about to set off the bomb.'

'Which means the risk of even more of a panic,' Claire added. 'Not to mention the possibility of innocent people being shot.'

Outside, a chorus of *Why are we Waiting?* struck up. The monitors showed a couple of outbreaks of jostling in the crowd as people tried to push their way forwards.

Flood folded his arms and let loose a couple of forceful obscenities. Even in this omnipresent, relentless cold he was sweating hard. 'Before we do this – are there any other options?'

He looked to Claire and then Adam. Both shook their heads.

★★★

The ambulance was on the dual carriageway and almost at the hospital. The time was ten to one.

'I don't understand this,' Chas complained. 'I can't find a thing wrong with him. You say he collapsed, clutching his chest?'

'Yes,' Dan replied.

'And he's been under a lot of stress?'

'That's right.'

'And he was in a bit of a state?'

'Yes.'

The paramedic rubbed at his nose. 'It all points to a heart attack. But his ticker seems fine. It's beating like a rhino's.'

The ambulance rounded a sharp corner, making Dan and Chas struggle to hold their balance. The paramedic almost stepped on El's camera, lying by his side like the rifle of a fallen soldier.

'Did he twitch there?' Chas asked, peering at the prone creature. 'I'm sure he moved.'

'It was just the ambulance,' Dan said quickly. 'But mind the camera, it's very precious to him.'

The hospital was just ahead, its car parks reaching out to the main road, its towers showing above some trees. They were shining in the harsh winter sun.

'It could have been the cold that brought on some kind of attack, I suppose,' Chas ventured.

'Just – let's get to the hospital,' Dan replied. 'I'll feel much better when we're there.'

★★★

The picture on the monitor suddenly jerked and zoomed in. A couple of the professionals were trying to scale The Wall. Police officers began running towards the pair, pushing through the rest of the group.

Flood swore again. 'This is getting out of hand.' He took out a mobile phone and stepped into the front of the van.

A posse of cops had reached the men and grabbed for their legs. Others formed a line and stood waiting to catch the pair. But they were hanging on hard, refusing to let go.

Some in the crowd began to shout and cheer. Security staff from Resurgam were also heading for the scene, trying to clear a space.

One of the men released his grip and fell onto the safety net of waiting officers. But the other was still clinging to the wall, kicking out, trying to free himself. Another policeman grabbed at him, caught a hold on his jeans and he too fell.

Flood climbed back over some body armour and re-joined Adam and Claire.

'That was Dance.'

'And, sir?' Claire asked.

'I told her she had to act.'

'And?' Adam prompted.

'She said there was nothing she could do.'

'That sounds familiar.'

The Tank's gun barrel levelled upon its target. 'Until I started talking about the laws on corporate manslaughter. She's going to bring forward the opening to two o'clock. She's only going to announce it a few minutes before, so no one gets overexcited.'

'Which means we can use it as a distraction,' Claire noted.

'So when she's addressing the crowd...' Adam said slowly, 'We move in.'

★★★

The ambulance sped past a line of cars and on to a roundabout. Almost all the traffic was heading into the city, long lines of vehicles tailing back.

'Everyone's going to Resurgam,' Chas observed, perceptively.

Dan's mobile bleeped with a text message. He had to read it three times to be sure he understood.

'Are you ok?' the paramedic asked. 'You look worried.'

'They're going to open Resurgam early. And I need to be there.'

'You do TV, don't you? Are you covering it?'

'We both are. Well, we were. Before...'

Dan screwed up his face and pointed to El. He was still lying comatose, eyes closed, but his breathing was now calm.

'Don't you worry,' Chas said, resting a hand on Dan's shoulder. 'I haven't lost one yet.'

The ambulance turned onto the road leading into the hospital. Sign after sign for various departments flashed by. Accident and Emergency was just ahead, the doors wide open, a doctor, nurse and orderly waiting.

'We're here,' Dan announced, loudly.

'Everything's ok now,' Chas replied. 'We'll soon...'

The sentence was stoppered in his mouth by movement from the patient. El sat up, took off the oxygen mask and grinned.

'Hey, what?' Chas objected. 'You're supposed to be dying.'

'I feel great,' El chirped. 'It's amazing what a little lie down can do.'

The back doors of the ambulance were opening, light sweeping inside, another paramedic waiting. He gawped at the modern day resurrection playing out before him, even if a less likely candidate for the position of saviour could scarcely have been envisaged.

'I feel so good I think I'll go for a little walk,' El continued. 'If you'll excuse me.'

He grabbed his camera, hopped down and headed towards the hospital's main entrance. Dan followed. They walked fast, ignored the shouts and calls, and certainly didn't dare to look back.

CHAPTER 28

If this was to be the place for the denouement of an extraordinary and touching story, there was no sign of it. The hospital looked as everyday as always. People came and people went, hurrying through the cold of the winter sunshine, the vast majority with grim expressions. Some carried gifts; flowers, food, newspapers and books, others looked too intent on their misery for any other considerations.

The main entrance was on a little crescent of road marked *Strictly No Waiting*. A parking attendant hovered, hunkered so low in his coat as to appear to be a man without a chin. At the slightest sign of any errant vehicle making a brazen attempt to linger for more than a few seconds the human vulture was upon it.

Dan and El halted a hundred metres from the entrance, behind a small line of unhealthy trees. It was the only cover on offer, and here the two devious hunters considered their strategy. The time was eight minutes to one.

A man usually averse, if not allergic, to any form of exercise, El had set the pace on the short journey from Accident and Emergency. He peered along the road towards the main entrance, the double doors set open and the constant stream of arrivals and escapees.

'Where's it gonna happen then?'

'Right here, I assume,' Dan replied.

'Assume?'

'As I explained, the clues aren't specific. They don't exactly give a grid reference.'

El raised the camera to his eye. He let the lens linger on the doors, then swept through an arc, along the long frontage of the hospital, to the car park, then behind and the many layers and angular depths of the building.

'The place is bloody huge.'

'One of the biggest in Britain.'

'And we don't know where the Cashman's gonna show up?'

'It's got to be here. Right at the main entrance. Where else for his final stand?'

'You sure?'

'It all makes sense. I hope so, anyway.'

El jutted out a dubious lip. 'It's one hell of a risk. Leaving Resurgam when that's the obvious place.'

'I told you about the clues. It all tied together, didn't it?'

'Maybe. It's just – now we're here, I'm starting to have me doubts.'

'Me too.'

'What?!'

'Just kidding.'

Once more the camera swept the hospital entrance. The time had moved on to seven minutes to one.

'He's leaving it bloody late,' El complained. 'There's not a dicky bird hint of anything happening.'

'You know what I'd like you to do?'

'What?'

'Be just like you were in the ambulance. I thought you made a great corpse.'

★★★

Once more they waited. El kept his camera focused unerringly on the entrance, Dan continually eyed his watch. It was remarkable how slowly the time was passing. Upon every glance he was convinced another minute had turned, but it was only a few seconds.

His mobile bleeped with a text. It was Claire again.

Did you get that last message? Important!

'Bugger,' Dan whispered.

'What?'

'Resurgam's opening early. When we're done here I need to get back - fast.'

'Me too. It'll be worth a few shots, 'specially if it goes boom.'

'Beautifully put. But the point is – how the hell do we get there?'

'What?'

'You saw the crowds around the thing. Plus the hundreds of other cars that were trying to get down to the waterfront. The cops are cordoning the area off. No one else is getting in.'

'You'd better do something.'

'How did I know you were going to say that?'

It was six minutes to one. Dan fumbled for his mobile, called Claire and explained his predicament.

'I'll put you onto the boss,' she said.

'I really hope this is urgent,' a very irascible Adam snapped. 'As I'm currently only trying to avert a terrorist outrage.'

'It is – to me.'

'Well?'

'I'm up at the hospital.'

The detective's tone softened. 'You ok?'

'Yep, fine.'

'Then what the hell are you doing there?'

'Never mind. But I need to get back. And there's no way. Unless…'

'What?'

'Could you send a taxi?'

'What?!'

'A special taxi. With a flashing blue light.'

Adam swore in a way usually reserved for the most distasteful of the criminal tendency. 'Since when did we become Copcabs?'

'I take it that's a no?'

'Well spotted. Now stop wasting my time.'

The phone was passed back to Claire, its short passage accompanied by background grumbling.

'How did the negotiations go?' she asked, sweetly.

'Not great.'

'It is a little tense here.'

'I guessed.'

'How important is it you get back?'

'Not particularly. I'll only be sacked if I'm not there for one of the biggest stories *Wessex Tonight* has ever covered.'

'That bad?'

'That's being optimistic and assuming Resurgam doesn't go up in flames. If I miss that Lizzie will probably take out a contract on my life.'

'Would it help what's going to happen this evening if there was some way of getting you back here?'

And now, bizarrely, despite a world that was growing ever more stressful and surreal, Dan smiled. 'Quite honestly, I don't think it'd make any difference. But I could certainly do with getting back to Resurgam.'

'That's the right answer,' came a reply filled with a matching smile.

★★★

Four minutes to one.

'Are you sure about this?' El bleated, for the umpteenth time.

'Still not entirely.'

'How much you sure?'

'You want a percentage?'

'Yeah. And make it a good one.'

'Say – maybe 60.' Dan saw his friend's expression, and quickly amended the guesswork mathematics. '70, then.'

El gibbered a little, but didn't reply.

A car drew up outside the entrance. The camera was at the paparazzo's eye in an instant. So eager was El that he was dangling forwards, hanging onto a tree for balance.

'Come on my beauty, come on!'

If desire alone was enough to create the Cashman from the invisibility of air, then he would surely have appeared. But instead an elderly lady picked herself slowly from the car and toddled into the hospital.

'Pants,' sighed El. 'I'm getting a bad feeling about this.'

'I know what you mean. But it all makes sense. Eight Cashman appearances and R, E, S, U, R, G, A, M. That can't be a coincidence.'

'And the times?'

'The first appearance at 6 o'clock in the evening, or 18 hundred hours. The second at five in the morning. They correspond with each of the letters. So the last has to be at one pm.'

'Right,' El said slowly, hampered by the burden of the mental arithmetic. 'And the locations?'

'All random, just so long as there are quite a few people about. With the critical exception of this last one, to point out the contrast of spending money on Resurgam instead of a hospital.' Dan wondered if he was trying to convince El, or himself. 'The pieces of paper in the bags are marked by letters, remember? From A to H. And where's the only place the H could lead you, from road signs or on a map?'

'Ok, but…'

'Combine that with who it is we think we're about to find and you've got it.'

'In which case, where is he?'

'He?'

'The Cashman.'

Dan raised an eyebrow. 'Or Cashwoman.'

★★★

The positive news was that there were no other media in sight, and not a sign of the foreign paparazzi. Dan tried to soothe El with the thought, only to be deflated by the rejoinder, 'There ain't no sign of the Cashman, neither.'

Another car drew up. El launched into his straining forwards mode again, and this time even began a low panting. It was like standing next to a starving dog.

The sun wasn't helping. It was shining on the car's windscreen, which made picking out the occupants difficult.

'There's at least a couple of people,' El muttered. 'No, three. This is it!'

Dan found himself leaning forwards too. 'You reckon?'

'Yeah. The Cashman, his helper, and that plonker Franklin who pulled out in front of us. It has to be.'

One of the doors was opening, the passenger side, but very slowly. The driver's door was opening too.

El's voice was breathless with excitement. 'Oh, great God of the paparazzi, deliver unto your loyal son El his pile of gold. He's a good snapper. He deserves it.'

'Shh,' Dan urged. 'Just concentrate.'

'I'm focused as a laser beam, baby.'

One of the car's back doors was opening. The attendant was hovering and watching, but making no attempt to intervene.

'Remember the plan,' Dan said. 'You know what to do.'

A woman climbed slowly from the front of the car. She was heavily pregnant. Another woman and a man joined her, shared a hug, and the man escorted her into the hospital. El slumped and deflated.

'He's not coming. We got it wrong. You got it wrong!'

Dan was finding self-defence difficult, and any remaining resources of hope even more elusive. 'He's – she's bound to wait until the last minute. That's the way it's worked before.'

El checked his watch. It was two minutes to one. 'We're missing the party,' he lamented. 'Back at Resurgam the Cashman's about to spring out and all those other bloody snappers are gonna fill their boots with El's gold.'

A couple of women emerged from the double doors. El raised the camera, but this time with much less enthusiasm. The pair paused for a second, exchanged a few words, then made their separate ways towards the car parks.

One minute to one.

'I'm gonna hang up me camera,' El moaned. 'The biggest gig going, on me home turf, and I'm diddled by a bunch of foreign fancy boys. I'm gonna take up basket weaving.'

A car was approaching the little crescent. It was moving slowly. And it looked familiar.

'Hang on,' Dan said.

The car passed through a patch of shade. There were two people in the front. And one was wearing a distinctive scarf.

'Holy flying saucers!' El gasped.

The car pulled up outside the main entrance.

'Come on!' Dan ordered and began striding forwards, closing the ground fast.

The driver was mouthing words, the passenger reaching into the back of the car.

'Come on, come on,' Dan urged.

It felt like being like an Olympic runner at the end of a marathon. He'd reached the stadium and was only metres from the finish line. There were no other competitors in sight, and all the work had finally paid off. Triumph, jubilation, and a symphony of relief were playing in Dan's ears.

They were almost at the crescent. The sun was blazing from the windscreen. But inside the car they could just about make out the person in the passenger seat putting something over their face.

Dan reached the door and knocked on the window. Looking back at him was the Robin Hood mask.

★★★

It should have been a moment of drama and delight. It was somewhat marred by the contemporary curse of the predatory parking attendant.

The window began to roll down and Dan was preparing his words. Something with a nod to history he thought, with suitable resonance for such a meeting. Something like, 'The Cashman, I presume?'

He was about to speak when a reedy and nasal voice, emitted unnecessarily close to his ear pronounced, 'You can't wait here.'

'What?'

'It's dropping off only. No waiting.'

'But…'

'No exceptions.'

'But…'

'Not even for you TV people and your friends.'

'But…'

'There are no exceptions at all. I've got a bunch of tickets and I'm not afraid to use them. And please, do not attempt to argue.' The irritating voice took on a note of pride. 'In my time I believe I've heard every excuse possible.'

'Not this one you haven't,' Dan replied, and stood aside to let the attendant see who was sitting in the car.

'Oh,' the chinless one faltered. 'Isn't that…'

'Yes, it is. On top of which, if you give me two minutes – just two – then what was about to happen here will still happen. And you'll be at the front of the queue, won't you?'

The calculations churned in the miniature despot's eyes. As time was limited and Dan very much didn't want any further complications, he added a little extra incentive.

'I don't suppose you get paid hugely well for such an important job. A little bonus would be the least you deserve.'

In fairness to the man, he might have been an automaton but he wasn't daft.

'In this case I can make an exception,' the model of officialdom announced. 'Please proceed.'

★★★

As the poignancy of the moment was now as lost as a pop star's humility, Dan merely said, 'Hello June.'

The mask was lowered. 'Hello Dan. So, you worked it out?'

'Eventually.'

'Well done.'

'Thanks. I think I know what this is all about, but I've got a few questions I'd like to ask – for the record.'

'Of course. I'd like it to all be on the record.'

It was curious how little people noticed of the world around them. The ceaseless procession from the hospital carried on with its comings and goings. Cars passed by, and no one spotted what was playing out in this small crescent of road.

El was standing back and taking snaps, leaning forwards and taking snaps, and jigging from foot to foot and taking snaps.

'And a little photo shoot for my excitable friend here too, if you wouldn't mind,' Dan added.

'No problem. I've got plenty I want to say.'

'I thought you might have.'

She was remarkably calm for this moment, the culmination of a wondrous story. But there was a little mistiness in the eyes, and a softness to the voice, which betrayed the power of feeling that had pushed her to act.

'There is one thing I need to do first,' June said.

'I'll get out of your way. It won't take long, will it?'

'It never does.'

Dan pulled away the fireball of excitement that was El. He was burbling delighted nonsense to himself, his face filled with a soppy grin. 'Let's hear it for Dan who found the Cashman,' he kept repeating.

And now came the final moment. The car door opened and out climbed the Cashman, bag in hand. Within seconds there was a crowd, grabbing eagerly at the last of the offerings.

El snapped and snapped and snapped some more. But as for Dan he just watched, filled with the colours of fields of spring flowers, an expanse of warmth and admiration that he had rarely known before.

CHAPTER 29

Daniel Groves had never thought of himself as a dreamer. Yes, he was sometimes prone to melancholy moods, although thankfully the Swamp of the depression that had always stalked him tended to strike far less often these days. For that, as he was gratefully aware, he had Claire to thank.

Dan might occasionally wander a little stroll of fancy, but that was one of the ways which helped him to solve crimes when Adam came calling. And he could sometimes just detach and admire the world, as when he was walking on Dartmoor with Rutherford, or marvel upon the people within it, as of now, watching June.

The problem was such traits didn't make for the greatest assets in his official job, which was more a getting stuck in and sorting out vocation. But the mechanism Dan had developed to warn him of such danger moments was in efficient working order, and now it activated again.

A miniature Lizzie materialised on his shoulder and began carping, 'Film it, film it, film it!' And, as though stung by an invisible bee, Dan took out his mobile and did just that.

When June had finished, she nodded nebulously to Dan and got back into the car. No one attempted to intervene. All were too busy celebrating their windfalls, gossiping excitedly, or scouring the area for overlooked booty.

The little car trundled slowly up to the expanse of car park and found a space. Dan and El followed and got into the back.

'So, that's that,' June said, with magnificent understatement.

Maggie reached out a hand and held her shoulder. 'You did it. Exactly the way you wanted. And now it's time to tell the world why.'

Both women looked to the back of the car, only to find Dan staring into space.

'It's time,' Maggie prompted, but to no avail, until the unsubtle intervention of a whack in the ribs from El.

'Err, what?' Dan said.

'What do we do now?' June asked.

'Sorry, I was elsewhere.'

Maggie nodded. 'We noticed. We just thought you might like to do some interviewing,' she teased, but warmly. 'Perhaps run a story. Given that you're the only journalist with the news everyone's been chasing.'

Kindly to the end, June asked, 'Are you ok?'

'Sort of,' Dan replied. 'It's a couple of things.'

'Which are?'

'Well, firstly finding you. The quest for the Cashman was such a huge thing. Now it's over I feel… a little lost.'

'I'm the same,' June agreed. 'It was an incredible time, hiding this great secret.'

'What was the other thing, Dan?' Maggie asked.

'Just the small business of Resurgam.'

★★★

The car was filled with yellow sunlight and felt warm, despite the pervasive cold outside. June wound down a window to let the crispness of the breeze circulate. El was happily spinning through the snaps he'd taken, examining each in turn.

'El's, all El's,' he giggled. 'Where are you now, Mr Italian? Chase El's farts!'

'What were you saying about Resurgam?' June asked, and Dan explained how it was opening early. In response, in that wonderful way which older people have, June swore with an erudite style. 'Oh bugger. I really wanted to be there to protest.'

'I rather wanted to be there too,' Dan replied, sadly. 'Being as my job depends on it.'

'And there's no way of getting back?'

However unspoken, the clock on the dashboard suggested not. The time was quarter past one.

'Your editor will understand, surely? Now you've got the story of the Cashman.'

'You don't know my editor.'

Dan must have looked impressively downcast, because both Maggie and June reached over and took a hand each.

'We'll look after you,' Maggie said, confirming the pair's status as modern saints.

A siren wailed in the distance. An ambulance no doubt, bringing yet another victim to this palace of suffering.

'I'll be ok,' Dan ventured. 'It's just – I'd have liked to be there to see Resurgam open, after all that's happened. And I wouldn't have minded a few more years of being a hack, either.'

The siren was growing louder. Dan's mouth felt dry. He gulped and said huskily, 'Ah well, I suppose it was good while it lasted.'

'What now, then?' June asked.

'We'd better take you back to *Wessex Tonight*. I can interview you, then plead prostrate before Lizzie for a stay of execution.'

The sound of the siren was overwhelming the car. It was coming very close. The ambulance must have overshot Accident and Emergency.

A flashing blue light appeared in the car park. It wasn't an ambulance, but a police car. And Claire was driving.

★★★

'I'm hoping you're here for the reason... I hope you are,' was the professional wordsmith's eloquent greeting.

'In which case you'd better get in. We don't have much time.'

Dan clambered into the passenger seat, and with a magnanimous afterthought looked over to El, June and Maggie.

'Yes, ok,' Claire conceded patiently, and the trio climbed into the back. It wasn't going to be the most comfortable of rides. El was in the middle, which meant both women were squashed against the doors like tomatoes in a tray. But at least they now had a chance of making it to Resurgam.

Claire switched on the sirens and blue lights and accelerated towards the main road. 'The law says I can only use the disco gear in an emergency.'

'And I suspect even the best of barristers would struggle to argue that transporting your boyfriend is such.'

'Yep.'

Dan thought for a few seconds. 'I should have said earlier,' he chirped. 'I must have forgotten in all the excitement. I've got an idea who might have the detonator.'

'Well, gosh-oh-mighty,' Claire replied. 'I'd better get you to the scene at once.'

The traffic at the roundabout froze as they sped through and slewed a hard left. Poor June, slight at the best of times, was being further reduced courtesy of the mass of El.

The time was twenty five past one. They dashed along the dual carriageway, heading for the city centre.

'How're things down at Resurgam?' Dan asked.

'Chaos. I'll get us as close as I can, but after that it'll be quicker to walk.'

The car dodged in and out of a line of traffic, the motion swinging their bodies from side to side.

'It'd be nice to be alive to cash in on the Cashman,' El muttered.

'As I owe you one I'll overlook that,' Claire replied.

'What do you owe him?' Dan queried. 'Look, what is going on?'

'I'll tell you later - maybe.'

They reached a roadblock, a couple of cop cars nose to nose, barring the way. Claire mounted the pavement and carried on. They were heading along North Hill, home to the university and Plymouth's student masses, almost at the city centre but still a mile from Resurgam.

The area was oddly quiet, the shops and streets mostly empty. It was as if the population of the city had all been drawn to Finale Friday.

Dan's mobile rang. It was Nigel.

'I'm on the way. Won't be long.'

'Good. Lizzie's been on the line. I told her you were in the loo.'

'Nice improvisation.'

Another roadblock was ahead, barriers this time, and manned by a pair of Community Support Officers. Dan swore to himself, but at the sight of Claire the men jumped into action and hurried to clear the way.

Now the crowd was starting to thicken, spilling onto the road, milling and meandering. Claire picked her way through as best she could. But they slowed, slowed and slowed again until progress was painful. The clock on the dashboard read 1.35.

Claire pulled the car into the side of the road. 'Time to run,' she said.

★★★

They adopted the shape of an armour piercing shell. Claire led the way, using a mixture of charm, diplomacy, authority and simple force.

'Urgent police business,' she shouted, in a remarkably loud voice, warrant card aloft. Just behind her, forming the shoulders of the round, came Dan and El and behind them June and Maggie.

Initially, progress was straightforward. There were hundreds of people, but not yet wedged together as a block. Resurgam was along one more street and around the corner. The time was 1.40.

'When is Dance going to announce the thing's opening early?' Dan asked.

'Five to two.'

'And when she's speaking you'll move in and...'

'Shh!' Claire warned. 'You're not broadcasting now.'

The street was narrow, cobbled, and the wedge of people was growing tighter. They were having to push hard, squeeze and sidle to make any progress. The mood was changing too. Where before smiles and nods had greeted their passage, now there was irritation.

'Who'd you think you are?' one sizeable man said, making no effort to remove his bulk from their path.

'CID,' was Claire's icy reply, and the obstacle shifted.

Most of the gift shops had closed, the owners hanging from upper floor windows to watch the opening. Cafes and take-aways remained open and were doing a magnificent trade.

The sun was blazing, the sky as clear as it had been all day. The temperature must have been no more than freezing, but the density of the mass and the number of bodies made it feel as warm as the summertime.

They eased around a corner. Resurgam was just ahead, dominating the sky, the police helicopter hovering protectively alongside. Now every hint of space was occupied. Claire was having to shout louder, push harder to make any progress.

It was noisy too, the roar of the aircraft competing with the hubbub of chatter. People were talking excitedly about what they planned to do when they finally made it inside the skyscraper.

The line of police vans was ahead, no more than a hundred metres away. But the gap might as well have been a solid wall, so many people barred their path. Claire took out her radio and barked a couple of orders. From the vans, four large cops began pushing towards them, forcing a route through the crowd.

'Our escort,' she said.

★★★

It was just after quarter to two when they reached the vans. Adam was inside, watching the bank of monitors, his eyes flicking from image to image. Each of the possible suspects was being watched, the cameras following every movement.

'The firearms teams are in position,' he said. 'Just after Dance starts speaking we go in.'

'I've got to be off,' Dan replied quickly. 'The day job calls.'

Claire followed him back to the street. 'Where are you going to set up?'

'By the gates, where Nigel is.'

She gave him a quick kiss. 'Be careful. We've still got no idea what's going to happen.'

'You too. See you later.'

Dan fought his way through the crowd, using whatever was required; smiles, charm, the sharp edge of his shoulder. El, June and Maggie followed. It was like a pop concert of teenage years and the ridiculous attempts to get as close to the band as possible.

The helicopter banked away, heading inland. Just behind the gates, around the stage, the black-clad security men were deploying.

'Dance must be about to do her thing,' El panted.

'Keep going. We're almost there.'

June and Maggie peeled away to join the protesters. 'See you after all this is done,' Dan called.

Nigel was just ahead, waving his hand. Dan saw a speckle of light in the wall of people and heaved through.

The media had been corralled into a pen beneath one of the stomach-ache statues. There was a line of cameramen and photographers, Nigel right in the middle. All the lenses were trained on the stage.

'The word is Resurgam's going to open early,' he whispered. 'Dance is about to make a speech. I've got us a good pitch.'

What Nigel meant was that, as ever, he'd secured the best position. There was a clear view to the stage. But looking behind, all they could see was the first few lines of people in the crowd.

'This is no good.'

'What?' the cameraman queried. 'But we've got the perfect spot.'

The banks of speakers beside the stage began to hum. With echoing loudness, a voice announced, 'Ladies and gentlemen, please welcome the woman who made this happen. The President of the Regional Development Council, Ellen Dance.'

Dan stared into the crowd. It was probably his imagination but he thought he could see cops converging on the suspects; earpieces buzzing with orders, guns hidden in jackets but always at the ready.

'What the hell's the matter?' Nigel demanded.

'We're looking the wrong way.'

Dance was walking up the steps, taking them studiously, regally. Her attire was nothing less than perfect. There was no nuance of even a stray hair or ruffled hemline, nothing that could detract from this time.

Just behind the stage, Denyer could have been in a trance. She stood perfectly still, clipboard pressed to her chest, watching Dance, willing her onwards.

'Get the camera!' Dan ordered.

'What? But...'

'Trust me. Just do it!'

Nigel looked baffled, but did as he was asked. Dan grabbed at the statue and hauled himself up. He took the camera and pulled Nigel up too.

The pained shapes of whatever the statue was supposed to resemble were reasonably flat, making for a usable platform. There wasn't much space for the two of them, but it was just enough.

Dance was gazing out over the crowd, eyes devouring their presence, as if the mass of people fed her existence. Hundreds of thousands here for her and her alone; her vision and now her reality. Instinctively, Nigel focused the camera upon her.

'Not that way.'

'What?'

'Turn round. Film the crowd. Now!'

'What am I looking for?'

'Just do it.'

With careful, measured movements, Nigel inched around and aimed the camera towards the masses. There were so many people, endless ranks and rows of faces, arrayed together, all gazing towards Resurgam and Ellen Dance.

'What the hell are we doing?' Nigel whispered. 'We're missing it.'

'Just keep filming.'

'Filming what?'

'Anything you see. And you will.'

CHAPTER 30

Picking out the targets felt an impossible task. There were countless people in the ocean of humanity. And plenty were wearing hats to shield against the cold, or shades to see through the blaze of the sun.

On the stage Dance was growing, building with oratorical momentum. With a black leather glove clenched in a fist of determination she held the microphone tight and stood supreme before the masses. The fervour was growing, the fire spreading.

They said it couldn't be done. But – together – we did it.

A low cheer rose from the crowd.

They scoffed and sneered – but we showed them.

More shouts and cries of yes.

We did it for our city – and our future!

And now genuine enthusiasm. People smiling, believing, carried along by the emotions of the mass. Applauding the hardest, evangelising along, was Denyer. She was no longer detached, part of the machine which built this skyscraper, but as captured by the moment as anyone.

Amidst the growing noise, Dan was trying to be methodical. To work his way through the people in rows. To start at the front, scan from side to side.

It took but seconds to know it was a fool's task. The numbers were overwhelming, the crowd too packed together.

'What're we doing?' Nigel asked.

'If we're lucky, filming a hell of an exclusive.'

'For our sake, I hope you're right.'

In a few minutes, we're going to open Resurgam for you to see... for you to be a part of. They said we couldn't make our deadline – but we've beaten it! We're going to open early!

Now there was real feeling from the crowd. They had become united in conviction and certainty. People were waving, some whistling, roaring out their approval. And Dance, at the head of it all, was beaming, delighting in her victory.

A couple of cops were standing on the roofs of the police vans, binoculars pressed to their eyes. Dan tried to follow where they were looking, but it didn't help.

'Shit,' he said.

El clambered onto a lower level of the helpful artwork and was doing his best to assist. But about the only obvious sight was the line of foreign paparazzi, the Italian amongst them, standing on a bench. And here too, the ethos of the group had changed. There were shrugs, scowls, none of the laughter of earlier.

For El, jubilant and elated, it was reasonably restrained that his only response was a resort to that childhood favourite, 'Na na na na naa!'

'Nothing's happening,' Nigel whispered. 'What am I supposed to be looking for?'

It's almost time to finally introduce you to the wonder of Resurgam.

Dance was winding up, her voice reaching election pitch. At any moment Adam would give the order and the operation begin.

Just below, close to the gates, a couple of figures were moving in the crowd. As they inched forward the sun shone from a plastic earpiece.

'That's it!'

'What?' Nigel asked.

'They'll be working in twos. Look for pairs of people slipping through the crowd.'

'But why…'

'Just do it!'

Dan peered through the relentless flood of dazzling light. The crowd was still, but there was movement within the mass, tiny currents, subtle and slow. Couplings of people making a quiet, watchful way, nudging and edging a passage.

The camera's motor whirred as Nigel zoomed in the shot. 'At the back,' he directed. 'By the police vans.'

The man was hiding; wearing large, dark shades and secreted into a gap between a van and a lamppost, but it was Steve Rogers, Kathy by his side. She was holding him very close.

'He's crying,' Nigel whispered. 'Hell, he looks traumatised, poor man. Why on earth did he want to come and see this thing open?'

Just below the statue the two men had stopped and were staring up at Dance, clapping with the applause.

It's almost two o'clock… nearly time to open the gates and welcome you to the wonder of Resurgam

It was close to convincing, but the second of the men would occasionally glance to his side. And there were Alannah and Jack, both looking to the stage. Jack's face was unreadable, but his daughter's was contorted with emotion. She was biting continually at her lip, chewing hard, clutching at the photo of Tommy. That overwhelming hatred, the one which would pound Resurgam back into the bedrock, had only grown in ferocity.

More movement in the crowd. Several people were converging on the pen where the protesters stood.

Let's count down to the moment. Let's roar it out to the world. Twenty… nineteen… eighteen…

The group split as they worked forwards. Some headed for one end of the barriers and Simian and the professionals, others to where June and Maggie stood with Seb, Esme and Mac.

Twelve, eleven, ten…

The crowd was joining in with the countdown, the noise building with each number. The security guards had deployed along the gates, ready to pull them open. The assault of noise from all directions was giddying.

Dan tried to shift his gaze between each of the suspects. There was no indication who might have the detonator. All wore thick coats, had plenty of space to conceal it.

Eight, seven, six…

Simian had spotted the men heading towards his group. He picked up a placard, held it out, ready for the fight.

'There,' Dan said to Nigel.

The police officers were moving faster now, closing the last few yards to their targets. Adam must have given the order to make the arrests, timed it for the cover of the most noise.

A cop reached Simian, but was pushed away. Others were grabbing at the big man, some reaching into their jackets, levelling guns, barking commands clear above the hubbub.

'Armed police! Put your hands where I can see them!'

As one the professionals stopped, ended their resistance in an instant and raised their hands. The game had become too real to gamble any longer.

People in the crowd had seen the weapons. There were gasps, a couple of screams, finding echoes as the alarm spread. Faces changed in an instant, fear replacing the enjoyment.

From the stage, over the speakers, the countdown continued, had almost reached its climax. But the applause was dying. People were trying to move back, push and heave, escape from where the protesters had been surrounded. Mac, Esme and Seb were all being arrested, June and Maggie too.

Only Seb offered any resistance. He was shouting, screaming at the cops, voice hoarse with rage. 'You fuckers, haven't you done enough? You want to kill me too, like you did Alice?'

The anger was enough to fight an army. Seb was thin but strong, a wiry power suffusing his young frame.

'I'll fight you all,' he was yelling. 'Come on! What the fuck have I got to lose?'

Guns surrounded him, but the futility of mere bullets held no fear for a young man who had already suffered such wounds. Only the urgent calming of Esme, June and Maggie saved him. It dowsed enough of the inferno to allow him to be led away, although still mouthing abuse.

By the vans Steve Rogers was being arrested, Kathy beside him. He was remonstrating, kept pointing to his face and that eye patch, as if any reminder was needed of the sacrifice the young man had made.

Claire emerged from the crowd, was standing by the gates, talking rapidly into a radio, counting off the targets. Ellen Dance stared down, frozen-mouthed at the despoiling of her sacred moment. Denyer was the same.

Around the stage, all throughout the mass of people, a fearful silence had spread. But the operation was working. Only Alannah and Jack remained to be arrested. The pair were closest to the gates, hardest to reach.

Two officers were fighting a way towards them. But it was furious work, like battling a rip tide, as scores of people strained and shoved, tried to get out the way.

With fast and frightened eyes Alannah saw the men converging on her. They were reaching into their jackets, about to draw their guns.

But she was too quick. She threw down the photo of Tommy, the glass shattering as it hit the ground. And from a pocket she pulled a small grey cylinder, held it aloft and screamed, 'No nearer or I do it!'

CHAPTER 31

There was so much to that single, resonating second.

For the rest of the crowd, seeing the guns, hearing the words, there was realisation and panic. People began battling to get away, pushing, shouting and screaming. They flailed and fought, blindly and desperately.

For the marksmen, for Adam in the control van, for Claire, there was perhaps a blink of an opportunity. Just a chance to take the shot, but rare is the human mind that can make such a fateful decision so fast and particularly not when presented with such an unlikely terrorist.

They hesitated for just long enough. And Alannah exploited it.

'It's a pressure switch,' she yelled. 'And it's armed. If I take my finger off the bomb explodes.'

It was a reflection of the moment that Nigel, most gentle of men, eschewer of all crudeness, whispered, 'Oh fuck.'

'Yeah,' El agreed, in an uncommonly subdued voice.

And Dan couldn't fault the analysis of either of his friends. They had a grand vantage point for the extraordinary spectacle playing out just below. But they were also horribly exposed. If there was an explosion, or gunfire, they were standing aloft upon a statue with no cover. Whether it was bomb, bullets or both, they might as well paint targets upon their chests.

'She told me how it works,' Alannah bawled. 'The bomb, the detonator. She was real proud of it, Esther was. She went on about it for ages – until I knifed her.'

Jack was straining forwards to reach his daughter, but being held back by a pair of policemen.

'Alannah, no!' he shouted. 'Don't do this. I lost Tommy, I don't want to lose you…'

'Shut up!' she yelled back. 'I lost Tommy, not you. And for what? For a scabby fucking building!'

A space cleared. It was as though a stage had been created, bounded by the gates and wall and a fading ring of people. Lit bright at the centre were Alannah and two sets of marksmen, guns trained on the young woman. And approaching, slowly and carefully, hands held high, was Claire.

'Let's take it easy now,' she soothed.

'No closer!'

Claire stopped. She was perhaps ten metres away, and as ever, even in this moment, she was calm.

'I only want to talk to you.'

'What's there to talk about?'

'What do you want to talk about? Resurgam?'

Alannah studied Claire, through eyes that were narrow and blurred. Her hand was tight on that little cylinder and it was shaking.

'Yeah, go on then. Let's talk about fucking Resurgam.'

★★★

Dan, Nigel and El stood as still as they ever had and watched the electric confrontation. Claire was waiting with her hands by her sides, her face gentle and understanding. Alannah was so brittle it was as if she might fracture at any moment; legs set apart and tensed, body rigid, taut finger always on that little cylinder.

El looked up from his viewfinder and whispered, 'It's got a switch and a button. But it must be a bluff, don't you reckon?'

'It's not a chance I'd be keen to take,' Dan replied.

The crowd was being ushered further back, police officers shepherding them along the access road.

'We're moving everyone away, Alannah,' Claire explained. 'I know you wouldn't want innocent people to get hurt.'

'Yeah, ok.'

'And I would ask...'

'What?'

'If you'd let us get the people out of Resurgam too.'

'No.'

'I know you hate it. I understand that. But there are hundreds of workers in there, and…'

'I said fucking no!'

Claire raised her hands placatingly. 'That's fine. You're in charge here.'

'Yeah. That's right. I am in charge – for once.'

In everything she said, each little tic and shiver, it was clear Alannah was grievously wounded. The hurt had subsumed heart and soul.

The crowd were virtually noiseless in their movement, the pervasive fear constraining any sound. It was so incongruously quiet that every word of the exchange between the two women carried clear through the winter air.

'You've achieved what you want, you know,' Claire said.

'Yeah?'

'Absolutely. You've really done for Resurgam. No one will be talking about the opening. It'll be all about you.'

'Good.'

'You and – Tommy.'

Dan heard himself draw in a breath. Claire had been on the police negotiators' course and found it surprisingly rewarding. She knew what she was doing. But she must be taking a risk, using his name.

'Yeah, me and Tommy.'

The voice was quieter now, distant. One hand rubbed at her eyes, the other stayed tight on that cylinder. At Alannah's feet, his face obscured by a web of broken glass, Tommy looked up from the photo.

'You loved him very much, didn't you?' Claire said, gently.

'He was the first one… the only one to – treat me properly. He never hit me. Never shouted at me. Not like them other blokes.'

'You were happy together.'

'Yeah.'

'Do you think he'd have wanted this? What you're doing now?'

Alannah stared at her, starkly uncomprehending. It was as though Claire had suddenly started speaking Norse. Slow seconds passed before a reply came, but when it did it was vehement, the words aflame.

'He hated the fucker too! That bastard skyscraper! He loved it when he used to patrol the beach. He didn't want this – thing.'

'But he'd have wanted the best for you. And this isn't it.'

'You reckon?'

'Yes, I do. And…'

'You know what I did earlier?' Alannah cut in, with vicious delight. 'Do you want to know?'

'If you want to tell me.'

'I did for Esther. I killed her. I stabbed her. I knifed her. And I fucking loved it.'

'But that…'

'You're going to have me for her murder. So what's it matter if I take out Resurgam and everyone in it?'

She held up a hand, the cylinder bright in the sunlight. It was bevelled around the top, darkened at the bottom with what looked like the lick of a flame. A couple of the marksmen shifted positions.

'Because those people are innocent,' Claire said gently. 'And Esther wasn't.'

Alannah didn't reply. She was staring at the cylinder, easing it back and forth, just a little, as though it was a lighter she was depending upon to find a way through the darkness.

'I only have to let go…'

Claire nodded. 'You can do whatever you want. It's all down to you how you're remembered.'

'What?'

'As a good person who suffered horribly, but was strong and came through it. Who people can thank for being merciful. Or…'

'Or what?'

'Or someone who let bitterness take them over and forced that on hundreds – probably even thousands - of others.'

Now, for the first time, Alannah took her eyes from Claire. Her head drooped and the cylinder came to rest by her side.

'I'm so tired.'

Claire took a careful step forwards. 'I'm sure you are, after all you've been through.'

'I was up all night. I didn't know if I could do it. I found the phone. The one she must have given him. I found some photos too. Of... the bomb. I knew what it was all about.'

Another step. 'I understand.'

'I rang her. I told her I wanted to do for Resurgam as much as her. I wanted to be there when she did it.'

'Yes.'

'So I came to see her.'

'Yes.'

'And then I did it – I did her.'

'I know.'

Alannah's head snapped back up. 'He was mine. Tommy didn't cheat on me. He wouldn't, never. When he met me, he dumped her. He wanted me.'

'I think you're right.'

'We were happy.'

'Yes.'

'But she had that hold on him. From before. When he planted the bomb.'

'Yes.'

'But he'd decided what to do. He was going to tell the police. That's why she done him. My Tommy was no killer. He thought he'd go to jail, but he knew I'd be waiting for him.'

'And you would.'

'Yeah. I would.'

Claire took another step forwards and held out her hand.

'Can I have it?'

'I'm so tired. I just want to sleep.'

'I know. And you can. Just give me the detonator first.'

Alannah's anger was dissipating under the gentle soothing. At this time of mortal danger for them all, Dan found himself once more amazed at the woman he'd finally allowed himself to believe in.

The two quiet combatants were only a metre apart. Claire was smiling, reaching out her palm. 'Let's remember Tommy the right way.'

The cylinder slipped a little and Alannah gripped it harder. She was staring up at the sky, sunshine filling her face.

Claire took one more step, stretched for Alannah's hand and slipped her fingers onto the cylinder. All around it was as if everyone released the tension they had held so hard inside. The world turned once more. Nigel let out a low groan, Dan felt his knees sag.

Tonight would be as it should. He and Claire, together and safe, sharing a moment he thought would never come.

Below, a policeman slapped jubilantly at The Wall, the sudden noise sharp in the silence. And Alannah recoiled and grabbed back the cylinder.

'He hated that!' she screamed. 'He hated that fucking wall, Resurgam, and everything about it.'

Claire lurched forwards, clutched for the cylinder, but it was too late. Alannah drew back her hand and with a force born of infinite rage hurled the detonator at The Wall.

Through the air it flew, tumbling and glinting, a slow arc, an easy passage to such a destructive end.

And all eyes switched to Resurgam. Expectant and fearful. Awaiting.

On and on the cylinder flew, spinning in the air.

Still they waited. For the crack, the boom, the rumbling of the blast. For the flames and the shrapnel, the shattering and the death.

A seagull squealed in the air. From the remnants of the crowd, way back along the road, came a low moan of massed voices, a choir of fear.

And now the cylinder reached The Wall and struck with a jarring, clattering impact.

Eyes searched Resurgam, up and down, back and forth, waiting. Watching for the spurt of orange and red which would herald the end of the skyscraper. The explosion of glass and concrete, the rush of singeing heat and the screams of the hundreds of people trapped within the mighty building.

But unmoved the monolith stood, as indomitable as ever, and all that came was the peculiar calm of this cold December morning.

CHAPTER 32

Ultimately it was an anti-climax. After all that was said, all that had happened, the armies of hype marched to the very top of the hill, they found no one to fight.

This time there were no speeches. There were no drum rolls, no trumpet fanfares, no countdowns. No crashes of cymbals, no fly by, no nothing.

At just before four o'clock it was announced, in a subdued voice on the public address system, that Resurgam would open at five. And come the hour, it did just that.

The gates were pulled back and the crowd, such as it was, wandered into the skyscraper. There was no running, no elbowing, no jockeying for position. No pressing, none of the crush of a great pack of people. It was an easy amble, as relaxed as a Sunday stroll.

The numbers were still well into the hundreds, but nothing like the tens of thousands that had threatened. Most had drifted away, contented themselves with a walk around old Plymouth, a breath of the sea air of the waterfront. Talk of terrorism and the sight of guns were ruthless dampeners for any festive mood.

Shop staff and assistants welcomed their visitors with smiles that were just a little too fixed. The music of the great aisles sounded muted. The noise of the few footsteps was like a small troupe of dancers rehearsing in a grand hall. There was no delighted reaction of an entranced audience, just echoes of emptiness.

Ellen Dance was absent, as likely to be found as the crock of gold at the end of the rainbow. Police officers still stood by in their scores, just in case. But as the minutes wore on, and the excitement obstinately refused to build, more and more were dismissed to begin their weekends early.

The hacks penned their reports. They were dominated by the showdown, armed police, the murder of Esther, those final minutes outside the gates. The actual opening of Resurgam barely received a mention.

A moment so long awaited had become nothing more than a postscript.

★★★

When Alannah was arrested the journalists flipped into flurry mode, filing their reports to all and everyone. Dan did the same, heading for the Satellite Truck and feeding the pictures of the confrontation back to *Wessex Tonight*.

'You ok?' Loud asked, with unusual concern.

'Kind of.'

'You look like rhino dung.'

The poetic words prompted Dan and Nigel to a quick précis of themselves. The engineer had a point. Both men were wild eyed, as pale as fresh snow, and pushing dishevelled to the very limits of the word's definition.

'It's wondering if you're about to be burned alive, lacerated by shrapnel, blown to pieces, or a mix of the lot,' Dan explained.

Behind them Resurgam was being evacuated, lines of staff filing out from the doors. Many hugged each other, some walked with a stupor as if they were the undead creatures of the night.

El lumbered up and was in a confused way. 'I got loads of great pics of the showdown. But where's my gal gone?'

'She'll be back. She promised and she'll stick to that. The whole Cashman thing is about principles.'

It would take half an hour to feed the pictures, so Dan wandered over to the police vans to see if he could find Adam. He discovered a surprise. The detective was sprawled in an unusually imprecise manner, tie well down his neck and drinking a pint of ale.

'This is entirely off the record,' he said. 'I just needed it after that.'

'And I bought it,' Claire added. 'So you can be sure Dan won't say anything.'

'Ok,' the malleable newsman replied, 'But there's a price.'

'Why is that always the way with you?' Adam asked, and passed over the nectar of the common man.

Dan took the glass and gratefully helped diminish the volume of liquid. 'So, what's happening now?'

'The technical boys reckon the detonator's real enough.'

'It was a pressure switch?'

'So they say.'

'Bloody hell.'

'Quite. And it's got a wireless transmitter. They're using that to track down the bomb.'

They sat for a couple of minutes, talking about the case. Of all they had worked on together, quite a parade of notables, it was one of the most remarkable. Dan was about to leave when word came back from the Eggheads. The bomb, such as it was, had been found.

'Has it been disarmed?' Adam asked urgently.

'More or less,' came the crackly reply over the radio. 'It wasn't such a tough job.'

The device, the man explained, was wired to a radio receiver, tuned to the frequency of the detonator and in full working order. But the bulging plastic wrappings to which it was connected, the ones captured in the photograph sent to Charles Cross Police Station, were filled with nothing more lethal than putty.

★★★

A polite knock on the door of the Satellite Truck heralded the return of June, newly released from arrest. With delightful modesty she said, 'I think you wanted to talk to me.'

The other hacks were engrossed in their stories, so El found a secluded corner and carried out a quick photo shoot. In a few minutes he had all the pictures he needed and it was Dan's turn.

'Forgive the provocative opening question, but we're a little short of time. You led everyone a merry dance, didn't you?'

'I didn't delight in it,' was the unruffled response, 'I did what I did for a reason and I believe it was justified, given what I was trying to say.'

'What made you do it?'

June hesitated and rubbed at her chest; tentatively, as though not wanting to awaken something which lay within. It was an everyday gesture, but filled with significance.

'I'd rather not say.'

'Too personal? Too difficult?'

She swallowed hard. 'Yes.'

Dan didn't push the point. Respect was due and the viewers would understand.

'But speaking generally,' he said, gently, 'It was about the way vulnerable people can be treated by our society?'

'That's exactly it. I don't have any family. I was thinking about giving away my house and everything I own to a charity, but that would have just happened quietly and never been noticed. I wanted to do something meaningful.'

'In what way?'

June smiled, but sadly. 'At my age you get used to losing friends. Some go suddenly, others take longer. More than a few have gone down to dementia. They've needed to go into homes for care – just basic things like eating, and getting dressed - and our so-called *civilised* society has forced them to sell their houses to get it.'

She stopped and Dan let the silence run. He didn't need to ask a question, just waited for the emotion to emerge. And it did, how it did. If the word civilised had been spat out with a rare passion, the explanation that followed was hotter by far.

'Making people sell their homes is theft. No, it's worse, it's robbery, because people are forced to give up what they have, just like if they were threatened with a knife. It's nothing short of a disgrace and a scandal. People who've lived decent lives, made their contributions to society, being robbed at the end when they have the cheek to finally ask for a little something back. And it's gone on for years, and nothing's been done about it.'

'But if I'm reading your own experience right, that wouldn't happen to you,' Dan pointed out. 'You'd have been cared for by the NHS.'

'That's not the point. This isn't a selfish thing. I wanted to draw attention to the plight of others who can't speak out for themselves. So I decided I'd sell my home and rent it back until the time came when I couldn't live in it anymore. And I'd find some way to make a statement about how older people are treated in this country.'

'So was created the Cashman?'

'Yes.'

'And you disguised yourself – hence the different appearances in the photos – ready for the final revelation of who you were, and why you were doing it.'

'Yes.'

'And Resurgam gave you the ideal stage?'

She nodded forcefully. 'Oh, how it did. I hated the thought of public money going on something like that, absolutely detested it.' June glanced with rank contempt towards the towering floors of the skyscraper. 'It summed up everything that's wrong. Don't worry about hospitals and schools. Don't worry about people in need. Let's spend our cash on a huge damned folly to our endless bloody vanity.'

'So you set the puzzle in the eight appearances and started the story of the Cashman.'

And now they looked to each other. Two people standing unnoticed amidst the iciness of a bright December afternoon, but holding between them a secret which would come to captivate millions. She was firm and defiant, but nonetheless with a melancholy distance in those clear, pale and so very principled eyes.

'So then,' Dan asked, quietly, a prompt for Nigel to zoom in his shot for the powerful close up. 'The final question - how would you like to be remembered?'

A rainbow mitten rose to rub away the trail of a tear. Finally, the long-readied words could be spoken, the culmination of such a journey.

'As one of the little people, who somehow managed to stand up and make the voice of the great mass of decent folk in this country be heard at last.'

★★★

At five o'clock precisely the gates opened and Dan and Nigel meandered inside. A group of the professionals stayed in the pen, to protest to the last. But the rest of the band braved the ire of their fellows and joined the visitors to see for themselves that which they had fought so hard to stop.

Seb, Mac and Esme were to the fore, amongst the first to slip through the doors. They were clustered as one, hugging each other, innocents in a foreign land. Seb was in the middle, his friends with arms of comfort and support.

Nigel set up the tripod and filmed as people passed by, wandering to check out the stores, examine the greenery, admire the cascading waters of the fountain. A couple sat down, whispered to each other and shrugged. The man held out his phone and went to take a picture, but the woman shook her head.

'I've seen church fetes with more excitement,' Nigel whispered.

A juggler was entertaining a group of children, his sparkling clubs whirling patterns through the air. One slipped from his hand and clattered onto the floor.

'All part of the act,' the man smiled. But the kids turned and slouched away.

June and Maggie walked slowly through the doors and stopped to stare around, at the layers of floors rising above. June was breathing deeply as if ingesting the air of this fabled place.

A trio was playing in the corner, all in evening dress. As they finished one tune, a brisk and light number, the woman set down her violin and looked to her watch.

Dan tried a couple of interviews with the visitors. The first three he waylaid didn't want to speak. To the question, 'What do you make of it all then?' the fourth, a young woman replied, 'It's alright.' He didn't bother asking anyone else.

'How many shots do you need?' Nigel asked.

'To properly immortalise this unforgettable moment for all eternity? Just a few - thankfully.'

The time was quarter past five. They were about to walk out of the doors when a yell stopped them. It was loud, penetrating through the half deserted arcade.

'Look at me! Listen to me! I'm going to do it!'

It was Seb. And he was on the third floor, standing balanced on the wall, arms outstretched.

★★★

Security staff materialised from where they had been hiding, secreted in doorways, and began trying to usher people away.

'No!' Seb shouted. 'Everyone stay where they are or I'll jump!'

Carefully, quietly, Nigel repositioned the camera. 'This bloody place is cursed,' he whispered.

All around there was perfect stillness and roaring silence. All faces were looking up to the young man, standing on the wall.

'It's for her,' Seb shouted. 'For Alice.'

Even from here, way down below, it was obvious he was shaking. It was in his stance, his voice.

'I loved her,' Seb yelled. 'I lost her – for this!'

He flung an arm at the innards of Resurgam and wobbled precariously. A security guard stepped forwards and called, 'Look now son...'

'Shut up! Shut the fuck up! Shut up or I jump!'

Along from Seb were Mac and Esme, both gripping at the rail that he stood astride. The rebellion was gone from Mac, beaten out of him by so many blows of the reality of life. He looked frightened, childlike, no longer at home in that long leather coat but drowning in it.

Esme was in tears, her face lost in misery and fear. She was begging and imploring, desperately trying to prevent the taking of another life by this shopping centre in the sky.

'No Seb,' she pleaded. 'I can't lose another friend. Alice would hate this.'

'How do you know? You don't know! You were only her mate. I was... we were...'

The voice vanished in the heaving of his breath. He rested his head on his chest and rolled his neck, circles and circles. It was as though Seb was counting away the last movements his muscles would make.

On the ground floor a baby started crying. A woman reached for her, mouthed soothing noises.

Seb raised his arms aloft, fingertips outstretched, as if preparing for a dive. Nigel groaned, others in the mall echoing the dreadful sound.

The young man closed his eyes. He was swaying hard, backwards and forwards, the momentum building. He was so thin now, so pitifully gaunt, and so lost. Below him waited not the reality of death on a cold stone floor, but the beauty of Alice and her loving arms.

'No!' came a voice, determined, but somehow kindly. It was irresistible, too filled with compassion to be ignored. 'No Seb, please.'

His eyes opened. 'June?'

'Seb, don't do this. Don't throw away your life.'

'I... but...'

'You've got far too much to live for. Believe me.'

'But – Alice...'

'I lost someone I loved too, Seb. My husband, years ago. I know how it feels. It seems like the end of everything. But it's not. We never forget them. But we don't betray them either. Not like this.'

'But... I lost her. We lost here. We'll always lose.'

'We didn't lose. Look around you. Do you think the opening of Resurgam has been a success?'

'But... the future. No jobs, no planet... no Alice.'

People were stepping back from June, leaving her alone in the centre of a ring of polished stone. No one wanted to trespass on the fragile link between these two fellows from different generations, a connection all sensed was so very critical.

'There's always something to live for,' June said with incontestable certainty. 'Listen to me Seb. I didn't tell you this before. I've hardly told anyone, but I want to tell you. I can tell you, can't I?'

He nodded, tense and determined, but unable to refuse the incantation of this extraordinary woman. And out came the confession; clear and dignified, but laboured with loss.

'I'm dying. I've got cancer. I savour every day I have left. I'd give anything to be like you – young and fit, with so much to look forward to. All of life is yours. Don't throw that away.'

'But I…'

'Please Seb. You've got everything to give to the world. And you will. Trust me. I can see it in you. I believe in you.'

'But…'

'You listened to me when we protested together, didn't you? It's even more important you listen now.'

He had stopped swaying, was looking down at June, those eyes so focused that there could have been no one else in this vast space, none of the hundreds of others, standing transfixed.

This was the fulcrum moment. With a shift of balance, just a few centimetres either way, the outcome would be life or death. And June knew it, just as she'd known so much this past year.

'Come down, please,' she said. 'I've got so much I'd like to talk to you about. Come down and let's talk.'

Seb stared, from June to the surroundings, the great modern cathedral of this mighty skyscraper. His eyes roved and gazed, looking far beyond the glitz and the glass, the shops and the friezes. And perhaps he saw the benevolent ghost of a beautiful young woman, whispering to him.

Slowly, Seb bowed his head and lowered himself down from the wall.

CHAPTER 33

And so the moment neared.

They discussed going out. To a fine restaurant to mark the occasion, but they weren't a pair for formal dining. They thought instead about walking to a local pub, but it was Friday night and not long before Christmas. It would be rowdy wherever they chose, and there was the risk of the dreaded shout *it's that man on the telly*.

And so they stayed home with Rutherford, a peculiar yet contented family.

Dan sat at the little table in the kitchen window, which had joined the flat's furniture soon after Claire's arrival. That was two months, one week and six days ago.

A tin of beer was evaporating nicely and they chatted as frying pancetta and bubbling tomatoes flirted with their stomachs.

'Are you going to ask me now?' Claire teased. 'While I'm wearing a pinny and smeared with tomato juice?'

'After dinner, I think.'

'You're not stalling, are you?'

'No.'

'No second thoughts?'

'None.'

'In that case after dinner it is.'

'How long before the feast is served?'

She smiled, bent down and kissed him. 'Twenty minutes.'

Dan disappeared into the bedroom and returned with the A4 diary which lived at the bottom of his cabinet. The poor thing rarely enjoyed a chance to see the light, but now was one of its moments.

'Ah,' Claire noted. 'The sacred book.'

'I'd like to spend a few minutes getting Resurgam out of my mind, so we can have the rest of the evening to ourselves.'

'Shall I chip in with some thoughts?'

'It's supposed to be a diary of my cases.'

'You're going to have to start getting out of the *my* mind-set and into the *our*.'

Dan took another swig of beer, opened the battered old book and began to write.

★★★

All those years ago, when Dan served his days at Journalism College, one of the lecturers had a pet saying; *Our mission is the search for the truth.*

Sadly rarely in his day job did Dan think he achieved the ambition, so adept at spin were the politicians, big shots of industry and other powerbrokers who dominated the news.

He came to understand it was equally the way in criminal investigations. In one of the lofty lectures Adam was prone to delivering, the detective said, *You usually get about eighty or ninety per cent of a case. Sufficient for a conviction, but not enough to really know what went on in someone's mind.*

And that would be the problem with the page of the notebook dedicated to Resurgam. Some of the main players were now residents of a world beyond questioning, so a little thoughtful surmise would be required.

He doodled a few ideas but nothing was really forming, so Dan asked of the professional detective, 'Why was there only putty in the bomb?'

'Tommy was no killer,' Claire replied from the realm of the fiery hobs. 'I'd say he ditched the real explosives somewhere, maybe in the sea, and replaced them with putty.'

'He was in thrall to Esther – before he met Alannah, anyway.'

'That'd be my guess. You said he didn't have much luck with women. He sounded lonely.'

'So Esther used him.'

'You don't know that. She might have liked him.'

'Then she had a hell of a way of showing it. Paying him a visit at full speed in a lorry.'

'That was when he forced her into a corner,' Claire pointed out. 'It sounds like he told her he was going to the police.'

'So Esther had to come up with some way of stopping him.'

'And she had to find a way to hide near Resurgam, so she could send those warnings and detonate the bomb. Hence the rucksack and rough sleeper disguise.'

'She was watching us,' Dan observed. 'There were often tramps about when Adam and I were at Resurgam. I remember one had a limp. I wonder if that was Esther. She probably hurt herself jumping out of the lorry.'

'She was said to be a good actress in her school days. She used that to take on a new character.'

'Do you think she really would have blown up Resurgam?' Dan asked.

'We'll never know. But given that she was driven to kill Tommy...'

Rutherford wandered to the door and patted a summoning paw. Dan got up to let him into the garden. It was another cold, but still night. Stars patterned the sky, fighting their traditional battle against the smear of the city's lights.

'Dinner's ready,' Claire called from the kitchen.

★★★

The rest of the afternoon at Resurgam had defied the habits of the building's lifetime and gone according to plan.

Lizzie pronounced the report Dan produced, filled as it was with natural drama and exclusive angles as *pretty decent*. He didn't bother attempting to elicit higher praise. Such campaigns tended to be a gruelling odyssey and rarely worth the effort.

Before he left for home, once again, Lizzie raised the *two truths and a lie* game. It was obviously bothering her close to the point of fixation.

'I want to know which was the lie,' she commanded. 'I can't imagine you want to present *Wessex Tonight*. But you wouldn't pour out your private life, just like that. And as for being a spy...'

'One day,' Dan interrupted, 'I might just tell you. But for now, allow me the luxury of a newsroom version of the Fifth Amendment. I need it.'

★★★

Tomorrow, *Wessex Tonight* would break the story of the Cashman, to coincide with El's splash in whichever newspaper bid the largest heap of gold for his wares. The photographer was giggling his delight and already planning a winter break somewhere well away from ice-bound England.

'Cuba's calling,' he said. 'El thinks he'll go down a storm there.'

Dan imagined, but managed not to vocalise, the reaction of the populace to the arrival of a pasty, chubby, burbling buffoon.

'Sounds splendid,' he said. 'Don't forget my cut. I think I'm going to need it.'

'Yeah, I know.'

Dan gave his idiot friend an askance look. The wind of perception was blowing once more. 'What do you think you know?'

'Nothing mate. Look, gotta go, gotta send these piccies off.'

★★★

They adjourned to the lounge for dinner. Once again, Dan found himself marvelling how the base ingredients of tomatoes, bacon and a few olives could be persuaded to taste so delicious. Claire was truly an alchemist of the kitchen. At the table in the bay window they sat, Rutherford at their feet, and continued the discussion between mouthfuls.

'What about Alannah?' Claire asked. 'Mr Breen's talking about a murder charge.'

'He would. He likes to bid high. But I can't see it. Manslaughter's more likely. She was obviously unbalanced.'

327

'She did try to blow up Resurgam. You can hardly have a charge of attempted manslaughter.'

The windows were steaming up, cosseting them in a lovers' cocoon. The recalcitrant tinsel had decided to mend its ways and cling to the wall. Tomorrow was the weekend, the beer was doing its soothing work and all felt warm and well.

'What happened to Ellen Dance?' Claire asked.

'No one knows. It was bizarre. She vanished faster than a magician's assistant. The word is she had a nervous wobbly and has gone into hiding.'

'And Jackie Denyer?'

'Likewise.'

'No one really came out of the whole Resurgam thing well, did they?'

Dan considered his sizeable forkful. 'Only June, I'd say. What a woman, and what a legacy she'll leave. But Resurgam is open and it's not going away.'

'It'll be a long time before its name means anything worthwhile though,' Claire concluded.

***

Mobile phones must surely be fitted with an app that detects tranquillity and a program to persecute it. Tonight, for a change, Claire's was the guilty party. She apologised, got up from the table and answered.

'Evening sir. No, not yet. I'll text you later.'

'Adam?' Dan asked, as she sat back down. 'What did he want?'

'I'll tell you in a while – maybe.'

Dan gave her a lofty look. 'I'm wondering if I already know.'

'Then we'll be able to see if that famous intuition has been on form again.'

The two plates were almost empty. Claire pulled up just short of the finish, as was her habit, and slipped the remaining pasta over to Dan.

'Come on then,' she said.

'Come on what?'

'You know full well what. I've been waiting long enough.'

'I haven't finished my supper yet.'

'Hurry up then.'

She sat back and watched him eat. When three tubes of penne were left, and Dan was slowly pushing them around the plate, Claire took the fork and ate them herself.

'Hey! I was looking forward to those.'

'And I've been looking forward to this moment. So get on with it.'

'Ok then, but one question first.'

'One?'

'Just one, I promise.'

'Go on.'

'I was set up, wasn't I?'

Claire sat back and folded her arms. 'I don't know what you mean.'

'You know exactly what I mean. Yesterday, Nigel was on his mobile just before I came home and found you packed and – with remarkable timing – about to leave.'

'Pure coincidence.'

'Then there's El knowing I need a fair bit of money for something. And Adam calling just now.'

'That might have been just a work thing.'

'They've been helping you, haven't they? That devious trio who dare to call themselves my friends.'

'Helping me what?'

'Helping you nudge me into finally sorting myself out.'

Claire turned to look out of the window. 'It's a beautiful evening.'

'That it is.'

'Care to make it even better?'

Dan ruffled Rutherford's fur and took another swig of ale. 'I suppose it is about time.'

★★★

Across the old wooden table they looked to each other.

'I'm out of beer,' Dan said. 'I could do with another.'

'You sit right there. You can have another later - if you get this right.'

'You sure?'

'Absolutely.'

'Ok then.'

'Yes?'

'Claire.'

'Yes?'

'I was wondering…'

'Yes?'

'I wanted to ask…'

'Yes?'

'If you…'

'Yes?'

'If you thought we…'

'Yes.

'If we…'

'Yes?'

'If we might get a television licence together.'

She sighed. 'Try again.'

'You want more?'

'Yes. I do.'

'That was quite a commitment for a man – well, a man like me, anyway.'

'I think you can do even better.'

'Really?'

'Yes.'

'Ok then. Are you ready?'

'Very much so.'

'Right then. I was wondering…'

'Yes?'

'If…'

'Yes?'

'If we might take advantage of certain perks which come courtesy of a special status granted under English law.'

Claire leaned forwards and pouted. 'You get - one – more – chance.'
'Just one?'
'One.'
'Ok then.'
Dan puffed out his chest, tipped up the beer can to seek out any last droplets of assistance and gave Rutherford a pat for luck.
'Last chance?' he asked.
'Last chance,' she affirmed.
'Right…'
'Come on. You can do it.'
'Can I?'
'You can.'
'Ok then. Claire…'
'Yes?'
'I was wondering…'
'Yes?'
'Whether…?'
'Yes?'
'If…'
'Come on. I have no intention of making this easy for you.'
'All right. Here we go then. I was wondering if… you might… just consider… possibly… seeing your way clear to… marrying me.'

And so, at last, it was said. And Claire began to laugh. And Dan joined in. And together they laughed and laughed and laughed some more.

The time was one minute to nine when Claire wiped her eyes, cleared her throat, gathered her voice and answered the question which had finally been posed.

'You're an idiot,' she chuckled. 'But you're my idiot. Yes, of course I'll marry you.'